The Women of
Skawa Island

Also by the author

The Adam Saint Mysteries:
When the Saints Go Marching In

The Russell Quant Mysteries:
Amuse Bouche
Flight of Aquavit
Tapas on the Ramblas
Stain of the Berry
Sundowner Ubuntu
Aloha, Candy Hearts
Date with a Sheesha
Dos Equis

The Women of Skawa Island

An Adam Saint Novel

Anthony Bidulka

INSOMNIAC PRESS

Cover design by Mike O'Connor. Cover image by iStockphoto.com.
Author photograph by Hogarth Photography.

Library and Archives Canada Cataloguing in Publication

Bidulka, Anthony, 1962-, author
The women of Skawa Island : Adam Saint book / Anthony Bidulka.

Issued in print and electronic formats.
ISBN 978-1-55483-124-1 (pbk.).--ISBN 978-1-55483-143-2 (ebook)

I. Title.

PS8553.I319W66 2014   C813'.6   C2014-907349-6
                                               C2014-907350-X

The publisher gratefully acknowledges the support of the Canada Council,
the Ontario Arts Council and the Department of Canadian Heritage
through the Canada Book Fund.

Printed and bound in Canada

Insomniac Press, 520 Princess Ave.
London, Ontario, Canada, N6B 2B8
www.insomniacpress.com

Acknowledgments

Writing a book, moving it from idle thought to coherent idea, from words cobbled together on a computer screen to being printed on a page (or replicated on an electronic device), to sitting proudly on a bookstore shelf, a bedside table, in a vacationer's carry-on, tasked with the job of entertaining, inspiring thought, laughter, tears, outrage, comfort, coziness, all this requires…deserves…a team: writer, editor, publisher, proofreaders, agent, marketer, bookseller, distributor, printer, reviewers, media professionals, and technical experts of all sorts. I am eternally grateful to them all. Without them, I would be less than I am. But with this book I acknowledge one of the most important members of that team: the reader.

Yes, of course, without you, the reader, reaching into your wallets—or virtual replacement of the same—the commercial lifespan of any book is about as long as a Sea-Monkey's. And I salute you, dear book purchasers, for supporting writers in this way. But readers do much more than that, perhaps at times without realizing it. Even today, after ten books and fifteen years in this career, it continues to boggle my mind to think that in addition to my magnificently supportive family and friends, someone wholly unrelated to me, someone I've never met and who has no vested interest in my career and no relationship with me, will not only read my book but will then take the time to write me a note, send a message or email, or contact me through social media and share with me their thoughts.

Astoundingly, the vast majority of these communications are resoundingly positive, uplifting, reassuring, kind, and generous. Sometimes they consist of little more than a simple "Thank you" or "I enjoyed your book and look forward to the next one." Sometimes they are lengthy expositions. Regardless of length or content, they are nothing less than daily doses of literary adrenaline for a writer whose fingers are poised above a keyboard. They propel me. They soothe me. They inspire me to do better. Thank you, teammates.

For the many wonderful women in my life,
who have made it so sweet.

And Herb.

Chapter One

People were streaming onto the decks, faces alarmed, crew members shouting as they scrambled to their posts. The young man, jostled by the crowd, didn't know the clanging bells and wailing horns were harbingers of an impending disaster that would forever change his life.

Confused by the commotion, helpless inaction overtook him. Instead of joining the scurrying hordes, he stood frozen against the deck's railing, white-knuckling the wooden veneer cracked by age and salt water. Trying to ignore the chaos, he buried his eyes into the tranquil blue that surrounded the vessel. This being his first time at sea, he'd never seen anything like it. Not the water itself but the immensity of it. It was as if he was seeing the world as it really was for the first time. He found it overwhelmingly beautiful.

Now this.

Still, nothing appeared amiss. The waters were calm, no waves higher than a foot or two. The only thing to look at was a tiny island, perhaps a kilometre away.

What could the fuss possibly be about?

"Darren!" a voice struggled above the racket.

He turned to greet the girl. Amanda. They'd met on board and immediately hit it off. He was certain she had a crush on him. He liked her too, but she was young, probably too young for him. Although the way she acted and the crazy, outrageous things that came out of her mouth made her seem older.

"What do you think is going on?" he asked when she was near enough to hear without his having to shout.

She shrugged.

"The boat has stopped moving, you know."

Amanda tossed a worried look overboard.

"It's a party in the dining room!" a boozy voice sailed over the others.

The woman was in her twenties but looked much older. She wore a short, tight denim skirt and a tube top that didn't quite fit. Dark tendrils of hair stuck to her sweating temples and neck like swirling snakes.

"Twila!" Amanda placed a hand on the woman's arm as she passed by, causing thick, green liquid to dribble over the edge of her plastic glass. "Do you know what's happening?"

"Oh, it's nothing," she responded with a phlegmy laugh, at the same time checking Darren out with a practiced eye. "Probably another friggin' lifeboat drill or something. Don't worry about it, hon. Grab a drink and join the party." With an unsteady sway of her hips, the woman winked at the couple and sauntered off.

Amanda searched Darren's face for answers. "What do we do?"

"It doesn't sound very serious to me."

"Everybody's going to the dining room. You coming?"

He smirked. "Nah, I think I'll just stay out here, enjoy the peace and quiet."

She stuck out her tongue. Something she did with irritating regularity. "Loser."

"Hey, I'm the only one who's not losing his head around here."

"C'mon," she urged. "Let's go." She turned, confident he'd follow.

Darren hesitated. He didn't want to be in that dining room. It was going to be loud. People were going to be shoving and pushing. The truth of what was happening would be told. He'd rather stay out here in the fresh air, look at the blue sky, the gentle water, and believe everything was going to be okay, even though his gut was telling him it wasn't.

But he couldn't let Amanda deal with this alone. She had nobody. Neither did he. They had to stick together.

Darren unfastened himself from the railing and went after her.

They joined the others streaming into the largest indoor space on the ship. Darren threaded his way through the crowd in Amanda's determined wake. Never one to miss a thing, she would want to get as close to the front, wherever that was, as possible. The passengers' chatter, growing increasingly rapid and agitated, was drowning out the ship's incessant alarms. As they passed their shipmates, Darren was reminded that most spoke a language he'd never heard before. Until this minute he hadn't thought it was a big deal. Now he wondered if understanding each other was about to become the biggest deal ever.

The young couple stopped near the edge of a stage meant for entertainers who'd never materialized. Two men were positioning themselves at the centre of the platform. One wore a white uniform, no doubt the captain. The other was a man Darren had met before, a man who looked like he'd be in charge wherever he was. His name was Smith. Hanging back in the shadows behind them was a third man, his complexion dark and as rough as a gravel road. He wore a robe similar to the ones worn by many of the others aboard.

Suddenly, the ship's alarm died and with it the competing voices. The abrupt silence was almost as deafening, but it lasted barely seconds before noise erupted again.

"Ladies and gentlemen," the man in white called out, his voice loud and forceful. "My name is Captain Rowley." He made a gesture with his right hand, and the noise began to wither. "I'm the commander of this ship." He waited again. When a reasonable quiet was finally restored, he continued. "You may have noticed we've come to a stop and dropped anchor." He exchanged a brief glance with the second man. "I'll ask Mr. Smith here to explain exactly what's going on." With that short statement, the captain stepped aside.

Darren tensed as Smith moved forward. The man stared into the crowd with serious intent.

Smith's firm jaw tightened as he prepared to address the passengers. For a brief moment, his solemn eyes settled on Darren. The effect was as if someone had opened a refrigerator door directly in front of him, a blast of cold shellacking his body. The young man shifted uncomfortably.

"Good morning," Smith began. "I'm going to do my best to tell you what's happening. But you need to be aware that, at this point anyway, we're not entirely certain of all the details ourselves." He cleared his throat. "At approximately nine o'clock this morning, roughly seventy minutes ago, we received a message from the Australian coast guard. They've ordered *all* sailing vessels off the seas."

Darren nudged Amanda's shoulder. "What's this guy

talking about? I didn't understand a thing he just said."

He was hoping for some of the girl's characteristic wit in return. Instead, Amanda shushed him, her eyes glued to the imposing figure on stage. Even though she was younger than he, somehow she knew this was a time for paying attention, not playing smartass.

Smith nodded to the third man standing in the darkness. Hesitantly, the man stepped forward.

Darren was startled by what he saw. The man was trembling and his eyes were moist.

In an unsteady voice, the man began to translate the words of both the captain and Smith into a language neither Darren nor Amanda recognized, a back and forth that would continue throughout the announcement.

When he was done, an audible rumble of alarm rippled through the crowd. The air in the room, already hot, grew stifling and reeked with sweat.

"A cataclysmic event has been forecast, and this event," Smith continued, "is massive in scale, with the potential to affect every continent on earth."

"Let's go home! I want to go home!" someone cried out, quickly followed by others.

"We can't go home," Smith responded firmly. "All we can do…all we can do is hide and hope for the best. I know you must be frightened. I wish I could tell you not to be, but I can't."

Darren felt his chest thump a quicker beat. His palms began to sweat and a hollow, sick feeling invaded his stomach.

"All we know is that this event is natural, an act of God. By that I mean it's not man-made. This is not a terrorist attack."

The word *terrorist*, even though he was making the point

it didn't apply to the circumstance, caused cries of dismay and drew worried looks. The crowd was growing increasingly unsettled with each passing second. Smith knew he had to get the information out fast.

He charged on. "By now some of you will have noticed a land mass off our port bow. This will be our haven."

As Smith waited for the translation and inevitable fearful reaction to subside, Darren felt Amanda move closer. Her warmth radiated through him. Despite the extra heat, he didn't budge.

Smith was back, his voice sharp. "Because of the shallowness of the reefs in this area, the captain has informed me we aren't able to get any closer to the island. For that reason, starting immediately, we will begin abandoning ship."

The robed translator did not wait for his cue, shouting the last words out to his people. Jagged screeches of concern punctuated the air like blasts from a shotgun. People began to jabber at one another, some yelling to get the attention of friends. Arms were flailing. A stampede was starting near the exit. The situation was running to a boil.

Darren's eyes moved wildly about the room. He thought that this is what it must feel like to be in a riot. People got trampled to death in riots. He saw Twila, the drunk woman they'd talked to on the deck. Her mouth hung open and her face was dead white. On the ground, her margarita glass lay overturned, its contents pooling at her feet. He pulled Amanda closer.

"Stop this!" Smith barked. "You must pay attention! It's the only way to guarantee your safety!" He turned to the translator with a harsh look, wordlessly commanding him to get control of the crowd. The translator looked as if he was about to bolt. Instead, he cleared his throat and began volleying words into the swirling mass of people.

It was no use.

The blast of sound that came next seemed powerful enough to blow out the windows of the dining room. All eyes fell upon Smith. Above his head he held a freshly discharged klaxon horn.

A fitful peace was once again restored, but for how long was anyone's guess. Smith coolly continued. "We will begin by ferrying all passengers to the island in groups of twenty-five. There is only one operating tender, so this is going to take at least five trips."

Smith's final words disappeared, as yet again the decibel level in the room grew exponentially. People were beginning to absorb the magnitude and severity of what was happening to them. This was more than simple fear or panic. Dread was taking hold.

Smith's eyes grew wary as tinges of doubt began to seep into his brain. Would he be able to hold onto control long enough to do what had to be done? "I'm telling you not to panic," he decreed. "If everyone remains calm and does what they're told, your chances of safety are much greater. We can get you to shore. Everything will be fine…"

"How do you know that?" someone yelled.

"You don't even know what's happening out there!" came an anxious voice rising above the din of foreign tongues.

"Is it a tsunami?" another passenger called out.

"What are we waiting for? Let's go now!"

And with that, a sea of people surged for the exit.

Darren felt a claw on his forearm. It was Amanda, her badly chewed nails red at the cuticles where cheap polish hadn't yet chipped off. He tried to smile until he saw the look in the young girl's eyes.

Terror.

Amanda was usually so confident. To see her self-assuredness vanish was the most frightening thing of all.

In that instant, he knew what he had to do. He would have to step up. He would protect this girl no matter what.

"Amanda," he said, turning her away from the crazed crowd clambering for the exits. "It's okay. We'll be okay. They do this kind of thing all the time."

"They do?" Faint hope.

"Sure."

"I thought you told me you'd never been on a ship before."

"Doesn't matter. Don't you go to the movies?"

"Not really, no, and I don't have a TV."

"You don't need one. When we get home, I'll teach you how to sneak into a multiplex. It's easy."

He watched as her eyes shifted away, over his shoulder, and registered the mounting pandemonium around them. Until today, they'd both looked at this trip in the same way, but what was once a crazy adventure had become an ill-fated folly.

"We should probably get going," she said, her voice no more than a peep. "Before all the seats are gone."

Darren's heart sank further. For the first time since he'd met her, Amanda sounded like the little girl she was. He was failing. He wasn't making her feel any better.

Darren fought to keep his voice confident, soothing. "Don't worry about that. You heard the guy. We have plenty of time. They only have one tender anyway. We'll take the next one."

"Yeah?"

"Yeah. How about I walk you to your room. You can pack a few things to take with you. There must be stuff you want while we're away. Maybe a bathing suit? I bet that island has an epic beach."

The girl's lips trembled into a tentative smile.

Darren felt her little hand, warm and moist, clamp onto his.

"Okay. C'mon," she said, turning away, once again taking the lead.

Whatever came next, Darren knew one thing for sure: They'd face it together.

Hours later, a total of one hundred and twelve people stood on a pristine stretch of sun-warmed sand. Some huddled together in groups, others remained solitary sentries. All eyes were fastened on the far end of the crescent-shaped shoreline.

Five times the Zodiac tender had appeared, making the trip from the ship, invisible behind the bend of the beach, and expelled its load of passengers. But for the last ninety minutes, nothing.

Gradual awareness of what must have happened stunned the onlookers into silence. The only sound accompanying their vigil was the sluicing of sea water as it rushed onto the beach, then just as quickly retreated.

As predicted, the cataclysmic event had arrived. There would be no more survivors arriving from the ship.

Darren and Amanda, standing hip to hip, looked at each other, a silent question hanging between them: *Was it coming for them next?*

Chapter Two

Bobby Drake never thought he'd be "this." He'd tried other things. He'd even gone to university hoping to become an optometrist. Unfortunately, his grades were so poor the dean's office cordially declined his request for a second year. Working retail was good, but the money wasn't. Finally, Lady Luck had kicked in. A talent scout spotted him at Noosa Heads beach, where he'd picked up weekend shifts lifeguarding. Next thing he knew he was a male model. Then, with similar speed but much less ceremony, he wasn't anymore. Left with expensive tastes in clothes and premium alcohol and even more expensive habits of the snorting variety, his options were few. The road to "this" was quick, steep, and downhill all the way.

He knew some of his so-called friends gossiped behind his back, saying all sorts of nasty things about him. But who cared? They were stuck in dead-end jobs hawking skinny jeans to tall poppies who shouldn't be caught dead wearing them. Meanwhile, he was spending a sweet, sunny Tuesday morning on the water.

Bobby had just launched his Jet Ski from the rear hatch of his lover's yacht. While riding the waves, he kept a close eye on the ship's captain and his assistant. They'd just made shore and were setting up lunch on the beach beneath multicoloured umbrellas. There'd be bay bugs and chilled shrimp and lots of champagne. Always lots of champagne. Then he'd have to pull down his trunks and do his duty before he could get back to the Jet Ski.

That's when he saw the child.

Damn it!

This was supposed to be a deserted island. The captain had guaranteed it. They…well, Colin…didn't pay all that money to be overrun by snotty-nosed kids cavorting in the water with their loud-mouthed mothers and boorish fathers chasing after them with sunblock and cheap cameras. Now he'd have to go back to the boat and make a scene. This was going to ruin everything.

Taking a closer sweep along the beachfront, Bobby saw that the child was a boy. He was maybe five and looked like some kind of wild thing, with long, matted hair and ratty, ill-fitting clothing. *He'd* obviously not arrived here by yacht.

Bobby and his benefactor, Colin Dunning, both having changed into lightweight whites, arrived on shore. They found the captain having a word with a woman who looked no less worse for wear than the child attached to her side like an extra limb.

"What's going on here?" Dunning, used to taking control, inquired of the captain as they approached the trio.

The captain regarded his employer, then the woman. "Would you excuse us for a moment, ma'am?" She only stared as he turned to address the portly man. "Mr. Dunning, perhaps we could have a word over there?"

The captain shepherded his passengers to a spot further down the beach.

"Will this delay lunch?" Dunning wanted to know.

"Can I get a drink or something?" Bobby requested as he pointed his beautiful face up to the burning sun in a way that he knew made it glow fetchingly. "I'm bleeding drying up here."

"Mr. Dunning, we have a situation." The captain's voice was low and conspiratorial.

"Situation?" Dunning huffed, half from indignation, half from being out of breath from all this to-ing and fro-ing. "What sort of situation?"

"This woman…and the child, she says they, well, she says they were shipwrecked on this island."

"What?" Colin and Bobby spoke almost together.

"Ten years ago."

"Woo," Bobby enthused, suddenly more interested in the whole thing. "That's maje."

Dunning looked at the young man, not sure what he meant. Deciding it wasn't important, he returned his attention to the captain and asked, "Exactly what are we to do about that? Rescue them or some such thing? We haven't enough room or provisions on board for a woman and most certainly not for a juvenile."

The captain did his best to hide his disdain for the man's self-serving concerns. "Apparently, there are *three* adults in total. *And* the child."

"Oh dear," Dunning fretted, waving a chubby hand in front of his perspiring face. "That is a problem then." He considered the quandary for a second or two, then announced his decision: "We'll send someone. After lunch, we'll return to the ship and contact the authorities. That'll sort it."

"I'm afraid it's not that simple, sir."

Dunning arched an unimpressed eyebrow. "Oh really? And why exactly would that be?"

"They aren't asking for our help. They have no interest in leaving with us."

"What!" Suddenly incensed, Dunning nearly choked on the word. "Is there something wrong with my yacht?"

The captain waited an extra second before replying. "Of course not. It's just that after what's happened to them, I believe they're afraid."

"Oh, they'll get over that," Bobby piped up. "Did you know I used to be afraid of water?" He waited for an answer. When none came, he finished off with: "Well, look at me now: King of the Sea."

"So what's to be done about them, then?" Dunning inquired.

"They *have* asked for something," said the captain.

"Well? Spit it out."

"The woman would like us to contact CDRA."

"CDRA?" Dunning responded in surprise. "You mean these people are Canadian?"

One needn't look too far back in history to see the roots of North American intelligence and national security agencies. Law enforcement and intelligence gathering began in earnest in Canada in 1864, when Sir John A. Macdonald, as premier of the colony of Canada West, created the Western Frontier Constabulary. In time, it merged with other forces to become the Dominion Police, and then the Royal Canadian Mounted Police, or the "Mounties."

In September 1945, a particularly serious event ushered

Canada into a new role on the international stage. A young Russian named Igor Gouzenko walked into the newsroom of the *Ottawa Citizen*, shocking everyone by announcing he had proof of a widespread Soviet spy ring operating in Canada. Gouzenko's allegations were a wake-up call for the country and the rest of the world. That event would cause a chain reaction of anti-Communist sentiments throughout the West. Like it or not, Canada was quickly and unexpectedly thrust into the Cold War. This was the first of a great number of factors that eventually inspired Canada to form an independent branch of IIA, the International Intelligence Agency.

IIA is not Interpol. Not CIA. Not CSIS. With a global perspective, IIA focusses on information specifically significant to its member countries. From Andorra to Zimbabwe, whatever needs knowing, the agents of IIA make it their business to know.

Each IIA member country maintains its own headquarters, home to the lead offices for each branch active within that region. In Canada, the Canadian Disaster Recovery Agency, or CDRA, is one of those branches. Its offices are in the Bay Wellington Tower of Brookfield Place, a major skyscraper in Toronto's Financial District. It was here that a man named Shekhar Kapur received a call, tossed fourteen thousand kilometres across the Pacific Ocean from an unknown island in the South Pacific.

The knock on the door was timid. Maryann Knoble, IIA's head honcho, detested timidity, in door knocks as in everything else. If you commit to doing something, she believed, do it with confidence, do it with zest, and do it with power. Anything else is a waste of time.

Already irritated with the author of the pitiful sound of intrusion, she glanced up at the monitor displaying the view directly outside her locked office door. Knoble had no time for personal secretaries either. Not that she didn't want people doing things for her—quite the opposite, actually— she just didn't want them loitering near her like barnacles on a destroyer. Alexander Graham Bell didn't go to all that trouble for humans not to give each other some space.

Standing outside the door was Shekhar Kapur. When the most recent head of CDRA was killed in Russia, Knoble had initially tapped its top agent, Adam Saint, as his replacement. Vexingly, that did not work out. Uninterested in other in-house sycophants vying for the position, Knoble decided to cast the net wider. She caught Kapur, who was head at IDRA in Udaipur, western India, but keen on making a change.

She hit the buzzer that unlocked the office door and electronically swung it open to allow her unexpected guest to enter.

"Kapur," her deep voice boomed, "it's customary to schedule meetings."

Shekhar Kapur was a tall man, and handsome in a Bollywood sort of way. He wore expensive suits that shouted quality and shoes that somehow kept their shine all day. His thick, wavy hair was cut short at the back and sides, the rest kept under control by fragrant oils that gave it a luxurious sheen.

As a young field agent, Kapur had been athletic and muscular, but now not even his well-cut jacket and trousers could hide a nearly skeletal frame. Maryann had begun to wonder if her new deputy had joined her organization under false pretenses, hiding an undisclosed illness.

Kapur remained outside the office threshold. "I'm sorry, Maryann. I apologize for the discourtesy. Of course, I will schedule meetings in the future. But you see, a matter has come up."

"Something I *need* to be aware of?"

"That's just it, Maryann. I don't know."

Knoble had been intent on her computer screens, each overflowing with matters of *legitimately* great importance *legitimately* demanding her attention. She looked up and saw that the man had not moved. "Oh for goodness sake, Kapur, come in."

He did as instructed.

Adjusting her silk Hermès scarf, one of a vast collection, she motioned for him to take a seat in front of her desk. The chair, by design, was uncomfortable, a silent communiqué about the desired length of stay and import of what should be coming out of the occupier's mouth.

"Forgive me, but," he began, "you see, in India, IIA is located in Mumbai, whereas my office with IDRA was in Udaipur. Very far apart, you see."

These were facts Knoble knew well. Very well. She knew almost everything there was to know about IIA the world over, including the location of every office. She was also quite familiar with the map of India. At the edge of her tongue was the urge to inform this dapper scarecrow of a man of these facts and to question who he thought he was to believe it appropriate to waste her time. But he was new. Instead, Knoble would demonstrate uncharacteristic and bountiful patience. Next week, she'd make mincemeat of him if need be. And somehow, she predicted, need there would be.

"Given such great distance between me in Udaipur and our head of IIA in Mumbai," he continued to explain at length, "I had very few day-to-day dealings with this office. Even though, of course," he hurriedly added, "Disaster Recovery is directly responsible to IIA regardless of how far apart the offices physically are. I didn't mean to imply otherwise."

If ever there was a time for Scotch, Knoble thought to herself, it was now.

"Which is why, when this unique request came in, I thought it best to run it by you before I acted."

Knoble considered her reaction. Despite her concerns over Kapur's deteriorating appearance, she knew he was reputed to possess superior intellect. Having a good brain and knowing how to use it overcame a great many shortcomings in Maryann Knoble's mind.

"From here on in, Kapur," she said, her bespectacled eyes unwaveringly intent on her subject, "I suggest you consider your office to be Udaipur and this office—my office—Mumbai. Do you understand?"

Kapur's face remained impassive as he took in the words. In ten seconds, he said, quite clearly, "I do."

"Fine."

"Excuse me, Maryann," he said, "but have you been to Mumbai?"

Knoble hesitated before slowly shaking her head to indicate she had not. Her eyes narrowed. *Is this man toying with me?*

"I have," he told her. "Many times. It is a very interesting city. You should visit sometime."

Briefly, Knoble studied Kapur's glittering, dark eyes and wondered if they hid something more than great intellect.

The Indian stood to go.

"Kapur," Knoble stopped him.

He looked down at her.

"This *request* you've received; you said it was unique. As you can imagine, *unique* is not a word tossed about lightly in this office."

"I would dare to say the same is true in India."

"So then, tell me, what makes this request *unique*?" She sat back in her massive, ergonomically splendid chair, giving the man her full attention. If he should feel he was being tested, he'd be correct.

Kapur took a moment for a deep breath, then began his report. "A short time ago, I received a direct message from the captain of a luxury sailing yacht. The vessel had recently dropped anchor near an unpopulated island in the South Pacific. Reaching shore, the captain discovered four people—three adult women and a child. These people claimed to have been shipwrecked on this island for ten years."

A curiosity, yes, Knoble admitted. Interesting, vaguely. Unique, hardly. She was about to look away dismissively until the new head of CDRA shared the next bit of information.

"The women refused all offers by the captain to rescue them."

Slightly more interesting.

"They *specifically* requested the captain contact CDRA."

Knoble shifted in her seat. So the survivors were Canadian. More curious. Rarely were citizens familiar with CDRA. Even though, in Maryann's not so humble opinion, they damn well should be. In layman's terms, the Canadian Disaster Recovery Agency was tasked with looking after the interests of any Canadians unlucky enough to find themselves in a disaster situation anywhere in the world. But people didn't care about that. Not until they were waist deep in it and didn't know how to get out. Just as, it would appear, these women now were.

Knoble waved the man off. "You know how to deal with this, Kapur."

He turned to go.

"Wait."

Kapur stopped near the door, thinking Knoble needed time to perform her magic spell to open it.

"You said they were found on an island?"

Kapur turned on the spot and regarded his superior. "Yes, I did."

"Where exactly?"

"South Pacific. Off Australia. According to the captain, the women call the island Skawa."

What happened next was unheard of.

Larger-than-life, powerful, ever-confident Maryann Knoble froze.

Chapter Three

When Sergiusz Belar was diagnosed with early-onset Alzheimer's disease, he was not entirely surprised. Having witnessed the suffering of his father, an esteemed Polish scientist, Belar knew only too well how the accompanying side effects devastated not only the person concerned but family and colleagues as well.

Belar had done the research. He knew the signs. He'd read the disturbing accounts of on-the-job mistakes and judgment errors made by those who suffered unaware or, even worse, those who knew exactly what was happening but chose to ignore it until they'd saved enough money or maximized their pension benefits. Belar was determined none of these things would happen to him. Early in his career as a social scientist, he'd begun saving like a madman. When he took a wife, it was with the non-negotiable agreement that the marriage would remain childless. Belar wanted no chance that he could pass the curse on to his own flesh and blood or subject an adopted child to the loss of love from a mentally deficient father.

Despite all of this, Belar managed to build a stunning resume bursting with accomplishment. First as a social scientist for the Government of Poland, and then taking on the same role with the International Intelligence Agency in successively more senior roles in three IIA member countries. Finally, he ascended to the top spot with IIA Canada. When the first signs of dementia were detected by his wife and soon confirmed by his physician, Belar dropped everything and stepped down.

Maryann Knoble, Belar's successor, was one of only a small handful of people who knew the true nature of the "personal" reasons Belar cited in his public retirement announcement. But, truth be told, it mattered little to her. She believed Belar had been in the position for too long anyway, hanging onto too many old-boys'-club ways of doing things. It was a new day at IIA Canada. The reign of Maryann Knoble had begun.

When she took over the post, the only purpose Belar served for Knoble was to answer her questions. Even so, the new chief of IIA preferred to figure things out for herself. Like Belar, she too was a dedicated researcher. In her first hectic months, she dug deep, sampling every pie Belar could possibly have had half a finger in. It was during this discovery phase that Knoble first became aware of Skawa Island.

The documentation was sparse, barely going deeper than to note IIA had funded the island's purchase for undisclosed research purposes. The transaction was peculiar enough to get her attention. But in taking the helm of an organization as vast and complicated as IIA, precious little time remained for investigating burning embers when bonfires raged. Yet, as soon as Knoble heard the island's name spoken again by Shekhar Kapur, she knew she'd made a terrible mistake. Embers left unchecked can ultimately cause the greatest damage.

There were many things in life Maryann Knoble did not like. Tardiness. Whistling. Cheap Scotch. Bad liars. Poodles. People who own poodles. Stupidity. Disrespect—although only when directed at her; otherwise, it had its purposes. At the top of the pile, however, was being uninformed. IIA was all about information: knowing when you needed it; knowing who had it; knowing how to get it; knowing what to do with it. In the minutes following Kapur's disclosure of the SOS from the shipwrecked Canadians on Skawa Island, Knoble found herself deplorably uninformed and, therefore, wholly discontented.

Although she had no reason to believe that a wolf had just waltzed through her door disguised as a lamb, deep down in her bones Knoble knew it was true. She could smell the fetid breath of a predator craving raw meat and fresh blood. Danger had arrived. She needed to move fast to defend IIA. And herself.

The timing couldn't be worse. IIA had recently found itself shoved onto a ledge. At the highest level of government, barracudas had begun to circle. It was a familiar formula. When the most powerful economies in the world begin to falter, politicians do the only thing they can. They cry out for fiscal restraint and fiduciary disclosure. Government responds, as it must, by seeking a scapegoat, the weakest in the army of organizations that prop it up. It was only because of the relationships she'd fostered with the men and women with the greatest clout in the country that Knoble knew IIA was in jeopardy.

The most dangerous of the lot was David Gilmore, a supercilious ass…in Knoble's personal opinion. His formal title was Minister of Public Safety. He was responsible to

Parliament for IIA as a whole and for its general direction. Which meant, like it or not, he held Knoble's leash in his grubby, little hands. And much too often he took inordinate pleasure in giving it a good shake or jolting yank.

Knoble knew how to handle men like Gilmore. She was confident she could steer the barbarian away from the gate of her treasured castle. Yet, she also knew that any controversy or scandal played out in public at the wrong time could just as easily bring everything tumbling to the ground. It was a dangerous time for IIA. Transparency was being demanded. Of course that was impossible. But the appearance of transparency was not. Knoble could make that happen. Whatever else might happen, IIA was not going down under her watch.

A persistent problem hounded Maryann Knoble. The same one which burdens every man and woman holding a position of power in uncertain times: human beings.

It was well known and well accepted that common, everyday people on the street are shortsighted and ignorant. They prefer governments to spend their tax dollars on minutiae like social services, health reform, highways, infrastructure, and the arts instead of big-picture necessities that keep them safe, healthy, and alive. Maryann Knoble appreciated art and good roads as much as anyone, but she knew they meant nothing without organizations such as IIA to ensure an environment in which they could be enjoyed.

Exacerbating the problem was that most of those same people had only a vague awareness of IIA, and even less so for its myriad divisions. Being the head of a powerful organization that most of the time flew under the radar was not entirely unappealing to Knoble, but now that same invisibility threatened the agency's existence and, by extension, her own.

Battling bureaucrats and dodging political threats were causing Maryann Knoble great irritation. The unexpected re-emergence of Skawa Island had created a permanent knot of uneasiness in her stomach. And there was one more thing further charring the edges of her already inflamed disposition: the shipwrecked women. How the hell had they known to ask for help *specifically* from the Canadian Disaster Recovery Agency?

Like CDRA, Aspen Downs was not well known. Its hidden location, in a verdant sanctuary ninety minutes northwest of Toronto, near the Grand River and Elora Gorge, was one reason. Money was the other. The luxurious long-term private care facility charged accordingly—and then some— for its solitude, impressive list of services, remarkably low resident-to-staff ratio, and its most valued offering of all: a guaranteed stress-free experience for the loved ones who left someone behind in the tender care of Aspen Downs.

Instructing her driver to wait in the car, Maryann Knoble entered the stately building. She took careful note of the quiet, peaceful atmosphere and barely detectable scent of cinnamon and hydrangea that lingered in the air. She wondered what it would be like to have this as one's workplace instead of the hectic, always-on-edge world of IIA and shuddered at the thought.

As promised, Loreena Kitzman was waiting for her in the reception area. The two women shook hands as they faced each other, Knoble wide and tall as a linebacker,

Loreena delicate and graceful.

"Thank you for agreeing to meet me here," Knoble began, silently assessing the other woman. She guessed Loreena Kitzman was in her early sixties and had benefited from subtle intervention, making her appear five to-seven years younger.

"Of course," Loreena responded with a sad smile. "I'm actually grateful for your visit."

Knoble didn't understand and her expression said so.

"I know that must sound odd," Loreena responded. "You see, for the last three years, it's been…a challenge… finding reasons to come here, finding reasons to stay."

"His condition has deteriorated that much?"

She nodded. "The first six or seven years after the diagnosis—after he left IIA—were really quite good. I am forever thankful he made the decision to leave work right away. It gave us time to…." She hesitated to swallow a lump that had developed in her throat. She was surprised by it—and glad. It had been a while since she'd felt anything but detached sympathy for Sergiusz Belar. "It gave us time to have a little more of a life together. And to prepare for… well, for this."

Knoble showed an empathetic face. Inside, her mind was roiling with disappointment and self-recrimination. Was she too late? Why hadn't she thought to confront Belar earlier? She'd left Skawa and a host of other things on the back burner for far too long.

"It took my people a while to find you," Knoble said, deciding there was no time for delicacy. "Your last name? You changed it?"

"Kitzman, yes," the older woman said, a faint smile flickering across her face. "I remarried a little over a year ago."

"Oh. I didn't realize you and B—Sergiusz were divorced."

"Yes. For a long time now. It wasn't my idea, believe me. But it was one of his 'rules' when he proposed."

"Rules?"

"He saw what this disease had done to his father, and then to him and his mother. He was so worried about my future should he ever develop the same thing that he refused to marry me unless I agreed to a list of rules. It's why we never had children. And if he received the diagnosis, the rule was that I would immediately agree to a divorce."

"Before he became too mentally incapacitated for you to divorce him legally."

"Yes."

Knoble nodded, admiring the dispassionate logic of Belar's decision.

"He didn't want a situation where he was intellectually unreachable and I was left married to a stranger who didn't know or care about me."

"As he is now?"

"Yes. Of course, I didn't want the divorce at the time. But now that I have Glen—my husband—I see how right he was. How selfless. Sergiusz could be a bit of a fuddy-duddy. And at times he was so distracted by his work I didn't think he even knew I existed. But that man…." She swallowed another lump. "…that man truly loved me."

Knoble waited for what she felt was an appropriate number of seconds before suggesting they make their way to Loreena Kitzman's ex-husband's suite.

At first, upon entering Belar's well-appointed room,

Knoble was taken aback. Not by how the one-time head of one of Canada's most powerful organizations had waned but rather by how he hadn't. Aside from a noticeably vacant expression in his gaze and the fact that he was wearing a comfortable sweater over a patterned shirt and cotton pants, instead of the tailored suits Knoble had been more accustomed to seeing him in, Sergiusz Belar looked much the same as the last time she saw him.

"Sergiusz," Loreena murmured as she approached the man sitting contentedly next to a window, apparently having been doing not much other than gazing outside. "I've brought an old friend to visit."

Knoble hid a frown at the inaccuracy of the statement. Belar and she had never been more than colleagues who knew each other in passing. Hoping the upturn of the corners of her lips passed for a kindly smile, she stepped forward and held out a hand. Instead of grasping it with his right hand for a shake, Belar held onto it with his left and squeezed tight.

Knoble winced at the surprising strength of the man. "Sergiusz, it's good to see you again. You're looking well."

"Yes," was his first word.

At least he can talk, Knoble reassured herself. Her eyes moved to Loreena. "Would you mind if Sergiusz and I had a moment alone?"

"Oh." She was surprised by the request. No one wanted to spend time with Sergiusz alone. And she wasn't entirely certain they should. "Are you sure? Sometimes he has flickers of recognition and he'll talk to me. He's not so good with other people, I'm afraid."

Knoble felt the corners of her mouth ache under the

stress of maintaining the unnatural position. But she knew she'd have to keep it up a while longer. The foolish woman hadn't even thought to ask her why she wanted to see Belar in the first place. She didn't want that to change. "Just for a minute," she said with a voice smeared with hope. "That's all. It's been so long since we've seen each other."

Loreena inclined her head to indicate she understood. "Of course. I'll be right outside if you need me."

"Thank you. Why don't you find yourself a cup of tea? You must need one." Women like Loreena Kitzman liked tea.

When the ex-wife was gone, Knoble pulled over a chair from where it sat up against a work desk that had probably never been used. She sat, her knees almost touching Belar's.

"You know me, don't you?"

For a long moment the man was silent. Knoble didn't care to interrupt the work of mutated genes doing their best to form an opinion.

"I think I might," he uttered with little confidence but with an increasing glimmer of recognition in his eyes.

"I'm who you used to be, Belar. I run the Canadian International Intelligence Agency."

He stared. Then: "Double I-A," he said, using the commonly used acronym.

Knoble smiled. This was better than she'd hoped for. But she knew lucidity was nothing but a passing fancy for Belar. She had to work quickly.

"Tell me about Skawa Island, Belar. Do you remember Skawa Island? You approved its purchase with IIA funds ten years ago. Do you remember that?"

His eyes shone, but he said nothing.

"I need to know why you bought that island. What did

you use it for?"

Belar's eyes darted to the window.

Blast it! I'm losing him.

"Belar, I need you to think about this," she commanded in a louder voice. "It's vitally important. This may be your last chance. Is there something I should know about Skawa?"

She could see it in his face. She was right. Something bad was coming. Skawa Island was a danger to IIA, a danger to her.

"Tell me, Belar, tell me."

Nothing.

"Tell me!"

"Excuse me?"

Knoble looked up to find Loreena Kitzman standing halfway through the doorway, her face quizzical. The woman had not gone for tea as she'd been told to.

"What are you doing? What are you asking him?"

Slowly rising from her chair, Knoble was content in the knowledge that she was never meant to be a sympathetic caregiver to the elderly or infirm. She didn't have the patience for it.

"I'm sorry, Loreena," she said in a sad voice laced with syrup. "You were right. For a moment there, I thought he was his old self again and knew me. I guess I got carried away with our conversation."

Not as easily swayed as Knoble had supposed, Loreena inquired, "What did you want him to tell you?"

Deceits came easily to the head of IIA. The chuckle that came with it less so. "You'll think this is ridiculous. I've been looking for a file. I thought your husband might have remembered where it was."

"You've been looking for a file for ten years?"

Knoble was done with this woman. Moving to join her at the door, she said, "I think it's time we left Sergiusz to rest."

"Skawa."

Like a lightning strike, Knoble's attention was immediately back on her former colleague. The single word had come from Belar. She searched his eyes, not quite focussed, but the gleam was still there.

"What did you say, dear?" Loreena asked, moving closer.

"Rex save Julia," he responded, at first mumbling, then repeating with almost perfect clarity: "Rex save Julia."

Knoble shot Loreena a questioning look.

Loreena shrugged apologetically. "Sometimes he talks about people we never knew."

Or, Knoble wondered, maybe he's talking about people *you* never knew.

She glared at the sick man. *Dear God, Belar, what have you done?*

Chapter Four

Late at night in her office, with everyone long gone and the brilliant light show of downtown Toronto at its zenith, was Maryann Knoble's favourite time of day. Good thing too, because she often found herself there.

Knoble had a routine, well known to those who worked most closely with her. Every evening at seven thirty she locked her office suite and met her driver in the building's underground parking lot. He ferried her to one of three favourite restaurants. All of them featured steak and starch at astronomical prices. She would finish her meal by nine and then have the waiting driver deliver her to the magnificent home in Toronto's exclusive Bridle Path neighbourhood, where she looked after the needs of an aging basset hound. Sophie was the love of her life. But by ten thirty, the doddering dog would be fast asleep, oblivious to the companionship they'd once exuberantly shared and her owner still desperately craved.

Knowing of only one way to stave off loneliness, Knoble made her way to her five-car garage, selected one of her little-used luxury vehicles, and drove back to the office, where she would drink one glass of Scotch, smoke one Arturo Fuente Opus X A cigar, and work until she deemed sleep the next reasonable item to check off her daily schedule.

Her back to the sparkling splendour dozens of floors beneath her, Maryann removed her oversized glasses and rubbed the bridge of her nose. For hours, she'd been studying—again—the files left behind by her predecessor, looking for anything that would tell her more about Skawa Island. But the only things she'd uncovered were more questions. Every time she thought she was on to something, the trail dead-ended in documents redacted beyond comprehension or simply unavailable, as if they had never existed.

Only one thing was clear.

Belar had kept secrets.

Why had he approved the purchase of the island? What did he intend to use it for? Did he actually use it? And, probably the most important question of all: With whom was he working? Whatever Belar had done on Skawa Island, he didn't do it alone.

Maryann was not surprised by this. Frustrated, yes. Surprised, no. She often did exactly the same thing. As the head of IIA, she occasionally found it expedient or necessary to take certain actions which, by their very nature, were required to be unburdened by electronic or paper trails. That thought brought her to a temporarily more pressing matter.

Replacing her spectacles and pushing aside the Belar files, she regarded the other pile on her desk. She opened the top folder and scanned the first page. It detailed the emergency laparoscopic surgery she'd recently ordered carried out at the IIA medical suite. Vocal cord removal. Controversial, possibly inhumane, but necessary. A fine example of something no one else needed to know about, however much it was for the greater good. The good of IIA. The good of Maryann Knoble.

Reaching over to the piece of equipment—perhaps her favourite—next to her desk, Maryann flipped the switch. She smiled as she fed the file into the shredder, listening to the sound she always found so comforting: "wwwwwwwr-rrrrrrrrrrrrrrrrrrrrrrrrrr."

Earlier in the day, using her higher-than-damned-well-everyone-but-the-Prime-Minister clearance level, Maryann had destroyed all digital copies of the report as well as sup-plementary files created by the IIA medical office. These, Maryann suspected with grim recognition, were the same steps Belar had taken two decades ago to hide what was happening on Skawa Island.

For the next while, with her exceedingly comfortable and expensive leather chair swivelled so she could appreci-ate the view of the city, Maryann finished her cigar and Scotch.

Later, rising from her desk to leave, she noticed some-thing odd at the top of her in-basket. The item was peculiar only because it looked like something she hadn't seen in quite some time. A relic of the past. A dinosaur. It was a personal letter.

She picked up the unopened envelope and turned it over. No return address. Using a diamond-studded, sterling-silver letter opener, she sliced open the top and drew out a single sheet of paper.

She read the handwritten note.

Then again.

It was from Milo Yelchin, until his recent death, IIA's house physician.

It was, in many ways, his suicide letter. Or rather an ad-junct to the one they'd found with his hanged body.

The letter was Yelchin's confession to Maryann of his complicity in a plot devised by her freshly "de-barked" and disposed of second-in-command, Ross Campbell. For reasons of his own, Campbell had been blindly intent on obtaining a top-secret asset under the protection of IIA's Asset Protection Unit: a cure for cancer.*

Blackmailed over his growing gambling debts, Dr. Yelchin had been coerced into cooperating with Campbell in an effort to convince CDRA's top agent, Adam Saint, to go after the cure. Saint was led to believe he was suffering from an inoperable, malignant brain tumour, the cure his only hope for survival. Yelchin had backed up his "diagnosis" with prescriptions for a combination of drugs designed to reinforce Saint's "symptoms." Even now, the agent believed his death was imminent.

Maryann judged the plan dastardly and ill-fated but superlative nonetheless.

Yelchin was sorry.

For this—and doubtless his many other sins, Maryann noted to herself—he'd taken his own life.

Milo Yelchin, Maryann decided, had been a ruinously weak man.

His letter asked only one thing. When Maryann told Saint of his horrible deceit, Yelchin hoped she'd also ask the agent to try to find it in his heart to forgive him.

A minute later, Maryann Knoble strode confidently out of her office, listening to the sound she always found so comforting:"wwwwwwrrrrrrrrrrrrrrrrrrrrrrrrrrrrrrrrrrrrr."

---

*When the Saints Go Marching In

My boot caught on a clod of dirt, baked to cement-like hardness beneath the harsh sun. I went down. The situation was about to rage out of control, and I'd just lost valuable seconds. I ignored the burning scrapes to the heels of my hands and scrambled to my feet. Threading fingers through unwashed, grimy hair, I surveyed the landscape and assessed my enemy.

Of the natural-born killers I've come across in my line of work, fire is one of the most dangerous and cunning, able to snuff out its victims in a multitude of ways—all horrible and deadly in their unpredictability. Paired with its natural ally, wind, as it was this morning, the danger factor was immeasurably multiplied.

On the opposite side of the narrow but lengthy line of raging fire, I could see two figures. They were moving through the haze of smoke, like ghostly wraiths, one considerably slower than the other. They were desperately attempting to snuff out the flames by tossing shovelfuls of dirt on top of them. An hour ago, just after dawn, when my father had first started the controlled burn, that might have worked. But no more.

"Adam!" I heard my father screaming when he caught sight of me. In all my years of growing up, I'd rarely heard him even raise his voice. When he did, it meant things were bad. Today, that was an understatement. "Grab a shovel!"

"Dad!" I yelled back as I ran closer, he and Anatole on one side of the fire, me and the vulnerable buildings of the farmyard on the other. Depending on which way the pernicious wind decided to blow, one side or the other was in imminent jeopardy.

"Grab a shovel!" he repeated through ragged dregs of breath.

Even obstructed by the curtain of smoke and blowing dust, I could see that my father was breathing heavily, his skin furiously red and damp with sweat. At his side, Anatole never looked up as he frantically continued to toss shovel after shovel of loose ground onto the mounting fire.

"Start over there!" Dad yelled, pointing to the far end of the fire line, about half a kilometre away. "We'll stop it from this end. We've got to hurry before it gets to the yard!"

I knew my father was feeling many things at that moment, anger and guilt at the forefront. Burning the straw stubble of a field after harvest was once a widespread practice throughout Saskatchewan. It was a quick and cheap way to clear a field and kill weeds. But eventually, farmers—and governments—began to realize the harmful effects: loss of nutrients to the soil, smoke pollution, and risk of fires spreading out of control and creating far more damage, at the extreme including loss of life. But Dad was old school. He'd have come out here before daylight and started the small burn in the typical calmness of early morning. He'd have kept diligent watch over the fire. But there was one thing he couldn't control: wind. And sometimes on the Prairies, a wicked wind can sneak up out of nowhere.

Fortunately, he'd had the sense to ask Anatole to come with him, something they'd likely been doing together every year since my nephew was a boy. Probably nothing had ever gone wrong before. But it just takes once. Then suddenly, you're facing disaster. It was Anatole who'd used his cellphone to call me for help.

"Dad, that's not going to work!" I shouted back over

the flickering wall of fire that separated us.

"Just do it!" he screamed.

He knew I was right, but he was desperate. Oliver Saint would never give up.

Neither would I.

"No, Dad, the fire's too big." The expanse of flame was simply too long for us to get to it all in time. The wind was picking up. Even if they worked at one end and I at the other, the middle would take over.

"Damn it, Adam!" His eyes were wild, his voice growing hoarse. "Grab a shovel and get to work!"

"I called the fire department," Anatole hollered at me, taking a few seconds rest from shovelling. The look he gave me told me two things: He knew I was right, and he knew the fire department would never get here in time.

I nodded, then turned and ran. Away.

"Adam!" I could hear my father's voice, a mixture of betrayal and sorrow, tear through the air after me.

One more shovel heaping pitifully inadequate loads of dirt on this fire was not going to defeat it. I had to find bigger ammunition.

Minutes later, I was behind the wheel of Dad's three-ton truck, barrelling toward the fire. It was none too soon. As I advanced, I could see Dad, leaning against his shovel for support, his chest heaving, his face a mask of sweat-stained soot. My sixty-five-year-old father was nearly done in. Anatole was still going at it, like some kind of machine. But he too looked as if he was about to either collapse from exhaustion or explode from the punishing effort.

I maneuvered the heavy vehicle to one end of the line of flames and positioned the nose so when I moved forward I would be driving directly over the centre line of the fire. My plan must have dawned on the other two men. They both stepped back from their battle and laid aside their shovels.

Only yesterday my father had travelled to the local gravel pit and filled the three-ton's box. His intent was to use the gravel to refurbish the yard and driveways that regularly wear down to bare ground and dirt over time. Instead, I would use the loose aggregate of small, pounded stones to put a damper on this fire.

Engaging the hydraulics, I raised the truck's box into the dump position and opened the rear hatch. I hoped my father kept the three-ton in good repair, especially the fuel line, as I had no desire to be caught sitting on top of an eruption. Even so, I did my best to travel at the top speed to make it down the blazing line fast, but slow enough to allow the truck to dump sufficient gravel onto the flames to either douse them or at the least tamp them down into something manageable until the fire department arrived.

As the truck rumbled by Dad and Anatole, I could tell by the expressions on their worn and exhausted faces that my strategy was working. Prairie fire was not going to win today.

I stood in front of my bedroom's full-length mirror, my body naked, caked with dust and reeking of smoke. My regular morning routine had been interrupted by the emergency call from Anatole about the stubble fire. But now, before I showered off the after-effects, I attempted the unflinching, professional assessment of my reflection that had become my morning ritual. I was looking for one thing: a sign that my disease had reared its ugly head, the appearance of which, I knew, was a matter of when, not if.

I don't know exactly what I expected to see. Perhaps a noted loss of weight, a sallowness in my skin, flagging muscles, unexplained bruises or marks, any signal warning me that the sickness was finally making its offensive move against me. I'm a big guy, 6' 3", with a sturdy, muscular build. I know my body. Any mark of physical deterioration would be readily apparent to me.

So far, so good.

Next came an evaluation of possible mental decline. I ran through a series of tests I'd developed, designed to confirm my knowledge of seven languages and access to detailed long-term memory. Things like reciting the Spanish alphabet, reviewing the seven cases of a Ukrainian noun, listing the names of the first three girls I kissed who were brunettes.

Satisfied that for one more day on this earth I was the Adam Saint I'd always been, I headed for the shower.

In many ways, however, I wasn't the Adam Saint I'd always been and never would be again. The worst day of my life occurred when my doctor, Milo Yelchin, told me about my glioblastoma multiforme, the most common and unfortunately most aggressive type of malignant primary brain tumour. Treatment is pretty much non-existent, survival completely so.

Except for some crazy headaches and some situations where I may have been seeing things, the thing, so far, had been asymptomatic. The good doctor said I could expect that, but not forever. Eventually, the seizures and vomiting and semi-strokes would begin. I could expect progressive neurological and personality changes. And then, sometime between now and a year from now, the pressure on my brain would be too much and I'd be done.

That not-so-cheery news is why I tendered my resignation to the CDRA and its mother ship, IIA. It's why my days were no longer spent visiting grisly crash sites, identifying charred Canadian remains at a nuclear power plant blast, or hiking the Austrian mountains in search of avalanche survivors. Instead, I was living in my childhood home on a farm in rural Saskatchewan.

The life of a disaster recovery agent is fast-paced, brutal, uncomfortable, exciting, and adventurous. All the things I love. Life on a Saskatchewan grain farm is none of those things. Yet there I was. Living with my father, Oliver Saint, and my nephew, Anatole. Occasionally, we got a visit from my sister, Alexandra. No more Koenigsegg CCX roadster that can accelerate from zero to one hundred kilometres an hour in 3.2 seconds. No more expensive wardrobe, fine wines, upscale restaurants. No more apartment in Yorkville's Four Seasons Private Residences with its Yabu Pushelberg—designed lobby.

Without the comfortable trappings of my former life, a raw admission was beginning to dawn on me. Something I feared made me a bad person, or, at the very least, a bit of a jerk.

I missed all those things.

What sense does that make? A dying man who still yearned for mere things and a job that might kill him.

But it was what I knew. Those things were a part of me. I must have loved them because I'd pursued them at great cost. I achieved them at the expense of my marriage and every other familial relationship I could lay claim to, including with a son who couldn't care less if I lived or died... even after finding out the latter was imminent.

Now all of it was gone. The career. The apartment. The car. The marriage.

After my diagnosis I came home. Because that's what you do when you learn you're going to die.

Right?

Maybe the only reason I came home was because I had nowhere else to go. But that wasn't true. I'd had options. I'd had options because I had money. Along with the extreme demands of my job had come extreme financial reward. I could have been anywhere in the world other than that cramped bedroom, living with an old man and a socially inept goth nerd.

No, I wasn't missing the trappings of my former life I was mourning them. Because I knew that life would never be mine again. I was on that prairie farm because something inside of me demanded it—demanded I reconnect with these people, my father, my sister, her son, and maybe, eventually, my own son.

And then, someday, I would die.

But not today.

Finished with my shower, I was surprised to find my father in the kitchen, cleaned up and working on a bowl of oatmeal.

"You doing okay, Dad?" I asked, eyeing him up for any signs of the overwhelming exertion he'd put himself through that morning. "Maybe you should lie down for a while."

"That machine of yours has been making noises," Dad grumbled without looking up.

By "machine" I knew he meant my laptop. As I poured myself a cup of coffee, the "machine" repeated the noise that had interrupted my father's breakfast. I knew the sound well and tapped the button that would answer the incoming Skype call. The image that appeared onscreen surprised me.

Maryann Knoble.

Even from two thousand kilometres away, the digitized version of IIA's chief exuded undeniable power and authority. Knoble's was not a pleasant face to look at. It was broad and square, even the rounded edges seemed as severe and unyielding as rock. Tiny eyes behind supremely shiny over-sized glasses were barely visible between slabs of skin, as if endlessly narrowed in intense scrutiny. Her hair was a barely controlled mess of tightly wound curls. I could easily conjure up the smell of sweet cigar tobacco beneath the musky cologne she favoured.

"Are you alone?" her husky voice greeted me.

"I'm done here," my father grunted as he got up to leave the table.

"I can go to another room," I told him.

"No need. Gotta go clean up the mess we made out there this morning."

"I can do that later. Why don't you take it easy today?"

He looked at me as if I'd just sprouted a set of antennae.

I watched as he made quick work of clearing his bowl, then grabbing a light jacket from a nearby coat hook, he exited by the kitchen door.

Maryann, sensing what was happening outside her line of vision, remained silent.

"Yes," I answered her original question. "What can I do for you, Maryann?" I was guessing I knew.

"It's time for you to come back."

As expected. "I already went over this with Campbell. He explained how you felt there might still be a role for a man on death row within the agency—although I can't even begin to imagine what that might be. But as I said to him and now I'll say to you, despite being honoured by the offer to use me up until my dying day, I must respectfully decline. I've got more important matters to attend to here at home."

Knoble did little to disguise a scoff. "That old farmhouse on the prairie? That isn't your home, Saint, and you know it."

Inwardly, I cringed at the words, at the possibility that she was the only one with big enough balls to tell me the truth.

"CDRA is your home. Your medical situation came as a shock. You've made decisions you wouldn't normally make because of it. I understand."

Is that so wrong?

"It doesn't have to be the end, Saint."

Doesn't it?

"What are you talking about, Maryann?"

"IIA and CDRA may be in trouble. You can help. You may be the only one who can."

She was pulling out the big guns. Although I didn't know Knoble all that well, I did know she didn't hand out easy compliments or false praise.

"I don't know if you understand my situation." My father was long gone but still my eyes darted to the door to confirm he was nowhere within earshot. Dad didn't know about my tumour. He was the only one left in my family who didn't. I couldn't bear to tell him. "I'm going to be very sick very soon, and then I will die. How can I possibly help you?"

"Trust me. You can."

Her request put me in a difficult position. Everything I knew about Maryann Knoble led me to conclude I did not like the woman. Yet, everything I'd seen and heard told me she was intelligent, strategic, cunning, and, like a bulldog on a bone, she would never let go of something she wanted. In my business, and for someone leading an organization like the Canadian arm of the International Intelligence Agency, these were traits to be applauded. But trust? Did I trust her?

"So what? You want me to come back and rejoin CDRA?"

I could not have predicted her next words. "No. Quite the opposite. The only way you can help me is if you don't."

I had to admit she'd piqued my interest.

"I need more, Maryann," I found myself saying. "Before I commit…." And that was as far as I got.

What was I doing? What was I saying? I had a finite amount of time left on this planet. Time I desperately needed to figure out how to tell my father I was dying, tell my son I loved him, tell my sister I was sorry for disappointing her. At the rate I was going, I'd need more time than I probably had.

I stared into those inscrutable eyes on the screen before me and announced my answer: "No."

She seemed miraculously unperturbed by my decision. Which meant only one thing: She'd been expecting it. Which also meant I should expect a Plan B. People like Knoble always had a Plan B. What I didn't expect was how Plan B would toss me on my ass and change everything.

Chapter Five

My sister works beneath a freeway on the southern outskirts of the city. Dirks, the bar she owns, is part biker bar, part skanky dive. Mostly, the crowd consists of an eclectic mix of self-respecting motorcycle enthusiasts, university students looking for cheap beer, and desperate singles who'd started at the swankier clubs downtown but downgraded after midnight. There are bars just like this all over the world. I've been in more than a few of them.

I'd spent the day mulling over the stunning message delivered to me that morning by Maryann Knoble. As a disaster recovery agent, I am the guy who needs to calmly collect information, make a decision, then act on it, usually within a short space of time. I am also a guy who is used to dealing with life-and-death situations. Often, the life at risk is my own. To help others, I occasionally put myself in jeopardy. This has never bothered me. It comes with the job; it's what I was trained to do. But this was different. This was about just me. My life. The kind of man I am. *So who am I?*

I needed…something. Guidance? A sounding board? Someone with a clear head?

With my father in the dark about my health, and me without a friend in my own hometown, the only adult I had to turn to in Saskatoon was my sister. Alexandra was neither pleased nor pissed when I planted my butt on one of Dirks's cracked leather bar stools. She was helping her team of beefy, dumbbell-pusher bartenders deal with last call, and business was brisk. People were ordering drinks as if the well was about to run dry, which I guess it was.

Doling out healthy pours of tequila into a trio of shot glasses on a waitress's waiting tray, she shot me a look, a dark eyebrow arched high. "Beer?"

I nodded.

"Can I get a brandymandarinorangechampagnespritzer, please?" a chirpy voice demanded over the waitress's shoulder.

Simultaneously finishing with the shots and starting on my draft, Alexandra landed her killer grey eyes on the gum-smacking princess for a count of three before responding with: "Fuck off."

I watched as the blond, too shocked to speak, was helplessly swallowed up by a passing pack of jocks, each barely managing a pair of overflowing pitchers in ham-fisted grasps and not caring about how much ended up on the already beyond sticky floor.

"Beer and tequila only night?" I asked my sister.

"Who the fuck does she think she is ordering shit like that in a place like this? Next thing you know she'll want a linen napkin and sushi. Jee-zuz!"

I shook my head and smiled. For the next forty-five minutes, I watched as my sister deftly handled seemingly endless hordes seeking to satisfy unquenchable thirsts. As the night wore on and alcohol did its magic on inhibitions, she effortlessly warded off the increasingly crude and charmless advances of every third dude and even a gal or two.

Some might tell you my sister bears resemblance to Lara

Croft, Tomb Raider—or Angelina Jolie depending on the genre of your entertainment pleasure—all dark and brooding, with the characteristic thick lips all us Saints share and a take-no-guff attitude about pretty much everything. Separated by seven years and my desire to get away from home as fast as I could, we didn't know each other as kids. I left her behind on the farm with a mother who favoured her son and a father who favoured his tractor.

Growing up wasn't easy for my sister. Alexandra's acting out and mood swings intensified after I left. Eventually, she was diagnosed as bipolar, but by then the damage had been done. Underage drinking led to drugs led to sex led to becoming a single parent. She'd be the first one to admit she didn't start out as a candidate for mother of the year, but from what I'd seen since being home, things had changed for the better between Alexandra and her son, Anatole.

When drinks stop being served in a bar like Dirks, things either get louder and rowdier as last shots are guzzled and sex connections are finalized or rebuked, or they die down in a hurry if cases of the former are greater than the latter. Fortunately for me, it seemed that Cupid was working overtime in Saskatoon that night. The place was clearing out fast.

"You look like you have something on your mind," Alexandra said as she deposited a fresh beer in front of me.

I gave my watch a pointed look. It was way beyond legal serving time.

"Perk of being the owner's brother. And you're paying for it."

My sister has a healthy disregard for rules and regulations and likes to make a profit.

"I had a phone call today," I started, guessing we'd probably have at least a minute or two of privacy. Patrons were slowly filing out with the encouragement of Alexandra's expert crew of employees. They themselves were encouraged by their desire to get the place cleaned up so they could get the hell out of there.

"I'm glad to hear you're making some new little friends," she threw out as she worked on rubbing down the world-weary bar counter between us.

"It was from Maryann Knoble."

This elicited an ugly curl of her lip. "What the fuck did that bitch want?" Although the two had met only once before in a difficult shoot-out situation, Alexandra had placed the IIA chief firmly in her "hate their guts" category of acquaintances. I doubted Knoble even remembered my sister's name.

"She says hello."

Alexandra gave me the finger and resumed her cleaning.

"She wants to cure me."

This got my sister's attention. She knew first-hand that something that sounded as outlandish as a cure for cancer actually wasn't. She stepped into the spot directly across from where I sat and stared at me.

"You know the story," I said. "IIA had the cure, lost it, I went after it."

"You're forgetting the best part. About how you let it slip through your fingers once you had it."

As it turned out, the cure was not some neat little confection in a syringe you plunged into your arm then hoped for the best. The cure was a kid named Jake. A ten-year-old boy who had something astounding in his genetic makeup that happened to cure some cancers. Unfortunately, it became quite obvious that if this incredible fact ever became known, his life would be sacrificed in the name of science. So, today, he—and the cure that lives within him—is hidden away where no one will ever find him.

The whole thing had been morally and emotionally shaky ground to tread upon. Do you save one life at the expense of millions of others? I was glad the decision was in my past, even if it meant that the one thing that could have saved my life was no longer available to me.

Until now.

"Maryann says there's a possible cure for what I have, after all."

"How?" Alexandra hissed, making a quick survey of the bar to ensure no one was close enough to hear us. "How can that be? Have they changed their minds about the kid?"

"No, but one of Maryann's Dr. Frankensteins has been working on a tissue sample of Jake's for years. He's found something."

"A cure?"

"Not really. Not yet. With all the regulatory red tape to get test trials certified, what he has won't even be safe for lab rats for a dozen years at least. But he's convinced it *will* work. So is Maryann, but she's no doctor. She admits this treatment could help me or kill me."

A tiny smile snuck onto my sister's glowering face, a slight but significant rearrangement that mystically morphed her features from harsh to beautiful. "But you're already half dead."

No beating around the bush with my sis. I like that about her. "Exactly."

"What is it? Like some sort of chemotherapy thing?"

"Nope. Just a serum with the aforementioned hoped-for miraculous reversal properties. It gets injected. We wait and see."

"You're going to do it." Statement. Not a question.

I hesitated and she knew why.

"She wants something."

"Of course."

"She wants you back."

I nodded.

Alexandra picked up the cleaning rag she'd set aside and used it to buff the counter between us as she thought about this. Behind me, I heard the late-night sounds of shuffling feet, scraping of chairs being pushed back from tables, and whispered promises that would mean nothing come morning.

After throwing back a random shot of whiskey abandoned near the till, Alexandra broke her silence. Her holler reached every dark nook and cranny of the bar: "You've got two minutes to get out of here, you losers! Get a move on, Gormley! I see you back there! Out! Now!" Mollified by a bit of satisfying screeching, she returned to her spot across from me. "That Wicked Witch of the West you used to work for would never consider just giving you this last chance of survival out of the goodness of her heart, would she?"

"She'd have to have one."

"Why does she want you back so bad? I know you used to be a big shit and all, but no one's that good. She's gotta be breaking about a million rules to do this for you."

"I'd have thought you'd be impressed by that."

"Well, sure." She smirked. "But, it still doesn't make sense. What's really going on here, Adam?"

"I think she's in trouble. IIA is in trouble. She needs someone who's outside the organization but knows it well and has the right training to fix things."

"What's the trouble?"

"That's the rub. I don't know yet. I'd have to sign on the dotted line first."

"I don't like the sound of that. You sell your soul to the devil, then she makes you do whatever she wants. And if you don't, by withholding the cure she's basically threatening to kill you."

Never let it be said that a bipolar single mother/bar wench can't also be brilliant. "Yup, that about sums it up."

We both heard the front door slam shut a final time and locks being shifted into place. Staff were hoisting chairs onto tables in preparation for the night cleaning crew.

"You've already made up your mind?" she asked, her eyes excavating holes into mine.

"Yeah."

"You're gonna do it."

"Anatole is working on flights right now."

"Well, you better tell him to book a second seat."

"Alexandra…."

"Keep your pie hole shut, brother. You're still a dying man. And until this serum shit starts working—and I hate to say this, but we don't even know if it will—you could keel over at any minute or have a stroke or who knows what. Right?"

"Alex…."

"Right?"

"Yes."

"And didn't you just tell me Maryann wants this done

on the hush-hush? Doesn't that mean you're going at this alone? Without the help of any of your CDRA buddies? Isn't that right?"

There was no stopping her at that point.

My head indicated the accuracy of her statements.

"So you think it's a smart move to go do whatever the hell it is this woman wants you to do, wherever the hell in the world she wants you to do it—alone? Adam, what if you get sick? I'm not kidding. What if you get really sick and you're in the middle of nowhere, all alone, with no one to look after you or get you home...."

And then the unusual happened. I heard it. She heard it. Her voice caught. The granite prairie lily was getting emotional.

"Well, screw you if you think that's the right way to go!" she covered with a bellow.

I understood. Anger has always been my sister's safe harbour.

Smouldering eyes vaulted over the bar toward a couple of employees who'd stopped to stare. "And screw you if you think I'm going to pay you to gawk instead of work!" If she were a dragon—and I'm not entirely convinced she doesn't have the DNA in her—fire would have spewed from her throat, smoke from her ears.

Obviously used to their volatile boss, they shrugged and went back to their closing-up chores.

"Get the hell out of here," she spat at me, yanking away my not-yet-empty beer mug.

Inside I was grinning. Suddenly, she'd become my baby sister again, pissed off that I didn't think she was big enough or cool enough to play with me.

"I'm not going to call Anatole," I told her calmly as I slid off my stool and headed for the door.

"Yeah, I got that. It's closing time. Now get out of here with the rest of the riff-raff."

"Okay. Have it your way. See you at six."

She frowned, licking lips that were no doubt burning. "What are you jabbering on about?" she shouted across the room.

"We have to be at the airport at six a.m. to catch our flight." I unlocked the door, pulled it open, and stepped outside. "I told Anatole to book you a window seat. I hope that's okay." With great and childish satisfaction, I shut the door behind me.

Chapter Six

Our first stop was Toronto. I had papers to sign and a miracle drug to inject. I also wanted to meet with Maryann Knoble to find out exactly what this was all about. It took her less than twenty minutes to bring me up to speed on Skawa Island and the shipwreck survivors who were requesting assistance from CDRA.

"I need you to tell me why you believe this is a problem for IIA." I was sitting in the insignificant chair opposite the monstrosity that was Maryann Knoble's throne.

"I don't know that it is," she replied matter-of-factly, gunmetal eyes steadfast upon me.

"Bullshit."

She didn't react.

"You see, Maryann, I have a policy. I have no issue with jumping headfirst into fire, but first I want to know exactly how hot it is."

"I can't tell you that, Saint, and not because I don't want to. I truly don't know. I've told you everything."

Undoubtedly not her first lie of the day.

"What I do know is that IIA purchased the island ten years ago under the direction of my predecessor, Sergiusz Belar. His reason for doing so is undetermined. On first inspection, the discovery of three women and a small child by the Australians appears to be innocent, an accident of fate. The fact they were deserted on Skawa for years but refuse to leave without the involvement of CDRA, well, I find that rather suspect. Don't you?"

"I find it unusual. A curiosity. But suspect? Why be suspicious of these women?"

"It's not them I'm concerned with."

I kept very still. If Maryann Knoble was ever going to tell me something entirely honest and vital to her true purpose, this would be it.

"It's how they got there."

"You think Belar, and therefore IIA, might have had something to do with it?"

She sucked in her cheeks and managed a perceptible nod.

"But why? Why can't you believe this is nothing more than mere coincidence?"

"The naïveté of your comment is precisely why I am the head of IIA and you…well, you are not. I *know* the world is a dark and dangerous place. You only believe it can be. You insist on the existence of light and hope, which I'm afraid to tell you,"—her stare was fire-hardened lava—"is a fool's game."

"You're wrong."

She snorted. "Which is why you were…are…amongst the best at what you do."

This wasn't a compliment. Yet, I was fascinated by it as a telltale clue of the inner workings of this woman's mind. "Oh? Why is that?"

"Your ability to pretend."

I was done with this. "Belar is our only source of information on Skawa?"

I'd had little to do with Belar when he was chief. At the end of his tenure, I was half a dozen years into my career and, as is typical for disaster recovery agents, spending every minute in the field. Belar had been the head of IIA, which meant he was no longer in the business of getting his hands dirty, if he ever had been.

"Sergiusz Belar is no longer available for questioning," she stated firmly.

I read Knoble's hard face. "Someone else knew what he was doing."

Knoble nodded her head in agreement. "There are three people I want you to meet. I've studied the records. During Belar's time here, there were three agents with whom he worked most closely."

"When do we meet?"

"They're waiting outside. But before they come in, you should know what they've been told about this meeting, and about you."

Knoble wanted my investigation of the shipwreck survivors kept confidential, so this would be interesting. I was about to learn the extent of duplicity Knoble was capable of. "Let's have it."

"Your recent and hasty departure from CDRA, although not your reason for it, was not a secret. For the purposes of today's meeting, these agents believe you to be returning temporarily as an independent consultant. Your past experience with this organization is being utilized to benefit an internal process audit instigated by the federal government. Your role is to select random past activities, projects, and cases carried on by the IIA; report on their legitimacy, adherence to agency mission, use of financial and

Gibsons District Public Library

Customer ID: 20886200151098

Items that you checked out

Title:
The dragon man : [a Detective Inspector
Hal Challis mystery]
ID: 30886000037008
Due: October-22-16

Title: God's spies : stories in defiance of
oppression
ID: 30886000182861
Due: October-22-16

Title:
Obstruction of justice : the search for
truth on Canada's Highway of Tears
ID: 30886001023437
Due: October-22-16

Title: I curse the river of time
ID: 30886000399226
Due: October-22-16

Title: The outlander
ID: 30886000019576
Due: October-22-16

Title:
The women of Skawa Island : an Adam
Saint novel
ID: 30886000584728
Due: October-22-16

Total items: 6
01/10/2016 1:38 PM
Checked out: 6
Hold requests: 0
Ready for pickup: 0

Thank you for using the 3M™ SelfCheck
System.

human resources, and eventual resolution; and ultimately deliver a success rating."

The only falseness I detected in Knoble's planned deception was my involvement in it. I had to wonder if in the lie lay a significant truth. Was IIA under the scrutiny of the feds? After all, they're the ones who pony up the cash to make it run. I liked the idea that even the mighty Maryann Knoble was accountable to someone.

"The purchase of Skawa being one of the projects under scrutiny?"

"In an ancillary manner only. Your actual investigation—the discovery of, or anything else about the shipwrecked women—is to remain confidential."

"For now."

Her lips tightened. "For now."

Knoble jabbed at a console button. A door different from the one I had entered through swung open. Two men and a woman immediately marched in. They'd obviously been awaiting their summons. I knew two of them. Scott Bellman was lanky and as pale as paper. When he was scarcely in his thirties, he'd created what was now known as the Cyber Investigations Unit. Three decades later, he was still considered a wunderkind in the field. I wouldn't be surprised if my nephew Anatole, a blooming computer wizard, might one day become just like him.

Next to Bellman's milquetoast milkweed, Jacqueline Turner was as vibrant as a spray of spring flowers. She wore a bright blue suit tailored to round each curve like a premium sports car, set off nicely against ebony skin that glimmered with vitality. I was surprised to see her. Only on rare occasions—usually catastrophic domestic events—do CDRA agents work together. I'm the first to admit I'm not particularly tied into, attentive to, or interested in office gossip, but I'd thought I'd heard she'd transferred to one of the Asian IIA offices.

"Elliott Bitterman is with Forgery Central." Knoble introduced the man I did not know once we'd all shaken hands and taken seats across from hers. Maryann's desk was so big that half a dozen of us could have been seated comfortably on the "visitor" side, yet there was unmistakably only room for Maryann on the other.

Like Turner, Bitterman was in his fifties and dressed in a serious suit, with a staid, vice presidential air about him.

After minimal pleasantries—none of us needed them—I translated a subtle tilt of head from Knoble as my starter pistol. "All of you understand why I'm here," I stated. "Each of you has worked under not only Ms. Knoble but also her predecessor, Sergiusz Belar."

Nods all around.

"For the moment, I'm focussing on certain purchase transactions made ten to fifteen years ago. As senior members of the agency, you'll have been privy to some of them. I dislike wasting anyone's time, so I'll get right to it. There are five procurements in particular that I'm interested in." I could sense Maryann's eyes burning into me. I ignored it. If she'd wanted to approve my strategy in this, she should have thought about giving me more than thirty seconds of warning before commencing the meeting. "Documentation is either abysmal or non-existent. I don't have to tell you how much the federal government is in love with paper."

The trio was remarkably patient. Silent. Listening attentively. Waiting for the shoe to drop and hoping it did so on the head of one of the two people sitting next to them.

"The good news is that four of these acquisitions have nothing to do with any of you."

Not a sigh of relief or change in facial expression, as befit well-trained senior agents. I was particularly impressed with Bellman, who'd struck me as the nervous type.

"I will be taking those up with other agents later today and into the night."

I sensed silent gratitude that whereas less fortunate colleagues might be struggling under my bureaucratically powered microscope into the wee hours of tomorrow, with any luck, it wouldn't be them.

I turned on Maryann. "Has an office been made available for interviews?"

Having no choice but to play along with me as I'd been forced to play along with her, Maryann tapped a sensor on the cord that hung below her neck and spoke quietly for a moment into her headset. Then, "Yes. You're set up in seventy-seven."

My strategy wasn't to piss Knoble off. Solely. If any of these three were actually privy to useful information about Skawa Island or what Belar was doing with it ten years ago, there was no way they'd volunteer it in front of two other agents. And if I needed to employ methods to extract information I felt was being kept back, there was no way I wanted to do it in front of those same agents. It was time to make this private. ·

"I'd like you to tell me everything you know about why an organization like IIA would purchase a tropical island in the South Pacific called...." For show, I consulted imaginary notes on my iPad. "Skawa Island?"

"I...I don't know what you're talking about." I was right after all. Scott Bellman *was* the nervous type.

"You must know about Skawa. You were working closely with Belar at the time he approved its purchase."

"I had nothing to do with that. I was working on an information portal and database collector unit Belar asked me to develop."

"What was the purpose of the portal?"

"He wanted a comprehensive facility to accumulate, monitor, and correlate all incoming meteorological, astronomical, and aeronautical information reports and studies from every space agency that reports to IIA. Do you have any idea how much information of this kind pours into IIA in any given week?"

"I'm guessing by your tone quite a lot."

"What he was asking was a massive undertaking. It was right after 9/11. Everyone was paranoid about everything. I believe his greatest area of interest had to do with astro-threat assessment. I'd be happy to discuss the basics with you over the next several days. But an island? I don't know about any island."

"Scott...." He'd asked me to call him by his first name. "Have you been to the South Pacific?" At random, I was throwing in a series of questions I could easily check the answer to. If he lied, I'd know I had something. Trickery is never foolproof, but it's a nice tool to keep at hand.

"I burn like crepe paper," he drolly reported.

I believed him.

The three interviews took nearly two hours. And then I was out of time. I had a meeting with my new best friend, the IIA doctor, who was waiting to pump me full of friendly poison.

"What did you find out?" Knoble asked when I came by her office to tell her I was done and heading for my appointment.

"I'm afraid nothing much," I admitted. "My hands were tied in too many ways. Keeping them believing I was less interested in the island's true purpose than whether they were complicit in a fraud perpetrated on Canadian taxpayers was maybe not the best tack."

She jumped on that. "We can't allow anyone to think we know what's really going on until we really do. I hope you understand that. I hope you understand our agreement fully, Saint."

Once again, I felt the full force of her eyes boring into me. Unsettling, I'd give her that. "I do. And I hope you understand that spending forty minutes with a suspect without time to access background information is not smart interrogation technique or in any way conclusive."

"Are you telling me one of these people may be hiding something?"

"I'm telling you that nothing I learned today tells me they aren't."

Her phone rang, and she answered through her head piece. She listened intently for a moment. Landing serious eyes on me, she informed me, "I have a call coming in. From David Gilmore."

I was quite certain the last person Knoble wanted to hear from at a time like this was the Minister of Public Safety.

A sharp incline of her head indicated it was time for me to leave.

In Udaipur, Shekhar Kapur's office had been one-third the size and had no windows. It had been amongst the most opulent on the floor in a building that by Canadian standards would at best be described as shabby. His work space in Toronto was unlike any he'd seen before. Everything gleamed. Everything smelled as if it was brand new. Everything worked. And everyone who was supposed to be a co-worker actually worked a great distance away.

As far as Kapur could discern in his short time with CDRA, this was not a place of teamwork; it was a place of solitude; the more successful you became, the higher up the corporate ladder you climbed, the more isolation you demanded. In India, solitude was nothing but a dream, isolation unheard of, no matter where you were, at work, at home, at the grocery store, taking a walk in a park. People, people, people. Everywhere. Kapur missed it.

So when he sensed someone approaching his open door, he looked forward to the human interaction. Until he saw who it was.

Like a blustery, cold wind, Maryann Knoble filled the room with instant disquiet and a biting chill.

"I've forwarded you a link," were the first words from the big woman's mouth.

Obeying the unstated command, Kapur opened his email and the message waiting there from Knoble. Eyes glued to his computer screen, he clicked on the link she'd sent him. A document appeared, a newspaper article with the headline in bold: "Canadian women found on desert island."

Kapur offered a silent prayer before shifting his gaze back to the woman who now towered over his desk like an imposing totem pole, her face a forbidding top carving. He knew what was coming next. Accusation.

"This will be in the *Toronto Star* tomorrow. James Romanow is hounding me for a comment. I asked you to contain this. I asked you to keep this quiet. How did this happen, Kapur?"

Shekhar stood to face his accuser. She was correct to be furious. She was not correct to lay the blame on him. Superior or not, Kapur was not a man to accept unwarranted culpability from anyone. If only she would stop talking long enough so they might have a meaningful discussion.

She kept at him. "Do you understand the jeopardy this puts CDRA and IIA *and you* in?"

Despite the circumstances of his upbringing, Kapur considered himself a true Indian. He was born in Howrah, the second largest city in the Indian state of West Bengal. Orphaned young, he was adopted and moved to nearby Kolkata with his new parents, a wealthy and well-educated British couple. Suddenly, he was Catholic instead of Hindu, enrolled in posh private schools instead of leaving school at a young age to support his family, and travelling the world in grand style instead of being victimized by its cold, harsh realities.

Despite his adopted pedigree and privileged upbringing, Kapur was aware, as were many Indians living in Europe and North America, of the existence of certain people, particularly Westerners, who outwardly treated physically identifiable foreigners as equals but whose actions oozed with barely veiled bigotry. Given her treatment of him since arriving in Toronto, Kapur had to wonder if his new boss was one of those people.

"Did you do this?" Knoble demanded.

"Maryann," he began, his voice strong, "until you walked in here, I knew nothing about this."

"Did you do this?" she repeated, her sandpaper voice ridged with menacing, dark edges.

"Of course not. I have no—"

"Then fix it."

The door slammed shut behind her.

Closing doors. Closing doors. Everyone wanted to be behind a closed door.

Shekhar calmly lowered himself to his chair and nodded to himself, content in the newfound knowledge that Maryann Knoble was not a bigot. She was simply an exceedingly unpleasant person.

There were a great many things about people that irked Alexandra Saint. Waiting for someone was near the top. She had twenty minutes to go before she was to meet Adam at the base of the Bay Wellington Tower. He hadn't invited her to join him on his ride up the massive downtown Toronto skyscraper where he used to have an office. This pissed her off. Did he really think she'd rather spend time traipsing through the overpriced boutiques and loitering in the snobbish eateries that littered the area like a parade of stuck-up poodles showing off for people whose hands they'd bite off if given half a chance? She'd spent part of the day touring the nearby Hockey Hall of Fame. That was cool. But now she was back in the lobby. Waiting.

It was interesting for a while, watching the antlike procession of businesspeople scurrying about in their stylish suits, nattering into cell phones, or worse, those goddamn pretentious headsets, each of them believing they were the ruler of the universe and the most important person in anyone's world. But if Alexandra was being completely honest with herself, she would admit that this place, these people, intimidated her.

Downtown Toronto was not her world. Not even close. Her world was a musty little biker bar tucked beneath a freeway overpass. At Dirks, she was Queen Bee, the most kickass, exotic, smart-mouthed bitch in the whole joint. And she owned the goddamned place, so if she didn't like something or someone, all she had to do was snap her fingers and they were gone.

She'd spent much of her youth being irritated. At people. At the stupid situations she was always finding herself in. At life in general. So it was good to be boss, good to be in a position where instead of taking it, she could toss it. But here, everywhere she looked, all she saw was something she wasn't and could never hope to be. But instead of being pissed off at the preening posers, the dark feeling that was filling her up like an expanding Rorschach blot was something new. It was easy being angry. She'd had a lot of practice. This was something different. Something worse.

Frustration.

She had to move before she stuck out a foot and tripped one of these assholes just for the pleasure of seeing the smugness wiped off their over-moisturized face.

Eventually, she found herself in a busy thoroughfare, like a greenhouse on steroids. Six stories of glass and façades that looked like they were from another era. She stopped to stare at the arched roof. It was, she grudgingly had to admit, impressive. People streamed by, never bothering to say "excuse me" or "sorry" when they bumped into her. With each shove, Alexandra bit into her lip and swore under her breath, until one particularly rough sideswipe breached her uncharacteristic fortitude.

"Drive a bus much, bitch?" The words slipped out of her mouth nearly before she thought about them.

The offending offended woman stopped in her tracks and whipped around.

"Oh shit," Alexandra exclaimed. "It's you."

Chapter Seven

When last the two women laid eyes on each other, they were sisters-in-law. Now, they were little more than strangers.

For a stunned moment amidst the chaos of the Eaton Centre, they simply stared at one another.

"What are you doing here?" Kate Spalding, the first to recover her senses, asked.

Alexandra assessed the woman who was once married to her brother. In better days, people had often commented that the two of them looked enough alike to be sisters instead of just sisters-in-law. They were both tall, with long, dark hair and sharp eyes. But Alexandra could see today just how different they really were. Kate wore her beauty with a confident ease, waving it around like some kind of lightsabre. *Look at me, I'm gorgeous.* Alexandra did little to flaunt her looks, instead making style choices that either cheapened or hid them, and not always on purpose. She saw how Kate's makeup was dramatic but subtle, whereas she looked as if she'd piled it on with a palette knife. Kate's work clothes were sophisticated, sexy but not overtly. Alexandra was also dressed for work. At a beer parlour.

"I'm waiting for Adam."

"Adam is here?" Kate fired off the question like a prosecutor who'd trapped a lying witness. "He's in Toronto?"

Alexandra wanted to slink away and extricate herself from this sticky, gooey mess. She didn't know exactly what had transpired between her brother and ex-sister-in-law, but she knew it was nothing good. They were in the process of finalizing their divorce when Kate got herself engaged to another man, some jack-off named Ross Campbell. All of them, Adam, Kate, Ross, worked for the same Clydesdale of a woman, Maryann Knoble. And then, somehow, someway, Campbell ended up dead, and Kate blamed Adam. Not exactly a good start to a harmonious divorce.

"He has a meeting," Alexandra hurriedly explained. "But we're leaving town right after that. We've got a flight and everything."

"Meeting? With who? Shekhar Kapur? Knoble?"

"Yeah, sure, one of them."

"Is he...okay?"

Alexandra detected a slight thaw in the arctic voice. Did Kate still care about Adam? She knew he was dying. Would it do her some good to know that maybe, just maybe, if the stars aligned, his fate might not be so dire? Would it help her get over her anger at whatever it was that happened between them?

"He's feeling good." When you didn't know how much to say, Alexandra always found it best to say as little as possible. Unless she was drunk, and then it was open-the-floodgates time.

"You tell him"—Kate raised a crimson-tipped finger between them—"if he's still alive the next time I see him, he'll wish he wasn't."

Alexandra watched as Kate strode away, dark hair flowing in her wake, the clacking sound of her heels crystal clear above the hubbub of the atrium.

Apparently the thaw was over.

For some, it's stressful. For others, their greatest fear. Some consider it a necessary waste of time. For me, flying is none of those things. Quite the opposite. In any given month, I might rack up anywhere from twenty to two hundred hours aboard an aircraft.

Pretty much any time I'm on the ground, my life is fast-paced, hectic, often dangerous and demanding, and sometimes death-defying. So when I board an airplane, especially for a long haul, I book business class and look forward to a good meal, some wine, entertainment, and relaxation. If I do have to work during a flight, it's done in a quiet, serene environment where the typical disruptions and complications of the outside world are thirty-five thousand feet away and can't touch me unless I want them to.

Getting us from Toronto to Skawa Island was not going to be easy. I'd delegated the task of figuring it out to my nephew Anatole, while Alexandra and I were dealing with things in Toronto. Having developed a business around his mastery of anything to do with computers, he'd proven himself indispensable while I'd been traipsing the globe trying to find my cure for cancer. Now that I no longer had a team of IIA people to arrange my travel and do my research, I needed him. And he seemed to be getting a kick out of being involved in something a little more colourful than his clientele of small-business owners and computer illiterates.

By the time I was done with my visit to the IIA doctor,

Anatole had emailed an itinerary. Air Canada would get us to Los Angeles, where we'd hop onto Air Tahiti Nui to Papeete. It wasn't until we were on that eight-and-a-half-hour flight that I reminded myself that my sister had had very little travel experience, never mind a thirty-two-hour blitz to the other side of the world.

We'd left L.A. at four thirty p.m. and with the time change would arrive in Tahiti at ten p.m. Perfect schedule for enjoying a nice meal and catching up on some reading, a movie or two, and maybe a few winks. When the trolley came around and pre-dinner drinks were poured without the attendant looking for payment or even a tip, Alexandra was uncharacteristically captivated. It helped that our steward was a sturdy, young Polynesian who seemed taken with my sister's vibe.

She'd started out by playing rude with him—her typical first move around any man—but he just ate it up like shaved ice on a hot day. I'd only flown this airline once before and found the business class meal nothing special, but by the time Alexandra had scarfed down her bluefish terrine and chocolate cake desert, she was like a different person. It turned out that my sister, at thirty-five thousand feet, mellow from wine that had turned her disturbingly coquettish in response to the attentions of the flirting attendant, was not a bad travel companion.

We arrived twenty minutes late in the French Polynesian capital. It was after eleven p.m. by the time a local cab dropped us off at the Intercontinental hotel for the night. From the little we saw of the resort, it looked like a perfectly lovely place with requisite acres of lush grounds and picturesque lagoon. We'd each managed a little nap on the flights, but we needed serious sleep in a real bed to prepare ourselves for what was coming next. I handed Alexandra a sleeping pill and attempted to shuttle her off to her room. But when she learned I was planning on Skyping with Anatole, she followed me into mine.

It was late afternoon in Saskatoon. We'd caught my nephew in his office, a.k.a. his bedroom. Because of the somewhat less than stellar parenting skill set demonstrated by Alexandra, Anatole had lived with his grandparents on and off throughout his life. By the time he was old enough to move out, and independent enough to afford a place of his own, my mother had died, leaving him and my father alone in the big, rambling farmhouse. Turned out they enjoyed being roommates, and Anatole stayed put. Besides, what better place was there for a socially maladroit pseudo-goth to hole up in? A swinging bachelor pad in the bustling downtown of a youth-friendly city like Saskatoon would be lost on him.

"How was the flight, Mom?" Anatole asked as soon as he saw Alexandra sitting next to me on the suite's bed, where she'd settled in with some treats from the mini-bar. "Did you feel the bump when you crossed the International Date Line?"

For a second, she was perplexed by the question, but she quickly recovered. "Don't be a smartass, kid. I might be far away, but I've got friends who can be there in four minutes to teach you a lesson."

"Speaking of petty criminals," he responded, unfazed, "I went by the bar last night. Keeping an eye on things like you asked."

"Yeah? Everything okay there? Jan and Paul should be pretty good about looking after stuff while I'm gone."

"No fires or police raids, and only two extra holes in the Gyprock since you left," he commented dryly. "So I'd say everything is business as usual."

In the unholy light of the computer screen set against the dimness of his bedroom, Anatole appeared ghostlike. His hair was even darker than his mother's, and the metal band tee-shirt he wore—one of a repeating cycle—hung loosely on his stick figure frame. Despite it all, at nineteen, he'd be a good-looking kid if he gave a damn and learned to crack a smile now and then.

I saw him check the time at the bottom of his display. "You're in Tahiti. Let me guess: hot and steamy?"

"I'm literally sweating bullets," Alexandra chimed in, swatting at her armpits.

I nodded. "What's next?"

He screwed up his face. "Well, I've got good news and not so good news."

Although not entirely unexpected, I didn't like the sound of that. With Skawa a deserted island, I knew that finding a way to get us on shore was going to prove challenging. "How close can you get us?" I asked.

"I've got you on an Air Tahiti flight tomorrow at one in the afternoon. That will get you to Tubuai Island. They only fly there four times a week, so we got lucky on that one."

I didn't know a lot about Tubuai except that it was one of a group of islands known as the Australs, at the far southern boundary of French Polynesia, the last traditionally charted islands in the Pacific before you reach the edge of the world at Antarctica near the 70th parallel. "And then what?" This was where the "not so good" news was likely to come in.

"Well, that gets you about six hundred and forty kilometres south of where you are right now. Unfortunately, after that, you still have another fifty to go before you reach Skawa."

"I hope you're not suggesting we swim?" Alexandra grouched, chewing on a five-dollar potato chip.

"They have cargo tugs called *goélettes* that move stuff between some of the islands out there," Anatole said. "They'll sometimes take passengers if you've got your own bedroll and don't mind a bumpy ride. I looked into it, but they won't stop at an uninhabited island. So you're pretty much left to renting your own transportation. There's a lot of fishing and water sport type stuff going on around there, so I wouldn't think it would be too hard to round up someone with a boat."

"What time do we reach Tubuai?" I asked, feeling pressure to get to Skawa sooner rather than later. Too much time had already passed since the women were discovered.

Anatole consulted another pop-up screen. "The flight's about an hour and a half, so you'll get there by two thirty tomorrow afternoon."

Doing the math in my head, I knew that even with the most powerful boat we were likely to find on the tiny island, it would take us at least another hour on water to get to Skawa from Tubuai. "Okay. Sounds like a plan."

"And what about once you get on the island, Uncle Adam? What happens then?"

For once, I was grateful to be conspiring with Maryann Knoble. I'd convinced her to reissue my satellite-capable phone and laptop. "Don't worry about us," I assured. "We'll stay in touch."

The locals call Tubuai "the island of complete peace and clarity." Temperate tropical climate. Sandy beaches in colours found nowhere else in the world: yellow, pink, and orange. All the lobster and giant clams you can eat. All surrounded by a glorious underwater world of tranquil turquoise. As far as I could tell, geographical isolation was the only thing keeping Tubuai from becoming completely overrun by organized tourism.

The next day's hour-and-forty-minute flight put us on the remote island mid-afternoon. It quickly became clear that although we might not be at the very edge of the world, it couldn't be far off. There are no taxis on the island and no hotels. Anatole had arranged for the owners of a local guest house, Chez Sam & Yolande, to pick us up at the airport.

I attempted to convince the driver that instead of taking us to the B&B, we wanted to go straight to a pier or dock where we might rent a boat. He was having none of it. Within ten minutes, we were being welcomed at the tiny six-unit boarding house in Mataura, the island's main village.

"Of course, of course, there is no problem," the woman to whom I'd explained our dilemma exclaimed confidently as she merrily led us to the rear of the B&B and showed us to a linen-covered table on a white-tiled balcony. "We have plenty of boats for a trip like this. Now, what can I get you and your wife to drink after your long journey?"

"I'm his sister," Alexandra hurriedly corrected our hostess.

"Oh, isn't that nice? We don't get many brothers and sisters on holiday together. Well, I mean when they are all grown up, that is."

I smiled with as much patience as I could manage.

"Nothing to drink right now," I said. "Who should we talk to about arranging a boat?"

"You talk to me, sir!" she said with a whooping laugh. "You talk to me! Madeleine! Now tell me, when would you and your sister like to go on this trip to…what was that island called again? I don't think I've heard of it, which is strange because I know of every island near Tubuai."

"Skawa Island. No one lives there as far as I know, so you may not have heard of it."

She nodded in understanding. "A lot of people come here, especially from America, trying to get away from all the racing with rats you do out there. You're looking for peace and quiet. We have plenty of that right here on Tubuai, you know. No need for this other island of yours."

"It's beautiful here," I agreed. "But friends told us about Skawa Island, and we thought, since we've come this far, we'd like to see it."

"Of course, of course," she repeated her favourite phrase. "There is no problem. Tell me, when would you and your sister like to go there? Wednesday, maybe? Thursday? The day after?"

"Uh, no. We were hoping we could leave right away."

The woman was flabbergasted. "Today? But it's so late in the afternoon already." She tried a rollicking laugh. "It's time to relax, maybe have a nice cold drink, a swim in the water."

I checked my watch. Not yet three. "I'm afraid we're in a bit of a hurry, Madeleine."

"I don't think this will be possible, but I will check," she responded in grave tones.

When I realized she wasn't moving, I said, "That would

be wonderful if you could do that for us. It's important." I handed her a paper on which I'd jotted down the exact geographic coordinates a sailor would need to get to Skawa. "Here are the directions. I understand it's only fifty kilometres away from Tubuai."

She studied the paper carefully as if trying to decipher a code, something that might explain the madness of anyone who would take the trouble to come all the way to Tubuai and not stay put. I could understand the confusion.

"Sally will bring you something cold to drink while you wait," she offered as she slowly sauntered off, I hoped to talk to someone about a boat.

Sally was not at all what I would have expected for a waitress in a place like this. First of all, she was Caucasian, the first we'd seen since we arrived. She was in her thirties and wore a rather simple costume of off-white khakis and sleeveless shirt. Dirty blond hair was piled into a messy bun at the base of her long, gently swooping neck her eyes were the same colour as the sea. Her greeting instantly gave her away as Aussie.

"I'll have a beer," my sister ordered.

"And you? Same thing?" As she asked the question, I could see a surprising seriousness behind her eyes, as if she were used to thinking about things more daunting than the daily special.

"I think I'll hold off," I told her. "I'm hoping we won't be here long enough to finish a drink."

She chuckled and began to move off, at the same time, murmuring, "Good luck with that."

"Wait," I called her back. "You don't think we'll get a boat, do you?"

She did a cool thing where her torso swivelled so that her face was looking directly at me but her shapely hips were still pointing away. "Nothing moves that quick around here."

"Nothing?" I'd had some practice at making double-entendres sound non-creepy.

Shrewd eyes sized me up a little closer than before. As she made her way back to our little table, I could see she was working hard to keep a smirk off her face. "She'll get you a boat," Sally told us, "but it won't be today. Or even tomorrow. Believe me, I've been here a few months. Time is not a priority on Tubuai."

"Is there someone you know who can be convinced otherwise?"

We all pretended not to notice Madeleine slowly making her way back from wherever she'd gone. Sally slipped two fingers into the back pocket of her pants and pulled out a card.

"I give these away to a lot of people who come here," she said with a sparkling smile. "For when they realize that peace and quiet can get a little boring." She pointed at the card. "I'll be there in half an hour." She looked at my sister. "You still want that beer?"

Alexandra wasn't exactly sure what was going on. She shook her head. "I don't think so."

"Wonderful news!" Madeleine rejoiced as she moved in to take the spot of the departing waitress. "We have a boat for you!"

I cocked an eyebrow, waiting for the other flip-flop to drop.

"Day after tomorrow, first thing in the morning. They will deliver you to this island of yours. And I will prepare a tasty picnic lunch to take with you. You like clam?"

"Nothing sooner?"

"Oh no! It's too late today. It will be dark before you know it. And you can feel it in the air, can't you?"

Alexandra's eyes whirled around her. "Feel what?"

"The heat."

My sister was not a fan of having the obvious pointed out to her. "No shit, Sherl—"

I cut her off. "A little warmer than usual?"

"Mm-hmm." Madeleine made the noise in a way that meant we were all in on the true meaning of the heat wave. For our North American benefit, she added, "Storm coming. If not tonight, tomorrow. So we make your trip the day after. Better safe than sorry, my mother always told us. Yours too, I would think."

I rose. Alexandra followed suit. "Is it all right if we leave our bags at the front?"

"Where are you going? Isn't Sally bringing you a drink?"

I'd seen Sally slip out the front door two seconds earlier.

"No, thank you," I said as I inched my sister toward the exit. "We told Sally we weren't thirsty right now. We thought we'd go for a short walk."

Madeleine nodded, still not sure what to make of us and doubting she'd said enough about what we should do next. "Of course, of course. No problem. It will be happy hour when you come back." She hesitated for a practiced two seconds, then added: "How do I know that, you wonder? It is *always* happy hour on Tubuai!"

Chapter Eight

It was aptly named The Shack, just down the beach from Chez Sam & Yolande Guest House. It looked exactly like the type of happily rundown place where wayward travellers and surfers and South Pacific adventurers would spend a few hours every day having drinks and meeting others of their kind. Alexandra and I didn't exactly fit in. First off, we were still wearing our airplane clothes. Second, whereas almost everyone else in the crowded little joint was either high on life or whatever the barman was serving, we were neither. The faint whiff of distraction and anxiety that wafted off us like heat waves from a scorching highway was easy to detect. We had a purpose other than conviviality or inebriation, and it was obvious.

We took the last two stools by the tiki type bar found only in South Pacific resorts and the backyards of one-time travellers desperate to recreate some of the relaxed vibe of long-ago trips. We ordered beers, and I watched my sister continue to melt. She was definitely a prairie girl unaccustomed to tropical humidity.

"I brought you this."

It was Sally. "It usually cools down toward evening, but not tonight. Thought you could use it." She handed my sister something that looked like a piece of cloth.

Alexandra looked down at it and then back at Sally. "I fucking love you."

Sally laughed and flicked her head to the right. "The loo is over there behind those potted palms. It's unisex. There's a lot of beer and tequila flowing tonight, so don't take too long."

Alexandra was gone before Sally was done speaking. The blond took the vacated space and nodded to the bartender. A few seconds later, he brought her a frosty glass of sparkling water along with our beers.

"Don't drink?" I asked, taking a fantastically soothing gulp of a pretty fine lager.

"In the right circumstances," she answered, her eyes never leaving my face as she sipped.

"Which isn't now?"

"I'm on the job. Sort of."

"Madeleine keeps you on call?" I said with less incredulity than I felt. Did the B&B owner really ask her staff to stay accessible on the off chance a guest might want something? Then again, this island was small enough to make it work.

"Not Madeleine. I'm a nurse. Me and another girl take turns being available in case someone on the island needs medical attention. I work at Chez Sam & Yolande just to keep from going squirrelly. As you can imagine, there are plenty of days around here when there's not much to do— for a nurse *or* a waitress."

"So why are you here?"

She beamed. "Look around. Occasional boredom is totally worth calling this place home, at least for now. I won't be here forever, but I'm not ready to leave just yet."

I nodded, indicating I was involved in the conversation and interested in it but not necessarily understanding it.

"You're expecting some story about me being here because I followed a boyfriend who came for the diving or fly surfing."

I gave a "maybe" kind of shrug.

"Actually, I did come out here with someone. We're kind of like you and Alexandra."

"What's like him and me?" Alexandra was back. The piece of cloth Sally gave her turned out to be a bright pink tank top. With my sister's complexion, she looked like she'd already spent a week soaking up rays on a Tubuai beach. She'd also somehow managed to transform her travel jeans into cut-offs, which were garnering plenty of attention from the male clientele.

"Looking sweet, girl." Our big blond bartender showed lots of white teeth with his wolfish smile. Pounding a full shooter glass on the bar top, he added, "In my books, that new look of yours deserves a free shot."

Sally offered Alexandra her seat back, but she declined. Better to show off her gams, I guess. She reached for the shot and downed it, giving the grinning barkeep little more than a peaked eyebrow in thanks.

"I was just telling…. Gawd!" Sally let loose an easy laugh. "I don't even know your names."

We introduced ourselves.

She started again. "I was just telling Adam that I also came to Tubuai with my brother. Just like you did." She'd obviously overheard our earlier conversation with Madeleine.

"Your boss thought it was kind of weird," Alexandra said, "a brother and sister travelling together. I know why we are. Why are you?"

"We can't help it; we're twins. We don't usually spend all our time together, but our folks passed away suddenly." She waved off our attempts at sympathy. "It's okay. It was months and months ago. Car accident. Actually, except for it totally sucking for us, it was kind of nice they got to go together, you know? Neither had to be sad or lonely without the other. But we were. So, Jess and I got to thinking we needed something to cheer us up. We figured a little adventure on a tropical island might not be a bad idea. So here we are, burning off our inheritance."

"What's your brother do here?" Alexandra asked.

"He's the one who's going to get you to your island," she said with a wink. "Tonight."

Learning that Jess, Sally's brother and our soon-to-be guide to Skawa Island, was also the big blond bartender with a crush on my sister was no big surprise. The two were fraternal twins, but the family resemblance was apparent if you looked close enough. Even having a beer at a beach bar on an island that barely ranks a dot on the map of the world, I was vigilant about my surroundings. At no time, whether I'm on the job or not, do I ignore people as inconsequential until I decide they are.

Wiping his hands on a bar rag, Jess said, "We gotta go now if we're goin', mates."

"Uh, don't you have a business to look after?" Alexandra, a bar owner herself, had little patience with disappearing employees.

"No worries there. Sally will look after things 'til I get back."

I eyed up the petite blond. Waitress. Nurse. Bartender. I was impressed. "Do you also happen to be the town mayor?" I asked her.

She grinned. "Only on Tuesdays, Thursdays, and Sunday mornings."

I turned back to Jess, my new favourite twin. "Let's go. Where's your boat?"

"Oh no. No boat, mate. Too slow. Sun goes down at six around here. We're going to lose light soon. And it smells like a wee bit of weather in the air. I've got a plane. My sister's not the only one with multiple jobs around here. I give bored tourists joy rides in the sky. I'll get ya to this island of yours in twenty minutes…." He hesitated a fraction of a second, then added: "Give or take." He gave me a pointed look. "If you've got the green, that is."

Now we were talking a language I understood. "I've got green."

With that, Jess was out from behind the bar and heading down the beach. Sally took his place as we exchanged smiles. It was important to get to Skawa as soon as possible, but on any other occasion, spending a little more time with this girl would have been my preference.

"Do you know where we're going?" I asked Jess when we caught up, following him to wherever it was he kept his airplane.

"Yeah, for sure. Sally texted me. Really, it wasn't that hard to figure out. There's not much of anything south of here until you hit some penguins. I've flown over your island plenty of times."

"It's deserted," I told him. "There's no airfield." An educated guess on my part. "Will that be a problem?"

"Nah. There's lots of flat space. Just like Tubuai. Besides, Bessy ain't so big."

"Who the fuck is Bessy?" Alexandra wanted to know in her delicate way. Despite her long legs, with Jess and me both over six feet, she was a bit short of breath keeping pace.

"Bessy's my girl," he shot back at my sister with a mischievous smile. I think he was hoping to make her jealous. "My plane. She's petite. So she doesn't need a lot of room to land."

"Wait a second…."

Alexandra is usually up for pretty much anything. But being an inexperienced flier and having just endured what must have seemed to her an intolerably long series of flights, she sounded concerned.

"Exactly how petite are we talking about here?" she asked the bartender-cum-pilot.

"You'll see."

We'd reached an open-air Jeep that appeared to be made more of salted rust than actual metal. Jess easily landed his long-legged body behind the wheel. The seat next to him was piled high with various sports equipment, including a surfboard, so Alex and I jumped into the back.

Fifteen minutes later, after a brief stop at Chez Sam & Yolande to pick up our bags, we were standing in a long, empty field next to a single-engine Skylane Cessna. It looked marginally better than the Jeep.

"How many people can fit in this thing?" Alexandra asked, the look of the aircraft doing little to calm her jitters.

"Four easy," he replied, winking at her, "but I hope you don't mind if you and I have to squeeze in tight."

Something told me I wasn't getting to ride shotgun on this one.

"So what's on that island?" Jess asked.

Knowing a thing or two about planes, I was following behind the bartender, both of us doing our own pre-flight inspection—me of him, him of the Cessna.

As he checked fluids, kicked tires, and wiped a suspicious-looking smudge off the window, he continued, "I've always wanted to land there. It looks a touch creepy though, you know. Some crazy cliffs and loads of trees for things to hide in. You know, like *Jurassic Park*. You don't own it, do ya?"

I shook my head, running a finger across a line of dents on the aircraft's body.

"That's nothing," he said with a relaxed laugh. "Me versus rock. Rock lost."

I gave him a look. I could fly this thing if I had too, so I wasn't too worried about Jess's abilities as a pilot, though I was sensing they probably weren't too shabby. The way he touched the body of his plane, almost reverentially, his eyes hitting all the right spots, I could tell this was a man who gave airplanes and flight the respect they deserved.

"So, why is it you two are headed there, then?"

That was on a need-to-know basis, and Jess wasn't on the list. I ignored the question and instead asked, "How much do I owe you for this and a return flight?"

"Three hundred each way."

"I'll give you seven fifty total, and no more questions."

He stopped what he was doing, straightened up, and fixed me with a stare. In three seconds, he made his decision. "Deal."

Either he was satisfied with what he saw or he really needed the cash. I'd have bet on the latter. After all, how many tourists flew all the way to Tubuai and wanted another plane ride? Jess probably made more in tips at the Shack than he did from his plane business. Flying was his passion, a beloved hobby, not a way to make money.

By the time we lifted off, both of Jess's predictions were coming to pass. The sun was beginning its colourful descent into night, and climbing up the same horizon to meet it like a fast-rising grey soufflé were storm clouds intent on destroying the brilliant display.

"So, sweetheart," Jess shouted at my sister over the sound of the plane's Lycoming engine and three-blade propeller, "you ever consider a life of surfing, clamming, and having a steamy, tropical-island affair with a hunky bloke who's totally into you?"

I had to give the guy points for reading Alexandra pretty well. She'd take blunt over bullshit any day.

"Are you out of your mind?" she yelled back.

Maybe I was wrong.

Then again, she didn't resist too hard at his suggestion to sit next to him up front.

"Can you believe this guy?" Alexandra twisted in her seat to give me her best incredulous look before turning it back on him. "I'm from Saskatchewan, dumbass. That's Canada. The Prairies. That sound like I'm the kind of girl who surfs and goes clamming?"

She really wasn't.

As we waited out a sudden shakeup of turbulence, I kept my eyes on the profiles of the pilot and his first mate. I marvelled at how people so different were often inexplicably drawn to one another. Jess was all blond and tanned and salty-skinned, bright-eyed and bushy-tailed, a lackadaisical jock who loved to fly and drink beer on the beach, whereas Alexandra was brooding and sharp-tongued with a preference for dark, smoky corners and hard alcohol straight from the bottle.

"Oh, come on," he chided good-naturedly. "Isn't it freezing cold most of the time where you're from?"

"Isn't it stinking hot and humid most of the time where you're from?" she countered. "Oh wait, that's here. Yeah, it is. I'm so hot, you could use my ass as a griddle."

"My pleasure, sweetheart. We land in ten minutes."

Another round of the Cessna doing its best to rattle our bones made the last statement rather appealing.

"Are you sure about that?" my sister goaded. "Doesn't seem like you can even fly this thing, never mind land it on a deserted island."

When he didn't respond right away, Alexandra shot me a concerned glance over her shoulder. Jess was suddenly giving his full attention to what was happening on his instrument panels and outside the plane.

"You *can* land this thing," she tried again. "Right?"

A shard of bright light accompanied by a violent shift to the left was followed by the two words you never want to hear from your pilot: "Oh shit."

Chapter Nine

"Shit! Shit! Shit!"

Alexandra Saint tightened her lips to disguise her smile as she regarded this swearing surfer man. He spoke her language. And he looked good all wet and woolly.

She fixed him with her best you're-an-idiot look. No reason to play easy to get. "I don't know what you're so upset about!" She had to scream to be heard over the howling storm laced with pelting rain. "You landed the plane! It's in one piece, and so are we! Isn't that a good thing?"

"But now I'm stuck here!"

"Is the plane broken?"

A sopping wet palm frond buffeted about by the near gale-force wind slapped him across the face. He gave her a lopsided look. "It's a bit windy," he coolly explained.

"I guess that's your problem."

Alexandra turned and stalked away, the whole time thinking she was really kinda sorta starting to like this big doofus with the wild beach-blond hair and bedroom eyes.

Bedroom eyes? Awww, shit!

It was exactly because of that kind of idiotic mooning sentiment that she found the whole flirtation thing boundlessly nauseating. Even thinking the term "bedroom eyes" was enough to make her gag. Normally, Alexandra was not the type of woman to ever think about any man in that way. She was a check-out-his-pipes-and-ass kinda girl.

"Where are you going?" he yelled at her over the storm.

"To find my brother. He might be a knucklehead for thinking he'll ever find shelter on a deserted island during a hurricane, but at least he's not sitting around crying about not being able to go home."

Jess caught up to her. "You see! You just called it a hurricane—which it isn't, by the way. Nowhere near it, actually."

"How am I supposed to know that? I'm from Saskatchewan. We don't have hurricanes."

"And I'm not crying about being stuck here. I had plans, that's all."

"With Bessy? Were you and your plane going out for a nice dinner and movie?"

Alexandra felt her arm being tugged backward. Her first response was to swing out the other in a karate move that would end up with the edge of her palm smashing into her assailant's throat. Instead—again inexplicably—she allowed herself to be halted, whisked around, and pulled into an embrace that was all pulsing muscles, whipping hair, and tongue.

When the strenuous kiss was over, Jess pulled back to assess the fallout. So far it didn't look like the crazy Canuck was going to kill him. Progress. Maybe he was a better kisser than he'd thought.

By now the couple was as wet as any two people could be. Only the thinnest sheet of rain separated them. Alexandra's eyes smoldered as she said, "Not here."

On this unknown island, there was only one place they knew of that would guarantee privacy. Jess pulled Alexandra toward the plane, up the stairs, and into the cabin, hauling the steps up after them. By the time he was done securing the plane, she'd already pulled off her sopping wet tank top. Her beauty stopped the man in his tracks. It wasn't just her plentiful breasts dripping with moisture that had him mesmerized. The rain had washed away her heavy makeup, the carefully applied artifice obscuring who she really was. Left behind was a youthful, brunette girl next door with eyes the size of saucers and thick pale-pink lips that trembled…with cold? Excitement? Uncertainty? A string of cussing?

He estimated she'd only get one chance to say no before his tiger urges took control. "Alexandra," he growled, "are you sure about this?"

She smiled because she was sure about one very important thing. She wasn't irritated by this guy. At all. That didn't happen very often. She answered, "Hell, yes."

"You made this?" My sister's croaky voice managed to reflect many things simultaneously: her amazement at the pineapple-sweetened, fire-toasted banana I handed her after she emerged from the plane's cabin; the fact she'd gotten very little sleep in a cramped, uncomfortable space; and her annoyance that I, who logically should have had even less comfortable sleeping arrangements, having been relegated to spending the night outside in the rain, appeared to be fresh and full of energy.

"This is friggin' fantastic!" Jess, looking and sounding considerably less cranky, followed close on Alexandra's heels. "How did you start a fire, dude? Good thing, though. Most people are surprised at how chilly it can sometimes get in these parts."

Perched on a generous slab of driftwood near the roaring fire, I ignored the question and started in on my own breakfast.

"I don't suppose you found a coffee tree?" Alexandra wanted to know, depositing herself next to me and reaching out to warm her free hand over the flames.

I shook my head to indicate there would be no Tim Hortons in her near future.

"Where the fuck did you spend the night? Did you find a Motel 6 in the jungle or something? And how do you look so good?"

I could see she was resisting adding: "For a guy with a tumour in his head."

"Experience," I said with a shrug. "I've done this type of thing a time or two."

"*This* is what you do?" she squawked, looking around at our sparse and tropically rustic surroundings. "You crash-land on islands and sleep in trees?"

"We *didn't* crash," Jess indignantly interjected. "It was just a bit of a rough landing. Remember the hurricane?"

Alex tossed a sour look all over the guy.

"So what are you two up to today?" the jovial pilot/bartender asked, easily deflecting the withering gaze. "A little shopping? Renting scuba gear? Maybe checking out a decent place for lunch?"

Alexandra shot our companion another look that quite clearly suggested he might want to shut up.

He wasn't taking the hint. "So I guess I'll get Bessy up and running and come back for you in…what? Two, three days? That give you enough time to check out all the museums and antique shops?" His eyes, sea-blue like his sister's, were chuckling at us.

Jess had managed to set the Cessna down in a rough, narrow clearing that ran alongside the beach. By the look of things in the morning light, we were lucky he was a decent pilot and the plane's brakes were in good working order.

I rose and approached him. "Didn't you say you always wanted to land on this island?"

He backed up a step, not sure of my intent. "Uh, sure."

"Well, what would you say to hanging out here a little longer today? Maybe the two of you could extend your date and do a little sightseeing."

Alexandra shot up like a sputtering rocket ready to meet the moon. "What are you talking about? First off, that wasn't a date. We were just getting to know each other in the privacy of…well, the privacy of Jess's airplane. And second, I'm coming with you. There's nothing you can say or do to change that, so don't even try. You know why I'm here, Adam. Nothing has changed that. And screw you for trying to get rid of me."

For a few seconds, no one said a thing. Then from Jess: "I'm good to look around on my own if you want me to stick around for a while."

I was growing to like Jess. Alexandra, not so much.

As I marched toward the plane, Alexandra yelled after me: "Where are you going now?"

I shouted back. "I'm getting our gear. Finish your banana. We leave in two minutes."

Like Tubuai, Skawa is an oval-shaped island surrounded by numerous islets known as *motus* and a large coral reef.

Abundantly fertile soil and a temperate climate work in harmony here. Flat, gentle plateaus mix with less hospitable remains of the island's volcanic past, both blanketed by verdant, almost prehistoric-looking, vegetation. Good for the sightseer, less so for the trekker. With its floor of slippery mosses and lichens, surprising stretches of marshland, and sudden craggy drops, I knew that making our way through the rainforest would not be easy.

I'd done my best to prepare my sister. I was used to harsh environments of every sort, and I knew well how weather, temperature, flora, fauna, and nature in general could be your friend or your very worst enemy, often getting the latter when expecting the former. A sun-mottled valley dotted with sweet-smelling flowers could be camouflage for poisonous snakes. A gentle breeze could be the harbinger of a killing dust storm. A defenseless fawn could signal the presence of a predator that cared not whether its meal was animal or human. My sister, the owner of a Saskatchewan beer parlour, was no stranger to predators and a certain amount of danger, but this was unlike anything she'd ever come across before.

Having taken my packing advice, Alexandra had changed into lightweight pants and a long-sleeved tunic. Her hair was pulled back into a loose ponytail shoved up under a Tilley knock-off. She was sporting a pair of hiking boots that looked well worn. Physically, she was in pretty good condition. Mentally, I could only hope for the best.

We were about twenty minutes in, tramping through the jungle in silence except for the sound of my machete carving a path through recalcitrant vines and unusually hardy ferns when she asked, "Why did you try to get rid of me back there?"

102 — Anthony Bidulka

"I wasn't trying to get rid of you, Alex," I lied easily. "I thought it would be safer for you near the beach with Jess."

"Safer how?"

That was a tough question to answer. In general, French Polynesia is not a particularly dangerous part of the world. Other than sun, mosquitoes carrying dengue fever, and the odd shark bite or coral cut, it's a rather benign place. There aren't even any poisonous snakes or insects I could dangle in front of her like a plastic spider on a string.

I tried out a better answer. "You're not used to this kind of thing, Alexandra."

"What kind of thing? Walking around in the woods? I'm a Saskatchewan farm girl. I do plenty of outdoorsy things. I live through minus-fifty-degree wind chill in the winter and horseflies in the summer. What makes you think I can't put up with a little heat and a few bugs?"

I grunted acquiescence and may have released a cheek height reed a little too late for my sister to avoid having it slap her in the face.

She didn't miss a beat. "It's whatever it is Maryann fuckin' Knoble has you looking for out here that you think isn't safe, isn't it? It's more than just some poor shipwrecked women. There's something else."

I stopped dead in my tracks and turned so I was nose to nose with my sister.

"I'm right, aren't I?" she challenged, standing her ground.

"Of course you're right. Or maybe you're wrong. That's the point, Alex. I don't know what we're going to find out here. I don't know what sort of shape these women are in, or how they'll respond to seeing us."

These were things Alexandra hadn't considered. "You think they'll be afraid of us?"

"Try petrified. Or hostile." I kept my voice even, my face solemn.

"I can deal with that. I can deal with a lot of things, brother dear."

"Okay," I said. "That's good, then. Let's keep going." I had no desire to erode my sister's admirable confidence and courage.

We only made it a few yards farther before she needed both.

Chapter Ten

"Shit on a stick!"

My sister is the proud possessor of a colourful vocabulary of curse words. Her use of the more mundane told me she was genuinely startled.

I rushed to where she'd landed, palms first, in a slimy quagmire. As powerful as it was, nary a ray of tropical sunshine could penetrate the thick overhead canopy of vegetation in this part of the jungle. As a result, our surroundings were bathed in dull, mossy green, and the air was surprisingly cool.

"Are you okay?"

"Better than that thing!"

I followed my sister's gaze to a dark globe about a metre and a half away. Frowning at the object, I worried that my suspicions about what it was would prove accurate.

"I tripped on it," she complained. Pulling herself up to her knees, she sat back on her ankles and cleared the dirt from the abrasions on her hands.

Wordlessly, I made my way over to the muddy, irregular-shaped sphere. Crouching down to get a better look, I first made a cursory inventory of the immediate area. Were there more? Had I missed any signs of impending danger?

Seeing nothing to warn me off, I reached down and

picked up the object. It was roughly twenty-two centimetres long, not quite as wide, with a circumference of about fifty-five centimetres. With great care, I began to wipe debris off its surface: rotted leaves, insect dung, and some sort of black material that smelled bad.

"What was it?" Alex asked. "Some kind of dog? Or a monkey? Are there monkeys here?"

I shook my head as my efforts revealed the object. A human skull. The neurocranium, the protective vault that surrounds the brain and brain stem, was fully intact. The viscerocranium, which forms the bones that support the face, only partially so.

Alexandra had made her way over, lowering herself next to me to get a better look. Covering our shared silence as we took in what we were looking at, the jungle made its own peculiar lowing noises. If there were songbirds here, they weren't chirping anywhere near this lonely burial ground.

Having never before seen a human skull, Alexandra reached out to touch it but quickly withdrew her hand before making contact. "Is this…could this be one of the women we're supposed to find?"

Again I shook my head. "No. This skull is old. Probably belonged to a man." I was far from being a forensic specialist, but the general larger size, sloping forehead, and squared eye sockets hinted at this being a male specimen.

"Thank God," she said in a hushed voice.

I raised an eyebrow.

"Not because it's a guy," she quickly clarified. "Because it's old." She waited a bit, then asked, "So you think this is some kind of caveman or something?"

"Not that old," I said, scraping off some last bits of

crud. "It's in pretty good shape. Still has some teeth."

"So he died not that long ago?"

I shrugged. "Maybe." I ran my thumb across a disturbance in the otherwise perfectly smooth frontal bone.

"What's that?"

I eyed my sister and decided she'd had enough excitement for now. "I don't know," I lied.

If I was placing a bet—which I've been known to do—I'd have said it was a bullet hole. Right in the middle of the guy's forehead.

It was after noon, and the damp heat was bearing down on us with unyielding intensity. We managed our hydration by making regular stops to rest and drink water. For lunch, I'd brought energy bars and fruit.

"Do we even know where we're going?" Alexandra wondered as she finished a papaya, juice dribbling down her chin. "Didn't the brainheads at CDRA tell you where to find these women?"

"They didn't know. The original rescuers never saw their camp. The women found them, not the other way around."

"So what's the plan? Walk in circles until one of them spots us and decides she wants to talk? For Chrissakes, you'd think they'd be desperate to get out of here."

"I had Anatole download a satellite image of the island. I plotted a perimeter route and search grid. We've been following the grid ever since we left the beach. Slowly but surely we'll cover every part of this island. If they're still here, we'll find them."

Alexandra's mouth hung open. "You mean they might

not even be here?"

"They *were* here," I replied matter-of-factly. "That much I know. Are they still here? That's what we're going to find out."

An impatient puff of air escaped her nose. "Damn, I wish I never gave up smoking."

We'd never directly talked about it, but I think she gave up the vice shortly after hearing I had cancer. It was going to be interesting to see how long that would last if my cure actually worked.

"How much longer is this grid thing of yours going to take?"

"I'd say about ten seconds."

"Wha…?"

Then she saw what I saw.

Partially hidden behind a nearby tree stood a woman, still as the stifling air.

We'd just found our first survivor.

Her name was Maybelline. She was twenty-eight years old. She looked decades older. Years on the island with little to eat—and what there was hardly following Canada's Food Guide—and poor protection from harsh tropical elements had worn the woman down. Her long hair, likely once thick and dark, had thinned and faded into pasty beige and hung off her scalp like dusty drapes. Far from sporting a glowing tan, the woman's skin was blotchy and in places red and raw from some sort of irritation. Her teeth were dull, like her eyes, and the nails on her hands and bare feet were serrated. This was a woman who spent her days rooting in the dirt, climbing trees, foraging as best she could to propel her sorry subsistence on this island. To her, this wasn't a sultry paradise with luscious greenery and golden beaches it was an unyielding, unforgiving prison.

"Are you from CDRA?" she asked after we'd exchanged names and little else. We were still standing several metres apart, none of us yet comfortable enough to make a move toward the other.

I nodded. "Yes. The men who first found you said you wanted us to come for you. Is that right?"

"Yes."

"I'm sorry it's taken us a few days to get here, but this island isn't very easy to reach."

"We been here a long time," she said, her voice weak from lack of regular use. "A few days ain't nothing to us."

"You'll take us to the others?"

Her head bobbed up and down, all the while her eyes made darting assessments of Alexandra, the first unfamiliar woman she'd seen in a decade.

Without a further word, Maybelline turned and ambled into the forest down a well-worn path. We followed. In less than five minutes, we arrived at the place the castaways had claimed as their home. The spot was wisely chosen. Instead of the beach, where there was little protection from sun and inclement weather, the camp was a short walk inland at a natural clearing in the jungle. There was a cave, where I guessed they slept, and, more important, a trickling waterfall. Of anything on the island that had allowed these women to survive, it was this that had saved them. Without a source of fresh water, they would have been as dead as the owner of the skull we'd found.

As is often the case in situations like this, situations of desperation or homelessness or extreme poverty in the outdoors, the centrepiece of the encampment was a firepit. Low-slung seats fashioned from rotted-out logs and driftwood encircled the fire, which was gently burning even though it was the middle of the day with temperatures soaring into the thirties and a punishing humidity that warned of· more unsettled weather. Sitting there were two other women and a young boy, maybe five years old. The child appeared the heartiest and healthiest of the bunch. The women had the same sickly dried-out flower look as Maybelline, though both were younger than she.

"My name is Adam," I said as we joined the silent gathering. "This is my sister, Alexandra." I crouched down next to the boy and smiled at him. "Hi. What's your name?"

"Theo," he answered, eyes bright but unsmiling. "Like Thee-oh-door. But shorter."

"Nice to meet you, Theo."

For a moment, it looked like he didn't understand me, but then he whispered, "Okay."

Alexandra lowered herself onto one of the logs and did her best to smile. "Hi," she threw out there.

Maybelline joined the circle, sitting next to the smallest woman, who was not much bigger than the boy. "This is Destiny. She's Theo's mom." She looked like one of those dolls whose head and eyes are much too big for the rest of its body. Whereas the other two appeared thin and malnourished, Destiny looked as if every bit of life had been sucked out of her.

Maybelline indicated the third survivor. "And this is Peri." Of the three adults, Peri looked to have fared the best. She wore her sandy-coloured hair in a loose ponytail. Her arms, pale and freckled, were surprisingly toned with long stringy muscles. Whereas the other two were wearing long-sleeved tunics over threadbare cotton slacks, Peri wore a tee-shirt and shorts.

Destiny and Peri did little more than tip their chins up and down to acknowledge our arrival. I couldn't yet tell if they simply had few reserves of energy to do more or if our appearance in their camp was unsettling them.

"We've come to take you home," I said. "Is there anything you need to do before we go?"

"Where?" This from the boy.

"Home," Alexandra said, trying for enthusiasm. "Back to Canada."

"What's that?"

Shock contorted Alexandra's face as the realization hit her. Theo didn't know Canada. He didn't know anywhere. He'd been born and lived his entire life on this island. This was the only home he'd ever known.

"You'll like it there," Alexandra said, doing her best to recover, but the words ended up sounding more like an order than a promise. She'd never been a real kid person.

I maneuvered into a more comfortable sitting position. "Can you tell us a little about how you got here?" Seeing as none of the group was chomping at the bit to leave, I threw out the question. Despite the pitiable condition of the survivors and the camp, I had to remember the reason Maryann Knoble sent me here. Playing white knight was not my number one priority. It was to find out exactly what this island was about, how it was being used by Belar and IIA, and whether these women were involved, and if so, whether they were complicit or merely incidental bystanders.

"We told them other guys," Maybelline responded, sounding defensive. "Shipwreck."

"That must have been terrible for you."

"Yeah, sure was."

"Do you know what happened?"

"What do you mean what happened?"

"To the ship. Did it hit something? Were there mechanical problems? Did it sink?"

Although Maybelline was playing the spokesperson for the survivors, each time, just before she spoke, her eyes jumped to her compatriots. Was she seeking comfort? Support? The correct answer?

"How am I supposed to know that?" she responded. "I wasn't driving the thing."

I nodded, adding to my up-to-now sparse collection of facts about the women and this situation. Now I knew that despite finding herself on a ship in the middle of the ocean, Maybelline most definitely was not an experienced sailor.

"How did you and the others get to the island?"

She stared at me as if I'd asked her to solve a quadratic equation. "I…we was…we swam. The boat sank and we swam."

"It was a yacht you were on?"

"Uh-huh. A yacht."

"What was the name of the yacht?"

Again confused hesitation. Again the jumping eyes. "It didn't have no name!" She said it with a smile from her dry, cracked lips, as if I'd been teasing her by asking a ridiculous question.

"Who owned the yacht?"

Nothing.

I stared at Maybelline. Then Destiny and Peri. Their eyes, staring blindly, seemed lost in the fire. Destiny looked as if she wished she could jump into it. How did these girls get themselves into this? Maybelline had been eighteen at the time, the other two were probably only fourteen or fifteen at most. Maybe it wasn't so surprising they couldn't answer me. I was questioning adults, but the answers—or lack thereof—were those of a child, which is exactly what they were when this happened to them.

"Maybelline," I started again, maintaining a pacifying tone. "Can you tell me how many people were on the yacht with you?"

Her chocolate eyes were filming over with tears. I was surprised her emaciated body could summon up the moisture. She simply looked at me, clueless, and shrugged.

There was one more question she had to have an answer for. "How many made it to shore?"

Her eyes brightened as she opened her mouth and lied: "Just us."

Chapter Eleven

"Why are you so sure they're lying to us?"

Alexandra was marching next to me as we made our way back to the plane. Maybelline, Destiny holding Theo's hand, and Peri trailed behind us. After ten years, the ship-wrecked family of four had little in the way of possessions they wanted to bring with them. Only Peri was carrying something more than a grocery bag of belongings: a leather briefcase wholly out of place in the Polynesian jungle. When Alexandra, offering to carry the hefty, looking thing for her, asked what was inside, the shy woman mumbled only one word under her breath: "Souvenirs." She declined to give it up.

"It's Maybelline who's lying," I responded, wiping away a line of sweat that insisted on forming on my upper lip no matter how often I attempted to dry it. The day had grown blisteringly hot and muggy. Jungle sounds were at a minimum. Most non-human inhabitants were wise enough to keep a low profile at midday. "The other two have barely said a word."

"I know you don't care what I think about things, but you're really starting to piss me off. I want to know. What's going on here, Adam? What is Maybelline lying about?"

Without breaking stride, our eyes locked. "A lot of

things as far as I can tell. But this isn't the place for an interrogation. The one thing she's not lying about is their condition. We have to get them medical attention and food."

"Maybe that's it. Maybe they're delirious from starvation and having to live the last ten years of their lives in this broiling hellhole. Maybe they aren't lying. Maybe they're just confused. Did you ever consider that?"

"Yes. I did."

"And?"

"How long did they tell us they've been on this island?"

"Ten years."

"How many of them survived the shipwreck and made it to the island?"

"They're all behind us," Alexandra huffed impatiently.

"That's it? Three women and Theo?"

"Adam!" she squawked her impatience.

"How old is the boy?"

"I dunno, four or five?"

"Who's the father?"

Alexandra stopped so suddenly I'd gone several feet before I realized she wasn't next to me. I looked back. She was staring straight ahead, a dumfounded look on her face, mouthing some not very nice words.

"What do you mean there's no room for all of us?" Alexandra was reaming out our blond pilot.

Jess was a smart guy. No way was he taking on the entire force of an unhappy Alexandra Saint by himself. His eyes landed on me, and Alexandra's followed.

"Alex," I said calmly, "the plane can only seat four. With

the three women and Theo, he's already over capacity."

"You knew this?"

I said nothing. Jess wisely followed suit.

"Why didn't you rent a bigger plane if you knew this mosquito couldn't carry all of us at once?"

"A bigger plane needs a bigger landing strip. Seeing as Skawa doesn't have even one, Bessy and Jess seemed the best choice. Besides, we weren't exactly overwhelmed with options."

Alexandra's nostrils flared. She knew I'd defeated her with the most frustrating of all weapons: logic.

She turned on the weaker link. "So we have to sit on our thumbs and wait for you and your girlfriend to come back?"

Jess shot back. "Actually, I thought sitting on your thumbs was why you two were coming here in the first place. Remember, this whole rescuing shipwreck survivors thing was just sprung on me."

Alexandra couldn't win and she knew it. She didn't like it, but she knew it. "So what'll it be?" She tapped the face of her wristwatch. "Half hour there, half hour back?"

"Sweetheart, I'm sorry, but I was only booked for one return trip. I do have another job to look after. Sally can't watch The Shack for me forever. Besides, it'll be getting late by the time we get back to Tubuai. Tell ya what, I'll make ya a deal," he said, turning to me. "I can come back tomorrow morning. Early."

"Tomorrow?" Alexandra crowed. "You want us to spend another night in this fucking jungle! Are you batshit crazy!"

"That sounds good, Jess," I interrupted my sister's growing head of steam. "Thanks."

Alexandra shifted her wrath onto me, eyes burning. "Are you kidding me? Where are we going to sleep?"

"Alexandra," I said softly. "It will be all right. We're on an adventure, right?"

For a brief second, shame passed over my sister's face. This was the girl who was up for anything. Being uncomfortable, put out, or even in danger didn't particularly bother her. Being in unfamiliar territory did. Our encounter with the castaways had thrown her off balance. I had to remember that for her the decision to come out here and everything it entailed had been little more than a vague concept. The grim reality of it, the condition of the women, meeting a child who knew nothing of the world but a deserted island, would be overwhelming for anyone. Disaster recovery agents deal with this kind of thing every day. Bar owners from the Prairies don't.

My sister is a tough chick. No doubt about that. But I was beginning to learn that in some circumstances her toughness is as dense as an eggshell, easily cracked and ground into powder. Alexandra was irritated with Jess, with me, with the situation. Being irritated is one of the things she does best. It was her go-to emotion. For a moment, she'd forgotten that, skulls and shipwreck survivors aside, she was also having one hell of a good time.

Together, we watched the aircraft take off. The small plane rumbled and roared as it fought sand and rock and a perilously uneven surface for every one of the four hundred and twenty metres it needed to get airborne. When it did, with queasily little room to spare, we both expelled a relieved breath.

Still watching the sky, Alexandra said to me, "This was

your plan all along." It was a comment, not a question, not an accusation.

"I need more time to search the island," I admitted. Maryann Knoble's intuition was dead on. There was something more going on here. I could sense it. I just had no idea what it was. Tomorrow would be soon enough to question Maybelline and the others. Including the boy.

"Your grid pattern thing," she said. "You weren't just looking for the women this morning, were you?"

"No."

"What do you hope to find here?"

"Nothing. I hope I find nothing."

She understood. "Then let's go."

We had experienced it once before. We knew the signs. The stunning heat. The overbearing humidity. An unmistakable scent in the air. A sudden wisp of wind, gone as soon as you felt it, leaving behind cool slivers against hot skin. The slow arrival of clouds, at first nearly translucent and benign but whose wake promised thicker, darker, roiling billows of tremendous power. There would be a storm in French Polynesia tonight. What we didn't know was when or exactly where. Would it once again pelt the shores of little Skawa Island? Or would it sideswipe us in favour of Tahiti or one of the larger islands nearby? Or would it miss us altogether, moving on to Kiribati or Fiji?

"How can you be so sure?"

We'd gone nearly an hour without talking. Alexandra was proving to be a good exploring companion, rarely needing more than the occasional stop for a brief rest and swig of water. She didn't need to fill the air with words, so when she asked a question, I knew it came as a result of serious consideration.

"Do you mean about finding something here?" I asked in return.

"That, and everything else. You left Canada after only one treatment of this supposed miracle drug, completely sure that you'd be well enough to make this trip, survive all of this, save those women, and eventually get back home. You're sure we can survive the night by ourselves on this island. You're not worried we're going to get eaten by tigers or attacked by poisonous ants in our sleep. You probably even know exactly where we're going to spend the night and what we're going to eat for breakfast. You're sure that if there's something to find, we're going to find it. You're sure Jess isn't some loser who'll get drunk and forget to come back for us. You're sure those women are lying. You're sure that Maryann Knoble is someone you can trust. It goes on and on, Adam. How do you do it? How can you be so fucking sure about everything?"

I kept on chopping away at troublesome vines and branches, clearing a path for us through the jungle. I didn't stop because my sister wouldn't want me to. Stopping would put too bright a spotlight on the question. On my answer. On us as a brother and sister who didn't really know each other very well.

"I *am* sure about a lot of things," I began as we continued fighting our way through the challenging terrain. "Mostly because I've lived this life for a lot of years. I know about jungles. I know about survival. I especially know about survival in places where it seems impossible. This place doesn't even come close to some of the places I've found myself in. I help people who are trapped in the maw of the world's worst disasters. I can only do that if I know how to be at home in hell. I do it by making it my business to know about every possibility that might keep me from getting my people back to safety, back home. That includes knowing about tigers and poisonous ants—there aren't any here by the way.

"But, Alex, I'm going to be straight with you. I'm not sure about everything. I just know what I know. I rely on that and on experience. Throw in a healthy dose of dumb luck and bullheadedness, and I move forward. My end goal is always clear. I'm dedicated to that. Always."

"But why? Why do this?"

I chuckled. "Well, in this case, as you well know, I don't have much choice. For me, it's die or maybe not die."

"Have I told you what a cow I think that Knoble woman you work for is?"

"A few hundred times, yup." We walked a bit more, then: "I believe in what the CDRA does. I believe I'm good at doing what I do, damned good. In many ways, we're a match made in heaven. I like helping people, Alex. But I couldn't be a cop or a fireman or anything like that. It just doesn't fit me." Now I did stop. "This"—I held out my palms to encompass our surroundings—"does."

"Is it worth it?"

I'd forgotten the unique brand of pain siblings could inflict upon each other, especially when mired in ugly truth. I knew what Alexandra was really asking. I knew the price she thought I'd paid for what I did for a living. It was a question I'd recently been asking myself quite a bit.

"It's…familiar."

My nose twitched.

Familiarity can be a bitch.

The scent was old but everlasting. I knew it well. It had been here for a long time. It would be here long after we were gone. My stomach constricted into a steel ball. The smell was putrid and primitive.

"Adam…what is it?"

My sister's eyes reflected what she must have seen in my face. Not shock. Or horror. Or even surprise. It was sadness. For here, once more, was a familiar foe.

Death.

I led the way. A disaster recovery agent is the perfect hound dog for this particular scent. It only took us another ten minutes to find the source.

At first, it seemed like nothing, just a tumbledown, primitive structure made from branches and mud plaster. But as we came closer, our eyes adjusting to the growing dimness of the deep jungle interior, our brains slowly processed the unimaginable, and we came to realize what was before us.

Alexandra cried out. I stifled a reflexive gag.

I'd thought I'd seen it all, every foul atrocity possible.

I was wrong.

Chapter Twelve

"Who are you?" The woman's voice sparked with irritation.

"My name is Shekhar Kapur." This was the second time Kapur had informed the caller of his name, when she had yet to share her own.

"Why can't I talk to who I want to talk to? I've been passed around from one person to the next, and no one seems to be able to help me."

"I can help you," Kapur told the woman in an unruffled voice meant to instill confidence. "Now, tell me how I can do that."

"Are you with CDRA? I lost track of who I was talking to two people ago."

"Yes. I am. I apologize for any confusion you've had to deal with until now," he said, playing up his British-tinged Indian accent more than usual. North Americans, particularly women, seemed to like it. "But now I'm on the line. So tell me. What can I do for you?"

"You can find Adam Saint for me. I need to talk to him right away."

"I'm afraid Mr. Saint is no longer an agent of the CDRA. Perhaps I can be of assistance to you?" How many times in how many ways would he have to offer this woman his services?

"No. I have to talk to Adam Saint. You say he's not working there anymore? I betcha I can tell you why. And I can tell you one more thing. He didn't have to quit. You know why? Because he isn't going to die!"

Kapur allowed himself a full five seconds to take in the woman's incredible claim. The details were sketchy at best in his mind, but he was aware of the circumstances surrounding the departure of the star disaster recovery agent.

"Do I have your attention now, Mr. Whatever-Your-Name-Is? Can I talk to Adam Saint now?"

"Kapur, Shekhar Kapur." Third time. "Who am I speaking with, please?" She'd been unwilling to give her name until now, which, no doubt, had been part of the cause for the aforementioned confusion and delays.

The woman hesitated, wondering if revealing her name to this guy was a good idea. Had she really thought this through? Was this still what she wanted? Yes, she reminded herself. If she was to have any hope of getting a full night's sleep ever again, she had to get this out. "Arla. That's my name."

"Arla…?"

"Tellebough. My name is Arla Tellebough. If you won't let me talk to him, I need you to tell your agent that he isn't really going to die. The whole thing was nothing but a big hoax."

Kapur cleared his throat. "Can you tell me how it is that you came upon this information, Ms. Tellebough?"

"From the guy playing the hoax. He told me all about it. He was drunk. And in a bed he probably shouldn't have been in—mine. He told me the whole thing. Pillow talk. You ever hear of that, Mr. Boss?"

"I have," Kapur replied quietly. "Ms. Tellebough, I would

like to meet with you at your convenience. I can send a car to pick you up and bring you here to my office. We can talk in private and in comfort, instead of on the telephone."

"A car? Like when?"

"Would right now be appropriate?"

The ensuing silence worried Kapur. At the least, he did not want the woman to hang up until the call had been successfully traced. As a matter of course, all telecommunications into IIA were recorded and tracked. "Or I could come to you."

"No. I don't think so." The voice had grown wary. "I think…I think…."

"Perhaps we'll just continue to talk on the telephone then?" Kapur speedily suggested.

"Okay." She sounded relieved.

"Can you tell me the name of the person who told you these things?"

"You betcha. Dr. Milo Yelchin."

With that, the seriousness with which Shekhar Kapur was treating the call rose to an entirely different level. He knew of Dr. Milo Yelchin. Or had. Before the IIA's in-house physician had ended his life by way of hanging.

"How did you and Dr. Yelchin come to be acquainted?" he asked.

"He *acquainted* me in a bar at Casino Rama and later in a hotel room. A couple of times, actually."

"What exactly did he tell you about Agent Saint?"

"The doc was bragging about what a powerful guy he was. He said he was doing all kinds of top-secret things for a top-secret government agency. I said, what sort of things could a plain old doctor be involved in that were so top secret? He said, lots of things. I said, like what? And that's when he told me."

Patiently, Kapur repeated his question. "What exactly did he tell you, Arla?"

"He said he'd been asked to fake someone's death… well, no, wait, not fake his death but fake him into thinking he was going to die. I said, why would you do something like that? He said he couldn't tell me or he'd have to kill me. That last part he said like a joke, y'know? I'd have never gone to bed with him if I thought he was going to kill me."

"Very wise of you, Arla. What else was said?"

"Lots of stuff. Most of it was pretty boring. And he must have thought so too because then he asked me if I knew what a disaster recovery agent is. He said Canada has a bunch of these agents. I said I didn't know that. Then he told me all these stories about what they do and that his job was actually more important than theirs because without him to help them stay healthy they couldn't do what they do. He must have thought I was getting bored again because he let the guy's name slip. Adam Saint. I remember it because my grandma used to tell me to pray to Saint Adam if I wanted my houseplants to live. Did you know Saint Adam is the saint of greenery or something like that? It never worked, by the way."

"That's unfortunate," Kapur murmured, serene words belying a spinning brain. Could this woman actually be telling the truth? It was exactly this kind of story, the outrageous sort, that often proved to be fact, especially here in North America. It was true that in India life tended to be filled with many problems, but most were far less complicated than those found in abundance in this country.

"Yeah, well, it's mostly my fault. I always forget to water them."

"I see." Kapur knew Saint and Yelchin only by reputation. Yelchin was dead and Saint had already resigned before Kapur had arrived. With so many other matters to attend to as the new head of CDRA, plus his own lengthy list of personal problems, he'd had little time or reason to learn more about them. But if what this woman was saying contained even a shred of truth, it was a most grave matter indeed and deserving of his full attention.

"I said to him: You must really hate this guy to make him think he's going to die. But he said, no. He said he actually liked this Saint guy and was sorry he had to do what he did. Like someone was forcing him to do it, y'know? And so I just got to thinking about how horrible it would be to think you're going to die when really you're not. Like, what about his mom and his best friends or, who knows, maybe this guy has kids? Do you know? Does this Saint guy have kids? That would be frigging horrible if he had to tell his kids he was dying. And obviously he quit his job. So he's not making money anymore. He's probably sitting at home alone, all depressed, his kids and friends all like sad and stuff, with no job and no money. I keep on waking up worrying about this guy and what's happening to him, y'know. It's terrible. Really terrible. Don't you think so?"

"Yes, Arla," Kapur agreed. "I truly do. Is your failure to complete a full night's sleep the reason for your call today?" It sounded to Kapur as if the woman was likely experiencing some level of guilt through association with the dastardly deed she described. "Or is there some other reason?"

She made an odd sound with her mouth as if she'd only

just considered the possibility. "Well, I guess so. What else could there be?"

Though he knew she could not see it, Kapur was nodding to himself. Although this woman was not admitting to any, Kapur could think of many more reasons. Perhaps she was a woman scorned, consequently grown unstable. Perhaps she desired revenge for a perceived wrong. Or perhaps she wished for money. Woman versus man. Yes, he knew this type of activity very well.

I glanced over my shoulder as I called out to my sister. "Alexandra, we need to keep moving."

"Get the hell away from me!"

My sister was doubled over, head behind a rock, retching her guts out.

Retching. I'd seen this many times before. When people are scared or in pain or, as in this case, horrified by something they'd just witnessed, they will vomit. In more extreme cases, they might urinate or defecate. The science behind the reaction is simple. Much of the energy used by the body is in the digestive system. So when the body is under extreme stress, it will empty the digestive tract to provide more energy for running or defence. All part of the fight-or-flight response. Animals do it too. When covered with excretory matter, they become less attractive to predators, both physically and sexually.

I stood there in the sweltering jungle, watching the familiar sight of a person experiencing punishing personal tumult. I felt myself shift into the mode of Canadian Disaster Recovery Agent Adam Saint, a glove that fit so well. As words formed on my lips, I hesitated. This wasn't just any person curled over herself, feeling wretched, stunned by what she'd seen, and embarrassed at the same time. This was my sister. Certainly, I could offer more.

I stepped forward. Lowering myself next to her, I placed a hand on her shuddering back. I thought she might shrug it off. But she didn't. Not right away, anyway.

Over the next thirty seconds, I felt the tension in her begin to subside. She was no longer throwing up but she kept her head low. Either she thought she wasn't done being ill or, more likely, she felt more comfortable keeping her face hidden, if only for a little longer.

"I'm okay, I'm okay," she finally uttered between short, quick breaths.

Alexandra pulled up as if to stand but instead fell back to the ground into a sitting position. Her face was the colour of a cooked scallop, her eyes pools of uncertainty.

"What the fuck is that over there?"

She meant the encampment we'd stumbled upon, only a few yards from where we were now.

"I'm sorry you had to see that."

"What do you mean you're sorry?" Her voice was strengthening, her spirit growing prickly. In this situation, probably a good sign. "You didn't know we'd find that shit." She hesitated, an uneasy look clouding her face. "Did you?"

"Of course not, Alex. I told you I didn't know what we'd find here. I tr—"

"I know, I know. You tried to keep me from following you. I just didn't think…. Adam, what went on here? What the hell happened on this island?"

Suddenly, I had to wonder if I'd been mistaken before

in letting my sister believe French Polynesia is not particularly dangerous. There *was* danger here, a dark, horrible, incomprehensible kind of danger.

Anthropophagy. The act or practice of humans eating the flesh or internal organs of other human beings. Cannibalism.

Aside from actually observing a human tear a piece of flesh from another and place it in their mouth, cannibalism is difficult to prove. Some say the act is nothing but a movie-propelled myth, urban legend, or fear-inducing story used by one tribe of peoples to ward off the undesirable advances of another. Nobody is certain how many cannibal tribes may exist today, if any. Some say none. Others say there are several. In tropical parts of Africa. And here, in the South Pacific. Fiji was once known as "Cannibal Isles." Kuru, the rarest disease in the world, also known as the laughing sickness, occurs only in New Guinea and is believed to be caused by eating human brain matter.

At first, what we saw seemed to be nothing more than the rest of the remains belonging to the skull we'd come across earlier in the day. The one with the suspicious hole in the forehead. I assumed some sort of scavenger had dragged the skull away from the rest of the body.

But then we saw more.

Many more.

Skulls. Bones of all kinds. Many easily recognizable as belonging to a human.

But it got worse.

Some of the skeletons, intact, were in what looked to be a rudimentary cages fashioned from bamboo and vines. These skeletons...these people...had not died in a natural environment. They'd been captives. Jailed. No doubt against their will. But for what purpose?

The only absolute indicator known about today that human flesh has been consumed by another human is the presence of human myoglobin in excrement. Myoglobin is a protein unique to human muscle tissue and can survive cooking, eating, and the digestive process. In 1994 in Colorado, at a 900-year-old Anasazi cave site, the discovery of coprolite, fossilized human feces, proved exactly that. Cannibalism exists. It can be ritualistic, customary, part of funerary rites, a war tactics, and occasionally practiced as a last resort by people suffering from famine, most famously the Donner Party, the *Mignonette* yachters, and the rugby players of downed Uruguayan Air Force Flight 571.

Even in well-publicized cases, irrefutable proof of actual cannibalism is difficult to find. I'm no specialist in the field, but I know what to look for. While Alexandra ran into the jungle in an attempt to disgorge her revulsion at seeing the mass uncovered grave, I took a closer look around.

The makeshift "cage" had long ago deteriorated. Over two years? Five years? Twenty? I couldn't be sure, given the unique environment. Today, it was no longer a fortification that would hold anyone prisoner, but the structure was still obvious, as was the intent.

Behind what had been the jail-like wall of bamboo bars were several skeletons, each mostly intact, sitting, lying, curled up into fetal positions. Outside the cage were even more disturbing finds. In one area were the skulls. Unlike the one we'd found in another part of the jungle, these were cracked open, some smashed into pieces. As if someone or something wanted to get at what was inside.

Near a spot that resembled the fireside sitting area where we'd found the shipwreck survivors were more bones. These were piled in a way that made it clear this was done by humans. No animal would have the ability or desire to stack the remains of their victims.

At this point, the alarm had not yet gone off in my head, despite the crushed skulls. But as I inspected the bones more closely, it began a slow, ominous clang.

Archeologists call them "butcher marks." I found dents and scrapes on the surfaces, the kind you'd see if sharp objects were being used to carve meat from a bone. Since we're the only species known to use tools in this manner, my grim suspicions were heightened.

Perspiration poured freely down my temples and into the neck of my already damp shirt. The heat was intensifying, hanging on me like a roasting cape. In the distance, the murmur of storm clouds warned of disharmony in the skies, invisible above the thick awning of jungle foliage.

I returned to the sitting area. There was no telltale utensil that might still have DNA evidence clinging to it. I scoured the area for something more. At first, I saw nothing, obvious or otherwise. Using a stick, I began poking and digging at the centre of the long-dead firepit.

Still nothing.

My eye caught the object on my next sweep of the surrounding area. Something large, almost hidden beneath the camouflage of ground cover.

Sidling up beside it, I used the stick to make first contact.

I heard a ding.

It was something hard. Metal?

I crouched down and slowly pushed aside the leaves. I

held my breath when I saw what it was.

A cooking pot.

I leaned in closer. It smelled. I couldn't identify the exact odour, but I knew it wasn't anything good.

I pulled the pot from its hiding place and brought it back with me to the firepit where the light was marginally better.

I maneuvered it to catch the sun and looked inside.

I cringed at what I found.

A noise to my right!

Alexandra had gone off to the left.

I dropped the pot and ran.

Chapter Thirteen

Shekhar Kapur would have been more comfortable using mass transit as he always had in India, but things were different in Canada. Being a person such as himself in a position such as his, in command of the country's Disaster Recovery Agency, demanded he drive himself or be driven. Kapur had never possessed a driver's license. In India, he had simply valued his life too much to take to the streets behind the wheel of any type of motor vehicle. In Canada, he was simply too busy to learn the rules. Many of these rules, he was certain, must have to do with courtesy and good manners and how to avoid honking your horn every few seconds, as they did in his country.

Usually, on the fifteen- to twenty-five-minute drive to High Park from the IIA office tower, Kapur would indulge in small talk with his driver. Often, it would be the most civil and enjoyable conversation he'd had all day. But today he was silent, sitting in the dark confines of the black sedan's rear seat. It wasn't because of the lateness of the hour, although it was later than usual. No, Shekhar Kapur was a worried man tonight.

Anyone in Kapur's position could anticipate having many worries. Any new day that did not add more to the list would be unusual indeed. Add to that his own personal woes, which were not inconsiderable. Of course, what person of his age—well past fifty—did not have their own share of personal issues? All of this he expected. But today his load had become significantly heavier. For the first time he wondered if he'd made a colossal mistake by taking on this new job, with its requirement of having to report directly to Maryann Knoble.

Kapur did not care for Knoble. He'd known it as soon as they met. This was not a problem. Not for him nor, he suspected, her. She was a power-hungry, ill-tempered, crass, condescending bully, but her reputation as a tough and steady leader who knew how to get things done expediently was well-known in the intelligence community. At the end of the day, Kapur cared less about the personality of the people he worked with and more about whether they accomplished their duties. All of this, and the fact that the position could not have been offered at a more fortuitous time, had convinced Kapur to accept it. Although it was the last thing he'd wanted to do, Kapur had known he needed to get out of India.

When Knoble first contacted him, Shekhar Kapur was the head of IDRA, headquartered in Udaipur, western India. Although Kapur was born in the east, he missed Udaipur more, as he would a hand should it be sliced off and thrown into a fast-flowing river. Udaipur was often referred to as the "Venice of the East," the "Most Romantic City in India," and the "Kashmir of Rajasthan," and not without reason. Tourists, especially wealthy Westerners, were known to flock to the enchantingly old yet modern town in the heart of the Aravalli mountains.

Still, even surrounded by all of its beauty, Kapur knew

that behind the façade, where the real people lived and worked, Udaipur was like most Indian cities. Overcrowded. Noisy. Dirty. Home to unspeakable poverty and other social, economic, and physical ills. None of these was of great concern to him. It was simply life in India as almost everyone knew it. Kapur's problems stemmed from issues of a more personal nature.

Kapur had been born Hindu in Howrah, the largest satellite city of Kolkata (formerly Calcutta). As a young boy, he was adopted by a well-to-do British couple living there. Thereafter, he was raised Roman Catholic, a religion to which he was as strongly devoted as anything else in his life. He loved everything about Christianity: the teachings, the age-old traditions, the rituals. He believed in all of the religion's basic tenets: God wants each and every one of us; in redemption there is power; God is omnipotent, omniscient, and omnibenevolent; and, perhaps most important of all, sin is bad, very, very bad.

It wasn't until he was a young man that he came to recognize the inherent problem of being a Christian in a predominantly Hindu country. Although you might find an Indian woman willing to marry you, you would rarely find a father willing to allow it.

Eventually, he did meet a young woman named Farha and married her. The situation was difficult because Farha's parents were devout Hindus and were against their daughter marrying a Christian. But they were elderly, Farha herself was not young, and they worried about her chances of obtaining a husband of any kind. So they relented. Kapur's relationship with his in-laws was always trying, with Farha's parents using every opportunity to malign and belittle him to whoever would listen.

Shekhar and Farha went onto have two daughters, Eenakshi and Priya. Soon after the birth of their second daughter, the marriage began to sour. Farha, spurred on by her parents, became increasingly angry about his desire to raise the girls as Catholics. About the same time, Kapur's wife began to show signs of a developing mental illness, with both Kapur and their daughters becoming helpless targets during increasingly regular bouts of verbal and physical aggression.

With the influence of his British parents and benefit of a top-notch American education, Kapur had been a perfect recruit for the Indian Disaster Recovery Agency. Starting out as an agent, he was considered particularly well-suited, having travelled the world more widely than most of his Indian counterparts. When a posting came up in Udaipur, he jumped at the opportunity to get himself and his children away from Farha's poisonous family. He hoped the distance would help the marriage and, quite possibly, Farha's mental state.

It turned out Kapur's worldly knowledge wasn't as much a boon as it was originally thought to be, as the vast majority of disasters IDRA responded to took place within their own country. Even so, Shekhar Kapur did well at his job and advanced quickly up the ranks of the organization. Unlike DRAs in other countries, the role of agent here was less swashbuckling hero and man-of-action, and more astute political wrangler and accomplished red tape splicer. Kapur excelled in these areas, taking on more administrative roles of authority, eventually landing the top spot at IDRA.

As mother ship, a country's International Intelligence Agency is responsible for the smooth running of each of its departments. A sudden departure or death of a key player at the wrong time could have grave implications. And so an essential duty of each IIA chief is to maintain an up-to-date list of possible and preferred replacements for every major post in those departments.

Sergiusz Belar, IIA Canada's former head, and Kapur had become lifelong friends after meeting at an IIA training facility in Switzerland. So when Kapur, who'd been head of IDRA for several years by then, learned he was on the replacement list for CDRA when the current head perished in an accident, the news was not entirely unexpected. He was, however, surprised to actually be considered for the role. Maryann Knoble, who'd taken over from Belar, no doubt had many options of her own she'd added to the replacement list and personally favoured, including in-house candidates.

Kapur was smart enough to know that part—if not all—of the reason he was being offered the job was Knoble's non-negotiable clause that the incoming head of CDRA accept and take over the position immediately. Uncharacteristically, Kapur had made a rushed decision. In an instant, he knew this was his chance to escape. Farha's parents were dead by this point, his daughters grown and living satisfying lives of their own. It was time to get away from his wife, who'd only grown more horrible and abusive with each passing year. Kapur informed Farha he was leaving India, and her, for good. He would file for divorce and leave her financially looked after. That same day, Farha committed suicide. Kapur moved to Canada as planned.

But it wasn't the pain of past personal demons that consumed Shekhar Kapur's mind when the IIA sedan pulled up to the driveway of the stately two-storey brick Tudor home in High Park. Tonight, all his thoughts were on Arla Tellebough and her assertions about Adam Saint.

Kapur knew Saint had likely been the preferred candidate for his job. Until, that is, he'd learned the former agent was dying. Now the Tellebough woman was claiming the prognosis was nothing more by a charade orchestrated by higher-ups within IIA. Who exactly was involved and why he could only guess at. Could someone so vehemently not want Adam Saint to become the head of CDRA that they would create such a horrible fiction?

Wishing the driver a good night, Kapur stepped out of the car. Despite the chill of the evening air making quick work of invading his too-slight frame, he stood on the street and watched as the vehicle silently slid away and its crimson taillights disappeared into the crisp darkness.

Even more worrying was another thought that had been burrowing its way through his brain all day, like a cancer of his own. Was the person behind the sham none other than Maryann Knoble? If so, God help him.

With my discovery that there might be cannibals on Skawa Island, I had two priorities. One: find them. Two: stay off their dinner plate. The best way to do the latter was to accomplish the former.

I was trying my best to speed up the process of searching the remainder of the island without causing my sister to worry. For the time being, I was blaming my rush on the impending storm that seemed intent on hammering the little island a second day in a row.

Alexandra had seen every bit of the skeleton-strewn

camp and jail structure, just as I had. We could only guess at what had happened there, when, and who was responsible. I vaguely suggested the site might be decades old, although I doubted it. I also didn't tell my sister what I'd seen in the metal cooking pot I'd found nearby.

Kettle polish.

The term refers to distinctive shiny marks striating the sides of cook pots. They come from only one thing: bone colliding against the inside walls of metal cooking vessels when being boiled. Together with the crushed skulls, butcher marks on the larger bones, and everything else we'd seen since our arrival, I was as confident as I could be without further scientific study that some sort of cannibalistic activity had taken place on Skawa Island, the purportedly deserted island in the middle of nowhere where my sister and I were stranded with no hope of escape until tomorrow. Discomfiting at the least.

Alexandra had proven herself strong, physically and mentally, but when I considered telling her the truth…an unsubstantiated truth…I decided that in this case the less she knew the better. I didn't want her thinking every noise or unexpected movement in the jungle might be prowling people-eaters. Even I couldn't ignore the fear factor of that possibility.

In the hour we'd been traipsing about the island since we left skeleton city behind, I'd dialled up my sensitivity metre to maximum. I kept Alexandra in front, because most attacks occur from the rear. Without her knowing, I'd rearranged my weapons arsenal—which I now considered insufficient, given the situation—for easy access. Blades in upper torso pockets. Handguns in a shooter's unholy triumvirate: waist, back, ankle.

As I've done countless times over the years, I silently blessed the powers of my recently returned special passport allowing me international travel accompanied by firepower.

"How much of the island have we got left to cover?" Alexandra asked without turning or missing a step.

"We're doing pretty well. I'd say we have less than a third to go."

"So let's see if I have this straight. In two-thirds of this supposedly deserted shithole, we've so far found a head with a hole in it, four shipwrecked Canadians, and what looks like a concentration camp full of dead people. I can hardly wait to see what's coming next."

"Good times, right?" I shot back.

"The best."

We reached a clearing and stopped to rest in the last bits of daylight. Dark clouds skittered across the sky like gangs of celestial thugs up to no good.

Alexandra wiped her forehead dry. She sipped at her canteen of water. Eyeing the tumultuous canvas above our heads, she said, "We're going to get hit, aren't we?"

I nodded.

"If I'm not wet from sweating like a rutting pig, I'm wet from all this bloody rain. I thought the South Pacific was supposed to be some sort of fucking tropical paradise…if you're a duck, maybe."

Movement to our left. Someone or something was in the bush. I fingered a knife I favoured for long-distance throwing. Alexandra hadn't noticed. Good. "We should keep going," I told her.

"Slave driver," she muttered. "Which way?"

"See that cliffside over there?" I pointed to the opposite

edge of the clearing. "We need to get on the other side of it."

"Oh good, more jungle," she murmured as she moved forward.

I held back to listen for any further sound from the treed area behind us.

Nothing. For now.

I followed my sister.

The storm arrived in earnest. Even through the thick foliage overhead the rain doused us, and within seconds we were entirely soaked. There are good things about tropical rainstorms. First, they're usually warm, like taking a tepid shower. Second, their intensity is so overwhelming you soon realize nothing you can do—other than take cover—will keep you any drier, so you just go about your business until shelter is an option.

Along with the rain came night. It was already dim in our jungle world, but now the dark grew absolute. Sluggishly, we moved through the wet, murky morass with the aid of small but powerful earpiece-mounted lights running on supercharged lithium batteries. Our progress was much slower than I would have liked. Nothing was as I would have liked. Of any time on this island, we were now in the most jeopardy. If indeed locals were hunting us, they'd doubtlessly be superior trackers in conditions they were far more used to than we were.

The situation wasn't good. I'd been in tight spots before but not with my sister at my side. As we slogged forward, I was battling a thought in my head. It scared me. Not the thought itself but the fact that I was not entirely focussed on the weighty matters at hand, although I desperately needed to be. But there it was: I could not escape the tormenting conviction that I had been an extreme idiot for ever having allowed Alexandra to accompany me to this island. If something happened to her, I would never forgive myself.

"Come on!" Alexandra was suddenly shouting.

I saw the door. I saw Alexandra running toward it.

"No! Wait!" I screamed a warning.

She stopped and turned, giving me a what-the-fuck? look.

In a flash, I was at her side, all my attention on the entryway. It was impossible, with the lighting and thick overgrowth, to determine how big the structure was or even what it was. Everything we'd discovered on the island so far had turned out to be an unpleasant surprise. Nothing told me to expect this sudden appearance of shelter to be anything but the same.

"What?" Alexandra crabbed. "Do you just want to stand out here and look at it?"

I have my own collection of looks. I gave one now to my sister.

She clearly understood and took a step back.

Grabbing Alexandra by the shoulder, I thrust her toward a small outcropping of boulders. I motioned for her to crouch down behind it. She probably thought I meant it as protection from the elements. In reality, I was hoping it would offer her a small bit of protection from unseen enemies.

I spent the next several minutes performing a rudimentary reconnaissance of the area and outside perimeter of what was turning out to look like a surprisingly expertly constructed building. Nothing about its exterior in any way revealed its purpose or what we might find inside, other than that who-ever built it had meant for it to remain hidden from passersby. The fact that Alexandra and I had spotted it at all was likely only a matter of one part luck and one part the ravages of time destroying segments of its camouflage.

The hand had barely touched my shoulder when I had it twisted up behind the owner's back, gun stuck into their side and lips in their ear growling: "Don't ever sneak up on me again."

Alexandra bent her knees and dropped to the ground with such speed I had to jump up and pitch forward to avoid landing on her—which she would have wholly de-served. I recovered from the roll quicker than she from her intentional collapse. She'd made a good move, but not good enough. On all fours facing my sister, I looked up from my ready position and waited. She did the same.

She eyed the gun I still held in my right hand. "Time to go inside?" she asked with a smirk. Her face was covered with muddy streaks already being washed clean by the rain.

"Sure," I responded casually, hopping up and throwing down a hand to help her to her feet.

"I just wanted you to know I'm not helpless," she said, grabbing onto my hand and hoisting herself up.

With a curt nod, I marched past her toward the build-ing, hiding my grin.

Standing at the door, I wordlessly handed my sister one of my firearms. I knew she was no stranger to guns.

It was time I admitted one of two things: Either my sis-ter needed to know the level of danger we might really be in or she already did.

The door opened with little more than a shove, uneven

surfaces scraping against each other. The unmistakable scents of mould and decay drifted over us. Our ear lights only illuminated a small portion of the space, but I immediately knew one thing for sure. I'd just found what Maryann Knoble was looking for.

Chapter Fourteen

When the lights came on, I glanced up from where I was crouched next to the portable generator and winked at my sister. "Told ya."

Sucking in her cheeks and nodding appreciation, she asked, "How did you do that?"

I stood up and slowly surveyed the newly lit room with greater scrutiny. "I'm familiar with this particular generator." It was a supercharged diesel-convertible-to-propane genset model, efficient, quiet, and using a fairly inflammable fuel source with a long shelf life.

"How can that be?"

I knew it the same way I was familiar with pretty much every piece of technology in the room. The same way I knew I'd found what Maryann Knoble was looking for. Everything in this place…this bunker…screamed IIA. Most of the equipment we were looking at—the power generator, computer systems, video and audio recording devices, cold and hot storage units—were top of the line, high-tech, and, the greatest telltale of all, proprietary to IIA. Only IIA personnel on IIA business would have had access to this stuff. Only IIA would have brought these items to this island.

I had used most of this stuff myself.

Ten years ago.

On closer inspection, I could tell the devices were out of date. Similar made-for-public-consumption varieties had likely hit Best Buy and Costco a few years earlier. IIA would have destroyed their own versions, having long ago moved onto the next generation of more powerful upgrades.

Knoble wanted to know what IIA's ties to Skawa Island were. I couldn't yet tell her what IIA had done here, but I could definitely confirm they'd been here.

"All of this stuff," I answered my sister, my voice louder than usual to make up for the rain and wind that relentlessly pummelled the building, even through the thick coat of foliage meant to keep it hidden, "it belongs to IIA."

"So what does that mean?" she asked, slowly circling the room, surveying the mess left behind. "Why would IIA be here? What would they be doing with all of this stuff?" After a beat, she added, "They sure didn't care about keeping things neat and tidy, did they?"

Understatement. The place was more than untidy the room had been ransacked. Files and papers had been pulled out of drawers and strewn across the floor. Furniture overturned. Equipment disconnected from power sources. Computer monitors smashed. Was this an act of simple vandalism? Calculated destruction? Anger?

"I don't know what they were doing here," I said. "That's what we're here to find out. All I know right now is that all of this equipment is out of date by about ten years."

"So that means IIA hasn't been here since then?"

"Maybe."

"Couldn't someone else have been using these machines after IIA was done with them?"

"Doubtful. Proprietary technology never leaves IIA

except to go to the crusher."

"So you think that's why it's such a mess in here? They were leaving, so they trashed everything? If they didn't want anyone else to use the stuff, why not just take it with them?"

Good points. "I don't think IIA did this."

Alexandra stopped what she was doing and turned to look at me. "What do you mean?"

"The equipment might be a decade old, but all of this," I said, referring to the chaos around us, "this was done recently, not ten years ago."

"How do you know?"

"Look at what wasn't tossed around."

Alex did as I instructed, screwing up her face as she did so.

"The dust!" she finally exclaimed. "If IIA did this ten years ago, all the stuff that's been thrown around would be covered with the same amount of dust as the stuff that wasn't. But it doesn't. It doesn't have any dust on it at all. Goddamnit, you're right, Adam! Someone just did this." She was getting excited. "Like, when do you think? Today? Yesterday?"

I shrugged. "Could be longer ago. The amount and rate of dust accumulation here isn't like at home. But, yeah, someone did this recently."

"Adam," she said almost breathlessly. "Those women. The ones we just let off the island with Jess. They could have done this."

I shot my sister a look.

She read it correctly. "Or…there's somebody else on this island."

I nodded.

"Adam! You need to see this!"

We'd been in the jungle cabin for about an hour, searching for any clue that might tell us who had been here and why. I had settled in to tinker with the least damaged pieces of computer equipment. If I could make any of it operational again, we'd at least have some chance at retrieving useful data. Alexandra had moved out of the main room to check out the rest of the structure.

I followed her voice down a short hallway that led to two doors. The first was a basic bathroom facility. The other, she'd discovered, was a bedroom.

"Someone was living here," she told me when I joined her in the tiny room.

I studied the space. It was dark and narrow with room for little more than a metal cot, a stand-alone wardrobe, and a small nightstand. The drawers of the nightstand were empty, but the wardrobe still held a collection of hastily hung clothes. Men's. About my size. Jeans, shirts, Tees, hoodies for warmth, nothing fancy. On the floor were a pair of well-worn sneakers and bedroom slippers. Next to them a cardboard box held an assortment of underwear and socks. The room and clothing smelled stale. Whoever slept here had departed for the last time quite a while ago and either left in a hurry or didn't care to wear these clothes again.

Alexandra held something out to me.

"What is it?"

"I found it between the night table and the wall."

The picture was faded and torn in half, as if whoever had kept it only cared about the one person left in the photograph, or really didn't want to look at whoever else was in it. The subject, a woman, was looking into the camera lens with studied intensity, as if she knew I was looking at her. If she did, I would tell her one thing: "Got ya."

The ten-thousand-square-foot Bridle Path house sat on three meticulously landscaped acres. Other than the thinnest slice of view if you were standing at exactly the right spot outside the front security gates, no one would see the house or its grounds unless invited to do so. The interior décor, chosen by a professional under strict guidance, suited the owner to perfection. Dark woods and fabrics; heavy, masculine furniture; nothing frilly, nothing purely decorative. Except one thing. Artwork.

Every wall of the house bore paintings, mostly oils or acrylic. A mix of contemporary and antique. All original. A few Masters. A few well-known Canadians: Verner, Murray, both Pratts, Hinz, and Hauser. Spread throughout the collection and throughout the house were several commissioned portraits, the subjects an adoring couple: Maryann Knoble and Sophie, the basset hound.

Maryann's favourite of the portraits was in her personal study. Inwardly, she chided herself for bothering to refer to the room as *personal*, as if there was another study somewhere for everyone else to use. She couldn't remember the last time someone other than herself, a domestic worker, or service person, had entered any of the mansion's many splendid rooms.

Gazing up at the special painting in the study, sometimes for an hour or more, was one of Maryann's favourite pastimes. Perhaps the closest thing she had to a hobby. She would fill a crystal tumbler with her preferred Scotch—ten-year-old Laphroaig—light up a cigar, and take a seat in the exquisite Caspani armchair perfectly situated for the purpose. The canvas was large, 300 cm x 215 cm. It showed her with Sophie in hand, several years earlier, on the resplendent estate's verdant front lawn. Somehow, the artist had made it seem as if they were in a magical kingdom, the house whimsically more castle-like than it actually was, flowers and trees in perfect bloom, song birds soaring overhead, the sky an ethereal, flawless blue.

As a child and into young womanhood, Maryann had considered herself a budding artist. In secret. In school, she had excelled at two things: painting and mathematics. Her intellectual parents, having no interest or patience for the arts, encouraged their young daughter to investigate the complex world of economics. In rare rebellious moments, Maryann would secretly visit museums or dabble on canvasses she hid beneath her bed. Despite this, she was not an unhappy child, equally contented by her developing skill with equations and computations and quantitative analysis as she was her hidden creative talent. As she grew older, Maryann developed newfound passions for political science and international relations. By the time her formal education was complete with a doctorate and several highly respected publications under her belt she was sought after by major corporations worldwide. Maryanne set aside her paint brushes forever.

Tonight, as she gazed affectionately at the beloved painting, Maryann reflected on what a perfect day it had been when the artist first sketched the drawing in preparation for the actual work. The job ended up taking another several weeks to get right. It was warm that day, but not too warm. Sophie had not yet begun to show signs of aging.

And for the first time since she'd recently taken over the helm of IIA, Maryann had truly felt in control of every blazing ball of fire she was expected to juggle on a daily basis. The feeling, she was soon to learn, would be fleeting and would only irregularly return.

Yes, that was a good day.

When the distinctive three-toned chime sounded, Maryann's forehead furrowed. She hadn't heard that specific pre-set warning alarm for quite some time. Fingering the Hermès scarf that perfectly matched her silk evening dressing gown, her eyes fell to the mother-of-pearl Gevril watch on her wrist. It was well past midnight; someone was up to no good.

Bringing her drink and cigar with her, Maryann approached the large desk that dominated the study, a replica of the one in her IIA office. On top was a computer strobing a visual warning to go along with the auditory one.

Settling herself in the desk chair, which over the years had formed nicely to her unusual shape, she entered an elaborate series of codes and passwords. When finally she had access to the contents of the warning, she read it over twice. Someone was attempting to access the personnel files of CDRA. And they were having some success. A limited number of IIA individuals did have admittance to these files without having to inform anyone, and they did so without setting off this warning. Something else was afoot.

Tapping at the keyboard revealed more. The person seeking to gain entry into this section of IIA's extensively protected data files did indeed have clearance. Except to one area: the files belonging to ex-agents, deceased, retired, or terminated.

"Well then," Maryann said to the screen as she jabbed out more key combinations. "First, I'm going to find out who you're looking for. Then I'm going to find out who you are."

And in that order she did just that.

The first revelation worried her.

The hacker was looking for Adam Saint.

The second revelation took her by surprise.

The culprit was none other than Shekhar Kapur, the new head of CDRA.

"You little weasel," Maryann hissed when the name appeared on the screen.

An all-too-familiar nagging doubt assailed her. Had she been too hasty in choosing Kapur for the post?

Once Krazinski was dead, Ross Campbell dispensed with, and Saint unavailable for either suddenly vacated position because he was dying, she'd had to move fast. An organization such as IIA could not appear weakened or incapable of fully delivering its mandated activities for any length of time. Other than Saint, there was no one else in-house she would consider. So she'd thrown the net wide, based on a list of potential replacements created by herself and past IIA chiefs. Kapur had been caught. Quickly. Maybe too quickly.

He'd seemed the perfect candidate. As the highly regarded head of IDRA, he was eminently qualified. At the time, the fact that he was a candidate put forward by Sergiusz Belar seemed like a good thing. That was before all this Skawa mess.

What was Shekhar Kapur up to? And did it have something to do with that damned island in the South Pacific? Had she unwittingly invited an enemy to live within the gates of IIA?

The timing couldn't be worse. David Gilmore, the baron of pomposity who was the current Minister of Public Safety and therefore her boss, had recently become a more irksome thorn in her side than usual. He'd been calling and keeping her on the phone with his endless, senseless jabber more often than was typical. Did he sense something was up? Under no circumstances could Knoble allow him to find out about the situation on Skawa Island. If he did, it would give him all the ammunition he'd need to hobble IIA and her right along with it, something she knew he'd take inordinate pleasure in. Like so many other men in positions of power, sometimes he liked to swing his sledgehammer just because he could. And if it happened to hit a powerful woman, all the better.

Knoble brought up a satellite video-link channel and initiated a call to Adam Saint.

No answer.

She tried satellite phone.

No answer.

As she typed a long series of commands into the computer to ensure Kapur would be spectacularly unsuccessful in his attempts, Knoble voice-activated another call, to a local number. A number she knew would answer. Soon, she would know a great deal more about Shekhar Kapur. "And that, my friend," she whispered, her voice gruff, computer keys suffering beneath her darting jabs, "will seal your fate."

"What exactly is IIA? Like, what do they do?"

Alexandra was sitting on a chair, feet up on the same desk where I was working. She was finishing off a bag of almonds from the stash I'd brought with me. I was back at trying to resuscitate one of the computers. I'd found an external backup drive that didn't look too damaged. All I needed was something live to connect it to.

"I'm just trying to figure all of this out," she followed up when I didn't immediately respond.

I tried a non-committal, I'm-busy-here kind of grunt.

She waved a boot in my face. "Hey. Adam? Sister asking a question here. IIA? What are they?"

As I tinkered away, I answered as best I could. "They basically like to collect information."

"Yeah? Information about what?"

"Anything that's going on anywhere in the world that could have importance to—in our case—Canada. Mostly technical and research data and intellectual property. Plus IIA is like the head office for a number of other sub-agencies."

"Like the CDRA, the people you work for?"

"Yes."

"What about Kate? Who does she work for?"

I was surprised to find the mere mention of my recently divorced wife elicit a reaction in me. Was it irritation? Anger? Maybe I'd just rather not hear her name.

"Kate works for the War Crimes Unit."

"I saw her, you know."

There it was again. *What the hell is that?*

Alexandra had grown quiet, but I could feel her dark eyes on me, like two burning cigarettes grinding against my bare skin. I looked up.

"You're frigging still in love with her? Aren't you?" Her tone was incredulous.

I went back to work. "No, Alexandra, I'm not."

"I saw you tense up when I mentioned her name. I saw

the look in your eye. Gee-zuz, Adam, not to put too fine a point on it, and I know you don't want us talking about this all the time, but if you're still dying, don't you think you'd make better use of your time finding someone else to moon over? She fuckin' hates you, bro."

Ah, yes, my sister, never afraid of the cannonball remark.

She was wrong though. I wasn't in love with Kate. I mourned for her, for what we once had, because it was pretty damn fine most of the time. My body physically yearned for her. Same reason. But I couldn't love her anymore. In every relationship, there's a line you just don't cross. If you do, there's no going back. Not only had Kate and I crossed that line, we'd gone around and crossed it two or three more times. I'd been complicit in a scheme that sent a man she loved, a man who wasn't me, to his certain death. Kate didn't know, but she suspected it. You don't come back from that.

Suddenly, the monitor in front of me made a popping sound. Then a tiny white dot at its centre grew until it filled the entire screen.

"Thank Christ," Alexandra said. "I was thinking we were going to have to get Anatole down here."

"Actually, so was I."

I held my breath as the screen came alive.

As with most tropical storms, this one was as strong and steadfast now as it had been from the start. It would show no signs of letting up until about two seconds before it actually did. The level of humidity in the windowless room had reached sauna proportions. I was glad for the roof over our heads but nervous with night approaching and us still here rather than in a decent hiding place that didn't stick out like a no-longer-hidden-cabin in the woods. One thing I know for certain about broken computers: the faster you urge them to do something, the slower they do it. All we could do was sit back, wait, and hope for the best.

Alexandra dropped her feet to the floor and pulled her chair closer. "Wow, I'm impressed. This thing looks like it might actually work."

Then, as if I'd logged in only yesterday, a familiar menu of options appeared. I knew this operating system. It was proprietary to IIA—ten years ago. I clicked this and that and eventually located the icon for the external backup drive I'd connected to the computer. Clicking the icon gave me the list of files available, admirably well organized.

I clicked on a folder labelled "Video." As they say, a picture is worth a thousand words. Within was a long list of video files. A quick scan showed that the most recent backup date was a decade earlier.

Alexandra's nose was inching closer to the screen. "What are these?"

My finger hovering above the mouse, I winked at my sister. "Let's find out."

I clicked on a random file near the bottom of the list.

A separate screen opened. A video player. I tapped the "Yes" button when asked if I wanted to play it.

The video began with a camera focussed on what looked to be jungle. It could have been any jungle anywhere in the world, but I was willing to bet it was the one right outside our front door. After a minute, a man came into the frame. He was very thin, Caucasian, wearing clothes that appeared to be almost threadbare, his hair and full beard long and unkempt. He appeared to be entirely unaware of the camera's presence.

The man moved into an area near the left side of the screen. Half-obscured, he began to urinate.

Then it happened.

From the right-hand side of the screen came three other figures. Except for the colour of their skin, which was darker, they looked to be in similarly rough shape. Their movements were stealthy; they were obviously trying to sneak up on the unsuspecting man as he relieved himself.

With stunning speed, the three fell upon the lone man like a pack of wolves.

The room had grown deathly quiet as my sister and I began to comprehend what we were seeing. The silence was eaten up by a heart-wrenching scream, belonging to the man who was being savagely attacked.

"Oh…oh God, Adam," came the first words from my sister. "Is this shit real?"

I was afraid it was.

From behind us, the front door of the cabin blew open with a deafening crash.

Just as we both spun about to see what was happening, three objects landed on the floor in front of us.

No! my mind shrieked as I jumped to my feet.

Accelerant.

I turned to tell my sister to run. But she was gone. Replaced by a giant ball of fire.

Chapter Fifteen

Instinctual or not, Alexandra knew exactly what to do when she found herself on fire. She dropped and rolled.

I'd seen an old coat on a peg near the hallway that led to the bedroom. I made quick work of retrieving it and fell down next to my sister. I used the coat to smother the flames intent on engulfing her. All around us the fire, aided by accelerant that smelled like gasoline, was flourishing, feeding on the flammable goodies strewn about the room. There was no time to think about who was trying to kill us or why. If we did, they would no doubt be successful.

Within seconds, Alexandra was free of flames and on her feet, looking like a smoking, pissed-off feline. There were char marks on her clothing, and her hair was singed, but otherwise she was okay.

I began scouring the room for the best escape route. There were pitiably few options. This building had been designed to keep people out but did the same job in reverse.

"The bedroom!" Alexandra shouted. "There's a window in there!"

Without a second's hesitation, we scrambled down the hallway toward the only room in the place with a possible way out. The opening was a small rectangle above the bed with a swing-up single pane. Jumping atop the mattress, I pulled Alexandra with me. I cupped my hands at knee level to give her a hoist up. With her left foot in my grasp, I lifted. She reached up to open the window and with my help began slithering through the tight space. Half outside, the driving rain and wind battering her, her hips suddenly brought all progress to a halt.

She struggled to move. I could tell she was beginning to panic. She appeared to be reversing her effort, giving up on the window. I couldn't let that happen. This was the only way out aside from the front door, but that was where the fire had originated and was at its fiercest. Getting her outside through this window was the only chance.

Roughly, I grabbed my sister's flailing body and began to rotate it. She fought back. Even above the storm and fire, I could hear the swearing.

The change in position worked. With her body at an angle, she would fit. Just.

I had no idea what…or who…might be on the other side of that window, but the only other option was grim. Using all my strength, I pushed.

I watched as my sister's feet disappeared. Success.

Within seconds, her face, mottled with mud and angst, appeared at the opening.

"Give me your hand!" she screeched. "I'll pull you through!"

I stepped back. Our eyes met. Hers wild and beseeching. Mine apologetic.

"I'll pull you through, Adam!" she insisted, louder this time.

I shook my head. There was no way I would ever fit through the tiny opening.

As she realized what was happening, Alexandra's face began to crumble. Tears mixed with rain sluiced down her face.

"You knew you couldn't make it!" she screamed at me.

I brought my face up to hers. "Alexandra, you have to listen to me now. Whoever did this is still out there. I want you to run. I want you to find a place to hide, near the beach. Don't move until morning. Don't come out until you hear Jess's plane about to land. Then you get to him and get the hell off this island!"

"You knew?" she repeated as if she hadn't heard a word I'd said.

"I'll be okay, Alexandra."

"No! You fucking won't! You won't. You're going to die in there!"

Our eyes were linked together, a bond I'd soon have to break.

"I know what you're doing!" she shrieked. "You don't think it's going to work, do you? You don't think the cure is going to save you. You think you're going to die anyway, so might as well do it now."

"Run," I told her.

I dropped the window pane over my sister's face, locked it, and leapt off the bed. Without looking back, I rushed into the hallway.

She was wrong again. I did believe Knoble's cure would work. I had to. Not to would be mental suicide. And it didn't hurt that I hadn't had a headache, nausea, or any other symptom since we'd arrived on Skawa. No, I wasn't ready to die. More than ever, I wanted to live.

I am a man who relies on facts. And reality. This was

simply a time when being a big, beefy guy was not going to work in my favour. Aside from chopping myself into bits there was no way I was ever going to get through that window. There was no point in wasting even a second thinking about it. I had to find another way out.

Back in the front room, I assessed the progress of the fire. Not looking good.

Aside from the hungry flames, the intense heat and smoke were becoming dangerous factors. In most blazes, the final killing blow is usually dealt by smoke, not fire. For a brief second, my mind returned to the morning of the stubble fire on my father's farm. I wasn't going to get out of this one quite so easily.

I surveyed the room again, looking for ways to save myself, however outlandish or preposterous. At this point, I'd take anything.

As a disaster recovery agent, the speed of your decision-making process can sometimes mean the difference between life and death. This was that kind of situation. I made up my mind and jumped into action.

Speeding back into the bedroom, I began yanking every piece of clothing off the wardrobe rack and pulling them on over my own clothes. Before long, I resembled a cloth version of the Michelin Man. Next, I eyed the cot and judged the best placement position for my hands. With every inch of brute force within me, I lifted the small bed, complete with mattress, off the floor.

The hall wasn't long, but getting the thing down to the front room was awkward, the place now more closely resembling an arena of fire. With the blaze engulfing most of the room, the heat was extreme. Perspiration coated my body. It was difficult to breathe. My lungs ached. Eyes burned. I had to keep moving before it was too late. Now or never.

With the front door obscured by raging flames, I could only guess at its location. I covered my head with the last piece of clothing I'd donned. Like my sister, I knew I might be rushing directly from fire into frying pan, but at this point, a frying pan was looking pretty good.

Positioning the cot in front of me like a shield, I rammed forward, bellowing like a bull. Frying pan, here I come.

Once outside the disintegrating cabin, I tossed the cot to one side and immediately fell into a roll. I did this for two reasons: in case I'd caught fire, and in case whoever set the fire in the first place was waiting for me. If they were and had guns, it would be harder to hit a low-rolling figure than some disoriented guy lumbering about trying to put out his sizzling clothes.

Coming to a stop, I immediately shifted to my feet and, still staying low, ran for cover behind a nearby bank of bushes. The rain was still coming down hard, and the clouds obscured any moonlight. For now, this was good news, aiding my chances of getting away unseen.

I counted to five and then ran.

I heard footsteps coming after me.

Shit!

Fight or flight? Or maybe vomit all over myself?

I can usually be counted on to fight.

Barely breaking stride, I shifted to the left behind a tree, pulled a gun, and readied for whatever was coming. I had a slight upper hand in that my pursuer would likely be expecting me to keep moving.

The sound of speeding footsteps was barely discernible over the sluicing storm and hissing fire doing battle only metres away, but it was enough for me to get a bearing. Biding my time, I waited until the last second before jumping out of my hiding place and grabbing hold of my pursuer. In a flash, I had one arm fastened behind their back and a gun at their temple.

Alexandra was not pleased. Again.

"What are you still doing here?" I demanded to know, letting my sister go. "I told you to get away from here!"

"I wasn't going to just leave you in there!" she rallied back.

"And just what did you think you were going to do?"

"I don't know!" she shouted back, not giving an inch.

"Alex…."

"I wasn't going to leave you alone to die," she cried.

I did the unexpected.

I reached out and pulled my sister into a hug. She hugged back.

Then: "And you're a shit-eating, pig-ass motherfucker for trying to make me!"

We pulled apart.

I had no time to react to my sister's assessment of my decisions because of the bullet that grazed across her shoulder.

Even the most practiced marksman would have difficulty hitting the side of a barn in these conditions. Driving rain. Dark. And we were doing whatever we could to make it even harder for whoever was shooting at us, moving fast through unfamiliar territory.

At least I hoped this was unfamiliar territory for the shooters. Certainly, it wasn't cannibals who'd orchestrated the fiery destruction of the cabin. Or maybe I was working with an outdated frame of reference for what the modern-day cannibal was capable of.

I took the lead in our escape, setting out on a zigzag pattern that would further confound anyone's ability to embed hot lead in our asses. Alexandra kept pace. We each had a gun, but with little knowledge of who was behind us, how far and how many, the smarter thing was first to elude our attackers and then to find a hiding place. I'd shoot the shit out of them later.

Fortunately, we'd covered much of this terrain earlier, in daylight. I don't exactly have a photographic memory, but I do enjoy excellent detailed recall and usually a faultless sense of direction. Even at night, I had a good idea of where we were going and what we could expect in terms of topography.

I slowed my pace just enough for Alexandra to come abreast. As we ran side by side, I said quietly to her: "In about thirty seconds, I want you to speed up. Stay as close on my heels as you can. When I raise my left hand, veer sharp left immediately. Sharp. Left. Got it?"

Breathlessly she nodded.

I moved slightly forward, increasing my speed.

We ran.

Faster.

I could hear Alexandra behind me. The front tips of her shoes nipping the rear of mine. *Good girl.*

Ten seconds.

Five.

Left hand up.

Simultaneously, we changed direction and darted left, barely decreasing our speed as we did so.

Four seconds later I heard it.

"Sonofabitch…!" the voice screamed. Then the unmistakable sounds of tumbling.

I'd come to know Skawa Island has more than a few surprises up its sleeve for the uninitiated. The rain helped too, making the ground a slippery mess. If my plan had worked, one of the gunmen was now on his way to the bottom of a craggy ravine. With any luck, a tender part of him would be introduced to the piercing edges of the rocks that lay in wait below, like sharp-toothed crocodiles in a bayou swamp.

"What just happened?" Alexandra questioned as we continued to race away.

"Just improving our odds."

There was one downside to my plan. Whoever was behind us…we'd just really pissed them off.

Too bad.

Bouts of gunfire increased.

The possibility of a lucky bullet hitting its mark grew.

We ran faster. Despite the benefit of adrenaline fuelled by fear, both of us were beginning to show signs of fatigue. Our breathing grew laboured. I spied Alexandra clutch her side as spasms of pain coaxed her body to slow down.

"Shit, Adam, they're going to catch us!"

"No, Alexandra, we can do this."

The foliage was getting thick. We couldn't continue side by side for much longer.

"Stay with me," I urged.

"Great idea," she muttered.

I smiled, winked, and moved ahead.

The thickness of the growth in this part of the jungle was slowing us down, but it would do the same for the people tracking us. Not to mention making it even more difficult for them to get a bead on us. As I moved forward, I realized that the rain had stopped, just as suddenly as it had started.

Based only on the sounds I heard behind us—which were pitifully faint—I guessed there were between two and four people chasing us. It might not seem like a lot, but the difference between two and four is massive when it comes to countermoves. With two, I could plan a potential trap that might just have a snowball's chance in hell of working. Even though all of us were armed, Alexandra was untrained. Realistically, I could only rely on her for self-defence. Two people I could take down on my own in a firefight. Four, I'd need a little help.

My mind was abuzz with possible scenarios for what to do next. Alternatives were not plentiful, especially when I would only accept ones where my sister had a good chance of surviving.

Should we split up? Normally, this would be the best thing to do at this point. Distract the gunmen even more, halve their chances of a successful takedown, and double our chances of one of us getting away. If we split up, they *should* go after me and leave Alexandra alone. But nothing about what had transpired so far tonight suggested these people were only after me. They weren't here enjoying target practice. They were here to kill.

We'd both been in that cabin. We'd both seen—or were about to see—something the gunmen didn't want us to see. By burning down the building and everything in it, they'd destroyed whatever they wanted to keep secret. The only thing left was to get rid of anyone else who knew about it, a.k.a. us.

There was only one other theory I could come up with that made any sense, an unsettling theory that was banging an eerie gong in my head.

Other than Anatole and a few unsuspecting Tubuaians, who else knew we were here?

One person.

Maryann Knoble.

Was her real purpose for luring me back into working for her now unfolding?

Did Maryann Knoble want me dead?

But why not let the tumour in my head do the job for her?

I had no time to debate the matter. I needed to clear my mind of suspicion and focus on escape.

Making a decision, I turned to assess how far behind my sister had fallen.

Too far.

Alexandra was gone.

Chapter Sixteen

Alexandra's disappearance changed things. Either she'd decided on her own that splitting up was the way to go or she'd been taken.

Or gunned down.

It didn't matter which was true. These assholes weren't hunting me anymore. I was hunting them.

First things first: I sped up to the maximum velocity I was capable of. I wanted them to believe I was still running away but at the same time I was putting as much distance between them and me as I could.

Not wanting to get too far from where I'd last seen Alexandra, I didn't want to keep it up for too long. Less than two minutes later, I saw what I needed. Deviating off track, I dove into a deep ground trough, likely created over decades of rainstorms and nicely shielded with ground cover. Lying low in the slimy depression, I coerced my breathing to slow and my body, vibrating with the strain of extended extreme activity, to still itself. I concentrated on the sounds around me. By picking out and ignoring normal jungle noises, I could focus on anything man-made.

I needn't have tried so hard. There were two of them. And they weren't trying to be subtle. Their heavy footfalls rushed by me at thundering speed.

Had they left someone behind to watch over Alexandra? Were there more of them coming?

I waited a full minute before moving. No one else appeared.

Thirty seconds more.

No one.

I pulled myself out of the trough and went after the men. I didn't know how expert they might be at tracking a human through jungle, but sooner or later they'd figure out I was no longer running. Shortly after that, they'd begin to suspect they'd lost me. In situations like this, hunters of any kind have the tendency to make the same stupid mistake. They wouldn't suspect I was actually behind them rather than in front—until it was too late.

Keeping to only a light jog, I followed the easy clues— broken tree branches and dishevelled ground matter. Before long, I was at the perfect distance behind them. Close enough to hear what they were up to but far enough away that I could keep them from detecting me. As long as I was careful. I am always careful.

After about two minutes the men slowed.

Dawning suspicion.

"Andrew, wait," one called out with a hushed insistence.

"What?" from the other.

"Are we going the right way? I don't hear anyone."

"What?"

"Stop, for Chrissakes."

They did.

I inched closer.

Closer.

I could see them. And their firearms. Powerful pieces. These guys weren't fooling around. Professionals? Mercenaries?

"Shit, you're right. I don't hear anything either. Now what?"

After a moment's consultation, the killers chose the only option that made sense. Split up to cover more ground. As far as they knew, I was unarmed, so even if one of them managed to catch my scent, they'd still have the upper hand.

Suckers.

I waited thirty seconds, then attached a silencer to my gun and followed the speedier of the two.

He quickly made a fatal mistake.

I let him finish the job and zip up his pants before putting him down.

The second gunman was more difficult. He was smart. He'd follow one path of possibility, an eagle eye out for signs of my passage. If he found none after the first minute, he switched directions. He did all of this swiftly and with sharp, precise movements, which made it difficult to get a bead on him at the distance I was aiming from. If I stopped too long, trying to get an accurate fix, I risked losing him.

I needed to change tack. I could follow this guy for half a day before getting a clear shot. I didn't have the time. I had to go back to find Alexandra. I just hoped it wasn't too late. These men didn't seem interested in taking prisoners. They wanted us dead. I was having the same feelings.

I took position and did what under normal circumstances would be unthinkable.

I coughed.

Suddenly, all the jungle was still. It seemed as if every sound other than the reverberating echo of my cough had disappeared.

The gunman would have to investigate.

From the position I'd chosen and where I'd last seen the man, I figured I had at least two hundred and forty degrees of clear sight in which I hoped to spot his approach. The other hundred and twenty was anybody's game.

Once again, things had changed. This was now a one-on-one battle to the death.

"Andrew?" the man called in a low voice.

Idiot. The sound placed him.

I stepped out of my hiding spot and levelled my gun.

No one there.

Turns out, the idiot was me.

He knew exactly what he was doing. Shouting out his buddy's name wasn't a mistake, it was a ploy.

I crouched down and swivelled, placing my best bet on where the man would appear behind me.

I was wrong again.

I felt him land on me from above like a sack of cement, a direct hit on the shoulders. Taking a page out of my sister's playbook, I allowed my knees to collapse and at the last minute pitched forward with as much power as I could. I thudded against the ground with such force that one gun flew out of my hand, a second from my ankle holster. Alexandra had my third. The other man landed heavily too, only inches away. I didn't know where my guns had ended up. All I was left with was brute force.

With two fists grasping onto the fabric of the man's pants for leverage, I pulled myself up his body and reached for his gun hand. At the same time, he was desperately trying to position it somewhere in the vicinity of my brain.

This was not the time for playing nice. I was in the region, so I slammed my fist into his groin. Even though this man wanted me dead, I had a momentary inkling of empathy as he howled in response.

Both of us still flat out on the ground, I tried again for his gun. But he was a strong bugger. Strong and smart, a deadly combination.

Trying to recover from his painful injury without losing control of his firearm, the man attempted to twist away from me. Bad move. Distancing himself from me also allowed me to maneuvre. As soon as we were clear of one another, I struggled to my knees. I threw myself on top of him just as his roll put him face down. This got me on his back. My arms weaved up under him and then behind his neck. I yanked up and jerked down hard. At the same time, I pushed down with my torso, putting extreme pressure on his neck and spine.

The gun popped out of his hand.

We each scrambled for it.

I got to it first.

That was the end.

Or not. I was barely standing when a hot shot grazed my hand, causing me to drop my newly won prize.

What the hell?

A third man.

Pistol aimed at me.

From the height of the barrel, I estimated the bullet would hit me directly in the chest.

In about two seconds.

I'm sorry, Alexandra.

It had been a long night, and it wasn't over yet. Sleep had been eluding her since the disturbing discovery that Shekhar Kapur was attempting to infiltrate Adam Saint's personnel files. Even shutting him down and calling in one of her private agents to investigate Kapur to find out what the hell he was after hadn't helped. Maryann Knoble did not like missing sleep. She needed a minimum of five hours every night. Without them, her morning demeanour was not her usual common black bear but rather ferocious grizzly.

She tried another finger of whisky. The complex Laphroaig from the Scottish island of Islay ordinarily calmed her. Even the meaning of the Gaelic word seemed designed to instill tranquility: *the beautiful hollow by the broad bay*. Not tonight. For Maryann, a woman who thrived in a world she controlled, to have as much uncertainty as had recently popped up around her, like recalcitrant heads of dandelion, was untenable.

One might believe that the only certainty in a job like hers would be uncertainty. But the opposite, Maryann believed, was actually true. Indeed, most of the matters that came across her desk each and every hour of each and every day were serious. Most of them were unexpected and in and of themselves uncontrollable. But the IIA's response—Knoble's response—was always the same. Gather intelligence, make a decision, assemble a team, delegate responsibility, and then act. Simple. The little details were always different and often complex, but the big picture remained the same, certain, with Maryann on top of the heap pulling the strings and pushing the buttons.

Yet now it felt uncomfortably like certain strings and buttons were being manipulated by someone else. Skawa

Island. Sergiusz Belar. Adam Saint. Shekhar Kapur. She smelled a big, fat, stinky rat here. She needed to chop off its head before it was too late.

The whisky did nothing. It didn't even taste right. The familiar and ordinarily enticing sea salt, wood, and peat fire smoke that met her nose was instead almost repellant. Maryann had heard it said that the atmosphere, ambiance, and company in which a good wine is drunk has as much influence on its enjoyment as the environmental conditions, soil, and climate in which the grapes were grown. Perhaps the same could be said for Scotch.

She roamed.

On nights like this, alone in the expansive house, Maryann Knoble felt desperately lonely. So lonely even the walls were in pain. She wandered the dim, long hallways, stopping here and there to admire a painting. It was the only thing that helped.

Tonight, she leaned toward the lighter pieces, ones with bright colours and fanciful themes. Eventually, she found herself in the one room she visited the least. The kitchen. Not fond of cooking, Maryann ate out almost every night of the week. On the rare occasion she did eat at home, the kitchen was only used to keep something cool or something warm until it was time to consume it. The cupboards were stocked with full sets of expensive dinnerware, flatware, and glassware, none of which were utilized on any regular basis. The items she found most useful, such as brandy snifters, crystal wine goblets, and of course the heavy leaded low-balls for her treasured whisky were kept elsewhere. There was, however, one important foodstuff in this room.

Oreo cookies.

Opening the cupboard where she stored them, Maryann noted that with only three full bags left it would soon be time to replenish the stock.

She opened a bag and immediately popped two into her mouth. No milk required.

With the front of her dressing gown sporting a few dark, chocolatey crumbs, Maryann made her way to the grand staircase that led up to her bedroom suite. It was time to try for sleep.

Her foot had barely touched the first step when she heard the sound, just barely, but it was there. She knew it that well.

Retracing her steps from earlier in the evening, she made her way back to the study. As was her habit, she'd left the computer on. She disliked wasting time with wake-up or start-up procedures every time she sat behind her desk, here or at IIA. At regular intervals, the computer was bleating out the information: "Email received."

Taking her seat at the desk, she glanced at her watch. Her man had done quick work. Had he uncovered something useful about Shekhar Kapur already? And why not? It might be three a.m. here, but it was early afternoon in India.

Fingers poised above the keyboard, Maryann hesitated, frowning at what she saw onscreen.

The sender was not her agent. Not only that, but the sender's address was unknown to her. This was not at all typical. Other than personnel high up in IIA or one of its subsidiaries, all with email addresses designed to be easily recognizable, the list of people who had knowledge of Maryann Knoble's private email address was short and well-known.

The spam filters and virus detectors protecting all IIA computers were of the highest calibre. Not much could get through without being destroyed, but not much did not mean foolproof.

Typically, Maryann would forward such an email to her assistant. The assistant would perform verification procedures before either routing it back or involving the IT department for possible follow-up should the message be determined to have malign intent. But not this time. This time, Maryann would have to assess the danger herself.

She knew better than to act rashly. Ever. Allowing herself time to evaluate and then re-evaluate the situation and her intended actions, Maryann sat back in her luxurious chair and withdrew a cookie from its bag. She carefully twisted apart the two sides of the dark cookie, one left with a slab of creamy whiteness, the other bare. She dipped the icing-free half into the glass of Scotch she'd left there hours ago. There was barely enough liquid to cover the bottom of the glass, but it was enough to give the cookie a splendid boost of piquancy.

She savoured the treat. When it was done, she was ready to act.

Leaning into the desk, she studied the email beckoning her from the computer monitor. Sender: Unknown. Address: Unfamiliar. Subject line: Skawa Island.

Secure in her decision, Maryann hit the key to open the message.

Blank.

Except for an attachment.

Video.

She punched in the commands telling the computer to

open and play the file.

As the first muddy, grimy, horrible images appeared on the screen, she recoiled and then nearly choked on a last bit of Scotch-soaked cookie.

Chapter Seventeen

The camera was stationary, recording its subjects from a distance. The lighting was poor. The sound crackling. But what was happening before Maryann Knoble's eyes was unmistakable.

The woman was being raped. By more than one man. The sounds were guttural. At first, she thought the woman was silent. Maybe dead? Then she heard it. A long, low, helpless moan, the sound of boundless, inexhaustible misery. Just as Maryann thought she might have to look away to save herself from becoming physically ill, the image changed. Someone had spliced in another piece of footage. From the texture of the film and background, it was immediately apparent this video was taken at a different location. The quality of the recording was much poorer, darker. This time, Maryann had to move closer to the screen, adjusting the position of her oversized trifocals.

Peering closely at the figures, two, maybe three men, she tried to make out what they were doing. They seemed to be hunched over something lying on the ground. Eventually, one of the men pulled back, resting himself on his heels as he took a break from the activity.

"What is that?" Maryann asked the empty room.

She brought her face to within three inches of the screen.

Lying on the ground was a fourth man. Very still.

Were these doctors? Ministering to a patient?

The glint was dull, but it caught her eye nonetheless in the otherwise stark and murky setting.

A knife.

One of the men was holding the implement aloft. Bringing it up to his face. To his mouth.

There was something on the knife's flat edge.

The man sucked whatever was on the knife into his mouth and began to chew.

The knife went back down.

For more.

"Mother of God!" Maryann cried out. With a violent shove, she pushed herself back from the desk and the offending images on the computer screen.

Mercifully, the video ended there. In total, it was less than a minute long, but to Maryann an eternity had come and gone since she'd hit "Play." She would always regret having done so.

As she sat there, barely breathing, barely capable of speech or rational thought, knowing she had to regroup her senses, fast, and focus on what to do, the blank monitor came alive once more.

The video was not over.

Maryann knew she couldn't bear to watch another second. But instead of images, a message began to scroll up from the bottom of the screen:

I hope you have enjoyed today's feature presentation.

What you have just watched is actual footage (not a recreation) shot on location at Skawa Island.

> *Directed, produced, funded by: The International Intelligence*
>   *Agency of Canada.*
> *In other words, Ms. Knoble: YOU.*

Maryann shuddered at the sight of her name. But the worst was yet to come. The concluding part of the message was short and simple:

> *Silence the women of Skawa Island.*
> *Or the next time you see this video—in its entirety—will be*
>   *on the nightly news. Everywhere....*

I stared at the gun directed at my chest, my own lost somewhere on the jungle floor. Years of training and experience had taught me never to give up. Always look for a solution, no matter how grave the situation. This was as grave as they get. Still my mind grasped for a way to save my life.

In the microseconds allotted me, I was coming up pathetically short.

So when the hefty log appeared behind my would-be murderer and with commanding force slammed into the back of his head, there were only two things I could do.

Sing hallelujah, and dive for cover from the bullet that had been fired upon the log's impact.

Having successfully dodged the killing projectile, I bounded up to find out what or who was behind the last-minute save.

Standing above the downed shooter, in all his blond surfer-dude glory, was our Australian pilot.

Gratitude and anger. Two things that rarely go together.

Two things a disaster recovery agent rarely finds useful. Of course, I was thankful to still be breathing air, but Jess was supposed to be on Tubuai, watching over the women we'd rescued from this island madhouse.

I shouted, "What the hell are you doing back here?"

He began mumbling something, but I realized his answer didn't matter right now. There was another more pressing priority. "Jess, we have to find Alexandra."

"He already did."

From the same dark corner a second figure emerged.

What happened next had never happened to me before. The tidal wave of relief that flooded up my body from the tips of my toes, up my calves, coursing through my torso, heating up my chest, and seeming to burst in my head like fireworks was momentarily incapacitating.

I stared at my sister. Only now could I admit to myself I'd thought she was dead.

I stood my ground and muttered, "You're here."

"Where'd you think I'd be? Holt Renfrew? You need to—"

In half a second, I covered the ground between Alex and me and slapped a hand across her mouth.

She struggled.

With my lips pressed against her ear and staring at a shocked Jess, I ordered them both to stay quiet.

She settled.

By the look on Jess's face, I knew he too had heard the noise.

Voices.

Not far away.

There were more of them.

We could either hide or make a run for Jess's plane.

Running silently through a jungle in darkness is not easy; actually, it's quite probably impossible. They were going to hear us.

The vote was unanimous. In the words of my erudite sister: "Let's get the fuck off this hot-scum-soaked piece of bird shit island."

We had the upper hand in knowing where we were headed. Our pursuers—I was guessing there were three to five of them—were still in tracking mode. They'd have to see us or hear us or find clues in an unforgiving terrain in order to stay on our heels.

However, they had some stuff going for them too. It took us precious seconds to locate my guns, without which I had no intentions of leaving. Even so, they outgunned us, likely outnumbered us, and if they were the professionals I suspected they were, they probably had night-vision goggles and telescopic gunsights. My only hope was that they had arrived on Skawa by boat. If they too had a plane, I wasn't sure how prepared Jess was to do battle in the air. At night. In a Cessna.

I ran lead. Jess brought up the rear with Alexandra between us. I warned them to say nothing unless they were shot dead and to stay as light-footed as humanly possible. Alex scowled at being ordered around but was doing better at it than Jess. He was as heavy-footed as a mob of drunken kangaroo.

Our pace was brisk but not an all-out run. I knew it would take us close to ten minutes to get to the beach where Jess left the plane, and I didn't want anyone tiring out before we reached it.

About two-thirds of the way there, the first gunshot rang out.

"Fucking hell!" my sister grouched.

"Don't!" I warned her to stay quiet, at the same time slightly picking up the pace. The shot had missed by a mile. They were desperate and trying to flush us out. They probably knew we were making a run for it rather than hiding, but they'd yet to pinpoint our exact location.

Soon they would.

Behind me came the sound of a collision, swearing, and then a groan of pain.

Alexandra had caught her foot on a vine and stumbled. Jess, too close behind, slammed into her, and they both went down.

I reversed course.

"I'm okay, I'm okay!" Alex insisted as I helped her up.

Another bullet. This one penetrated a tree right above where Jess's head would have been if he'd gotten up any faster.

"Run!" I ordered.

Jess, now having his bearings, took the lead. Alex followed.

Until she realized I wasn't.

She stopped. "What are you doing? Come on!"

"Alex, go! Catch up with Jess. I'll be right behind you," I told her.

"Don't be a fucking hero! You're getting on this plane with us."

"I have every intention of doing that. But I can keep them at bay if they get too close before we all get on."

She began to argue.

I held up a gun in front of my face. "Alex, I know how to use this. I know what I'm doing. I want to stay alive, if for no other reason than to kick your ass for wasting time!"

She turned and ran. I took cover and focussed my attention on what was coming up behind us.

I could hear thrashing through the foliage. They were too close.

Searching the ground, I selected the heftiest and longest piece of deadwood I could find that fit my intended purpose. It was an old trick but a good one. One I hoped would give us the extra seconds we were going to need.

Aiming for the area with least obstruction, I pulled back the piece of wood, javelin style. Breathing in, I angled it upward. With as much power as I could generate, I propelled it forward.

The projectile sailed up and away a good distance before leaves and vines slowed it down and gravity pulled it back to earth. I didn't wait to see where it ended up. I turned and ran in the opposite direction, the direction of the beach and the waiting plane.

Seconds later, I heard the sound of my makeshift javelin landing on the ground. The sound that I hoped would send the remaining gunmen running in the wrong direction. At least for a while.

As I broke from the edge of the woods, I saw Jess climbing up the steps and into the plane's cockpit. Alexandra was standing there waiting, watching, arms crossed. As soon as she caught sight of me, her face cracked into a movie-star-wattage smile I'd seen less than a handful of times before.

I was halfway across the expanse of thick sand when I heard them.

They were smarter than I'd hoped, not easily fooled for long.

The plane's engine roared to life. The three-bladed propeller spun into a blur.

There was no hiding it now. They knew where we were and what we were planning to do.

Still several metres away, I hollered at Alexandra, "Get on!" Once the shooters broached the beach, we'd be easy pickings.

Alexandra held out her hand. "Come on!"

Why won't she ever listen to me?

With the sand slowing my progress, my calves screamed with pain as I pushed them into triple time.

Alexandra boarded the plane right before I reached her. I climbed up behind just as the first bullet whizzed into the sand near the landing gear.

They weren't trying to hit us anymore.

They were aiming for the plane. In particular, its fuel source.

Debilitate the plane, debilitate us.

It's what I would do.

The plane began to roll before we had the hatchway off the ground.

Jess was yelling commands, most of which we didn't hear or care about and probably had to do with—given the situation—unrealistic safety precautions, such as taking our seats and fastening seatbelts. Pilots will do what pilots will do. Hard habit to break, even with a cabal of gun-toting hooligans on your tail.

The Skylane needed more than four hundred and twenty metres to take off.

Jess did it in under four hundred. In a hail of bullets. I was right in my assessment of him as a pilot. The guy knew what he was doing.

Below us we saw the three remaining men firing on us as they scrambled to catch up. A well-placed shot could still mean our doom. The atmosphere in the cabin was tense. Except for the exertions of our ascent, silence pressed down on our ears. Jess pushed the plane higher and faster.

We all began to breathe easier as the Skylane ferried us further and further away from the island, burying it into the folds of a dark night. I was betting we wouldn't be seeing Skawa Island on a South Sea vacation brochure any time soon.

"Can you fly this thing at night?" Alexandra piped up, suddenly super aware of the cocoon of blinding black that surrounded us.

Jess shot her a glance and assuring smile. "Fair dinkum, I can. Been back and forth so many times these last days I could probably do it blindfolded."

"Really?"

I knew Jess's plane was outfitted with Synthetic Vision, but he left that part unsaid, preferring to impress my sister with his manly talents. I let it be.

But there was one thing I couldn't let go. "Not to down-play how grateful I am to you for saving us," I began, "but what the hell are you doing here?"

"I came in chased by that bugger storm. Probably why you...or those other drongos...didn't hear me. Who are they anyway?"

I ignored his question. "But why did you come back at all? You're supposed to be on Tubuai watching over the women and the boy."

He shifted his head to look at me. "No worries there, mate. Sally and Madeleine are looking after them. You said they needed medical attention and food. No one better for that than them."

I couldn't be too pissed with the guy. This wasn't what we planned, but in the grand scheme of things, it turned out for the best.

"Besides," he followed up with a mischievous wink for Alexandra, "I hadn't seen this one in yonks. Missed her."

Good grief.

Chapter Eighteen

Dawn was approaching by the time Alexandra and I returned to Chez Sam & Yolande on Tubuai. Madeleine and Sally were in the dining room, preparing it for the breakfast crowd, which looked to be only us.

"Well!" Madeleine exclaimed upon seeing us, clapping her hands together to exaggerate her point. "That is about the longest walk I ever heard tell of!"

We smiled sheepishly and took the seats offered. We were dirty and sweaty and unimaginably exhausted, but at that moment there was nowhere else I'd rather have been. After what we'd just been through, the charming little dining room overflowing with warmth and sunshine and amazing aromas coming from the nearby kitchen seemed preposterously heavenly.

What we really needed was to excise from our brains the horrific things we'd witnessed on Skawa Island. Hopefully, a good breakfast and pleasant surroundings would do it. For Alexandra. For me, I knew it wouldn't be so easy. I'd tried over the years to find a way to rid myself of the sights and sounds and smells that permeate scenes of disaster. Alcohol helps. Driving a nice car too fast. Sex. An overpriced meal. Loud music. But none of it lasts forever.

But maybe for Alexandra it would be different.

I hoped so.

Sally brought coffee and we exchanged smiles.

I liked that girl's lips.

"So what now?" Alexandra asked when Sally left with our order.

I studied my sister. Even after our experience on Skawa, the appalling revelations in the hot jungle, surviving fire-bombs and gunfire and barely escaping with our lives, she was up for whatever might come next. I was impressed with my baby sister. She'd told me she was tough. Now I believed it. She'd demonstrated pluck, fighting skill, bravery, willingness to face danger head-on with a *Fuck You!* attitude. The attitude was nothing new. But I could see that my sister meant to be in this with me, no matter what. And I was glad of it.

"Alex, why are you doing this?"

She scoffed at the question. "You know why." She took a deep drink of the strong, good coffee.

"I know you said it was because you thought I might get sick or keel over and die out here with no one to look after me, but there's more."

She looked away for such a long time I thought she was simply going to snub the question. And me. Then: "You're right. There is more. You're a smart guy. You know what it is. Don't make me say it."

I kinda had to. "Alex…."

"It's Anatole, okay?" she blurted out.

"Anatole? What does he have to do with this?"

She looked at me like I was a Ford Fairlane on a Lamborghini car lot. "Adam, I'm bipolar. And there's probably loads more shit than that wrong with me. You know that."

I shook my head. "I'm missing something here, sis."

"Do you know how many people in Canada commit suicide every year?"

I shrugged. I did. "Less than one percent."

"Yeah, well, you make those people bipolar and suddenly it's twenty-nine percent. Twenty-nine!"

"Alex, where are you getting this information?"

"What? You think I can't read? You think I don't know how to google?"

"You can't believe—"

"Adam, shut up. Even if it's not exactly twenty-nine, it's a whole fucking lot. More than any other psychiatric disorder. And at one point or another, I've had all the risk factors. Depression. Substance abuse. History of suicide in the family."

"Wait, wait, what history of suicide in the family?"

"Mom."

Suddenly, the cheery room grew dark and the air choking.

"What the fuck are you talking about? Our mother did not commit suicide."

"Didn't she? Maybe not with a knife or a gun to her head, but face it, Adam, Mom did not want to be who she turned out to be. She didn't want the life she got saddled with. She didn't want us, especially not me."

I pulled back from the table. My breathing was erratic and rough. I stared at my sister, shocked by everything coming from her mouth. Shocked but not entirely surprised.

"More coffee?" Sally. The second she saw our faces, she began to move off.

"Fuck, yeah," Alexandra answered, holding up her cup to be refilled.

"Uh…breakfast will be out in a couple minutes…unless…."

"That's fine," Alexandra told her.

Sally gladly moved off.

The revelation about my mother needed to be put aside. We couldn't deal with that here. Not now. It would take…. Gawd! I had no idea what it would take to get to the bottom of who my mother was, what she'd done to her life, her husband, her children, and why.

I took a deep breath and continued. "I must be really dense or just really tired right now, Alexandra, but I still haven't connected the dots."

"Adam, the chances of my committing suicide are stacked against me. Mom is gone. Dad is…well, he's not exactly old—but he's getting there—and he's going through all this stuff now. That leaves you, brother dear. You're all Anatole has left. If something happens to me, I don't want him to be all alone in this screwed-up world. So you have to live. This drug has to work. Because if it doesn't, I don't know what I'll do."

I couldn't believe my ears. Was my sister telling me she was hedging her bets in the very likely case she was going to kill herself at some unknown time down the road? Alexandra had always been a deep but scattered thinker. There've been times when thoughts so profound came out of her mouth I'd be dumbfounded, and other times when I considered having her committed. The problem now was that I wasn't entirely certain which this was.

"Alex, Alex, Alex, nothing is going to happen to you. You're going to be around for years longer than Anatole is going to want you around. You are *not* going to kill yourself. Ever. I won't let that happen."

Sally was suddenly at the table, handing out steaming

plates of vibrantly yellow scrambled eggs, thick slabs of ham, and brown toast plump with butter. Alexandra was eyeing me as if she didn't believe what I'd just said. I didn't blame her. Based on the last several years, I'd given her no reason to trust that she could count on me. But I must have been doing something right if she wanted someone like me in her son's life.

I gave Sally an apologetic look as I accepted my breakfast. It can't have been enjoyable serving our table that morning.

"Maybe I'll make you the same promise," Alexandra said, her voice shushed like that of a mother soothing a wounded child.

"Deal."

"You didn't answer my question."

"What question?" I asked.

"Now what?"

It was a good time to move on. The new subject matter wasn't, however, all that much easier. The original plan was to get the Skawa survivors back to IIA. Now I wasn't so sure that was a good idea. Since the day I met her, I've never been certain if I could trust Maryann Knoble. Now I was wondering if she was out to end my life, one way or another. Was I being paranoid? Were the drugs she'd had pumped into me affecting my thinking? Was my tumour acting up? Or was my gut sending me a warning I'd regret ignoring?

"Alex, once we get some food into us, we both need sleep, and I need time to think."

Fortunately, we had a bit of time. The women and the boy were safely ensconced in rooms next to ours, getting the rest and whatever medical attention they needed prior to the long journey that lay ahead. The soonest Anatole could get us off Tubuai was twenty-four hours from now. By that time, the survivors' travel documents I'd ordered from my guy who does that sort of thing would arrive.

"Let's talk about it tonight. Deal?"

"Deal," she agreed.

Chapter Nineteen

Not surprisingly, many of the patrons of The Shack looked as though they hadn't moved since I'd last been there two nights ago. Same sun-kissed people. Same cold beers and umbrella drinks. Same happy-go-lucky attitudes. Different bartender.

I had a pretty good idea where Jess was. When I'd called Alexandra's room to see if she wanted to meet for dinner, she told me she was still tired and planning to stay in and have a long bath. It sounded as if she was reciting the excuse from the palm of her hand where she'd hastily jotted it down, assisted by Jess.

The new guy served me up a second draft, then silently moved on. He could tell I wasn't up for chatting. Maybe it was the laptop in front of my face. I could have done this in my room, but it was a cramped space that, despite claims of air conditioning, maintained an average temperature best described as warm soup.

After sleeping for several hours, I'd awakened rested but not refreshed. I grabbed a cold shower, put on a fresh pair of shorts and cotton tee, and went for a long walk to think. I ended up here just after sunset.

I'd spent a couple hours researching, and now it was time to contact Anatole.

The Skype connection was a bit jerky with a half-second delay but not bad considering I was where I was and Anatole was in his bedroom/office on a farm in Saskatchewan. It was nearing midnight on the Prairies, but I knew Anatole to be a night owl and a homebody, so I was pretty certain I'd catch him. Besides, he seemed as intent on following our exploits as he was the latest season of *Game of Thrones*.

"Good timing," he said by way of greeting. "I just confirmed your flights. You're out of there tomorrow. You and the four people from Skawa Island are on your way to Toronto. Mom back to Saskatoon."

"Great. Now I need you to change it all."

His pronounced Adam's apple did a bit of a dance in his slender, long throat, white as a swan's. "D-d-did I hear you right? You want to change your flights? You know there are only four flights a week in and out of Tubuai, and if you—"

"No, no, the flight tomorrow morning is okay. But after that, once we get back to civilization, the final destinations need to change."

"Which ones?"

"All of them."

He shook his shaggy head and smirked. "Your life is crazy, dude."

"Tell me."

Fingers poised on top of a second keyboard, he asked, "Okay, so who is going where?"

"Your mother will be travelling with the three women and the boy."

"To Toronto…." His fingers busy.

"No. I want you to bring them home, Anatole. To the

farm. All of them. Keep it quiet. Tell no one." At first blush, this might seem like a pointless instruction, given the lack of any evident circles of friends in my nephew's life. Real friends, that is. But his stable of online acquaintances, I was coming to learn, was considerable, and with great potential for leaks. "Not even Dad. Until you have them there, of course."

"Really?" His face lit up at the thought of suddenly becoming an active character in the adventure. "Like here? In this house? You want me to hide three women and a kid here on the farm?"

"Can you do it?"

"Oh yeah."

Good kid. "Good man."

I could see his brain was already growing distracted with details.

"I have to check how many beds we actually have in this place. You might need to give up your room...."

"No problem," I told him. "I won't be there."

I had his full attention again. "Where are you going to be?"

"I want you to get me to Copenhagen." I named a hotel and the rental car company I wanted to use. When he had all the information he needed to make arrangements for the next couple of days, we said our goodnights.

It was even later in Toronto, and despite the perverse pleasure I might get from waking up Maryann Knoble and seeing her sleep-puffed face and hair askew, I decided instead to send her a text. It was a better option for me anyway. I didn't want her getting suspicious about the sudden change in plans and figuring things out until I was ready. So

I was surprised and a little annoyed when a return text immediately popped up on my iPhone.

"Change?" she wanted to know.

Fuck.

"Have survivors," I typed. "Transport issues. Passports taking longer 2 process w/o IIA assist." I smirked as I firmly placed the blame for the delay in getting the women back to Toronto on Knoble's decision to do all of this clandestinely. As a CDRA agent, I could have gotten new or faked passports issued in a matter of hours. As an independent, I was having to resort to less reputable sources. She didn't need to know that my sources were nearly as quick and that the passports I needed for Maybelline, Peri, Destiny, and Theo were winging their way to Tubuai at this very moment.

"Timing?" came back the swift reply.

I felt a small hand fall onto my shoulder. I turned to see the deep pools of ocean that were Sally's eyes. Smiling eyes. Inviting eyes.

"Will keep u informed," I hurriedly jabbed out my reply.

Then I powered down and took Sally up on her generous invitation.

Shekhar Kapur sat patiently in the front passenger's seat of the dark-coloured sedan. He'd seen no one on either side of the street in the nearly fifteen minutes he'd been there. Just as he'd hoped. It was nearing three a.m., so any movement would be unusual, immediately suspect, and cause for him to sound the alarm.

In his hand, he held an iPhone, a pre-typed text at the

ready. All he had to do was hit "Send." He glanced down at the message he hoped he wouldn't have to transmit: "Get out."

Two minutes later, the driver's side door opened and the man he'd contracted got in. He was wearing all black. Black slacks. Black jacket. Black balaclava. As planned, there was no exchange between the two. Instead, the driver removed the balaclava, started the vehicle, and drove away.

Fifteen minutes later, the car stopped on a side street where little traffic other than delivery trucks would ever venture. Perhaps it was overkill, Kapur realized, but he was a very careful man. He felt best when nothing was left up to chance. He could not allow anyone to see him in this car, with this man, or looking at the information the man was about to give him.

Wordlessly, the driver pulled two small items from his pocket and handed them to Kapur.

Kapur pulled out his laptop and powered it up. As the computer came to life, Kapur first turned his attention to the iPhone his companion gave him. He opened the Photos app and began swiping through the series of seventeen photographs. Using his fingers, he magnified certain parts of each.

The pictures were all similar. They showed pages from the paper file the man had found in the late Dr. Milo Yelchin's office, closed since his recent suicide. The fact that Yelchin was a sole practitioner was a good thing. It made the break-in easier to plan and the probability that Kapur would find what he was looking for much greater. Sealed in his office, Yelchin's files would remain untouched until patients came forward to claim them.

The deceased doctor's clients were primarily but not exclusively IIA agents and other employees. The fact that Yelchin had insisted on an office outside of the IIA building was another thing working in Kapur's favour. It was much easier to obfuscate his real purpose in asking a hired burglar to break into a neighbourhood business rather than a high-security government facility.

Finishing his scan of the photographs, emailing a copy of each to himself before deleting them, Kapur's suspicion that the paper trail would be thin was proving true. Other than some general notes and administrative documents, Yelchin kept little hard copy information in Adam Saint's medical file. Kapur hoped the second item provided by the driver would produce more.

Kapur's nose wrinkled at the unpleasant scent of the man sitting next to him. Even the fragrance of his own cologne, a special blend made especially for him, couldn't obscure that his companion was a meat-eater. Briefly, he wished he'd told the driver to simply take him home, but it was too far from the clinic, and Kapur had known he'd want to verify the information—and its existence—as soon as possible. At least the man was keeping quiet. He would put up with the stench a while longer.

Kapur slipped the memory chip into the correct slot on the side of the laptop. He clicked on the single folder icon that appeared onscreen. Within seconds, several other folders popped up, organized by year. Holding his breath in anticipation was not an option, as he was attempting to breathe solely through his mouth. He clicked on the correct year. More folders, this time arranged by specific date. He selected the most recent. Two more files. He opened the first.

The file was a detailed formal medical report likely submitted to Yelchin by the laboratory that had carried out the tests ordered by the doctor. Kapur scanned the document but was soon lost in technical jargon he didn't fully comprehend.

He opened the second file.

There it was.

Yelchin's notes on the results of Adam Saint's last physical. For some reason, Kapur had been blocked from Saint's IIA and CDRA personnel files, but he was still able to put together a rough timeline around the agent's departure from CDRA. The timing of the medical report and these notes fit. These were the documents on which Yelchin would have based his death-sentence diagnosis.

Anxious to see if the claims of Arla Tellebough could possibly be true, his eyes moved quicker than his brain could process the written words.

Now Kapur did catch his breath as he read: "...patient remains in superb physical condition...."

They made a strange quintet at the Saskatoon airport. A tall, handsome, dark-haired woman wearing too much makeup and tight clothing, alongside three other women, whose emaciated state made anything Alexandra picked out for them at an airport clothing boutique appear oversized, and a little boy, whose eyes barely stayed in their sockets as he took everything in.

"There they are!" Anatole announced to his grandfather, pulling him along to greet his mother as she entered the arrivals area.

Mother and son embraced briefly, followed by an awkward silence as the women and boy with her stared at the old man and tall, gawky teen who'd appeared before them.

Alexandra introduced each prairie newcomer by name.

More strained silence.

"Are you hungry?" Oliver Saint asked. "I have a roast in the oven for supper."

"We have to wait for my bag," Alexandra said.

"What about their bags?"

"They don't have any."

Oliver frowned. "They're visiting all the way from Toronto without suitcases?"

Alexandra shot her son a look, wondering what story he'd come up with to explain the sudden appearance of four house guests. But he was oblivious, too busy exchanging shy glances with Peri, the youngest and certainly most attractive of the women.

"Anatole!" she barked to get his attention.

"What?" he finally responded. "Not deaf here."

"Or blind," she shot back with a raised eyebrow. "Would you see if my bag is on the carousel yet? It's the big black one."

"Oh great, that'll be easy to spot," he muttered as he slunk away.

Alexandra smiled at her silent father, who smiled at the silent women.

"How old are you?" Theo asked Oliver. He'd heard about old people, but it was only since the beginning of this voyage that he'd actually seen anyone older than his mother, Maybelline, and Peri. This was the first time he was close enough to one to talk to.

Oliver looked down at the boy and said, "I just had a birthday. How old do you think I am?"

Theo answered quickly, "One hundred?"

Destiny grabbed her son's hand and gave Oliver an apologetic look. "I'm sorry, mister. He ain't seen many old people." She winced when she realized what she'd said. "Not that you're old. I meant older people, not old."

"That's fine," he said. "I am old."

"Really?" she said. "You're not, are you?"

"Not what?"

"A hundred?"

"I bet he's way older than that," Theo piped up, inching closer to get a better look.

Oliver, straight-faced, glanced at his daughter, who was stifling a laugh. "What's so funny over there?"

"Nothing, Dad." She turned to Theo. "He's sixty-five. Still pretty young, right?"

Theo shrugged. "Not really."

"I didn't know you still had friends from high school," Oliver commented, thinking it was a good time to change subjects.

Alexandra stared at her father and then at the women. They were anywhere from five to ten years younger than she was, although the last decade had aged them prematurely, especially Destiny and Maybelline. Peri was ignoring the fascinating conversation and instead focussed on keeping her eyes on Anatole's progress at the luggage carousel.

"Oh yeah," Alexandra said, giving a lame grin to the other women, hiding her surprise that her father might believe they were schoolmates. "We're still really tight."

Oliver nodded but had little else to say. If it hadn't been

a rainy day, he'd have been outside doing farm work, a good excuse to have turned down Anatole's request that he come to the airport with him. Should have done it anyway, he thought to himself.

It was late when I arrived at Kastrup Airport. Within forty-five minutes, I was in my rental car and on my way to Hotel D'Angleterre on Kongens Nytorv.

I have a fondness for elegant, older luxury hotels. This one, the grande dame of Copenhagen since 1755, had recently undergone a major overhaul. Some said it was the most ambitious hotel restoration in Danish history. The last time I'd stayed here in 2013, the doors had just reopened with only a small number of rooms available and considerable noise from the nearby Metro construction site immediately in front of the hotel. Yet, even in that not-quite- dressed state, she'd won me over. The service was impeccable, the promise of sound-proofed windows fulfilled, and the new Balthazar Champagne Bar suited my taste and was my first stop after checking in and having my bags sent up to the room.

Forgoing a stool at the bar, I instead chose one of the muted rose-coloured benches under a tall window with a table large enough for my laptop, food, and drink. Aside from a few small groups at the other end of the room, the place was mostly empty. After ordering a glass of a champagne I was unfamiliar with—when in Rome—and a few dishes from the tapas-style menu, I brought my computer to life and settled in to do some research to expedite my activities over the next couple of days. Time passed quickly. Before I knew it, I'd wrapped up the business portion of the night and moved onto harder liquor. That's when I made an uncharacteristically imprudent rookie move.

I picked up the phone.

I checked my watch. It was after midnight, making it just after six p.m. in Toronto. I hit the speed-dial number I'd once used often. Now, never.

"War Crimes Unit, may I help you?"

I hesitated. This was a mistake. I shouldn't be calling my ex-wife. I was half-drunk. Halfway around the world. Feeling...what? Lonely?

I missed her. I missed my wife. I missed what we had. Maybe Alexandra had been right when she accused me of still being in love with Kate.

Was that wrong?

"Hello? May I help you?" the voice at the other end of the line inquired a second time.

My eyes slid over the few patrons still hanging out at the bar. Maybe one of them would psychically know what I was about to do and warn me off.

No such luck.

"I'd like to speak with Kate Spalding, please."

Now it was the voice's turn to pause.

Why?

"I'm sorry. Agent Spalding is unavailable. Can I help you?"

"This is Adam Saint. I'm Agent Spalding's...husband. It's important...." Was it really? "I wonder if you could check if she'd take my call, please." This is where killing the messenger might work in my favour.

Another pause before the woman replied. "I'm sorry, Mr. Saint, but Agent Spalding isn't here."

At least Kate hadn't instructed her receptionist to block my calls or tell me to leap off the nearest thirty-storey building if I tried to contact her. Either that or she was letting me off easy.

I knew she probably couldn't or wouldn't give me any useful estimation of when Kate would return, so instead I said, "Could you leave her a message, please?" This was probably for the best anyway.

"Uh…well, I could, but I don't know when she'd see it."

"Oh?"

"Agent Spalding has taken a leave of absence."

This was surprising. Kate had suffered a blow with the death of her fiancé. But in this regard, she and I were alike. We were warriors. Nothing short of our own deaths would keep us from our jobs longer than a day or two. It was why our marriage had worked as well as it did, and at the same time, why it had to end.

"Do you know when she plans to return?"

"No."

"Do you know where she is?"

"No."

"Thank you." I hung up and immediately dialled another number. Kate's cell.

No answer.

Kate's home number.

No answer.

No answering machine or message manager. Worry began to flicker in my brain.

Had she taken Ross Campbell's death harder than I'd thought? Kate had a thick shell, like a beetle you couldn't crush with the stamp of a boot. She was impervious to outside factors that would bring most people to their knees. It's what made her a good agent. And, I'd thought, a good wife too. I never had to worry about the emotional landmines or mental gymnastics I'd heard tell of from other men discussing their relationships with women. Kate was straightforward and tough. If she didn't like something, you knew it right off with no sugar-coating or double-talk required. If she was upset or sad, she simply said so. Tears were seldom involved.

I dialled again.

Anatole's cell.

"Hey," he answered.

As a matter of course, I always block caller ID for outgoing messages. "It's your favourite uncle."

"Uncle Adam. What's up? It's…"—he did the math—"…gotta be after midnight in Copenhagen."

"Just checking in," I lied easily. "Everything okay there?"

"Yeaaaaaaaah…." He drew it out in a way that told me there was more to the story.

"Tell me."

"These women were starving when they got here. I guess Grandpa fed them a bit too much too fast. They got pretty sick. I couldn't get into a bathroom around here for hours. It was epic. But they're okay now."

"That's my fault," I said. "I should have warned you that their stomachs wouldn't be used to eating much. Especially not Dad's type of cooking. They need to go slow, get their bodies used to a regular diet. And regular life for that matter."

"Yeah. By the sounds of it, they were getting by on fruit and tree bark. No wonder they're so skinny. The kid's okay, though. He wasn't as starving as the rest. I guess he never knew any different, being born on the island and all. He's pretty cool. So is Peri."

"Good. I'm glad you're all getting along. Remember, Anatole, keep them on the farm for now. Don't take them into the city. Don't let any of the neighbours see them. Not for the time being anyway, okay?"

"Sure."

Dead air.

"Anatole, there's one more favour I need you to do for me."

"Shoot."

Leave it alone, my mind insisted. "Your Aunt Kate," I spoke over the sound of the voice in my head. "I need you to find her for me." *Stay out of her life. She doesn't want you in it.*

"Is she missing or something?"

"No, nothing like that. She's just…well, she's taken some time off work and I can't reach her. I just need to know where she is. And if she's all right. Can you do that? Without her finding out?"

"I can." After a beat, he added: "But aren't you two, like, divorced and stuff?"

"Yeah."

"Okay, then."

"Thanks, Anatole. We'll talk soon." I hung up quickly before I had a chance to change my mind.

Chapter Twenty

Morning in Copenhagen dawned sunny. I was refreshed from an early run. I'd jogged to the city's iconic Little Mermaid statue perched on its rock off Langelinie promenade and then back to a still-chilly Nyhavn harbour for coffee. By eight thirty, I was motoring down Amagerfælledvej, headed for one of Copenhagen's newer business districts, Ørestad City on the island of Amager. I knew the offices of Lungaard & Jørgensen opened at eight, and the trip, depending on traffic, would take me roughly twenty minutes. I was giving the L&J people about an hour to settle into their day. By then, I hoped, they'd be prepared to deal with the unexpected.

I presented myself at the business's front desk, manned by an officious-looking gentleman. I displayed my CDRA identification, which, if I do say so myself, looks rather impressive.

"And how may I help you, Mr. Saint?" the front man asked after carefully inspecting my credentials. His English was flawless.

"I'd like to speak with Ancker Kjaer, please. I don't have an appointment, but I'll only need a short time." My previous night's research indicated that Kjaer was the person in the International sales group most likely to have enough seniority and knowledge to be able to answer my questions but not too senior and knowledgeable to feel above indulging an unscheduled interruption to his day.

"Just one moment. I'll see if he is free."

Several minutes later, I was in a speeding elevator headed for the eighth floor. Kjaer's office was on the fourth. Something was up.

The plaque on the door read: Else Madsen, VP International. I'd definitely been bumped up. I shook hands with the woman who rose to greet me. Madsen was in her fifties, only an inch or two shorter than I, handsome in an outdoorsy, athletic way. Her grip was firm but not overpowering, unlike some executives who use bone-crushing handshakes to communicate supremacy to first-time visitors.

She indicated a circle of chairs. They were the ultramodern Danish variety that look stunning, unfailingly win prizes for design, and are impossibly uncomfortable. As we sat, she offered a drink, which I turned down.

"I hope you don't mind," she began, "but when the call came up for Ancker, it was automatically transferred to me. Unfortunately, he's out with allergies today. But Ancker does work for me, so hopefully I can answer your questions with at least half the intelligence he possesses," she said with a good-natured chuckle. "But I cannot guarantee it!"

I smiled. "Well, I hate to take up your valuable time for such a small matter."

"No matter is too small when it comes to the needs of our valued customers," she responded smoothly. "I understand you are with the Disaster Recovery Agency, Mr. Saint. By your accent I'd say from the American offices?"

"Canadian."

"I'm sorry. I'm not very good with English accents. Yet, I can tell you with great confidence if someone is from Aalborg in Nordjylland or Sorø in Sjælland. Funny how the ear works, *ja*?"

"Well, I'm afraid my question for you has more to do with memory than accents."

"Ah well," she said enthusiastically, "it shouldn't be a problem then. Who needs memory when we have computers?"

We shared another smile. I pulled a paper from my pocket where I'd jotted down the description and model numbers of the IIA equipment I'd found in the cabin on Skawa Island. The descriptions came from memory, the model numbers from IIA inventory listings I'd sourced online. I handed the list to Madsen.

She took a few seconds to scan the document, then looked up at me. "What is this, Mr. Saint? Of course I recognize the items as being manufactured by Lungaard & Jørgensen for IIA. But if I'm not mistaken, these model numbers are quite old. Perhaps a dozen years or so." She let out another of her short laughs. "I do hope you're not here looking for replacement parts!"

"No, no," I assured her, keeping my tone light and airy. "You see, I'm working with IIA on an internal process audit that involves these items." I handily stole Maryann Knoble's lie for when I interviewed the agents who'd worked with Sergiusz Belar. "I know, Ms. Madsen, that when—"

"Else, please. We are not so formal here. I think the same is true in Canada?"

I invited her to use my first name as well and began to wonder if all this nicey-nice was really nothing more than clever misdirection. "I'm aware that when IIA purchases this type of equipment from Lungaard & Jørgensen, it's done on a custom basis. All of it remains proprietary and confidential. What you make for us, you make *only* for us."

She nodded slowly but said nothing. Creases around her mouth told me her concern level about the matter at hand was on the rise.

I kept on. "As such, I expect you are quite familiar with what the equipment does and its intended purpose."

Still nothing.

"I recently happened to come across the items I've listed on that paper. They were in an unexpected location. I'd like to know who purchased them and for what purpose."

Her eyes scanned the list a second time. She looked up. "Can you identify this location for me?" Her voice was edged with the first flinty signs of steel.

"At the moment, no."

"Mostly, these are computers and recording devices," she said, her voice slipping back into its lighter tones. "None of these model numbers, from what I can recall, are for any type of machine that does anything unique or special in any way."

I shrugged. "Perhaps not." I was beginning to wonder if, like myself, Else Madsen had superior memory allowing her to recall model numbers of equipment her company produced over a decade ago.

Again, she looked down at the paper, as if searching the words I'd written there for some hidden agenda or meaning. She stood and retraced her steps. Once behind her desk, she began typing on her computer's keyboard. I followed but stayed on the guest side of the desk.

After a moment, Madsen stopped typing and stared at the screen, which was invisible to me. I waited.

"Well," she began, "I was right. These are computers. Printers. Video recorders. Audio recorders. All quite high-tech, of course, even by today's standards. As far as I can tell, they have no special capabilities other than the obvious. Nothing to hint at IIA's purpose for utilization. Other than speed and processing power and the ability to operate at almost one hundred percent capacity under almost any conditions."

Like in a steaming hot, dirty jungle and powered by generators?

She glanced up with apologetic eyes. "I'm sorry. I can't tell you more than this, Adam."

"Can you tell me who initiated the order?"

Reciting a date from a decade earlier, she confirmed what I already knew. "Purchase authorized and processed by Sergiusz Belar."

Damn. There had to be someone else. Belar might have signed the cheque, but he didn't order, create specs, inspect, and pick up a bunch of computers and digital recording units by himself.

"There must be someone else from IIA attached to this acquisition. Maybe someone who called for updates or arranged for the equipment to be shipped when the order was completed. Can we identify someone like that?"

For the next quarter hour, Madsen worked the computer like a beaver on a dam. Her fingers moved across the keyboard with the confidence of someone who knew exactly what they were doing. At each roadblock, she grunted her dissatisfaction, then tried another tack.

Eventually, she looked up from her screen and with

finality said, "I'm sorry. There's just nothing here. Nothing more I can think of to try. I see no other names associated with IIA or any of its subsidiaries connected with this file."

"Is that unusual?" I asked.

"Today, I'd say yes. Ten years ago, maybe not so much."

I had one last gambit. I retrieved a photograph from my pocket, the same one I'd found on Skawa Island, and handed it to Madsen. "Do you recognize this woman?"

She carefully studied the face, then slowly shook her head. "I'm sorry. No."

I nodded understanding. I scanned my brain for any remaining possible ways I'd not yet thought of to get useful information from this woman and her computer. After a moment of silence, I sensed I couldn't push any further without wearing out my welcome. Madsen had given me all she was going to. It was time to leave.

Never underestimate the power of downtime around a sunny table with good food, hard liquor, and plenty of mindless tourist buzz. It's like dumping random thoughts into a blender. You might be pleasantly surprised at what comes out.

When time and circumstance allow, I make it a practice never to leave Denmark without having one of my favourite local meals: a herring buffet. I returned to Nyhavn, which stretches from Kongens Nytorv to the harbour front, just south of the Royal Playhouse. The two sides of the lively waterfront canal area are usually jumping with tourists when the weather is right, and today it was. The food and drink, as in most busy entertainment districts around the world, don't come cheap, but unlike many, they do come good.

A little ahead of the lunch rush, I found an outdoor table below the tall, bright-blue façade of Nyhavn's Færgekro, with a nice view of the water. I ordered a Carlsberg beer and a shot of aquavit. The place offered assorted flavoured varieties of the strong spirit, but I prefer the original with its sharp taste of caraway. At the buffet, I selected from a colourful collection of hot and cold dishes: marinated herring, herring in herbed cream sauce, fried herring with horseradish and caviar, rollmops, smoked herring, baby potatoes. I then heaped a side plate with rugbrød—a Danish rye bread—chopped chives, red onions, and crunchy pork rinds.

Settled at my table, I made slow work of the food, enjoying the sun on my face and watching the canal filled with bobbing boats. Before long, an influx of people just beginning to think about lunch crowded into the area, looking for a table like mine. All the while, the niggling thought that had begun as soon as I'd arrived at the offices of Lungaard & Jørgensen earlier that morning persisted. It zigged and zagged through my head like an arcade pinball looking for the right hole to fall into.

In my work, I often find myself in situations where knowledge of a language other than English or French can come in handy. Over the years, I've become a dedicated student of languages. I find their similarities, and at times astounding differences, fascinating. To date, I claim knowledge of seven—five fluently and two passingly, with several others in process.

When it came down to learning a North Germanic language, my choice was clear. Studies have shown that speakers of Norwegian generally understand both Danish and

Swedish far better than Swedes or Danes understand each other. So as I practiced dialogue for the upcoming call I planned to make, I focussed on the best Norwegian I could muster rather than Danish.

Taking a shoring-up sip of aquavit, I dialled the number I'd found online.

"Lungaard & Jørgensen, how may I direct your call?"

"I'd like to speak with Ancker Kjaer, please," I responded in a deep Norwegian accent, keeping my voice thick and slow. "This is Herloff Engebretsen with Skandinaviska Enskilda Banken." My hope was that a phone call from a major bank would be met with all due seriousness and few questions.

"Just one moment, please, Mr. Engebretsen."

I waited.

"*Hej*? This is Ancker Kjaer."

The niggling paid off. Either Kjaer had made a remarkably speedy recovery from his allergy problems, or Else Madsen had just spent her morning lying to me.

Chapter Twenty-One

Not once during his childhood did Anatole Saint have reason to believe that who he was or anything he did or was interested in would lead him to live a happy life. Growing up as the single child of a woman like Alexandra Saint was not easy. Even early on—maybe especially early on—Anatole had the feeling he wasn't exactly a welcome presence in her life. She was constantly irritable, quick to anger, and stingy with anything that approximated gooey maternal love, the kind he regularly witnessed being slathered upon the other kids he knew. As he grew older, he convinced himself he was actually the lucky one. Who wanted an adult smothering you with affection? Watching you like a hawk? Giving you stupid rules to follow?

Every so often, when things got tough for his mother, Anatole would be sent to live with his grandparents on the farm. "Tough" meant only two things: She'd lost a job and couldn't afford to feed him, or she'd screwed up her drug regimen and couldn't get her shit together enough to feed him. Sometimes it was both.

Even though the farm was only minutes outside the city, this was not a simple transfer of his life. Of course, his mother and grandparents didn't seem to think it was such a big deal. But it wasn't they who had to either switch schools or get up an hour earlier to catch a bus to go to the regular place. It wasn't they who hated the outside and dirt and then had to live in a place that was all about outside and dirt. It wasn't they who couldn't keep friends because he never hung around long enough to make any. Well, that and because most kids thought his mom was weird…and yes, they thought he was too.

Spending time with his grandparents, Oliver and Eva Saint, really wasn't so bad though. He knew his mother and grandmother did not get along because his mother said so. But he didn't see all the bad qualities she insisted the older woman possessed. From Anatole's perspective, she was certainly a tough old woman who didn't take guff from anyone. But she always had a hearty meal on the table, never forgot to buy school supplies or new runners when he needed them, and even forced hugs out of him every now and then. Grandpa Oliver was even better. He was a good guy who never once made Anatole feel useless or incompetent or unworthy just because he didn't want to help out in the fields or milk a cow or learn how to fix a broken tractor. Oliver tried to include his grandson in farm activities, of course, but it was more like testing the waters. As soon as he realized Anatole had no interest in anything that had to do with being a farmer, he backed off and let him be.

The circumstances of his upbringing aside, Anatole believed he grew up in a Golden Age. The Internet Age. It became his refuge, his salvation, his educator, his guide through tough times, his best friend. What would he have done without it? He welcomed with open arms every new aspect of digital life as quickly as it was created. From surfing the web and sending email, to everything online—communications, making purchases, reading books, listening to music, social media, blogging. It all made sense to him. And as the world of what computers could do expanded, so did Anatole's expertise.

For eleven-year-old Anatole, there was no better way to spend a day than rooting around on the Internet and making his computer do wondrous things. The tougher the better. He thrilled to a challenge. He frequented a plethora of online chat rooms dedicated to computer devotees and loved nothing more than to be the one who solved a particularly problematic and complicated issue.

When he created a spectacular website for a grade eight class project, things really began to change for Anatole. His teacher told other teachers, and classmates told their parents, who then told friends and acquaintances. The timing could not have been more perfect. Everyone and his pet parakeet seemed to want a website or blog site, and they were willing to "pay the little kid to do it."

Individual clients became business clients. Clients who first wanted help with a website would later come to Anatole when they had other computer problems, anything from installing new systems to printing matters to the famous "my computer won't…" concerns. Anatole could always help. By the time he was in grade eleven, he had incorporated and was pulling in more than forty thousand dollars a year—part-time, after school.

Contrary to what Anatole understood other parent-child relationship progressions to be, instead of his mother being all adoring of her newborn and then becoming more and more distant and a stranger to her developing tween child, the older he got, it seemed, the more interest she took in him. Gradually, Anatole even began to believe his mother actually found him okay to spend time with. She was far from a typical mother, but she was coming around.

Unfortunately, this period in their relationship coincided with tough times. Alexandra had been in a good place. She'd had a fairly stable relationship with a biker named Scruff. He was a decent guy—for a biker. He was the one who'd pushed her into buying the bar. She'd never have had the guts to try something like that on her own. But then bad things started to happen. Scruff was killed in an accident. Business at Dirks floundered. Things got so rocky they once again had to move back to the farm. This was never a good thing. Not for his mother anyway. Even so, and to her credit, Alexandra refused to take even a penny from her son's growing bank account. Before long, she left again, leaving Anatole behind until she "got back on track." But just when that happened and she'd set up house in a small but clean apartment for the two of them, Eva Saint died. Back they went to the farm to support the grieving Oliver. Eventually, his mother moved out. Anatole never did. He had lived with this widowed grandfather ever since.

Anatole loved his bedroom/office in the farmhouse he now considered his home. It was big and outfitted with blackout blinds for the days when the sun was just too bright for him. Lined up on three interconnected desks were his babies: an ever-growing collection of computer hardware, a sophisticated telephone system, and specialized wireless capability equipment. Today, his office had an extra little something in it: a former Skawa Island resident and shipwreck survivor.

As soon as Peri stepped into the arrivals area at the

Saskatoon airport, Anatole knew there was something special about her. He could barely keep his eyes off the girl. At nineteen, he'd still never had a girlfriend. He'd had crushes on some of his online friends, virtual relationships based on nothing more than the girl's photograph and ability to chat intelligently about computers or world affairs. Some might say this wasn't such a bad place to start. But his feelings always remained unproclaimed and unrequited, enjoyed only by him and only in his dreams. Peri was different. She was a real live girl, and she was close enough to touch.

At first, she'd been wary. Exhausted by her recent decade-long experience as a shipwreck survivor living on a deserted island, her reluctance to talk was understandable. But before too long, she began opening up to Anatole. She started spending time with him alone. Peri appeared to be fascinated with his work and asked him endless questions about it. Finally, thought Anatole, here was someone who truly did like him for who he was and what he did. Life had actually gotten pretty sweet since he'd begun helping his Uncle Adam with stuff he could do on the computer. But this was something altogether different.

With little experience under his belt with such things, Anatole could have gone weeks or months or even the rest of his life failing to recognize his feelings for this girl. It wasn't until breakfast one morning that he realized what was happening inside him.

Oliver Saint was not the kind of man to say anything about such things out loud, so it was nothing more than an odd look from him—an unusual occurrence—that caught Anatole's attention. Neither being chatty in the morning, normally the two men ate breakfast in genial mutual silence. Then Oliver would head outdoors to do farm work, and Anatole would make his way back upstairs to begin his own workday at the computer. But that day, Anatole happened to look up and caught his grandfather staring at him, his expression either confused or bemused. It wasn't until he caught his own reflection in the screen of his laptop—which he kept at the breakfast table for casual use during mealtimes—that he understood. He was grinning from ear to ear, like some kind of drunken clown. Suddenly, he knew why.

He'd been thinking about Peri.

She made him feel this way.

Happy. Ecstatic. Anxious to see her when she came down for breakfast.

And now he knew one more thing.

This is how love feels.

So, the first time Peri asked to come up to his room to watch what he did, he'd readily agreed. He couldn't imagine doing this for anyone else. Anatole valued his privacy. He liked being in his dark room, by himself, with no distractions to take him away from whatever activity was happening in cyberspace that day.

Over the next few days, her visits became a habit. She'd join him after breakfast. Every so often, she would ask a question about what he was doing, but usually she just sat there and watched, her eyes darting from here to there as his fingers flew across the keyboards and made things happen. He loved her even more.

But one question plagued him. Could this girl have the same kind of feelings for him? His look wasn't exactly the kind girls typically fell for. He was too tall, too thin, his dark hair too shaggy. Anatole had heard himself described as "goth," which was *so* way wrong. Just because his hair was jet black, his complexion pale, and he favoured black tee-shirts, that didn't make him a goth. Goths were mysterious, exotic creatures with complex features who wore black fingernail polish and eyeliner. Anatole looked the way he looked. It wasn't planned or contrived. He simply just didn't think about it too much. He wore what he wore. The easier the better. The less often he had to actually go to a store or barber shop the happier he was.

"So, you can find out almost anything there is to know out there, can't you?" Peri asked out of the blue one morning.

As Anatole typed a stream of commands, he mumbled, "Pretty much, yeah."

"Could you…could you find a person?"

Finishing what he was doing, Anatole turned to look at the girl. He noticed how just a few days of good home cooking and sitting in the late summer sun had done wonders for Peri. Whereas Destiny and Maybelline still looked tired and ragged, despite spending most of their days doing nothing, Peri had bloomed. Her skin and hair looked healthier, and she'd even gained a few much-needed pounds. The other women still kept pretty much to themselves or spent time with young Theo. Peri wanted more.

"What do you mean find a person? Like, could someone have found you on that island? That's not how it works." Anatole considered his answer more. "I suppose if I linked up to a satellite feed that happened to be aimed directly at the island…."

"No. I don't mean that. I mean, what if I was looking for someone?"

Anatole's eyes widened. He knew very little about who these women were, what had happened to them, when or why, what their lives had been like before the shipwreck. He inferred from his Uncle Adam's instructions that it was best not to know too much. For now. "Are you looking for someone?" he ventured.

Her gaze flitted off. She chewed a nail, then looked at him. "Maybe."

"Like a boyfriend kind of person?" It killed him to ask.

Peri grinned. "No, silly boy. I've been living on a deserted island for ten years. How would I have a boyfriend?"

Anatole moved his head in a familiar way that he knew would cause a long, dark swath of hair to fall across his eyes. "Just asking," he muttered.

"I've been missing so long they've probably forgotten about me anyway," Peri threw out, unfolding her right leg from beneath her and getting up from her seat. "Forget about it. I should probably go down and see if your grandpa needs help making lunch."

"No wait!" He would do anything for this girl. To feel needed by her was awesome. Maybe his uncle wasn't the only hero in the Saint family. "Who are you looking for? Maybe I can help."

Peri sat back down and stared at him. "Really?"

"Maybe. I do stuff like that for my uncle all the time." He knew he was exaggerating a tad, but isn't that what guys were supposed to do when they wanted to impress a girl?

She pulled her chair closer. "Wow, I don't know anymore. It's scary, y'know?"

"What is?"

"Trying to contact my family after all this time."

Anatole nodded. "I guess it has been a long time. But you shouldn't be scared about it. After the shipwreck, they probably thought you were dead. They'll be so pumped to hear you're not."

Peri winced. "It's a little more complicated than that."

"More complicated than that?"

"I wasn't exactly close to my family before all this happened. I was young and a bit wild, I suppose. I just took off."

"You ran away from home?"

She nodded.

"Where'd you go?"

"Here and there. No place good."

"Oh."

"Before all this, I hadn't talked to my folks for a couple of years. They probably thought I was dead before I ever even got on that boat."

"Oh."

"But now…after all I've been through…well, I've been thinking it might be a good thing to try. Talk to them, I mean. Tell them I'm alive. And maybe…." She stopped there, her eyes glued sightlessly on a computer screen.

"Maybe what?" Anatole pushed.

"Well, I've just been thinking about when all this is over. I won't really have anyplace to go."

Anatole resisted blurting out the words that immediately jumped to mind: *Stay here. With me.*

"Then you're right," he said instead. "We should try to find them. I'll help you."

Peri jumped up from her chair and threw her arms around Anatole. It was the first time they'd touched. Anatole felt as if he was being embraced by a blanket of sparking electricity. When she was done and had pulled back, he was embarrassed to think about how red his usually embalmed-white cheeks probably were. It felt as though they were on fire.

"This is so great. How do we start? What do we do?" she chirped excitedly, then suddenly her face scrunched up with worry. "But wait! They don't need to know that we're looking for them, do they? Nothing you type into your computer is going to show up on theirs, is it?"

"No, of course not. We can do all this confidentially. No one has to know you're looking for them until you want them to."

Relief escaped her mouth. "Good. Because I wouldn't want that, okay?"

"Okay."

Spirits back up, she asked again: "What do we do first?"

"I'm going to need information about who we're looking for. Where they live. What they do. That sort of thing. But first things first: I need names."

Eyes fastened on Anatole's, Peri hesitated as if reconsidering, then said, "My mother is dead. But maybe we could look for my father? Then maybe my grandfather?"

Anatole smiled. He liked the smile he got in return. "Sure."

Chapter Twenty-Two

The community of Lovely Lake is located on the southeast shore of its tree-lined namesake. The encircling mounds of the Monashee Mountains watch over the Okanagan Valley town and its clear, cool lake, and to the east, the jagged Selkirks rise high and mighty. On almost any summer day, when the lake is serene and the fishing good, it would be difficult to imagine a more idyllic place to be…until a bomb goes off.

As Jacqueline Turner stepped over the debris left behind, she took special note of the ruined fragments of rubble that elevated the scene from disaster site to gut-wrenching tragedy: mangled pieces of metal that had once been students' desks and lockers, a calamity of school supplies and gym equipment, the telltale signs of where six youths and two adults had just lost their lives.

"This was the primary detonation site," Abe Dalton, a bomb expert flown in from Vancouver, explained. "There were three bombs in total, but the other two were either less powerful or didn't discharge properly."

"Or maybe this particular part of the school—and whoever was in it—was the principal target of the explosion," Turner speculated.

"We're not convinced this was a targeted action."

Without taking her steadfast eyes off the grisly scene, Tuner asked, "Why not?"

"This is…was…a school. The bombs went off on a Saturday morning. That timing suggests the perpetrator's main intent wasn't to kill anyone."

Turner scowled. "I guess fate wasn't on their side. Why *were* those kids here?"

"The children were attending an English as a second language summer session. One of the adult victims was a teacher, the other a parent who'd decided to wait in the school until the class was over."

Turner nodded, remembering, as her training taught her, not to think too hard about the humans behind the tragedy.

"What about you?"

Turner stopped and looked at the investigator. "What about me?"

"Why are you here? This is a town of seven hundred people in the middle of the Kootenay rainforest. The dust is barely settled, and IIA already has an agent on the ground. Something big is going on. I need to know what you know if I'm going to carry out an investigation that means anything."

For the first time since meeting the man less than an hour before, Turner took the time to really look at him. She considered herself an excellent judge of character, a skill CDRA agents would flounder without. She didn't have time to waste in Lovely Lake. If she wanted to get, she was going to have to give. "IIA was monitoring some unsettling chatter that involved Lovely Lake School."

"Chatter? What kind of chatter?"

"A short while ago, during routine monitoring, it was discovered that blueprints were being downloaded for a public building in a relatively small British Columbia community."

"Routine monitoring?"

"Mr. Dalton—"

"Call me Abe."

"Abe, either you'll stop interrupting and accept what I'm willing to tell you without question or we're done here."

"Gotcha."

With a curt nod, Turner accepted his acquiescence to her terms. "None of this would have raised alarms except that the building in question was a school. This school. A school not currently or recently under construction, nor scheduled for any maintenance work that would require blueprints. Chatter surrounding the downloads became increasingly bothersome."

"Then why the hell—" A withering look brought Dalton's protestations to a speedy conclusion.

"Believe me, Abe, no one wanted this to happen. A warning would have come down if we had actually known anything. But public privacy issues demanded IIA obtain court authorization before we could dig deeper to see if there really was a problem here. Quite obviously, it's too damn late for that."

Dalton swore.

Turner reacted with a sour look and words to match. "Sometimes our laws protect us, sometimes they kill us."

Less than forty-eight hours before I'd arrived in Copenhagen, Jacqueline Turner had been dispatched to the site of a school bombing in rural British Columbia. It was because of what she'd found there that I was now in a cab rushing from Lennart Meri Airport in Tallinn to Hotel Telegraaf in the Estonian city's Latin Quarter.

Following protocol, Turner had first confirmed that the needs of the bombing victims and their families were being met by local agencies and caregivers, then quickly shifted her attention to the cause of the disaster. She'd been specifically selected for the assignment because of her aptitude with matters related to computer-assisted crime.

In 2003, newly available software allowing voice communication over the Internet took the world by storm. Suddenly, people could reach out to each other by a simple microphone plugged into their computer—they could video chat via webcam, they could send instant messages over the Internet, all of it for free. Less than a decade later, Skype would have over half a billion users and be scooped up by Microsoft for $8.5 billion.

Where did Skype come from? The Baltic. Janus Friis from Denmark, Niklas Zennström from Sweden, and three Estonians, Ahti Heinla, Priit Kasesalu, and Jaan Tallinn. IIA only became interested in Skype in 2009, when the Canada Pension Plan Investment Board invested in the company to the tune of $300 million for a fifteen percent stake. It turned out to be a wise move. Microsoft's acquisition grabbed Canadians a net profit of over half a billion. Not bad for a twenty-month investment.

As with any other heavily used international communication service, IIA developed a surveillance program to monitor Skype user behaviour—chat, uploads, downloads—for suspicious activity. CDRA had had no involvement with Skype or its surveillance. Until this week. Until an explosion tied to suspicious downloading behaviour sent Turner to Lovely Lake, BC.

Turner knew her investigation would benefit from being closer to the source of the technology and those who knew it best. Microsoft's Skype division headquarters are in Luxembourg, but most of the development team and employees of the division are still situated in Estonia. And now, so was I.

Tallinn is an old city, the oldest capital in Northern Europe, a fairy-tale old town with a profusion of eye-catching red tile roofs. It sits on the southern coast of the Gulf of Finland and struggles to maintain a population above four hundred thousand. When I arrived, it was still sunny and the temperature was holding onto mid-teens. I entered the hotel's dark-walled lobby and approached the front desk. In Estonia, you have about a fifty/fifty chance of finding someone who speaks Russian. The closest I come is Ukrainian. We made do.

Once I was signed in, I asked the clerk if my friend, Ms. Turner, was still staying in the hotel. He answered in the affirmative. I acted thrilled that we'd be crossing paths and wondered if he knew whether she was in her room now. He thought so.

Instead of heading directly up to mine, I took a seat in one of the lobby's charcoal-coloured armchairs. I was hoping timing would work in my favour. Turner was on the job. If she was like me, she'd work long hours with no set time for meals or rest. I dialled her cellphone number. I'd kept it since my interview with her at the IIA offices in Toronto prior to my trip to Skawa Island.

She picked up on the first ring. "*Da?*" She knew Russian.

"Jacqueline, it's Adam Saint."

"Saint. Twice in less than a week. Can I just be that lucky or is this no coincidence?"

"I'm the lucky one. I happen to be in Tallinn and heard through the grapevine you were too. I wonder if we might meet up for a drink." I highly doubted she bought my lie. But she'd pretend to.

"When?"

"Now. I'm downstairs." I was giving her little choice. She now knew I was in her hotel and knew that she was in her room. There was little she could do but agree to a meeting.

"I'll do you one better," she said. "It's been a long day, and I'm starving. I was about to go down to the hotel restaurant. Why don't you grab us a table for two?"

Might she be leading me on? Get me away from the elevator banks where I'd catch her if she tried to give me the slip? Clever. She was returning the favour and giving me little choice. Unless one of us was willing to reveal our actual game, for now we'd have to play this one.

"I'd love to," I said.

"I'll be down in fifteen minutes."

Restaurant Tchaikovsky is a stunning room with silver chargers and sparkling glassware atop crisp white linens dramatically setting off slate-grey walls, all beneath a domed glass roof. I was offered a deuce next to a bookcase and ordered a glass of white while I waited for my date, hoping not to be stood up.

I wasn't disappointed. True to her word, Jacqueline Turner strode into the dining room fifteen minutes later, a ravishing sight in a tight purple dress. I rose to greet her. The maître d' assisted her into her seat.

"The food here is fantastic," she said to me, her hand still on the maître d's arm. "I know it's late," she fluent Russian, looking up at the man with a brilliant smile on her face, "but is the *menu degustation* still available?"

"I'll see what I can do, madam," he responded.

"Tell my friend about it." She said this in English. Either she didn't know if I understood Russian or it was a subtle move on her part to exert dominance.

The maître d' described six courses beginning with poached asparagus followed by grilled trout, blini with classic garnishes and caviar, halibut fillet, Estonian beef with lard, potatoes and wild mushroom sauce, and finally a Grand Marnier baba with rhubarb ice cream for dessert. By the time he moved off to see whether the chef was willing to make an exception for the nine p.m. cut-off, Jacqueline was confidently perusing the *veinikaart* for a proper wine to have with our meal.

"They'd do a wine pairing if you'd prefer, but I'm in the mood for red tonight, if that's all right with you?"

I sat back and gave in to relinquishing decision-making. "Splendid."

Her eyes inched above the menu, assessing my status. Satisfied, she returned to the listing, smoothly commenting, "I appreciate a flexible dining companion."

"My pleasure."

A short time later, the ordering was done, the wine arrived and poured, and our waiter had moved off to await the preparation of our first course.

Turner held up her glass in toast. "To a pleasant dinner together." Then she added: "I hope the pleasure is not short-lived."

She knew something was up.

Eyes meeting over the table, we touched glasses and drank.

"Tell me why you're really here, Saint. Did you follow me?"

"Of course not. CDRA agents always know where their colleagues are."

"But you forget. You're not an agent anymore. Or did I get that wrong?"

I pulled a small envelope from my pocket and laid it on the table between us. Her sparkling brown eyes did a slow tour of the room before settling on my hand and what lay beneath it. I slid it forward. Her hand fell onto mine. Suddenly the heady scent of her perfume swirled into my nose—for a moment, nearly overpowering.

"If I ask what this is before I open it, will you tell me?"

"It's a photograph."

I could tell by the look on her face she was mildly surprised. And curious.

Wordlessly, she took up the envelope and pulled back the flap, peering inside. Frowning, she withdrew the fading picture. The one Alexandra had found behind the bedside table in the hidden cabin on Skawa Island.

Her cheeks sucked in, she asked, "Where did you get this?"

"Do you recognize it?"

"Of course I recognize it. You know as well as I do that it's a picture of me. I might be a few years older now, but not all that different."

"No," I agreed, "not all that different at all."

We paused a moment as our waiter delivered our

asparagus served with mussels and herb butter sauce and refilled our wine and water glasses.

When he was gone, Turner shoved the photograph back into the envelope, placed it on the tabletop, and with a red-nailed finger pushed it away. "Here you go, hon. You can put it back under your pillow." The words were taunting, but her face was grave.

"That's not where I found it."

"And I suppose now you're going to tell me where you did?"

"Do you already know?"

"I have no idea. That picture has to be a dozen years old. It's probably a copy of a copy. Who knows where it might have been."

"Or where it shouldn't have been."

"Stop this, Saint. Neither of us has time for games. What are you after?"

She was right. I had hoped she'd take one look at the picture and blurt out something useful. I wasn't surprised to find she was smarter than that. It was time for the direct approach.

"That picture was found on Skawa Island, in the South Pacific. In a cabin filled with ten-year-old IIA surveillance equipment. Care to tell me why?"

Her wordless response was unexpected. No denial. No anger or guilt. But, rather, sweet satisfaction.

The sprawling square footage of extortionately priced real estate, high in the sky in Toronto's Bay Wellington Tower, was impressive at any time, but especially so at night. Its wraparound windows were like massive video screens displaying the glittering wonders of Canada's largest city. I rarely visited Maryann Knoble's office and never this late. Tonight, it seemed more dark lair than place of business.

When she buzzed me in, I immediately detected the scent of her cigar. The building had a strict no-smoking policy, but civilian rules weren't made for Maryann Knoble. She was standing at a window, staring out, her silhouette a bulky, black smudge against the glass. Dithering clouds of smoke hovered above her head.

"If you drink Scotch, help yourself," the raspy voice invited. "I don't keep anything else."

The room was dim, but the bar at the far end was well-lit. I made myself a short drink and took a position on the other side of the large platform that was her desk. Just where she'd want me.

I'd come straight to the IIA offices from Pearson airport. The trip home had been uneventful, except for the turbulence in my mind as I considered all I'd seen and heard since I'd last left Toronto. Discovering the hell on earth that was Skawa Island. Finding the shipwrecked women. Knowing they were keeping secrets. Uncovering IIA involvement. Barely escaping the place with our lives. Searching for clues and information in Copenhagen and Tallinn. Coming up short...but not entirely empty-handed.

Sometimes, the act of refusing to contribute information as Else Madsen and Jacqueline Turner had done—under the guise of faked bewilderment—was its own brand of evidence. Madsen had told me only what I already knew: Sergiusz Belar had requisitioned the equipment I'd found on Skawa. What she didn't tell me was that she'd lied about

Ancker Kjaer, the Lungaard & Jørgensen employee I'd planned to question. She'd told me he was out with allergies. The question was: Why would a senior vice president bother to take it upon herself to answer what should have seemed like innocuous inquiries about outdated equipment manufactured by her company? I'd confirm it at a later date, but I was putting my money on greed. Madsen had likely been paid off by whoever was behind the destruction of the equipment and the creation of the threatening video. I had to give the mastermind credit. They were one step ahead of me. I hate when that happens. I planned to ensure it never did again.

At least Madsen had made an attempt to appease me with a falsehood. Jacqueline Turner hadn't even bothered to do that much. She simply claimed ignorance. She'd said she had no idea why a photograph of her turned up on Skawa Island. Had she been there? If not, then who? And why would they carry a picture of a CDRA agent with them?

There was an even more troublesome issue. The men who first tried to firebomb us, then shoot us. Presumably, their goal was twofold: to end our lives and to destroy all evidence of IIA presence on Skawa Island. At the moment, the best suspect I had for arranging that party was three metres away, her back to me, puffing on an overpriced cigar.

Standing there, taking a brief sip of the excellent Scotch, it dawned on me that in all of this mess, I'd forgotten one other serious matter. My impending death. Or would Knoble's experimental drug change all that?

"I need to see Belar," I announced.

"And I need to see the three women you pulled off of Skawa Island," she responded, unmoving.

I addressed the dark outline. "I'm still having trouble with travel documents. I expect the issues will resolve soon."

Until I had a better grip on the game being played by Knoble, I wasn't about to trust her with the safety of three women and a child. IIA and Serguisz Belar were involved in some crazy stuff on that island, of that much I was certain. Belar could not have been acting alone.

As far as I could tell, there were only three options for Knoble's role in all of this: One, she knew nothing and was as interested in the truth as I was. Two, she knew nothing and wouldn't care much about what had happened on Skawa as long as her precious IIA was not adversely affected by it. Or, three, she knew everything, was an accomplice to Belar, and was using me to gauge the potential possibility of the secret's being revealed and how best to quash them.

"Bullshit." Her voice was liquor-soaked, thick, and deep, but nowhere near being impaired. Maryann Knoble had her full wits about her.

I let her assessment of my story sit between us. The fact that it was accurate wasn't about to make me flinch.

"I want to know what you know," she said.

"Then we want the same thing."

Slowly she turned. Like a heavy freighter moving stealthily through enemy waters, she approached the desk and lowered herself into the chair that waited for her there. She nodded, an invitation to follow suit. I sat.

"What makes you believe I would care what you want, Saint?"

"I don't. But if our motivations are the same, or at least complementary, there shouldn't be a problem."

She thought about this for a second or two, then: "We are not a team. I am the head of IIA, and you have been contracted to perform a service. Everything I've heard about you tells me you are a man of your word. I hope that continues to be the case. We made a bargain. I upheld my part. Now it's time for you to uphold yours."

"I will," I told her, not entirely sure I was telling the truth. "But first I want to talk with Sergiusz Belar. I can find him if you won't tell me where he is."

Expelling a large plume of smoke, she sat back in her chair and eyed me, her lips a tight line across the square face. "Go right ahead," she finally said. "I'll have my driver take you to him."

I waited for the other shoe.

"But you should know that Belar is incapacitated by Alzheimer's."

I'd heard the rumours. Something about Knoble's manner suggested there was no falsehood in her words.

"Did you really think you were the first person I turned to for help with this?" she said with poorly camouflaged derision. "I visited Belar. You can try if you want to waste time, but I know you won't get anything more out of him than I did."

"*Did* you get something out of him?"

Another puff. "In a roundabout way, yes. I'll tell you what I found. But first, I want a full report on what you found on Skawa. A report I am rightfully due. Your forcing us into this absurd tennis match, volleying bargaining chips back and forth, is making me cross."

Knoble was right. I would put Anatole on the hunt for Belar to confirm her story, but I suspected she wasn't—in

238 — Anthony Bidulka

this specific instance—leading me astray. There was no obvious reason for her to do that. And so I began.

Over the next forty-five minutes, I described my trip to the South Pacific with Alexandra—what we found there, and what we were forced to leave behind. I told her about my side trips to Copenhagen and Tallinn but left out any personal opinion on what I'd thought about Madsen's and Turner's responses to my visits.

Knoble was a good listener, only occasionally interrupting for clarification of a certain point of interest. Her scowling face grew progressively blacker as I confirmed her worst fears. Something horrible occurred on Skawa Island a decade ago. IIA was irrefutably involved. And someone knew about it and was willing to kill to keep it quiet.

Only when I was done did Knoble rise from her seat. Saying nothing, squinting eyes deep in thought, she crossed the room, retrieved the bottle of Scotch, and returned, pouring each of us an inch of the liquor before settling back into her chair.

A full minute and a half passed in silence.

"So there it is," she finally muttered, the words crushed gravel beneath thick-treaded tires. By the look of her, she might not have known she'd said it aloud.

"Yes," I said, more to wake her from her trance of concentration than to signal agreement.

Her eyes slid up from the bottom of her glass, regarding me with curiosity and perhaps a smidgen of disdain. "You think it was me who was behind the attack on the cabin."

"The thought had crossed my mind."

She did her best impression of a smirk. "Then it's either

very brave or particularly foolhardy of you to have come here tonight. Alone. Not unarmed, I presume, but alone. Ready to face your murderer."

I said nothing but was increasingly aware of the subtle weight of the weapons resting against my body.

"Clever, isn't it?" she said. "Saving your life by allowing you drugs to destroy the tumour in your head and then turning around and having someone blow it off."

"Not an entirely ill-conceived strategy," I agreed.

She answered back with a glower, heavy with a challenge. Dare to believe. Dare to doubt. Dare to trust. Dare to suspect.

Knoble had brought me here late at night, when no one else was around. I thought about the door behind me. Was someone on the other side? An assassin waiting for a sign from Knoble?

"I guess we've come to that point," I told her. "It's time for you to either finish the job…." I counted to three. "or start talking." I was hoping for the latter.

Chapter Twenty-Three

It wasn't enough. Shekhar Kapur knew that even though Adam Saint's medical notes prior to his diagnosis with a deadly brain tumour showed no such thing, it could be argued there were more recent test results, files that Kapur's hired man had failed to find when he'd broken into Dr. Milo Yelchin's office.

Kapur hated the fact that he'd had to resort to common thuggery to support Arla Tellebough's claim, but he'd had no choice. He'd been unsuccessful in accessing any of Saint's files in the IIA or CDRA databases. There was so much more he didn't know. If Saint had been lied to, who was behind it? And why would they do such a thing?

Inside his head, a name was being whispered. He hoped the voice was wrong. If not, he'd be forced to do something he found distasteful. He would have to rise up against his immediate superior. The woman who'd hired him for the job that allowed him to leave India. Maryann Knoble. Had he escaped one hellish relationship with a woman only to suffer another?

As much as he personally disliked Maryann Knoble, deference to one's superior was a trait Kapur found difficult to shake, unless that superior was doing wrong. Then all actions taken to reveal it would be justifiable. But if he was going to toss that particular stone, he'd need to be certain its heft was great enough to do some damage.

Tonight, walking into the "gin joint," as he thought of it, was not easy for Shekhar Kapur. He didn't visit such places. He saw no point in it. They were loud, usually the lighting was kept dim presumably because the owners wished to save money on electricity, and alcohol flowed much too easily.

As an agent, Kapur had been required to do many things he found offensive. This, simply, would be another.

IIA's policy of recording and tracing all communications that came into the agency had been invaluable to Kapur. Little had Arla Tellebough known that just by placing a telephone call to his office, floodgates had opened through which he was able to find out everything he needed to locate her. Rather than confront the woman in her home, he decided his best first step was to observe her as a stranger might. Was she someone you could believe, someone whose word you could trust, an unimpeachable witness? Or was she, as he suspected, just another silly Western woman with breasts that were too large?

The bar was on Yonge Street, another place Kapur would normally avoid. Even its name was misleading. With block after block of filthy, cracked sidewalks, rundown buildings, and peculiar smells that emanated from businesses selling cheap food and sex, there was nothing youthful about this street. But Kapur understood that these same things were what attracted hordes of people, locals and tourists alike, drawn in by the widespread appeal of sensual seediness.

Stepping into the bar, Kapur was immediately assaulted

by noise that passed for music and the mixed scents of yeasty hops and drugstore perfume. Only the gaudy luminescence of neon signs and the spotlights over the bartender's station kept the place from being drowned in bilge water darkness. Quickly assessing the layout, Kapur moved to one side of the large room where he'd spotted the only available spot, and he hoisted himself onto a single stool next to a high-top table. As expected, the cheap bit of furniture proved exceedingly uncomfortable.

For several minutes, he sat there, surveying the crush of people, sometimes being elbowed or side-swiped as Boy X tried to get to Girl Y, or a gaggle of self-indulgent young women passed by, engrossed in their phones rather than looking where they were going. Carefully, he considered each feminine face, looking for a match to the photograph he'd found online from the woman's Facebook page.

"Sorry for the wait, cutie. What can I get ya?"

Kapur turned to find the owner of the voice. She'd come up behind him. He almost choked when he saw her.

It was she.

Arla Tellebough.

This woman's hair was darker than her Facebook photograph had shown, but he was confident it was the same person. He glanced down at the nametag bobbing up and down on breasts barely covered by stretched white cotton. Big breasts. Certainly much bigger than he'd ever touched. Farha had rarely allowed him that pleasure, even during their irregular bouts of lovemaking. The tag read: "Arla."

Following his eyes, she grinned and commented, "It's a short name, hon. Shouldn't take you so long to read it. So what do you say?"

Kapur's eyes moved up to hers. They were dark brown and rimmed in coal black, a combination he found unaccountably attractive. He stuttered, "Well, yes, I suppose it is a short name."

She smiled. For real this time. "I mean, what do you want to drink?"

It took him a second to respond. "I'd like a glass of water, please. No ice."

"Ooooo, a big spender, huh?"

"I'll gladly pay for it," he quickly added.

The waitress gave Kapur a strange look, as if she were trying to figure something out, then began moving away. "No problem, sweetheart. I'll be back."

"Thank you."

Arla Tellebough stopped dead in her tracks. Slowly, she rotated back to look at Kapur. She was accustomed to strange men making strange requests. This was something different.

She took the three steps back to the high-top and stared. "You're him, aren't you?"

Kapur could feel an uncomfortable heat begin to seep up his collar. This was not how this was meant to go. He was here to observe her from afar, to judge her credibility.

"Him? Him who?"

"There's something about the way you talk. And your accent. I recognize it from the phone." For a moment, she looked unsure, doubting herself. "It's you, isn't it? You're the guy I talked to about Adam Saint. You're the CDRA guy, aren't you?"

Kapur's one shortcoming as an IDRA agent had been his inability to maintain a convincing lie. This was a skill

244 — Anthony Bidulka

which came in handy, especially when dealing with grieving family members who didn't need to know the *whole* truth of what had happened to their loved ones. Kapur had never been able to disguise much of the truth.

"Yes," he admitted, at the same time noting that the woman's proximity allowed him to breathe in the flowery sweetness of her perfume. Or maybe it was the soap she used? Arla was older than he'd expected, at least in her mid-thirties. Her face was much more intelligent and thoughtful and kind than her online image had suggested.

Arla regarded him, braver in the safety of a crowded bar, her own turf, than she might otherwise have been. "So, are you following me or is this some kind of crazy coincidence?"

Again he stuttered his answer, cross with himself for doing so. "I was hoping I could ask you a few follow-up questions, on the matter we discussed."

Her eyes widened. "Here? Are you kidding me?"

"I see now this may not be the most opportune time. You're busy."

She hesitated before responding, studying the man's face, noting the nervous way he intertwined the long, dark fingers of one hand with the other's. "Yes, I am." She didn't move away. She gave him a closer once-over. Good-looking. Gorgeous eyes. Well-dressed. He smelled great. He was skinny, though. Beefy was the usual type of guy she went for. She was surprised to find she didn't mind it. There was something about him that was kinda sexy. "Do you wanna maybe wait for me? We could have a drink or something after I get off."

Kapur was stunned by the request. He didn't quite understand what was happening. Did she have more to tell him about Adam Saint? Had she been waiting for an opportunity to do so?

"When is that?" he asked awkwardly.

"Two a.m. That too late for you, hon?"

"No," he blurted out before thinking, even though it absolutely was too late. Nothing about this was right. He did not like this bar. He did not like staying up after midnight. He did not like that his plan had gone awry so fast and so spectacularly. He did not like how confidence and intelligence had abandoned him in favour of the awkwardness of a teenage boy.

But, God help him, he did like this woman.

The images were far beyond disturbing. Even for a woman like Maryann Knoble, who'd witnessed her fair share of atrocities. The brutal rape. The cannibalism. The raw, coarse soundtrack of abomination. And finally the eerie message.

> *I hope you have enjoyed today's feature presentation.*
> *What you have just watched is actual footage (not a recreation) shot on location at Skawa Island.*
> *Directed, produced, funded by: The International Intelligence Agency of Canada*
> *In other words, Ms. Knoble: YOU.*
> *Silence the women of Skawa Island.*
> *Or the next time you see this video—in its entirety—will be on the nightly news. Everywhere.*

Maryann Knoble hit the stop button and searched the face of Adam Saint for his reaction. It wasn't what she'd expected.

They were still in her office, having reached temporary détente and an agreement to share information. Her offering was the video she'd received by email from a mysterious source.

Saint thought the video was useful, the gritty images helping to, if not exactly make sense of what happened on Skawa Island, at least place a few more pieces in the puzzle.

"Now we know what the IIA equipment we found on the island was being used for," Saint said, his brain clicking away a million miles an hour. "Someone wanted to record what was happening there."

"Who?" Knoble demanded to know, even though she suspected her agent didn't have the answer. "And why in God's name would you want to make a record of such a thing?"

Saint dipped his head toward the screen. "Maybe we just found out why."

"To what...? Blackmail me? Destroy IIA?"

"Possibly. Yet, it seems that whoever wrote this note is as blindly interested in protecting IIA and hiding their involvement in this as you are."

Maryann grunted her displeasure at the backhanded slam.

"Along with the evidence I found on the island, I'd say chances are good they aren't lying about this not being a Hollywood-type dramatization. What we saw on the screen really happened. Including the rape. Which also supports my belief that the women we rescued from Skawa were lying to me. They weren't the only ones on that island."

"So where are they?" Knoble barked. "Assuming you're correct and the men who tried to kill you weren't the men in the video, where are these cannibals, these rapists? From what you told me, you covered every inch of that island. Is there any way you missed seeing them? Could they still be there?" Maryann stayed quiet about one other thing that worried her. If Saint missed seeing the men, were there other women still left behind on that island? Being tortured, raped…eaten…by the same savages?

Saint shook his head. "I don't see how. But I can't guarantee it. Our departure was hasty to say the least. We were off the island before I was done. We need to go back."

"No," Knoble snapped. "There's no time. Not now, anyway."

Saint had assured her the cabin and everything in it had been destroyed, along with any evidence of IIA's presence. For now, that was the most important thing. She would eventually send a team back to Skawa to guarantee a clean sweep, but that needn't involve Saint.

"We need to focus on finding out who sent this message," she said. "And then we need to stop the bastard before he makes good on his threat. Whoever he is, he quite obviously wants the three women and the child dead."

"Are you worried about them?" Saint challenged. "Or is it IIA you're more interested in protecting?" He didn't add the third option: Was Knoble acting only to save her own skin?

The head of IIA scowled. Saint was a frustrating man. He didn't fear her at all, not even one little bit. Perhaps it was the shadow of his own death that propelled his imprudent courage, and perhaps that wasn't such a bad thing. At least she needn't concern herself with any hidden agendas with this one. He'd laid his cards on the table. What he was forgetting was that the table belonged to her.

"As far as I can see, none are mutually exclusive," Knoble pointed out.

She was right, Saint knew. And for the time being, they were stronger working together than apart.

"Tell me about Belar."

"I'm afraid we'll find little help there. The man's brain is almost entirely atrophied. When I asked about Skawa, he had nothing but nonsense to say."

"But he did say something? What was it?"

"It was nothing. Gibberish. Even his wife didn't know who he was talking about."

"Tell me anyway."

"Rex save Julia. That was it." She shook her head. "The names mean nothing to me and nothing to his wife. I spent hours combing over personnel files from ten years ago, but I found no reference to a Rex or a Julia, as first or last names. Dead end, Saint."

"Maybe."

Maryann was visibly uncomfortable with the question she was about to pose, rarely, if ever, having done it before: "What now?"

Saint blew an exasperated shaft of air through his nose as he regarded the woman. "There's a common thread weaving its way through every morsel of this thing."

"What's that?"

"Lying. Everyone is lying about something. I'm going to find out why."

Saint stood, throwing a shadow across Knoble. She didn't like it. Bringing herself to her feet, she demanded to know: "Where are you going?"

"I don't exactly know yet. I'm still working on it."

Actually, it was his nephew Anatole who was working on it, but as far as he was concerned, the less Knoble knew about his family the better. "One more thing," he added, hoping to move her off the topic. "I want to do some work on the video. See if I can figure out where it came from. I imagine given the secrecy of what we're looking into, you probably haven't called in IIA techs to look at it."

Knoble pursed her lips. He was right. Something else she didn't like. Knoble was no slouch when it came to computers, but something like this, a forensic procedure, was beyond even her prodigious talents.

"You've asked me to trust you," Saint pushed on. "Now you'll have to return the favour. I'll need passwords and a way to get through the security firewall."

Considering the outlandish request, Knoble returned to the grand window display, showing the agent her back. They stayed like that for nearly a minute before she answered. "Then I want something also." Saint steeled himself. The bargaining game was not quite over. "What is it?"

"I want the women. Here. The child too." She didn't give him time to respond. "Don't bother with the travel document bullshit. I know you're lying. Any agent worth his salt can create a fake passport in his sleep. I know you have them. Given the circumstances, I would have done the same, but things have changed here tonight. We've talked out our differences." She turned, she-wolf eyes burning into him. "Haven't we?"

Saint debated his answer. Wisely ignoring his first impulse, he responded with a curt nod.

Chapter Twenty-Four

I could have gotten into the secure building if I'd wanted to.

Actually, I did want to. Badly.

But I knew it was wrong. I shouldn't be here. If Kate decided to go off the grid, then she had a reason. If she had wanted me to know why, she'd have told me. I think.

Not long ago, she'd come to my rescue. Immediately after Milo Yelchin gave me my death sentence. The words that sealed my fate still echoed in my head: "*We call it GBM*," Milo'd said. "*Glioblastoma multiforme. We saw it on your MRI. It's the most common of malignant primary brain tumours. And the most aggressive.*"

I'd gone home and proceeded to find the bottom of every bottle of alcohol I owned. A couple of days later, Kate entered my apartment—with the key I'd given her "just in case"—and she found me. She cleaned me up, made love to me, then asked me to sign divorce papers.* The last part wasn't so great. But at least she was there. She got me through the worst of it.

But now, as I sat outside her apartment building, a thought occurred to me. When I'd given her that "just in case" key to my home, she hadn't given me one to hers. Maybe she knew this day would come. A day when I'd be

*When the Saints Go Marching In

desperately worried about her, desperately wanting to see her, touch her, make sure she was all right. A day when I was probably the last person on earth she wanted to see.

I stepped out of my rental car, but instead of bursting my way into my ex-wife's building, I started to walk. Within ten minutes, I was on the city's Waterfront Trail. The full moon laid a glittering blanket across Lake Ontario. It was a sultry night in Toronto, the humidity high as I made my way down Queen's Quay. As I got closer to the Harbourfront area, it would get busier, but for now, I had solitude, with only an occasional couple on a romantic, late-night stroll for company.

The irony was almost painful. Did I want what these couples had? Did I wish it were Kate and me walking hand in hand, oblivious to the world around us, loving each other on a hot summer night? Is that what we once had but didn't know it? Had I carelessly thrown it away?

Settling on a cement ledge next to a giant spherical art installation that resembled the Death Star, I pulled out my phone. Not yet midnight. Rowan, my son, was seventeen. It was probably early evening by his standards. I dialled his cell.

After three rings, his very precise diction informed me that he was unavailable and to leave a message. I remembered Kate mentioning that he was spending some time over the summer at a friend's family's cabin in Muskoka. My mouth opened to say something, but nothing came out.

The last time my son and I had spoken, he'd calmly notified me that he was aware of my terminal state and wondered how it might affect him and his financial ability to attend art college. The words stung. I knew he didn't mean them. He was being a typical teenager, too pissed off at his father—for good reasons—and unable to see beyond his own needs, to think about and accept the finality of the fact that his dad was dying. Some day, Rowan would wake up and be devastated by what he'd said. I just hoped, for his sake, that day wasn't a day too late.

I was gazing out at Toronto's islands across the inner harbour, contemplating calling Rowan back, when I detected the tail. The foot traffic in the area was light and always moving, and other than me, no one was sitting alone in the dark, so the guy stood out. He was probably blissfully unaware that a small patch on his right arm was highly reflective in the moonlight, making him easy to spot.

Not in the mood for coy, I put my phone away, made a mental inventory of my weapons, and headed straight for him. As I got closer, he began to pull back into the shadows.

"Hey!" I called out.

He turned and ran.

Great. I'd missed my workout that day.

First heading north, I thought he'd make for the busier Queen's Quay. Better chance of getting lost in a crowd. Instead, he navigated around the boat basins. He stuck to the trail and eventually clipped west, with the Power Plant gallery on one side and the tall ship *Kajama* on the other. Then he made his way toward the Harbourfront stage area. Dumb decision.

Given a clear path and the fact that I was faster than he was, I was easily catching up. He took the footbridge over the next inlet, heading straight for the basin directly beside the marine police station. Unwanted attention here would cause complications for both of us, so I slowed my pace as we traversed around the watery parking lot populated by law enforcement speedboats.

The runner headed north and then shifted direction again to cut through the Rees WaveDeck into HTO Park. As he moved toward the beach at the water's edge, I decided this was the best place to end our little parade.

I stepped up the pace, feeling each pump in the muscles of my calves and hamstrings.

Sensing I was making a move, he tried to speed up.

In ten seconds, I was almost abreast of him, coming up on his left.

"G'devening," I greeted him companionably as we raced side by side.

He looked at me, incredulous. I could see perspiration dripping down his face. Strain marks around his eyes and mouth told me he was tiring.

At the right spot, I made a sudden veering motion into him.

The man stumbled onto the sand of the tiny beach, the unexpected change in surface throwing him off stride. If he was any good, the destabilization would only last a second. I had to make it count. Using an old football move, I wrapped my arms around his mid-torso and used my legs to push us sideways.

He fell to the sand. I landed on top of him.

Immediately, he swung into a defensive rolling motion, threatening to toss me off. I knew I couldn't let go.

For ten seconds we struggled. Only one of us was going to win this one. He was strong. And determined. Eventually, like a rider atop a bucking bronco, knowing that any second I was about to eat dirt, I clamped my hand against his face, torqued left, and pressed it into the gritty sand. Reflexively,

254 — *Anthony Bidulka*

he forgot what the rest of his body should have been doing and instead focussed on closing his eyes and reaching out for me. In that microsecond, I clamped my other hand around his throat and squeezed.

"Stop this!" I urged him.

It took another ten seconds for him to decide my advice was sound.

I released his face and in a flash had a gun kissing his forehead. My other hand, still around his neck, loosened when I could see his eyes reflect a resentful acceptance of the situation.

"Who sent you to follow me?"

He glared. Idiot.

"I've got a gun. I've got water to dump a body in. I don't see this ending well for you. Unless you start talking."

"You won't do it," he croaked.

I tightened the neck hold. "Wanna try me?"

His pupils told me he was worried.

But not worried enough. And that told me exactly who'd sent him. Someone who knew me.

I leaned down into his face. My voice spewed over him like hot magma. "Tell Maryann that the next time she sends a goon to follow me, I'll send him home in a body bag."

Chapter Twenty-Five

When Anatole Saint stood up and stretched, he could almost touch the ceiling of his room. He did it not because it felt particularly good but because he'd read somewhere that it was a wise thing for people like him to do after spending many hours hunched over a computer screen. That done, the lanky young man folded himself back down into his chair and regarded the collection of screens that encircled him like a rotunda of digital art.

Several years ago, he'd invented a swivel pad that rested on his desk, on which each screen was situated side by side. He could take the monitor on which he was working (although he often worked on more than one simultaneously), and simply swivel it—instead of himself—directly into the perfect line of sight. Of course, each of the monitors had multi-window capabilities, but he preferred this set-up. He got more done and could casually consider what was happening on one screen while dedicating the rest of his attention to another.

The two screens on his furthest right were typically used for client matters. The furthest left was dedicated to gaming. The one next to it was primarily used for research. The centre screen was committed to personal matters and social media. It was on this screen that he now refocussed his attention.

It was late, the house quiet, dark outside and in, but as was his habit, he was far from finished with his workday. Night was his preferred time to get stuff done. He liked to pretend he was one of only a few diehards trolling through Internet sites, studying, exploring, gathering information, while the rest of the world was fast asleep.

Tonight, it wasn't client work that had him probing the world's digital depository of information. This was personal. He typed in a query, and immediately 1,347,343 results appeared. He scoured the first page and selected the one that seemed the best match: *Ten Ways to Tell If Someone Is Gay.* Anatole liked lists.

Number one: What is his favourite TV show? If it's Modern Family, Project Runway, Top Chef*: Gay.*

Number two: How does he describe most things? Never good or okay, but fabulous*: Gay.*

Number three: Does he smell good for no reason?: Gay.

Anatole rolled his eyes. Noting the source of the list, he closed the window, adding the name to his own mental list of Internet sites to ignore.

As he referred to the results page for another more credible option, he heard a knocking sound followed by a hushed "Hey, are you there?" It was his after-midnight ring tone setting telling him he had an incoming call. Given the late hour and the fact that the caller ID was blocked, he guessed it was his uncle.

"Hey," he answered.

"Anatole, it's Uncle Adam."

Anatole called up his uncle's itinerary on one of the screens. "So, how're things in Toronto?" Now that his uncle had lost his supercool apartment, he'd booked him into the

Fairmont Royal York on Front Street.

"Fine. How are things with our house guests?"

Anatole silently chastised himself. All it took was the mention of the Skawa rescuees, not even Peri's name specifically, for his face to warm up. "They're fine." His cheeks grew toastier as he made the conscious decision not to tell his uncle about the special research he was doing for her.

"Nothing unusual has happened since they've been there?"

"Uh, no."

"You're confident no one knows about them?"

"I haven't said a thing to anyone. And you know Mom and Grandpa. They don't talk to people any more than they have to, anyway. Unless someone recognized them at the airport—and who could that be?—I think everything is still top secret around here."

"Good. They haven't been anywhere?"

Horizontal ridges formed on Anatole's pale brow. He knew his uncle was a cautious guy, but this was beginning to feel more like a warning than casual interest. "No," Anatole assured him. "These are definitely city girls, but I think they're getting used to life on a farm."

"I hope they haven't gotten too used to it."

"What do you mean?"

"I just got off the phone with your mother. I've asked her to bring them to Toronto."

Anatole froze. Peri was leaving. Just like that. "What are you talking about? Why didn't anyone tell me about this?" He blurted it out before thinking. His uncle's silent response confirmed just exactly how asinine his demanded expectation to be consulted on this matter was.

"I'm sorry," he quickly added. "That came out wrong." His voice sounded weird. High and whiny. "It's just unexpected. I thought you said they'd be safer here. I think they are. Don't you?"

"Anatole." His uncle's voice was gentle but firm. "You and your grandpa have done a great job of taking care of the women and Theo. But things have changed. They need to be here now."

"Okay," he mumbled his acquiescence. He knew there was no use trying to explain the strange, unfamiliar, but wonderful feelings he was having for the youngest of the female survivors. He barely understood them himself.

"Okay?" Saint confirmed.

"Yeah. Okay."

"Good. Do you have anything else for me?"

Speedily typing some instructions on a keyboard, a second screen came to life with windows packed with information. "I do. Some weird stuff, actually."

"Weird how?"

"This shipwreck that supposedly happened ten years ago—I can't find anything to tell me that it actually happened. I've checked maritime records for the area and time period, give or take five years, and there's nothing that even comes close to what the women described to you. Now, Uncle Adam, I've never done this before, so maybe I'm not looking in the right places. But it seems kind of weird that there was no mention of something like this, at least in the local papers of some of the bigger islands nearby."

"Agreed." Stony-voiced.

"These gals aren't talking much about themselves, so I haven't had much luck that way, but I've been digging into their backgrounds with the little I do know, like you asked. Facebook and Twitter and most other social media weren't around before they were lost, so I can't rely on that, but there still should be more out there than I'm finding, some sort of records or background info that's made it online. From a virtual world perspective, Uncle Adam, these girls were almost ghosts even before they went missing."

"Almost?"

Anatole grinned at how quickly his uncle picked up on his clue. "Theo's mom let it slip the other day that Destiny isn't her real name. Garbage in, garbage out. With the right information, I had better luck. I haven't told her yet because I'm not a hundred percent sure, but I was able to track down some people who I think are her parents."

"Tell me more."

Anatole spelled out what he'd learned. In return, Saint told him what he needed done next.

"Good job, Anatole," Saint praised his nephew. "And you were right not to say anything to her. Keep it that way. Do you think the other women are using fake names too?"

Anatole thought he could hear frustration in his uncle's voice. Maybe that was why he was sending for the women. He needed to interrogate them. If he couldn't come home, the women had to come to him. He shrugged. "Dunno." Then: "Uncle Adam?"

"Yeah?"

"I know this may sound weird, but…well, instead of Mom, what about if I brought them to Toronto?"

There was another short silence. Anatole was glad they weren't on Skype, which was their usual mode of communication. He couldn't bear the questioning look that was probably on his uncle's face right now. And it would be hard to hide the discomfort that was spreading across his like a crimson rash.

"Anatole, I need you there. At your computer. I have another big job for you. Something that's going to take all of your attention and skill."

This made the young man's pink ears quiver. "What is it?"

For the next ten minutes, Saint described for his nephew the video he was about to send him, its importance to what they were doing, and what he was asking of him.

"I know you've hacked into CDRA before, Anatole, but this is something different. Maryann Knoble has agreed to give you access to areas of the IIA system that I doubt even you could have found your way into without her permission."

"I don't know about that," Anatole replied matter-of-factly, emboldened and enthralled by his new assignment.

Saint chuckled. "You may be right there. But I want you to be careful with this. I don't want Knoble to know who you are. I only told her you're a specialist I've used before and that I trust you one hundred percent."

Anatole blushed with pride.

"Once you're done, she'll have all the passwords and protocols changed faster than you can tie one shoe, but until then, you'll have free range. Be aware that she'll likely be monitoring everything you do, so do whatever it takes to keep your identity private."

"I understand," he said, trying hard but not entirely successfully to keep the thrill out of his voice.

"First thing tomorrow, I want you to get half a dozen disposable, untraceable phones. Do you know how to do that?"

"Duh."

"If you need anything from Knoble or have to ask her any questions to do what you need to do to trace that video's origins, call her but do not identify yourself. Use a phone only once. After you use it, destroy it."

"Man, you really don't trust that woman. Isn't she, like, your boss?"

Saint ignored this. "One more thing, Anatole."

"Shoot."

"This won't mean anything to you, and quite possibly doesn't mean anything to anyone, but while you're digging around in IIA, see if you can find any reference to someone named Rex, or maybe named Julia, specifically how they might relate to Skawa Island."

Anatole typed the names into an open document he'd been using to make notes about the things his uncle was tasking him with. "Weird, but got it. Anything else?"

"I think your to-do list is long enough for now. Your mom should be contacting you about making travel arrangements. I'd like to have them here within the next couple of days. You'll tell your grandpa about the women leaving?"

"Sure." He was still plenty bummed about the loss of Peri. He'd have to toss and turn about that one some more to figure out why.

"Anatole," his uncle said. "Thanks."

Anatole gazed at the long list of way cool stuff he was going to get into and knew it made up...well, sorta...for how he felt about losing the girl. It had been bound to happen anyway. Guys like him never got to keep the girl. "Thank you back," he replied, meaning it.

Just as he was about to hang up, his uncle called out his name again.

"Something else?" he asked.

Saint waited a beat, then: "Your Aunt Kate. Did you find anything?"

Anatole wondered if this was truly a last-minute question, or much more important than his uncle was letting on. "Nothing other than confirming what you already know. She's not at work and not responding to messages. Don't worry. I just need some time to dig a little deeper."

"Okay. Thanks." The line went dead.

The timing was almost too perfect. The very second Anatole hung up from his late-night call with his uncle, he heard the noise.

It was nothing more than a gentle thump. But it was unusual at this hour in the typically quiet-as-a-tomb farmhouse.

He strained to listen for more.

He couldn't be sure, but something didn't feel right.

Anatole scanned his room for something to use as a weapon.

Quite quickly, he established that his was not the type of room where one could easily procure such a thing.

With nothing else at the ready, he swiped up an unused surge protector bar. He reasoned that if he swung it by its metre-long cord, he could use it to do damage.

He stepped out of the room.

Stopping on the landing near the top of the staircase that led to the lower floor, Anatole listened again. He hoped to either confirm or refute what he thought he'd heard.

A second passed.

Several more.

There it was.

This time, the sound was more of a shuffle, as if someone was rifling through papers. Definitely coming from downstairs. Anatole peered through the dark hallway to see if there was any light coming from his grandfather's bedroom, but the slit below the door was dark. He debated waking him up.

What if it's nothing? Which was most likely the case. Weird noises in old country houses were more the rule than an exception. *So why is this particular noise getting me all worked up?*

Wake him? Not wake him?

If he did, the house would be thrown into an uproar. Not only would his grandpa be disturbed, but the women and Theo would be too. They'd been through enough of being scared for one lifetime. And if it was nothing but a mouse or wind through an open window, he'd be left looking like a fool. In front of Peri.

No way.

With his surge-protector weapon firmly in hand, Anatole slunk his way down the stairs. He stopped every two or three steps to see if he could catch another bit of the sound and identify it as something benign.

No such luck.

Once on the ground floor, the noise suddenly became more pronounced. Whoever or whatever was in the house had either grown bolder, wasn't very good at being sneaky, or, worse, didn't care.

The sounds were coming from the living room, not the kitchen. This wasn't good. Anatole was very familiar with the kitchen but rarely went into the living room. Why would he? Other than a place to put up a Christmas tree, he didn't have much use for it. At least in the kitchen he'd have access to a smarter weapon than a glorified plug-on-a-string. Then again, so would the intruder.

As he inched toward the archway that led from the house's entrance hall into the living room, another fearsome thought hit the young man. When he'd tried to reason that the women and Theo were perfectly fine here on the farm and didn't need to be shipped off to Toronto, his uncle's response was: "…*things have changed. They need to be here now.*"

What had he meant by that? Were the women in danger? Was someone after them?

Another thump from the darkened living room.

Was it already too late?

Someone was definitely in there. This was no rodent or errant gust of wind.

Maybe I should scream?

Maybe I'm wrong.

Still, his manly ego would not allow him to call for help.

He shuffled forward.

Inch by inch.

On the threshold of the living room, he raised his right arm so the surge protector was now swinging from its cord at waist level, ready to strike out like a snake.

Taking a last step forward, Anatole winced as his left hand shot out and scrambled to find the light switch on the wall. This was it. Now or never.

Bright overhead lights flashed on like a strobe.

Anatole raised his weapon and took aim at the intruder.

Chapter Twenty Six

"Anatole! Stop! It's me! It's Peri!"

Still twirling the surge protector like a lasso above his head, Anatole stared at the girl. Relief flooded over him, quickly overtaken by confusion.

"What are you doing down here in the dark?"

There was little the young woman could do to hide the fact that she was doing something suspicious at the small desk Oliver Saint used for various chores. It was where he sorted through mail, paid bills, and stacked newspapers and magazines he'd likely never get around to reading.

Setting his makeshift weapon aside, Anatole approached the girl, glancing down at the desk as he did so. His grandfather was no neatnik, but it was obvious from the mess of papers and opened drawers that she'd been searching for something. Wordlessly, his face filled with hope for a good explanation, he looked up.

For a moment, Peri said nothing, debating her options. Without warning, her grey eyes, tinged with flecks of blue and green, clouded over, and suddenly her pale face was awash in thick, fat tears. Throwing herself against Anatole, she wrapped her thin arms around his narrow waist and sobbed into his tee-shirt.

Not sure what to do, Anatole looked down at the

shuddering little head, more than a full foot below his own. Clumsily, he moved his long arms until they'd encircled the young woman. It felt weird, unnatural, but so very good. The longer she stood there, the less awkward it became. Instead of focussing on the crying, he breathed in the clean scent of the girl. She smelled like soap and a bit like the fresh hay they fed the horses.

When the outburst was over, he felt her tiny body gently push against his chest. He took this as a sign that the comforting was over and she wished to be released. Dropping his arms to his sides, he stepped back, his eyes anywhere but on hers. It had been a strangely intimate moment, and once again he felt uncomfortable and unsure of what to do or say next.

"I'm sorry, Anatole," she told him, drying her face with the sleeve of her pullover. Actually, it was his pullover. One of the many pieces of clothing he and his mother had contributed to the non-existent wardrobes of their house guests.

"It's okay," he said, not exactly sure what he was talking about.

"I shouldn't have come down here." She shot an uneasy glance at the disturbed items on the desk. "I made a mess of your grandpa's things."

"We told you if you needed anything to just ask," Anatole said.

There was a moment of silence.

"So...what *did* you need? What are you looking for?"

A pained looked crossed the girl's face. She wrapped her arms around herself as if cold. "Money. I need money, Anatole. I know your grandpa does his bills and stuff here, so I was hoping I'd find some."

"Is there something you need to buy? Uncle Adam told us to get you whatever you want. I can drive into Saskatoon tomorrow and pick up what you need."

She shook her head. "That's not it."

Anatole narrowed his eyes. He had never had a girl-friend. If he were being honest he could lay claim to very few friends of any kind, in person that is. Online was another story. Via various social media outlets, Anatole had made plenty of friends from around the world. Rarely, however, did their conversations steer far off a familiar range of topics. They discussed economics, politics, and especially information technology and what was new and hot on the Internet. But every once in the long while, there was talk of personal relationships. One of the people he chatted with most often in this regard was Aneel, who lived in Taiwan. Aneel talked about these "games" his girlfriend played. Mind games. Very confusing games. Games where what she said was not what she really meant. Anatole wondered it that's what was going on here.

There was only one reply he could think of to make. "I don't understand."

"Do you remember how I told you I'd like to find my dad and my grandpa? I know you said you'd try to help, but you're so busy with your work and doing stuff for your uncle that you probably don't have time. I need the money to go look for them myself. I can't sit here and wait for…well, I don't know what we're waiting for. I need to go, Anatole. I want to find my family."

Anatole felt a stab of guilt. He had promised to help Peri, but she was right. Not only was his regular work keeping him busy with clients experiencing more than the usual number of meltdowns, but late summer was a hectic time on a Saskatchewan farm. Not that he did much of the "farm work" per se, but it had long been an unspoken agreement that when his grandfather was extra busy with seeding, harvesting, or haying, Anatole would step up his responsibilities around the house and yard. He made sure the animals were fed, the eggs collected, the barn mucked out, the horses exercised, the garden weeded, the flowerbeds watered, the laundry done, the house cleaned. On top of all that, keeping up with his Uncle Adam's requests for help with travel, research, and playing host to three women and a five-year-old boy sucked up any free time he might have had.

He didn't regret any of it. For the first time he could remember, Anatole was beginning to like pretty much everything about his life. He loved his work. He didn't exactly love being outside and getting dirty, but after all his grandpa had done for him over the years—like giving him a place to live and food to eat when his mother couldn't—he did like looking after things for him. He certainly loved having Peri around. And he most definitely was grooving on becoming wingman to his adventurer uncle. He'd never be Indiana Jones, but he could be his brainiac assistant.

"I'm the one who's sorry," Anatole said. "I should have told you sooner."

"Told me what?"

"You're right. I have been busy with lots of other things. I haven't had as much time to look for your relatives as I wanted. But I have been trying when I can. I guess I was waiting until I found both of them."

The girl's face brightened. Anatole's heart swelled.

"What did you just say?"

Wiping away unruly, dark bangs from his eyes, he said, "I found your grandfather. Or at least I'm pretty sure I did. He's got a unique name, so I'd say it's him."

"Really? You did? Where is he? Let me get a pen or something to write this down!" she blurted out excitedly, searching the desk for blank paper and something to write with. "Where is he? Where is he?"

"Don't worry about a pen. I'll print something off for you," he said, a tentative smile trembling on his narrow face.

Suddenly, Peri stiffened. "You didn't tell him, did you? You didn't say anything to him about me, did you? Did you actually talk to him?"

"It's okay," Anatole soothed. He remembered well her desire to keep this on the down-low until she was sure she wanted direct contact. There'd been strain in family relations before she' was lost at sea. He could easily understand why she'd want to take this slow. "I didn't talk to him. All I know is where he is. And whe—" Anatole stopped there. Suddenly, what had been the worst thing to happen to him ever—melodramatically speaking—had become something really good. For Peri.

"What?" Peri persisted, still nervous. "What is it? Is something wrong?"

"No. Something is really right. Your grandpa—he lives near Toronto."

Peri looked confused. "Why is that so really right?"

"I was…well, my mom was going to tell you this tomorrow. She's going to be taking you and the others to Toronto. Probably tomorrow or the next day. You'll be right next door to where your grandpa lives. I know you're not sure if you want to see him, but at least this way, if you decide to, it'll be a lot easier. I can give you money to go see him or whatever. If you want."

For the second time that night, Anatole found himself with a crying woman in his arms.

With eighty percent of the city of New Orleans flooded by Hurricane Katrina in 2005, it's virtually impossible to find any home or person that wasn't affected. For disaster recovery agencies, Katrina was one of only a handful of instances where agents from all parts of the world, not just nearby Canada and Mexico, were dispatched regardless of the nationality of persons in jeopardy. Fat lot of good we did, but we tried our best.

New Orleans is known as the Big Easy. The origins of the nickname are obscure, but never more than now, since Katrina, had I understood it as well. When it comes to natural disasters, political corruption, social issues, and disease, this is a city that has put up with some plain old hard living. But it bounces back like nowhere else in the world. New Orleans celebrates recovery with loud music, spicy food, free-flowing alcohol, flashy costumes, and a people bearing an irrepressible spiritual exuberance.

Despite a section of natural high ground, the storm damage to the predominantly middle-class and racially diverse Gentilly neighbourhood was pretty severe. The people came back, but things are still far from normal. So I wasn't surprised when, on a sweltering early evening, I pulled up to a modest house with much of the exterior badly in need of repair. A small group was gathered on the front porch, which was bordered with elaborate wrought ironwork that would have been stunning were it not rusted to bright orange. Drinks were flowing, and music coming from some other house down the street lent to the party scene.

Seven pairs of eyes followed me as I stepped out of my rental and followed a crumbling sidewalk up to the porch.

"Howdy," one of the men said, not unfriendly.

Up three steps, and I was standing beneath the metal arch entrance of the porch. No one stood up. "Hello. My name is Adam Saint. I work for the Canadian Disaster Recovery Agency." I could see the shade of well-earned mistrust of pretty much any government agency mist over several of the faces. "I'm looking for Mr. and Mrs. Shoemaker."

"I'm Billy Shoemaker," said a man of generous proportions, wearing a golf shirt that strained at both belly and shoulders. He nodded to a woman sitting next to him. She was a third his size. "This is Tilda, my wife."

"I'm sorry to interrupt your visiting, but I wonder if we might talk in private."

"What's this about?" Billy wanted to know before he was willing to budge an inch. I didn't blame him.

"It's a family matter," I answered, giving them an opportunity to keep this business to themselves if they preferred.

Billy sipped from a glass of beer and chuckled. "All my family is right here."

I dug into his eyes a little deeper. "All?"

Tilda jumped up and hopped over a few feet and knees to get to me. "Why'n't you stay here with everybody, and I'll go talk with the man," she said to her husband. "Anything you need to hear, I'll call ya," she suggested.

I could see Billy was used to having his wife look after things. He waved us off and dove back into conversation with the man sitting nearest him.

"You wanna come inside?" Tilda asked in a way that told me she wasn't too keen on the idea. "It's a fair bit hotter in there than out here though, I'll warn ya."

I smiled. "Why don't we just step down into the front yard?"

She nodded. "Not much of a front yard. Not yet anyway. We'll get to it someday."

I followed her down the steps to a spot under a tree. Its branches were twisted and bark mottled as if suffering some kind of disease, but it had leaves, and with leaves come shade.

"Shoulda asked before we come down here," she fretted. "Can I get ya something cool to drink?"

"Thank you. I'm fine."

She nodded quickly, her eyes moving back and forth between me and the crowd on the porch. "So what's this about a family matter? Has something bad happened to somebody?"

It was understandable that people in this barely dried-out city would be something less than an optimistic bunch. "No, nothing like that."

"You said you're from some sort of disaster agency. What now?"

"I've come with good news, Mrs. Shoemaker." I'd start there. My real reason for being here would have to wait.

The way the woman's eyebrows lifted at hearing my words made her appear owlish. "Good news? Well, ain't that something? What is it?"

"Mrs. Shoemaker," I began, doling out my words in slow rhythm, "we believe we've found your daughter. Arlene." Destiny's real name.

"Arlene?" she crowed. "You found her? Didn't even know she was lost."

Chapter Twenty-Seven

It was just the three of us left on the Shoemaker porch, the neighbours and friends sent home. Because Mrs. Shoemaker insisted, I sat before a lukewarm beer that tasted surprisingly good. The light of the dying summer evening was beginning to fade away, slipping through the curlicues of the ironwork railing, leaving suffused, watery patterns on the rough wooden floor. The temperature, however, wasn't anywhere near ready to break.

"She used to be a good girl," Billy Shoemaker huffed. "But that didn't last long."

"Oh, stop," Tilda disagreed but with little vehemence. "She was just spirited, that's all."

"Ran away like a wild dog every chance she got," he kept on. "Starting when she was barely twelve. She'd come back dirty and drunk and probably high. Who knows what sorts of things she and those other girls she hung around with got into. Last time was when she was sixteen. Never came back after that for more than a night or two. Usually to get something to eat or more money. Always money."

Tilda sat in a rocker, head nodding, eyes not quite focussed on anything.

"I came out and asked her one time if she was selling it," Shoemaker said, his gruff voice straining from how he really felt about what he was admitting. "She just looked at me like I was nobody and said 'yeah.' Just like that. Like it was nothing."

Shoemaker's eyes were damp. Tilda just kept nodding and rocking.

Here was a new bit of information. Arlene Shoemaker a.k.a. Destiny a.k.a. Theo's mother had been a prostitute. In my head, I was debating whether or not to tell the couple that they were grandparents. But I hadn't come here for that. I'd come to root out the reason for a lie. It had been obvious to me since I first met the women of Skawa Island that they were holding something back. Nothing about their story rang true.

They would undoubtedly continue to lie. To counteract this, I needed to discover as much truth about them as I could. Nothing crushes lies better than pure, bald fact. It's why I'd asked Anatole to dig into their backgrounds. Any good lawyer, investigator, or dictator can tell you: Interrogations go much smoother when you know most of the answers before asking the questions. I'd soon have my time with the women, but to successfully shoot down their deceits, I'd need plenty of ammunition.

"When exactly was the last time you saw Arlene?" I asked.

After a bit of disagreement between the two, they settled on a date that coincided with a time period immediately before the shipwreck off Skawa Island.

"Did you notice anything strange or unusual about your daughter on that visit?" I asked.

"Mr. Saint, we knew what our daughter was," Tilda Shoemaker responded, unhelpfully. "We didn't agree with it, but we accepted it."

I could see there was something troubling big Billy.

"You know," he finally said, "now that you ask, there *was* something different about that last time she came home."

"Like what?" Tilda asked before I could.

"She didn't ask for money." He looked at his wife. "Remember? We even talked about it after she was gone." His beer-blurred gaze covered me. "She told us she was about to come into some cash." Back to his wife. "Remember, Tilly? She even was kinda bragging about it. How she was gonna come back and take us all out to dinner somewhere fancy in the Quarter with all her new money."

Tilda picked up the story. "That's right. She said she'd have to be gone a year, though, in order to get it. She said things would be different when she got back. We jus' thought she was giving an excuse for why we wouldn't be seeing her for a while, that's all."

Billy's head bobbed up and down in sad agreement.

"Did she tell you anything about how she was going to earn this money? Or where she was going?"

Tilda shook her head, downing the rest of her tepid drink.

"Guess we didn't really ask her about that, neither," Billy confessed. "I suppose we shoulda."

Tilda shrugged.

"Did you hear from her again after that visit?"

"Nope," Tilda said. "Like she said, we didn't hear from her for a year. Then before we knew it another passed and another. We figured she just got her money—or more likely didn't—and forgot about us."

The City of New Orleans is divided into eight NOPD districts, each headed by a district commander and with its own staff and geographic jurisdiction. I'd called in a favour with the police commander of District Five, a man I'd worked with closely during Katrina. He vouched for me with Commander Johns of the third district, which included Gentilly.

I arrived at Johns's office on Paris Avenue late in the day. After a minute of professional courtesy chat that neither of us was really interested in, we got to work. I'd brought along photographs of the three Skawa women: Destiny, now identified as former Gentilly resident Arlene Shoemaker; Maybelline; and Peri. The last two had given last names of Johnson and Winkle, respectively.

It didn't take long for Johns to pull up a sheet on Arlene. As her parents already informed me, she was a well-known local prostitute with the typical list of cop shop incidents, all of which had come to a sudden halt ten years before.

"We assumed she moved onto riper territory or finally got her act together," Johns said. "But really," he added with a shake of his head, "I doubt anyone gave it much thought at all."

Peri's name and photograph netted nothing. Maybelline was a different story. One that pretty much duplicated Destiny's. Maybelline's real name was Debbie Kilmer. She and Destiny were hooking on the streets at the same time. They got picked up for the same variety of petty infractions and then disappeared off the cops' radar screen pretty much simultaneously.

Instead of answers, I was left with more questions. The biggest being: What were two—likely three—common prostitutes from the U.S. doing aboard a luxury yacht in the South Pacific?

Every time I find myself in New Orleans, I try to eke out some time with my friend Greg, a local newshound who knows the best places to drink and eat. Early drinking is usually done in the French Quarter, late drinking and eating pretty much anywhere but there. Over the years, we've gluttonously enjoyed discovering the many faces of New Orleans dining. Tonight, Greg was intent on introducing me to the barbecue scene. His choice, an eatery called the Joint, is located off the beaten path in the Bywater neighbourhood. In New Orleans, I'm used to getting good eats in places that in any other city would be classified as dumps. This was another one, the building nothing more than a one-storey cement brick painted sickly yellow and poo brown, squatting next to a scruffy patch of dirt that had been baked to the death of everything but a collection of weeds.

Whenever there's a choice between dining in or out, Greg likes to eat outside, this time in the restaurant's backyard at a long wooden table. The place was hopping, and the vibe good-natured. This was a place to eat meat, laugh loud, and drink a lot.

The menu featured pulled pork, beef brisket, ribs, mac and cheese, and slaw. We settled on a little of each. We were pretty much done our meal and settled into arguing over which drinking hole we'd head to next, when I felt an insistent vibration against my thigh. Thinking it might be an update from Anatole, I apologized to my host and checked the display screen of my phone. Not what I expected.

The text was from Jacqueline Turner. She was in New Orleans and requesting we meet. Now.

"That look on your face better not mean you're not buying the next round," Greg muttered, the curl of his lip indicating he already knew the answer.

"It's a colleague," I told him. "She wants to meet at Catores. You know it?"

Greg frowned. "Strange."

"Why?"

"Catores's been closed for years. Tried to sell itself as a boutique hotel, but it was never more than a rat trap. The only thing going for it was the courtyard restaurant."

"There're lots of those around in New Orleans," I countered. "Good chef?"

"Cute chef," he responded with practiced dryness.

I grinned. "Well, I guess she wants to meet in private." I threw some cash on the table. "Listen, if it's not too late when I'm done, I'll text you to see where you're at."

He gave me his trademark snarl. "Not holding my breath."

Pulling up to the Catores Hotel, I ventured another reason for the business's failure. The dark building was located on a seedy street at a far edge of the French Quarter, the kind of place most travel agents would warn their clients to stay clear of, regardless of how good the room rate.

"*Where are you*?" I texted Jacqueline.

During the drive over, I'd considered potential reasons for the CDRA agent suddenly finding herself in New Orleans and how that reason might coincide with her late-night request for a meeting. I knew CDRA had no current business in Louisiana. Was she simply returning the favour of my surprise visit in Tallinn? Or had she thought better of things since she'd stonewalled me? I'd confronted her with the photograph of her we'd found in the cabin on Skawa Island. She'd claimed no knowledge of how it could have gotten there. Was the truth about to come out in this rundown, boarded-up hotel in New Orleans?

"*In the courtyard,*" she texted back. "*Side door, half way down north side of building. It's open.*"

I followed her instructions, creeping down the side alley to the door and letting myself in. As I'd guessed from the outside, there were no lights on in the building. Without the help of the nearly full moon, my eyes needed a few seconds to adjust to the stark blackness.

"Jacqueline?" I called out, my voice thrown back at me in an eerie echo that reverberated against bare walls.

No answer.

My hand searched a nearby wall for a light switch. After a moment, I found a plate of eight and flipped them all into the up position.

Nothing.

The power had long been cut off.

I called out again, pulling my handgun from where it nestled between the waist of my jeans and small of my back.

"In here!" I heard her voice respond.

My eyes travelled in the direction of the sound. I could just make out a faint flickering that indicated a light source somewhere nearby.

I inched down a long, narrow hallway that led to another shorter one and ended up in a large room. Given the mess of overturned tables and chairs and scatter of broken glass and ceramic, this had likely once been the indoor section of the hotel's restaurant.

At the far end of the room were three banks of double doors. Only the centre set was open. It was through this opening that the light and Jacqueline's voice had originated.

"Jacqueline?"

"In here," she beckoned, less forcefully this time, no doubt aware of my proximity.

My gun leading the way, I carefully stepped over the detritus of the abandoned, vandalized restaurant toward the doorway.

On the other side was the outdoor courtyard Greg had mentioned. During the hotel's heyday, this would have been an extension of the restaurant, offering an al fresco option for diners, common in New Orleans. Dining courtyards come in various sizes and upkeep standards but usually feature an open roof, lots of greenery, and often some form of fountain or water feature. This one had all three, except the potted plants had been left for dead and the fountain was dry, cracked, and being eaten alive by weeds.

The light came from a big blue moon and an industrial-size flashlight. The flashlight stood on its battery base on a bistro table, once likely a romantic rendezvous point for any number of couples who couldn't afford the pricier establishments in the better reputed parts of the Quarter. Next to the table I saw a lone figure. Only a shadow at first, but as I moved further into the courtyard, the indistinct gloom began to morph into features. Jacqueline, as still as a statue.

"Is that a gun you're pointing or are you just glad to see me?" The sound of her voice hinted at none of the carnal playfulness of the words.

"Just a precaution," I said, lowering the weapon but not putting it away. I stepped closer.

"Why don't you stay where you are," she suggested.

Odd.

"I thought you wanted to talk."

"I do, but let's do this first before we get all cozy."

Odder. I fingered the gun, its firm, cool smoothness reassuring.

"Do what? What's this about, Jacqueline?"

Even in the dark, I could see her jaw tighten before she answered.

"I think you know." She had one hand in the pocket of her raincoat. There wasn't a cloud in the sky.

"Have you changed your mind about telling me the truth about the picture?" A guy can hope.

"I want you to tell me where they are."

Oh shit. "Where are who?"

"Saint, don't screw with me on this. The three women you found on Skawa. Where are they?" By the play of shadow and light across the fabric of her coat, I could see her hand moving in the pocket.

"I don't know what you're talking about."

"The fuck you don't. I'm not fooling around here. I lied to you, Saint. Now you're lying to me. We both know it. What you don't know is that the game you're playing is not the one you think it is."

"Okay. Then why don't you tell me what I don't know."

Her breathing pattern changed. Heavier. Faster. Nothing drastic, but it was there.

A subtle shift in the moonlight showed me something more. The look in her eyes wasn't threatening. It was pleading.

Turner was right. I had no idea what was playing out here.

"There's no time for that. Saint, you need to tell me where the women are." She stopped for a brief moment, then: "I promise you no harm will come to them. You can trust me."

"Why in the world would I do that? You know, just for future reference," I said, "you would have had a better chance over dinner in Tallinn than bringing me out here for this cloak-and-dagger set-up."

She looked away, then quickly back. "I suppose you're right about that."

For five seconds, we stared at one another. I was mentally placing bets on what was coming next. She was probably evaluating whether our stalemate was irreversible. I soon got my answer.

"Then I'm afraid this is the end of the line for you, Adam."

The words were barely out of her mouth before Jacqueline Turner fell to the ground, proving herself fatally wrong.

Chapter Twenty-Eight

Long before the first shot felled Jacqueline Turner, I knew I'd stumbled into an ambush. Even before she'd uttered her threat: "*Then I'm afraid this is the end of the line for you, Adam,*" the writing was on the wall.

What I wasn't so sure about was if they'd get her first or me. That was why I hit the ground seconds before she did. I leapt backward, rolling to the floor and indoors away from the once charming courtyard that was now a kill zone.

Other shots quickly followed the one that murdered Turner. Hasty estimation led me to believe there were at least three, if not four, shooters at various spots throughout the building. The shot that ended Turner's life came from above, so I knew at least one of them was on the second floor. He'd have taken aim from the window of an abandoned hotel room that would once have boasted a "courtyard view."

Although I dearly wanted to get back to my car, I knew doing so would be lethal. If the posse had any smarts, they'd anticipate the possibility of my escaping the initial shootout. Especially since they'd obviously planned to assassinate Turner first. Which meant my way in and my car would be well covered by snipers. If they didn't get me in the courtyard, they'd get me trying to leave the same way I'd arrived.

One other thing was working in my favour. Why kill Turner first and not me? Either it was a dumb call or they wanted me alive. They'd set up Turner for one reason only. Obviously, they—whoever *they* were—had learned I'd visited her in Tallinn and what we'd talked about. They knew I'd been on Skawa Island. They knew I'd rescued the shipwreck survivors. It didn't take much to conclude that I was dealing with the same group of killers who'd tried their best to destroy what we found there by blowing up the cabin with Alexandra and me in it.

They wanted the women of Skawa Island and thought they could use Turner to find out where I'd stashed them. They killed her because she'd failed. She was no longer any use to them. They didn't kill me because I still had something they wanted: information.

As I ran through my options for escape, I was relatively secure in the knowledge that I was dealing with a take-down-and-kidnap scenario here. This would likely be followed by some rather unpleasant torture-'til-I-talk activity rather than my immediate death. They needed to take me alive. For the safety of the Skawa survivors—and probably my sister, too—I couldn't allow that to happen.

Although the team of shooters would likely mistakenly expect me to head for the exit and my car, I still had disadvantages. I was badly outnumbered and unfamiliar with the building. The fact that it was pitch-dark didn't bode well for either side.

Taking my chances that there were more of them on the main floor than anywhere else, I made the move a million groaning moviegoers would have warned against. I headed up. On my way, in I'd seen a set of stairs, so I knew where I was going. Stealth was the key. If I could make it to the second floor without a telltale noise, I had slightly better than a chicken's chance in a cook-off kitchen of getting out of this.

The second floor was typical hotel, narrow hallways and rows of doors. I crouched on the landing and swore under my breath. The floors were uncarpeted, either by design or because of the cheapness of the owners. Bare old wood is creaky and hard to sneak on. Immediately, I was proven correct.

A series of scurrying footsteps alerted me to the fact that I wasn't alone.

The original shooter. He was still up here.

With only seconds on my side, I had just enough time to dodge into an alcove that held a gutted icemaker and bashed-in snack dispenser. I pushed back against the wall and held my breath.

The footsteps rushed by, only inches from where I hid.

Then they stopped.

For the moment, I had the upper hand. I knew where he was, and he, at best, only suspected my presence. It would be easy for me to shoot him, but the noise would bring the others. I'd be doomed. The only thing that would save me was remaining undetected. Soon enough, they'd figure out I was still in the building and would come upstairs to look for me, but I was counting on the precious moments between now and then to get out of this.

My brain whirred with possible moves, calculating their probability of success.

I made my decision and stepped out of the alcove.

My movements were lightning quick. And silent. I'd just

come from where my adversary was currently standing, on the landing above the set of stairs that led down, his head cocked listening for telltale activity. I knew the exact distances involved.

I stepped out of the alcove and whipped my arm around the gunman's neck, at the same time clamping my other hand over his mouth and nose. I pulled him back into the murkiness of the alcove. I used the leverage of my greater height to keep his bucking feet off the floor. I was hyper-aware that even the most insignificant but unusual noise would bring his friends running.

Visualizing the death grip of a boa constrictor against an ill-fated rodent, I continued to press hard, feeling my bicep muscles groan with the increasing pressure. In a surprisingly short time, I felt the writhing body grow less and less resistant. I could only hope the sounds of my enemy's death throes were muted enough to keep our position unknown.

Out of the corner of my eye, I saw good news and bad.

As consciousness faltered, the sniper's gun hand had begun to relax, falling to his side. The good news was that our battle was about to end. The bad news was that when it did, the gun would fall to the floor and make a whole lot of clatter. I had no free hand with which to catch it.

Suddenly it was over. The man grew limp. He had lost. The gun began to slide from his grasp. The only thing I could do was position my foot in such a way to break its fall just enough to keep it from landing too loudly.

I was only halfway successful.

The gun slipped out of the man's hand and down my leg. But eventually it had to drop to the floor. The sound was not as dramatic as it might have been, but depending on where the other shooters were, it would get some attention.

If someone downstairs accurately identified the sound as coming from up here, I needed to do whatever I could to throw them off. Quickly. Instead of allowing the weight of the man's sagging, unconscious body to drag him to the floor, I pulled up, then used the momentum of the dead weight to drop the body head first into the empty hull of the ice-making machine.

He fit just right.

I lowered the lid, whipped up the killer's gun from the floor, fitted it into my waistband, and slipped out of the alcove and down the hall.

At the far end was a right turn, another hallway, and another right turn, hotel room doors on both sides. Eventually, I found the matching staircase to the one I'd used earlier. I looked up and down. No one in sight in either direction, but there were definitely sounds of shuffling and whispering from below. That was enough to send me up to the third and final floor.

If Turner's killer had shot her from a room on the second floor, I saw no reason for another shooter to be stationed on the third. They'd only send someone up here once they realized I wasn't on the first floor and was still in the building. There were a lot of places to hide in the hotel. They'd start on the first floor, but when they found their buddy in the icemaker, they'd focus on the second, then the third. So I gave myself at least three to five minutes to figure out how the hell I was going to get myself out of here.

When I reached the third floor—which took longer than I'd wanted because of the potential for a betraying noise with each and every step—I was pleased to see one more set of stairs leading up. The building was three stories high, which meant these steps led to only one place: the roof.

It was only after I'd made the final, achingly slow climb up and opened the door to the outside that I realized how stiflingly hot and humid the old hotel had been. The temperature hadn't really cooled much since the afternoon, but up here there was a soft breeze that felt more refreshing than an ice chip in hell. That's when I made my mistake.

My grip on the heavy rooftop door gave way, slipping from my sweating palm. I grabbed at it but was too late. With a bang that I imagined could be heard down Canal Street, the door slammed shut. I reached for the knob, turned, and pulled. The door opened. It hadn't locked. I poked my head inside and heard the worst.

Footsteps.

A lot of them.

Moving fast.

Up the stairs. Like a horde of ants from the depths of their hill, converging on an unexpected dropped crumb, ready to devour it.

Being that crumb is not a good feeling.

I inspected the door. Rooftop doors lock from the inside, not the outside. They could lock me out here. I could not lock them in.

I shut the door again and scanned the area for something to block their access. There was nothing. I was caught.

A million groaning moviegoers were right.

I raced to the edge of the roof. Looking down three stories, I saw the narrow alley I'd used to reach the side entrance of the building. The alley was narrow because the building next to it was barely a metre away, quite likely against numerous city ordinances and building codes. Unfortunately, the neighbouring building was five stories high compared to the Catores's three. There'd be no hopping rooftop to rooftop for me.

I had only one idea for a way out of this.

And no time to think about how stupid it was.

I shifted my body so that I was now sitting on the edge of the roof, feet dangling over, facing the brick of the opposing building. I swung my feet up and braced them against the other building. Then, curling up at the abdomen, I wedged my body into the metre of space.

I've climbed mountains, rappelled down tall structures, bungee jumped off bridges, but none without harnesses or some type of rope or pulley device to keep me from free-falling to my death, as was the case now. I didn't know if what I was attempting was even possible. But I couldn't allow myself to consider failure. All I could do was move and make up rules as I went.

And so I went.

Slowly at first, as I figured out the combination of movements that netted the best results. Time wasn't on my side. As soon as the shooters figured out where I was, all they had to do was wait for me below. I'd have no choice but to drop right into their hands.

My muscles quickly began to complain from being contorted into positions they'd never trained to be in.

Down.

Down.

Aside from being caught in the act, my greatest risk was losing the perfect position of shoulder and foot brace between the two structures. One slip, one false shift, and my body would plummet onto the bare concrete below. Nothing would break my fall but my own skin and bones.

Down.

Down.

I guessed I was about half the distance when I felt the fabric of my shirt give way where it was being scraped mercilessly against the building's rough surface. Now all that was left was my skin, screaming in burning pain as it took the brunt of the grating movements.

Down.

Down.

I heard voices. Coming from above. They were on the roof. Confused. Yelling at each other.

Then it happened. Facing upward I saw it all. First one head popped over the ledge. Then a second and a third.

The strain of what I was doing was affecting my body in ways I could not foresee. It felt like blood was sloshing around in my head, throwing off my spatial perception and hearing. I couldn't quite make out the words dropping on me from above like verbal bombs. It sounded like they were arguing.

One head pulled back. It quickly returned along with a long arm at the end of which was a big, black gun.

They were going to pick me off. It would be easy, like shooting a fish in a barrel.

More arguing.

I could only judge my current position by the distance I was from the top. Unfortunately, I figured I still had too far to go to chance a drop. With nothing to land on but hard cement, the possibility of dying or breaking something was pretty high.

The voices were getting louder.

They were probably coming to the same conclusion I had. They wanted me alive. They didn't have to shoot me. They just needed to be on the ground below me when I ended my crabwalk down the side of the building.

Suddenly the voices stopped.

The heads were gone.

Oh shit.

They'd left the roof. It was a race. They were running down the three sets of stairs to beat me to the ground.

I had no choice but to speed up.

It seemed impossible. This was simply something you couldn't do fast without risking a fatal move.

I had no choice.

Down. Down. Down. Down. Down.

In my mind, I pictured their progress down the staircase. I'd made the same journey up. I knew how long it would take.

I was running out of time.

They would be bursting out of the side door at any second.

Taking a deep breath, I rolled my head forward toward my knees and pushed my aching body into a ball.

At the same time, I heard the unmistakeable sound of a door opening below me.

I dropped.

Chapter Twenty-Nine

Unable to twist my head far enough to see exactly what was happening beneath me, I'd had to rely on my hearing to make a do-or-die judgment call. I heard the side door of the Catores's building open. Three men were about to come through it. Three men with guns. I had only one chance to get this right.

Mumbling a quick prayer, I relaxed my grip on the opposing walls, crimped myself into a tight ball…and fell.

The soft landing I was looking for appeared at just the right moment.

Gunman One made a loud "oomph" sound as the weight of my sudden appearance on his head sent him to the ground. The only upper hand I could claim in the situation was the benefit of expectation. I knew—hoped—I was about to flatten this guy by landing on top of him. He was expecting to exit the building alongside his two buddies, guns in hand, and wait for me to crabwalk the rest of my way into forced captivity.

Step two in my plan was crucial: Block the door with the momentarily debilitated body of Gunman One before Gunmen Two and Three had a chance to get through it.

Step two didn't work.

I adjusted. As Gunmen Two and Three exited, they

were greeted by the sight of my firearm against the temple of Gunman One.

Dragging my hostage into a standing position, his body shielding me from his friends, I shouted a warning: "One step further, and you'll be wiping his brains off your faces." The secret to a making a good threat is believing it.

This was quite obviously not how they'd thought this would go. The two men glanced at one another; their guns remained level and pointed our way.

The guy in my custody was understandably unhappy with his circumstance. He was struggling, making me un-happy. "Stop it!" I growled in his ear. He probably hadn't taken into account that my bleeding shoulder was screaming in pain and making me very prickly. "This only ends one of two ways. We both live or we both die."

That seemed to settle him down a bit.

Slowly, we inched backward down the alley. The street and my car were less than half a dozen metres away. With every centimetre, I figured my chances for getting out of this alive would soon put me on the right side of the 50/50 mark.

Just before we broached the sidewalk and the welcome illumination of streetlamps, I stopped.

My guy tensed, sensing I was about to make my move. "You're going to regret this," he snarled.

"But not this," I said, clocking him upside the head with the butt of my gun.

He dropped like a sack of beignet flour. As I rushed for my car, left hand searching my pockets for keys, right hand tight on my gun, I could hear scrambling down the alley.

Keys found, I beeped open the lock just as the first wild bullet buzzed by me and hit a street sign. I opened the door, dove inside, and hit start. As I fishtailed out of there, I wondered how I was going to explain the bullet holes to the rental company.

I drove like a madman for several minutes, tripling up on speed limits and making last-minute turns, right then left, and racing down back alleys until I was certain I had no tail. That done, I screeched to a halt on a dark street that looked like a nighttime scene in a ghost town. Most of the houses were abandoned, doors and windows boarded up, lawns overgrown, fences badly in need of repair.

I slammed my fists into the steering wheel and let loose with a long list of my favourite expletives. Some of them I used more than once.

I had to get my brain around what had just happened and why and how all of it was going to propel me forward.

I'd thought Jacqueline Turner was the key to this whole thing. She'd been working with Belar. She knew what happened on Skawa Island ten years ago. She'd probably even been there. But was I wrong? Was she nothing more than a pawn? Then? Now? I should have pushed her more when we met in Tallinn. I should have brought her in. Sicced Maryann Knoble on her. Instead, I had waited until I knew more. Now, Turner was dead and I knew less.

Who sent Knoble the video? Who wanted the Skawa women dead? Why? If it wasn't Turner who was Belar's accomplice, trying to protect herself and hide her role in the heinous acts that occurred on that island, then who the hell was it?

At this point, only one thing was clear. The women of

Skawa Island were in peril. But how could I protect them without knowing from whom?

Checking the time, I hoped my sister would still be at work at the bar. I dialled her cell.

No answer.

I dialled the bar's direct number.

"Dirks," a male voice answered, typical bar noises almost drowning him out.

I pictured the steroid-brained bartender. "I need to speak to Alexandra. This is her brother, and it's an emergency." I hoped he wasn't about to tell me she was out of town. When we first discussed her taking the women to Toronto, I wasn't in a rush to get them away from the farm and into Maryann Knoble's hands. And having just gotten home from our trip to Skawa Island, Alexandra needed a day or two to catch up with things and check in on her business before leaving again. I'd agreed.

"Hold on," he said before clunking the phone receiver down on a hard surface.

"Make it quick," came my sister's no-nonsense voice thirty seconds later. "I've got a bar full of numbnuts to look after."

"Plans have changed."

"What?" She sounded annoyed. "You don't want me to take the women to Toronto?"

"I want them in Toronto, but I'm coming home to get them instead."

"Where are you?"

"New Orleans."

"I don't get it. I can get them from here to Toronto and back again twice before you can do it once. We have flights out first thing tomorrow morning. Why don't we just meet you there?"

I could either order my sister to just damn well do what I wanted her to, or try to explain. Knowing full well the latter would take less time and have a much greater chance at success, I spent the next ten minutes describing the events of my last thirty-six hours.

When I was done, she took about ten seconds to think it through and reach her conclusion: "I know you can be an idiot, but I never took you for being all-out stupid."

I knew what she was thinking, knew she was right, and knew I didn't need her to spell it out for me but she would do so anyway because that's what sisters do.

And so she did: "I get that things have changed. I get that the women are in danger. I get that you want to get them away from Dad's place the sooner the better. But you can't seriously believe that coming here yourself isn't the stupidest move of all.

"They obviously know you have them. But they don't know where. Even if they screwed up and let you escape in New Orleans, don't you think they'll try to follow your ass instead of hunting and pecking until they find the women themselves?"

"Of course."

"Then what the hell, Adam! Just let me do this."

"It's t—"

"And if you say it's too dangerous, I'm gonna come over there and make you eat my knuckle sandwich. It's dangerous. Yeah. That's your life and now it's mine too." She caught herself there, not sure if she'd said something she didn't mean to. She quickly recovered. And then some. "At least until all this shit is over with. At least until we're sure Knoble is holding up her part of the bargain and she's really cured you and not just hopped you up on some crazy drug that'll keep you going until you do all her dirty work for her."

"You think that's what's happening?" I asked quietly.

"Yeah, I do," she blurted out. "Don't you?"

"I think there's a strong possibility."

We let it be quiet for bit.

I hadn't thought about my illness for quite a while. At least not consciously. In real time, the period between my initial diagnosis and today was only weeks, but in some ways, it felt as if I'd been living with this forever. I was tired of thinking about it. Tired of wondering how to get myself out of this ultimate life-or-death dilemma. Tired of rallying against all common sense that told me this was a fight I was always meant to lose.

Alexandra was right about a number of things. I couldn't get back to Saskatoon fast enough to make any difference to how safe the Skawa women were or weren't. I'd given my sister serious responsibility. She'd accepted it. I needed to let her follow through with what really was the best course of action, despite my deep reservations.

"Tell you what," Alexandra broke the silence first, anxious to move on from the subject of my impending death. "I won't let them out of my sight. None of them. Not the women. Not Theo. Not Dad or Anatole. The staff can close up. I'll go home right now, get my things, and spend the night at Dad's house with everyone else. I'm not gonna let anyone hurt any of them, you can believe that. Tomorrow morning, Anatole takes us to the airport. We meet you in Toronto. Done."

It was a sound plan. "Okay."

"Okay?" She sounded surprised.

"Okay."

"Well, okay then."

"One thing."

"Oh frigging hell. Here it comes. What? Do you want me to call you every fifteen minutes? I'm not doing that."

I let that sit in the air for a few seconds. "No. That's not it. When you get to Toronto, I don't want you to take the women to IIA."

"If I don't have to see that warhorse Maryann Knoble, that's fine with me. So where do we go?"

"Have Anatole book a hotel. Downtown. Big. Lots of people around. Tell him to text the details when he has them. When you arrive in Toronto, go straight to your room, lock the door, and stay in until I get there."

"I can do that."

"I'm counting on it."

"Adam?"

"Yeah?"

"I'm not scared."

"You should be."

Saying goodbye to Peri at the airport left Anatole feeling wrung out. They'd both pretended it wasn't a big deal and that they'd see each other again when things returned to normal.

But what was normal for a girl who'd spent the last ten years on a deserted island? Whatever it was, he was betting it wouldn't include him. She had to get back to her old life. Figure out who she was. Find her family. At least with that last part Anatole could be of use. He'd found her grandfather and was still working on locating her father. Maybe that would be the string that would keep them connected. They'd have to keep in contact at least until Anatole had some news for her. Then, who knew where things would go?

Complicating matters at the airport was his mother. He didn't want to come off as some lovesick puppy in front of her. She'd never let him live it down. As it was, she regularly needled him about finding a girlfriend to "make him miserably happy." And to top it off, she was acting all jumpy already. She was accompanying the women on their trip to Toronto despite Anatole's plea to his uncle to be the one to do it. He knew it made more sense for his mom to be the escort. She was the one who had brought them to Saskatoon in the first place. She'd travelled with them before. She knew all of them, whereas Anatole only had eyes for Peri. Although he had gotten a kick out of spending time with the kid. Theo had started off life disadvantaged in many ways, but he was smart. Anatole had no doubt he'd catch up with the real world in record time.

Now they were gone. His mom had it half right. That girl *had* made him miserable. Miserably sad.

Returning to the farm after dropping everyone off at the airport, his grandfather busy in the fields, Anatole had the house to himself. After fixing himself a quick bite to eat, he trudged up the stairs to his room. He stopped halfway. Suddenly, he truly realized what a toll the loss of Peri's company was taking on him. Usually, there was nothing he liked better than to get behind the bank of computer screens in his darkened room and dive head first into the virtual world. It was there that his own personal brand of style and capabilities and skill sets and experiences outshone almost everyone else's. It was there he was king.

But not today.

Today he was dreading it. For the first time, he felt reluctant to step into the dark pit he called an office. What was usually a sanctuary today seemed like an inescapable hole thirsting to suck him in against his will.

Boy, do I need a change.

His eyes moved down the stairs to the kitchen, where he kept a laptop. It was a sunny day. Warm. He could change out of the jeans and black tee-shirt he usually wore into a pair of shorts and…a black tee-shirt, take the laptop outside to the picnic table, maybe help himself to a cool beer…the kind of stuff his uncle Adam was always hounding him to do.

But he had so much research to do. Peri's father. His Aunt Kate. The Skawa Island video. Rex. Julia. Never mind the needs of his own clients. It was all doable, but not by sitting outside with nothing but a single laptop.

His legs took him the rest of the way upstairs. At the door to his bedroom, he hesitated, reached for a light switch and flipped it to the on position, then entered.

Setting his plate of sandwiches and glass of milk on his desk, he muttered to himself: "There are windows in here somewhere."

There were actually four sets of windows in the room, each covered with blackout blinds. One by one, Anatole pulled the cords that rolled up the coverings, revealing lush countryside vistas. He went one further and pushed open one of the windows, allowing a soft breeze to deliver fragrant fresh air into the room.

It looked like a different place. Bigger. Messier.

Plopping himself down in his chair, a spot he privately referred to as the command centre, he regarded his five computer screens, two of them busy working at tasks he'd set them to before leaving for the airport.

He chewed on a sandwich and gave the room another once-over.

He didn't like it one bit.

Is that a bird singing?

Just as he was about to jump up to restore his lair to its original and preferred setting, a ping from one of the computers grabbed his attention. Lowering himself to his seat, he began to read the document one of his searches had delivered. When he was done, he uttered two words: "Hello, Rex."

Chapter Thirty

"Maryann Knoble."

Hearing her voice for the first time made Anatole's young heart beat a thready rhythm. To hear his mother tell it, this was a woman who'd sooner mow you down than push you aside.

"Uh…hello." Inside, he chastised himself for not thinking this through more thoroughly. He'd let his excitement overrule clear thinking. "This is…uh, Adam Saint's guy. You gave me access to your computer systems to—"

"I see. Well, Adam Saint's guy, what have you found?"

"You can call me Starbuck." Anatole loved *Battlestar Galactica*, the original and every reboot. His uncle had warned him about revealing himself to the IIA head, so this was a perfect time to use the alias.

A count of three before: "Well, *Starbuck*, have you found the source of the Skawa video?"

"I haven't, but—"

"Then what is this about? Finding whoever sent that video is top priority. I was led to understand you knew this and would deliver results."

"Yes, I know." Anatole's dark eyes under dark, heavy brows moved to another screen where a long-shot search program was again showing disappointing results. Once again, the source code of the video sent to Knoble's email address was pinging back and forth between countless locations across the globe in an infinite loop. "But I can't find who sent it."

"I'm just hearing about this now?" she huffed. "From you? If you're unable to do this, I'll—"

Anatole returned the favour and cut off Knoble. He didn't care who this woman was. No one derided his computer skills. It was the one thing he knew he was good at. "Uncle Adam told me what you wanted, and I tried. But whoever sent the video knew what they were doing. I could find them. If I had unlimited time over five years and some luck. But I'm guessing that's not gonna work here."

The sweat began to drip down his temples before he was done. Outbursts were not his thing. His clients liked him because not only was he good at what he did, but he always kept his cool, understood frustration, and displayed infinite patience beyond reason. Quite obviously, he told himself, this thing with Peri was adversely affecting him.

"You're correct," came the stiff reply.

He was expecting a dial tone.

Instead, she continued. "So I'm guessing you have another good reason for calling this number."

"I do," he replied tentatively, now not sure if he'd made the right decision in contacting the woman in the first place. But without her, he was at a standstill. He had to plow ahead. "I found Rex."

"One moment," she replied, terse.

The line went silent. IIA wasn't the type of place to use elevator music for their line holds. Anatole imagined Knoble was either closing a door or yodelling an order to an underling to ensure she wasn't disturbed while they continued to talk.

It was a full sixty seconds before the hard voice was back. "Tell me exactly what you found."

"That's why I called. I don't want to use up your time or anything...." Anatole felt bad about his earlier smackdown and was trying to make nice. "But I came to a roadblock in your system. I found out about Rex, and I think I can find Juliet too. But I need more access. I can tell you— or maybe your IT guy?—exactly what I need."

It had been a major frustration. It was like being given free rein in a candy store, told you could have anything you wanted, but when you reach for that final piece of sweetness, the one you really, really wanted, your hand is slapped and you're turned away, and no matter how many times you come back or change how you try to reach for it, the result is always the same.

Anatole knew it was a big deal to be given access to the IIA system. It was understandable that they wanted him in and out as fast as possible. He suspected the impenetrable wall he'd come up against had been an oversight. A portal they'd neglected or forgotten to open to him. Or maybe he simply hadn't gotten to it fast enough and his privileges had been revoked too early. Desperate to make that final foray into the depths of IIA's virtual world where he was quite certain he would find Juliet, he'd dialled the number his uncle gave him. The one he'd been warned to use only in the most exceptional circumstances, a last resort. And now here he was, talking to Maryann Knoble, needing her help.

"For your purposes, *Starbuck*," She made the name sound derisive, "I am the IT guy."

"Okay," he quickly agreed. "Well, if you have the system

up on your screen, I want you to go to—"

"Tell me about Rex first," her voice steady, almost inviting.

Anatole took a deep breath. Typing into his keyboard, he pulled up several documents on two screens and then began talking into his headset. "Do you know about the New Frontiers Program?"

"NASA," she immediately replied. "They sponsor a series of space exploration missions. Scientists from domestic and international organizations submit mission proposals for projects."

"Uh-huh. The very first two projects are already in progress. But it's the third one that's interesting."

"Why is that?"

"First of all, it's got a way better kick-ass name."

Knoble gave no sign of being amused.

Anatole continued. "Projects one and two are called New Horizons and Juno. Project three, set for 2016, is called Origins Spectral Interpretation Resource Identification Security Regolith Explorer."

"Why is this important?"

Anatole puckered his brow. She wasn't getting it. How could she not get it? "Origins Spectral Interpretation Resource Identification Security Regolith Explorer. Also known at Project OSIRIS-REx."

He heard an intake of breath. As it was expelled, out came the word: "Rex."

"Uh-huh." He allowed himself a self-satisfied smile.

"What exactly is the OSIRIS-REx mission?"

Anatole referred to the details onscreen. "To study the carbonaceous asteroid 1999 RQ36 and return to earth with a sample for detailed analysis."

"IIA was behind the project?"

"Not exactly."

"Then give me exactly." The words as sharp as knives.

"IIA is part of a consortium of sponsors behind an unplanned fourth mission. Project OSIRIS-REx II."

"And what *exactly* is the difference between projects one and two?"

"The original REx isn't slated to launch until 2016. By the time it reaches the asteroid, does what it needs to do, and returns to earth, it will be 2023. The cost is expected to be eight hundred million dollars. And that doesn't include the rocket or whatever it is they'll be sending out there, which will probably be another two mil." He waited a count of three, then added: "The second project, REx II, cost almost twice that much."

"What? Why?"

"Because they wanted to launch immediately."

As she digested the information, Anatole imagined he could hear the grey matter gnashing in Maryann Knoble's considerable cerebral cortex. She'd understand that forcing such a massive undertaking into a severely condensed time period would command a skyrocketing price tag. The manpower budget alone would be staggering.

"When did this happen?" Knoble asked.

"Roughly a decade ago." Without exact dates to work with, Anatole couldn't be certain, but he knew OSIRIS-REx II was ordered in the same general time period as the shipwreck off Skawa Island.

In addition to the imagined brain sounds, Anatole could now hear the familiar ticking and clicking that said only one thing. Knoble was furiously tapping away at her computer's keyboard, checking everything Anatole had told her, and maybe more.

"What else?" she asked.

"Well, that's what I've been trying to tell you. The 'what else' part I can't get to. I'm being blocked. I need more access. I've come across vague references to Juliet, but any documents I open have been digitally blacked out. But there are tons of links that I know will tell me the whole story. Who knows? Maybe she was one of the scientists who oversaw REx II. Or maybe Juliet is the code name for another NASA project we don't know about yet. But I can find out. I know I can." Anatole could feel his original excitement building again. This was so cool. So exciting. He needed this more than he needed food. "But I need your help," he told her. "It's why I called."

What came next nearly caused his heart to explode. "You've failed at your task, Mr. Starbuck. I thank you for your efforts, but your services will no longer be required by the International Intelligence Agency. From this moment forward, *all* access is denied." *That's what she was doing on her computer!* "Any attempts by you to enter IIA domains will be met with swift law enforcement and legal action. Do you understand?"

Anatole was speechless. Which mattered little. The line had gone stone-cold dead.

Maryann Knoble's fingers scrambled across the computer keyboard like spiders over webbed prey. The file she was after was the same one she'd quite recently protected from another potential hacker. Adam Saint's personnel file.

She had what she wanted in a matter of seconds, the reflection of the display screen glittering across her shiny trifocal lenses. As she replayed the telltale words, made in haste and error, she scrolled down to the segment of the document she sought and smirked to herself. "I've got you," she said aloud to herself, "Anatole Saint."

Chapter Thirty-One

"Mr. Saint, I need to speak with you immediately."

I turned to find the man who I'd learned had replaced my friend, Geoffrey Krazinski, as head of the Canadian Disaster Recovery Agency. I'd not yet met Shekhar Kapur in person and saw no reason to now. "I'll have to get back to you," I responded brusquely, continuing on my route to Maryann Knoble's office.

"Mr. Saint…."

This guy was obviously intent on catching me: He was following me down the hall.

I stopped and faced him, surprised by the serious look in his eyes. "Mr. Kapur," I said. "My apologies, but I'm rather in a hurry. Perhaps another time."

"No," he insisted. "It must be now. We must talk *now*."

The man was displaying signs of unease and a sense of immediacy I couldn't quite understand. I was no longer a CDRA agent, and we'd had no dealings since he'd arrived to take on the post. I checked my watch. I'd just arrived from New Orleans and come straight here. Texts from Alexandra told me the Skawa women were safely holed up in the Royal York Hotel. I knew the chances of Knoble's spies grasping my tail the second I touched Canadian ground were better than good. She'd be bursting at her

Chanel seams to yell at me and demand to see the women. I thought it best to beat her to the punch.

"What is it?" I asked Kapur. "I don't have a lot of time."

"You have more than you think."

Cryptic words. He had my interest. I moved closer.

"Come to my office, please." He turned to lead the way.

"Mr. Saint! Wait!" another voice called out from across the office.

A young woman on impossibly high heels was running toward us, looking frantic. I didn't know her.

Kapur seemed to. "Jessica, whatever it is will have to wait."

"I'm sorry, Mr. Kapur, but I just got a call from Ms. Knoble. She insists Mr. Saint come up to her office. *Immediately.*"

I followed Kapur's gaze to a crook in the ceiling. It was well disguised, but I knew what he was looking at. Security camera or spy cam, either way it did the same thing. I peered into the thing knowing I was staring into the face of Maryann Knoble.

"I'm sorry, Mr. Kapur," I said as I moved toward the fretting secretary. She was likely not used to being called into action by IIA's most superior officer, and was beginning to look like a songbird about to have a heart attack. "It looks as if this will have to wait, after all."

He knew he'd been trumped. He said nothing as he watched us go.

I followed the girl to the elevator bank. "I can take it from here," I told her. She gave me a grateful smile and moved off. No one wanted to get on the elevator and push the button that took them to Knoble's floor. It rarely turned out to be a pleasant experience.

312 — Anthony Bidulka

Even though Knoble knew damn well I was in the building and on my way to see her, when I reached the unmanned door to her office, it remained resolutely closed and undoubtedly locked. She wanted me to go through the process of ringing the bell and waiting for her to respond. I did.

She was sitting behind her gargantuan desk, Hermès scarf, frizzled helmet of hair, trifocals all in place. Wordlessly, the tilt of her head instructed me to take a seat. I did so.

"You disappoint me, Saint," was her opening.

"Why is that?"

"You haven't upheld your part of our bargain. In exchange for allowing your man access to IIA's digital vault and computer systems, you were to deliver the women of Skawa Island to me."

"I only promised to bring them to Toronto. I've done that."

"They're here? In the city?"

I nodded.

"Where?"

"I'm not quite ready to tell you that yet."

Watching a person get angry is an interesting thing if you can remove yourself from focussing on how the end result will affect you. Maryann Knoble was a hard woman to read. Most times her face revealed nothing but long-suffering disdain and a feeling of superiority over whoever happened to be in her company. Power and confidence oozed from her pores. I would have imagined she'd long ago discarded the emotion of anger as being utterly useless. People responded much better to threats, manipulation, domination, all things she had mastered. So I took some small pleasure in seeing the sides of her nose betray a flare and the beady eyes, already steely, begin to gleam with pinpricks of killing silver.

I let her stew for a few seconds, then: "Let me explain why."

"I would enjoy that," she said, joy nowhere evident in the words.

Knoble sat silent, her face frozen, as I described to her the events which led me to believe that the lives of the three women and the young boy we'd rescued from Skawa were in imminent danger. I told her I had them in a secure location, where they would remain. At least until I had time to interrogate them with the goal of finding out who wanted them dead.

"What makes you think they know who that is?"

"The story they told us was a lie," I responded. "They aren't who they say they are. They weren't the only people on that island. There were others. People they knew. People who were systematically picked off, one by one, kidnapped and tortured, beaten, raped, then murdered and eaten as if they were nothing more than animals.

"These women are acting as if they had no idea what was happening on Skawa Island. I don't believe them. I'm not even convinced there was a shipwreck in the first place. I want to find out who they are, how they got on that island, and why. And most of all, we need to know if they have anything to do with what's happening right now."

Knoble jerked back in her chair. "You think these three women could be behind this? Firebombing the cabin. Sending the video. Threatening their own lives."

"Who initiated first contact? The women. They're the ones who asked the Australians to contact CDRA. Why?

We've only treated them as shipwreck survivors because they told us that's what they were. Suppose something else is actually true." I didn't know if I believed the theories myself, but I needed to put Knoble off balance. I needed her to agree to give me a little more time before I handed over the women. I had no misconceptions about how difficult she, with the full clout of IIA behind her, could make things for me if I tried to go it alone from this point on.

It was a long, cold, hard stare. Then: "You have two hours."

For the third time in the past ten minutes, I felt my iPhone vibrate in my pocket. This seemed like a good time to take a break before I said something I'd regret. I pulled out the phone and checked the messages.

All were from Anatole.

All said the same thing.

"Knoble knows about Rex. What about Julia?"

Maryann Knoble knew she wasn't going to like what came next, so she left it up to Saint to make the move.

He put away his phone, regarded her for an extra long moment, then asked, "You found out what Belar meant, didn't you? About Rex and Juliet?"

Irritated, she responded with: "Why waste my time with the question when you already know the answer?"

"I haven't had time to get details from my guy yet, that's why. Tell me."

Knoble made short work of reporting everything she'd talked about with Anatole Saint. There was no reason not to. It would come from the nephew if not her. As she recited the facts, she used her considerable ability to multitask and studied the man sitting across from her.

She disliked men who were too handsome. Wearing their good looks casually, as if they weren't important, as if they weren't a weapon used against women every day in every way. She knew Saint wouldn't have given a moment's thought to how a man's looks would affect a woman who looked like her. All her life she'd needed to not only excel but dominate any situation she was in, whether it was getting the highest mark on a test, competing for a job, or even something as pedestrian as getting the attention of a barista at a busy coffee bar. If she let her guard down for even a second, the spoils and everything else that went along with that particular battle went to someone else, usually a good-looking man.

For some reason, she could forgive a beautiful woman. The more made up, the more they dressed to kill, the more she understood them. After all, they were fighting the same war, only using different artillery. Of course, none of that mattered now. Or ever again. But still, she couldn't help it. Sitting so close to a man like Adam Saint riled her and sent her temperature rising.

The agent appeared deep in thought as he spoke. "So IIA was part of a group who spent a shitload of cash sending a rocket into space to study an asteroid. What could this possibly have to do with what happened on Skawa Island? Are we barking up the wrong tree here?"

As he said the words, Saint's mind kept on returning to his interview with Scott Bellman. The scientist had told him that Belar had asked him to develop an information portal. He'd wanted data on meteorological, astronomical, and aeronautical activity from every space agency in the world. The question was: Were the two things truly as unrelated as Bellman had claimed?

"Maybe you were right, Maryann," Saint mused. "Maybe Belar's rant was nothing more than that. Just a random thought with no connection to the island."

Like it or not, Knoble was having to admit to herself that for this occasion only, she was in bed with Adam Saint. Hell, she'd pulled back the covers, scooted over, and invited him in. There was no one else to turn to. They were putting a puzzle together. She had pieces. He had pieces. Without each helping the other, the picture would never come together. When it did, they might very well be shocked at what they saw. But this was just like any other of the many horrors that existed in the world. You had to accept it, embrace it, and give it a good chewing up before you could spit it out as nothing more than a gooey mess on the floor. Of course, the way she intended to deal with this might radically differ from Saint's plan. More than likely so. But that was the least of her worries right now. Right now, she had to tell him everything.

"No," Knoble said. "Belar knew exactly what he was saying. Rex save Juliet has *everything* to do with Skawa Island."

"How do you know that?"

"Because of what I didn't allow *your guy* to find."

"Juliet?"

"Yes."

"Why did you shut him out?"

"Because he'd already pointed me in the right direction. Once he told me about Project REx, I knew where to look for the rest. Well…" she corrected herself, "not all the rest.

But the next part of the story. Civilians aren't meant to know everything IIA knows. It's the reason we exist. We protect them. You should be grateful I turned him away when I did."

Saint didn't need to hear more. The threat implicit in the words was clear.

"You know Sergiusz Belar is Polish." She didn't wait for an answer. "In Polish, the word *skala* is pronounced 'skawa.' Without getting into linguistic intricacies, *skala* roughly means 'a big rock or boulder.'"

"Like an asteroid."

"Yes. Belar named his newly purchased uncharted island after the big rock Project REx was created to study."

"So where or how does Juliet figure into this?"

Knoble made a disgruntled sound. "This is where things begin to get more interesting. Shortly after the 9/11 attacks in the U.S., a team of scientists in Finland identified an asteroid with a trajectory putting it on a collision course with earth."

Saint sat up even straighter in his chair. As an agent of an organization that dealt with disasters, he was not unfamiliar with events that would induce shock and awe in most people. This, however, was a new one even for him.

"Best estimates were that the collision would occur anywhere from nine to eleven years in the future. Projections—and they were surprisingly accurate with this, even a decade ago—indicated the impact site would be a town in Tennessee. Mount Juliet."

Saint whispered the words. "Rex save Juliet."

"Yes," Knoble said. "Juliet was the name of the town the asteroid would destroy first. And eventually the code name for the asteroid itself. We know that an asteroid with a diameter anywhere near five hundred kilometres would sterilize the planet. Theory speculates that it was an asteroid only ten kilometres wide that decimated the dinosaurs. Stop me if you're already familiar with any of this."

Saint shook his head.

"NASA tracks any asteroids in earth's vicinity larger than one kilometre. Possible impact from a rock that size would be taken very seriously and require international involvement. Where things get tricky is when we're dealing with something smaller. Take a rock half that size. Something like that hitting earth could cause continental-scale damage…."

"But not global," Saint uttered. "That's the problem."

"Exactly. Efforts to deflect or destroy such an asteroid would cost billions of dollars. But who foots the bill? If it's going to hit your country but not mine, why should I pay? And if the efforts result in a deflection so the asteroid now hits me instead of you, well, that's cause for war."

"How big is Juliet?" Saint asked.

"That," Knoble said, "is what makes this messy."

"Juliet is under a kilometre in diameter," Knoble reported. "About half a mile. Her size was a grey area, so the subject of what to do about her caused a great deal of controversy. At the time, the degree of certainty that she would actually hit earth was only one percent. And if she did, there was even greater uncertainly about the level of damage an asteroid like Juliet, considered on the small size, would cause. And size wasn't the only problem."

"The timing was all bad," Saint correctly guessed. "The OSIRIS-REx project wasn't set to leave for several more years and wouldn't return with its payload for several more after that. They needed that data to figure out what do about Juliet, but it would arrive too late."

"Exactly."

"Enter Project REx II."

"Yes. The decision to immediately send out a mission was made, with support from most of the Disaster Recovery Agencies around the world. It wasn't an easy call. As you can imagine, there were a great many obstacles and opportunities for failure. The chance the mission would get financed and launched, carry out a successful retrieval, and bring back information that would result in a definitive strategy for destroying or deflecting Juliet within the tight time frame before she hit was, well, less than optimal.

"The resources it would take to carry out the mission were, excuse the pun, astronomical. Economic and political environments were less than ideal. The world, particularly the U.S., was still reeling from 9/11. There was an undeniable public exhaustion with disaster scenarios, real and suspected. To publicly announce that an asteroid was rushing toward earth with a one percent chance of hitting us was simply not an option."

"So it was done in secret."

Knoble shrugged. "As many things are."

"How do you know about all of this?"

"As you can imagine, the sheer mass of files related to former chief Belar's tenure with IIA is prodigious. When I first heard about Skawa, I knew nothing but its name and that he'd purchased the island with IIA funds. I couldn't find any other files related to the project. Of course, I had no way to know that I should be searching for Project REx.

320 — Anthony Bidulka

But once your man connected the two, I went back into the archive vaults. I found Project REx, and all the data related to Juliet."

"And Skawa Island? The women? The cabin with IIA equipment? What happened there? How does it all tie together?"

Frustrated streams of air plumed from Knoble's nose. "It doesn't."

"What? So we're back to square one? After all of that? You're telling me REx and Juliet don't connect to Skawa Island at all?"

"They do. I just don't know how. In the files on Project REx and Juliet, it's clear those events led to Belar's ultimate decision to purchase Skawa. What isn't clear is why and what he did with it once he had it. Those files are either missing or never existed in the first place."

"How can that be?"

"I have a couple of theories."

Saint's eyes narrowed. "The asteroid…."

Knoble stingily gave Saint credit. He wasn't just a lump of muscle who bullied his way through bureaucracy to do his job after all. The man was intelligent.

Saint followed through on his train of thought. "If Juliet was supposed to hit earth a dozen years or less after its first discovery…." Saint's eyes bored into Knoble. "Maryann," he said quietly, "is Juliet still coming?"

Chapter Thirty-Two

Suddenly, my medical situation became pitifully insignificant. What did a malignant tumour in my head matter if millions of people or maybe even the entire world were about to be decimated by an asteroid?

"No," Knoble finally responded, waiting just a fraction of a second too long to do so. "Juliet is not about to hit earth. Actually, within eighteen months of her discovery, it became clear she never would, not even close. Project REx was cancelled."

"That's why you think there are no files tying REx and Juliet to Skawa Island? If Belar purchased the island for some reason attached to the asteroid hit, then: no asteroid, no island."

"Perhaps."

I could tell there was something more. On any typical workday, Knoble wasn't a sharing kind of person. Information was on a need-to-know basis, and rarely would she deign to think anyone other than herself needed to know much of anything. She gave orders, not details. But that simply wasn't going to fly here. "You said you had theories. Plural. What else is there?"

After a moment of chewing the inside of her cheek, Knoble relented. "About the same time as Juliet was rendered benign, Sergiusz Belar received his own diagnosis."

Oh shit. "Early-onset Alzheimer's."

She nodded gravely. "Which means dementia."

"Good God, Maryann. If Belar was losing mental facility, who knows what he might have decided to do with Skawa?"

"His symptoms weren't full blown at the time, but, yes, his decision-making process may have been...compromised."

"Then the sooner I get information out of the women, the better." As I stood, anxious to get on with it, I wondered what other leads we might have. "Jacqueline Turner's dead, but what about Scott Bellman and Elliott Bitterman?" Belar's other colleagues.

Knoble rose, agreeing with my thought process. "I'll have someone interview them again. More forcefully this time. As well as anyone else we can come up with who might have had a connection with Belar back then."

"Good," I said, preparing to leave.

"One more thing, Saint."

I stopped and turned.

"Shekhar Kapur."

I knew Knoble'd witnessed Kapur attempting to talk with me when I'd first arrived at IIA. She'd had me whisked away before he could reveal what he so desperately wanted to tell me.

"Kapur was a known associate of Sergiusz Belar."

This added a new wrinkle. Suddenly, I saw Kapur and whatever information—or misinformation—he'd been meaning to share with me in a new light.

"Belar taught Kapur at the Swiss facility. They remained friends," Knoble elaborated. "Belar was the one who put

Kapur on the list to be considered for the job of CDRA chief."

"Why are you telling me this? Do you suspect him of something?"

A granite mask accompanied her revelation. "I suspect everyone of something."

Once again I turned to go.

I only made it as far as the door.

"Don't screw me on this, Saint," came the ugly voice. "You have two hours."

I swivelled on my heel and stared at her. I said nothing. Only waited. The remote control door, locked and solid as stone, would do nothing without her permission.

She waited.

"I will do my best," I told her.

"You'll do better than that. Otherwise, I'd hate to see federal prosecution charges for computer hacking of a Canadian government intelligence agency brought against your nephew. Such a young man, Anatole. To have his life ruined like that would truly be a shame."

In this matter, call me sexist if you must. If Maryann Knoble had been a man, I would have rushed across the room with the speed of a bullet train and buried my fist into her face. And that would only be the introduction to the hell I would visit upon her for threatening a Saint.

Instead, I counted—slowly—to five.

I'd warned Anatole not to reveal himself to Knoble. I'd instructed him how not to. Obviously, he'd made a mistake. He wasn't a trained agent accustomed to keeping secrets. I shouldn't have been surprised.

I heard a click that indicated the door had been un-locked.

I walked through it and left IIA.

While I waited in my suite at the Royal York for Alexandra to bring me the women, I set out provisions. Jujubes, chocolate, and Pinot Grigio. Three things Alexandra told me the women craved and indulged in whenever they had a chance to since returning to the real world. It made sense. On a deserted island, processed sugar in any form is about as scarce as a desert waterfall.

"Come in," I called out in response to the expected knock on the door.

Looking nervous and wary, Destiny and Maybelline stepped into the room, followed by my sister. I hadn't seen the women since we'd rescued them. They'd filled out some but still looked comically inconsequential next to the Amazon-like stature of Alexandra, with her strong, dark features a stark contrast to their wilted haggardness.

"Where's Peri?" I asked as the two women immediately moved toward the table where I'd set out the goodies and began helping themselves.

"She's sick," Maybelline answered before Alexandra had a chance. "She's been in her bedroom all day, throwing up and stuff. I think she ate something bad last night."

I glanced at Alexandra. She shrugged. "I told them to order whatever they wanted from room service."

"She'll be better tomorrow," Maybelline added.

"I guess I have to go back to Destiny's room to look after Theo?" Alexandra asked in a way that told me there was nothing less she wanted to do.

I smiled encouragingly. "You want to take some jujubes with you?"

She scowled. "Thanks, but I think I have it covered." She left.

I joined the women at the table, where they'd taken seats. Destiny had pulled the bowls of candy in front of her, taking one piece at a time, chewing it, then immediately taking another, no resting in between. Maybelline had poured herself a glass of wine, filled to the brim. Obviously, Alexandra had done some shopping for the women. They were each outfitted in only slightly toned-down versions of Alexandra's own wardrobe of tight jeans and tighter tee-shirts, but on the gaunt women, the clothing had a much different effect.

"Is everything else okay?" I began lightly. "You're both feeling all right? Your rooms are okay?"

They both nodded, wide eyes regarding me with suspicion.

"And the farm? Did you enjoy your stay there?"

"Your daddy—he's a sweet guy," Maybelline ventured. *He is?*

"Good, good. I know we've been moving you around a bit. I'm sure you're wondering why and what's happening."

Nothing about their silent responses indicated I was right about that. Destiny chewed. Maybelline sipped.

"Now that you've had some time to rest, get some food, and recover a little from your ordeal, I wanted to go over your stories again."

"Stories? They ain't no stories," Maybelline pointed out. "It's what happened to us. We told you everything already."

"Did you?" I waited a beat, then: "Debbie?" My eyes moved from Maybelline to Destiny. "Arlene?"

The chewing and sipping stopped. Mouths hung open.

"I've just come back from New Orleans." I focussed on Arlene/Destiny. "I saw your parents."

She said nothing and began popping more jujubes into her mouth.

"I had a chat with local law enforcement too. I know both of you were working the streets before this happened to you."

They neither confirmed nor denied. Their silence sounded like confirmation to me.

"Was Peri working in New Orleans with you?"

Maybelline shook her head. As on the island, she was acting as the spokesperson "No. We didn't know Peri before…before all this shit. Don't know where she's from."

"You first met on board the yacht?"

She nodded.

"Who invited you?"

She gave me a perplexed look. "Invited me to what?"

"Invited you on board the yacht."

Her eyes moved to Destiny. Got no help there. She took a long sip of her wine. "This man, I guess."

"A man invited you, both of you, to go sailing on his yacht?"

"Yeah. There's nothing wrong with that, is there?"

"Of course not. Who was this man? What's his name?"

"Don't know his name."

"Destiny? Do you know his name?"

She shook her head.

Back to Maybelline. "So he was a stranger, then? You accepted this invitation from a man you didn't know?"

Maybelline's nose flared. "You knows we was prostitutes," she said, a bit of sass seeping into her voice. "That's who we do all our business with: strange men."

I couldn't argue with that. "Did you board the yacht in New Orleans?"

"That's right."

"Debbie—"

"My name is Maybelline now."

"Maybelline, you said this boat was small, a yacht. Are you telling me you sailed on this yacht down the Mississippi River into the Gulf of Mexico, then ended up all the way in the South Pacific Ocean? Exactly how long did that take?"

No dummy and recognizing a trick—excuse the pun—when she saw one, Maybelline kept her mouth shut tight, her eyes flashing.

"Maybelline? Is that what happened?" I pushed.

"No," she spit out.

The first admission of a lie. This was where the real interrogation would begin.

"It's time you told me what really happened."

Anger and fear burbled up in the ensuing silence, like onions spitting on a hot grill.

This was interesting. Why would the women of Skawa Island ask to be rescued by CDRA if they weren't going to talk to us or tell us the truth when we did? Not to mention these two women were American. Why not ask for USDRA instead?

"It's okay," I assured. "You won't get into any trouble. You can talk to me. I just want to figure this out and help you if I can."

Maybelline twisted her lips, puckering first one side then the other, her jittery gaze flitting around the room until it finally landed on me. She'd been thinking about what to say. I could only hope part of it would be true. "We was flown to someplace in Australia—don't ask me where, I don't remember what it was called—and we got on the boat there."

"Okay. Who got on the boat?"

"What?"

"Who got on? You, Destiny, Peri. Who else? The man who invited you? Anyone else?"

"Yeah, the man." Her eyes zipped to Destiny, then back to her wineglass. "And others."

"How many others?"

"I don't know. I'm not no math teacher."

"About how many? Five? Ten? A hundred?"

"There was quite a few, I suppose. I don't know exactly, so don't ask no more."

"Who were they?"

"Don't know. I just talked with Destiny and Peri. Don't know who else."

"Did you talk to the man?"

She shrugged. "I suppose. Some."

"What did he say? What did he tell you about the trip you were on?"

Eyes pierced into me. If they were arrows, they'd have been poison-tipped. "He wasn't much for talking, on account of we were fucking all the time. You *know* why we was there." She said it like a dare, like if I wanted details about that, she'd happily give me some.

Of course, Maybelline had no idea who she was dealing with. Her tough talk and increasingly hostile attitude weren't going to put me off. Quite the opposite. She didn't know it yet, but Maybelline was about to slip up and say something she didn't want to.

"So this man paid you to come on the boat to have sex with him. Was he also having sex with Destiny? And Peri? And others?"

"I don't know what those other whores was doing. I only know about me."

"Destiny?" I tried again without much hope.

Eyes down, Destiny mumbled, "I guess."

Maybelline was going to be my fount of information. It would be she who led me to the truth. I turned my focus back on her and asked, "How many men were you having sex with on the boat?"

Steam might have issued forth from her ears. Her lips curled as she hissed, "I just told you. With the man. That's it. That's what I was paid for. That's what I did."

"What was his name?" I threw in again, hoping to catch her off guard.

"I don't know!"

She was still lying. I believed she was a prostitute. I had supporting evidence for that. I might even believe she ended up on a ship because she was a prostitute. But everything after that was bullshit.

"Then what happened?"

"When?"

"Tell me about the shipwreck."

"Like I told you before, I don't know much about that. They told us to get off the boat, so we did."

"Who told you?"

"I dunno. I guess the guys who was driving it."

"Was the boat damaged somehow?"

"I guess."

"How do you guess that?"

"It wasn't moving."

"The boat had stopped? Someone told you to get off?"

"Uh-huh."

"How?"

"How what?"

"How did you get off the boat?"

She reached for the bottle of wine, now room temperature, and refilled her glass.

"We got in this littler boat."

"Who did?"

"Me and Destiny and Peri."

"No one else?"

"That's right."

"Why not? If the yacht was in danger, why didn't the man or other people on board or even some of the crew get in the smaller boat with you?"

"I don't know!" she shouted, some of her wine sloshing out of the too-full glass. "The boat was too little, I guess."

"Were other lifeboats launched?"

"Yeah, that's what happened. They all got on those other boats."

"What happened to those people?"

Her shoulders moved to her ears. "Dunno. I guess they didn't make it."

"Was it storming?"

"No."

"Was the water rough?"

"No."

"Was it night?"

"No."

"Then what happened to them?"

She glared at me.

"You didn't see what happened to the other lifeboats? Or to the yacht?"

"That's right. We was kinda busy saving our lives, ass-hole!"

"There's no record of the shipwreck."

The statement sat between us like a weighted anchor. The women exchanged uneasy glances. Destiny was too upset to even eat jujubes anymore.

I let the silence spread.

"Well," Maybelline, unable to bear the uncomfortable quiet a moment longer, whispered in a hoarse voice. "That's none of our fault, now is it?"

Round two.

"You told me that you and Destiny and Peri were the only people to survive the shipwreck. Is that right?"

"Didn't I just say that?" The fight in her was far from worn out.

"The man didn't survive? He didn't make it to the island with you?"

"That's right."

"No one else made it to the island with you?"

"That's right."

I turned my entire body toward Destiny. "Then where did Theo come from?"

Chapter Thirty-Three

The chortle was anything but a happy sound.

"If we have to explain to you where babies come from," Maybelline snorted, "you got bigger problems than trying to get us to answer your dumb-ass questions."

I kept my eye on Destiny. It was her baby we were talking about. If ever she was going to open her mouth for something other than a jujube, now would be the time.

"Did you give birth to Theo on Skawa Island?" I asked her.

She nodded, her eyes fidgeting from me to Maybelline to the bowl of colourful candies.

I sighed. "As Maybelline has already helpfully pointed out, I know you're not math teachers. But if you were on the island for ten years, and Theo is only five, and no one else survived the shipwreck, how did you get pregnant?"

Both women gasped. The jig was up. Unless they were about to claim Immaculate Conception, no lie was going to work here.

Destiny began to cry.

Maybelline reached over and laid a hand on the other woman's shoulder. It was the first sign of tenderness and real friendship I'd witnessed between the two. She too began to tear up.

Part of me felt bad about what I was doing. I hate making anyone cry. My whole career was based on the premise that I was the guy who took tears away, not created them. This wasn't exactly a browbeating, but we weren't doing the two-step either. There was more at stake here than hurting the feelings of two women who had been through something irrefutably traumatic. Not only were their lives currently in danger, but something atrocious had happened in the South Pacific. Someone needed to be held accountable. The skeletons on Skawa Island, whoever they were, deserved justice. Their not-so-carefully constructed web of lies needed to be ripped apart. Now.

I picked up the remote control that sat on the table. I powered up the flat-screen TV positioned not far away in the sitting room. When I was sure I had the attention of the women, I hit "Play."

By the end of the short video that had been sent to Maryann Knoble along with the threatening message that called for her to "*Silence the women of Skawa Island,*" Maybelline and Destiny were inconsolable in their grief.

Understandable.

Except….

There was a marked difference in their reaction from that of myself or even Maryann Knoble. They were equally as horrified by the disturbing images. They were not, however, surprised. And suddenly I knew one more piece of truth. They'd not only seen these images before; they'd lived them.

I gave the women some space. I poured each of them a large glass of water. They'd need the liquid to replenish their tears and soak up the wine and sugar they'd consumed.

After a ten-minute hiatus, I returned to my seat at the table and faced the two women. Solemnly, I asked them to come clean. "How did this happen?"

Maybelline had the good sense to look ashamed. "I mighta lied to you a little bit," she admitted in a tiny voice.

If I'd been my sister right about then, I'd have said something like, "No shit, Sherlock."

"It was those animals!" Destiny spit out the words through jaws clenched so tight they might have been made of steel. "They did this to me."

I was surprised by her outburst. Until now, I'd heard nothing but one- and two-word replies from the diminutive woman. Abruptly, a horrible thought slammed into me. "Was that…was that you on the video?" Could Destiny actually have been the rape victim whose face was obscured in the footage?

"No," she said, her words dripping with bitter acid. "But it may as well have been. What happened to that woman happened to me too. Happened to all of us. That's how I got Theo."

I took a few seconds to think about the varied implications of the words. So many paths to go down. Which to take first?

I began. "Who were the men in the video?"

Destiny shook her head. The words, the memory, the dredging up and confessing to what had happened—all of it had cost her. Once again, her eyes glazed over as she slid back into the safety of silence.

"We never knew," Maybelline said. "At first they was just like us," she added.

What? "How is that?" I asked. "How were they like you?"

"They was on the boat. Just like we was."

"I don't understand. Do you mean they were invited on the yacht as guests?"

She let out an ugly sound, like a grunt. "Was no yacht. Was a big, old, dirty cargo ship. We was crammed on it like buns in a bag."

"Maybelline," I said slowly, "now that we're telling the truth, let's go back to the beginning. You and Destiny were approached by a man in New Orleans?"

"Yeah, that much is right. He knew what we was. And he was offering money. Lots of it. But not for sex. He wanted something else."

"What did he want?"

"Don't know exactly."

She must have seen my budding protest because she stopped me before I could voice it.

"No, it's true. Listen to me. Me and Destiny—we worked the same street at the same time when we could. One night, this man come up to us. Nothing weird about that, right? He asks us if we want to earn a bunch of money. Like, I mean, a bunch. But he tells us it wasn't for sex or nothing like that. He tells us he works for the government and they needs some people for this top-secret experiment. He said we could make all this money, but we couldn't tell anyone about it. And we'd have to be away from home for a long time. Maybe even a year. Said we could only do this thing if nobody would worry about us being gone that long."

"Didn't you think that was suspicious? Never mind risky?"

"Of course we did. What? Do you think we're stupid as

shit? We told the man to fuck on off and leave us the hell alone unless he had cash and wanted a blowjob or something."

No use turning away a bit of business.

"What happened then?"

"He gave us an envelope. Had money in it. Five thousand. Each! He said it was a like goodwill, something like that. He told us to take the money and meet him back on that same corner the next night. If we did, he said we'd earn twenty times that amount doing this experiment thing."

"So you agreed."

"Damn right we agreed. I don't know about you, but I don't make no hundred thousand dollars in cash every day. I was just eighteen years old. Destiny was fourteen. So yeah. We went out and partied hard on that money that night. Came back the next, and there he was. We told him we'd do it. He told us to take care of our *affairs*…." She said the word as if she'd never use the hoity-toity term herself. "And he'd call us when he was ready for us."

"What happened then?"

"It took about a week before he called. We thought he mighta forgot about us. We didn't care. We was having fun with our five grand. Each! But then he called. He told us to meet up at the same street corner with one suitcase and be ready to go. We did it. Hell, as far as we was concerned, this was our ticket outta that stinking life."

"Where did you go?"

"Like I told you before, that part was real. We flew to someplace in Australia. It was a big city. We got put in some cheap hotel. We sat there for days. I guess they was waiting for everybody else to get there."

"Everybody else?"

"Everybody else who got on that boat."

"How many?" I asked.

"I don't know exactly, but there had to be over a hundred in all."

My head was spinning. What was going on here? The only good thing was that this time the story coming out of the woman's mouth sounded authentic.

"Who were these people? Were they all prostitutes?"

She shook her head. "Nah. Actually, there was hardly any women at all. That kinda made us nervous at first. But nothing we could do about it then. So we got on the boat with the rest of them. Mostly they was these dark guys—not dark like me but like an Indian or something like that, except they was wearing these robes and things on their heads and talking some strange language. Even on the ship it was kinda us and them. Mostly because we couldn't understand anything they said. And they was old and gross, and they smelled."

The description was too vague for me to venture more than a guess. The men were likely of some African or Middle Eastern descent, speaking Arabic or French or maybe even Berber.

"So there was a large group of these men. Out of the hundred, how many would you say?"

"Dunno. Maybe twice as many as us."

"Who are the 'us'?"

"The rest of us. Who could talk English. All of us just regular black and white folks, I guess. It's not like we was there to party and get to know one another, y'know."

"What *were* you there for? Why were you on the ship?"

"He told us we was going to some other place in Australia, to a…I dunno, he called it some fancy word…

like maybe a testing facility or something like that. It was where we was going to stay for the year to do the experiment. He didn't tell us what it was yet."

"He? The man you talked about? He was on the ship with all of you?"

She nodded.

"Maybelline, did he ever tell you his name? Or did you ever hear anyone call him by a name?"

"Oh sure."

My heart skipped a little faster. "What was it?"

"Smith. He said his name was Mr. Smith."

Great.

"Okay. You're all on this boat. You head out to sea. What happened then?"

"Well, me and Destiny, we was getting a little freaked out by then. It was all pretty weird. And neither of us had been on a boat in the ocean before. And all these strange men hanging around everywhere. So we pretty much stuck together and kept to ourselves. But then the boat stopped."

"In the ocean? Or did it arrive in a port of some kind?"

"In the ocean. All we could see was this little bit of land. Didn't look like much of anything."

"Skawa Island?"

"Turned out to be, yeah."

"Everyone was sent to the island?"

"Not really sent. We was told something bad had happened. Like really bad. In the world. They said it was some kind of disaster thing and we had to get off the boat right away. We thought it was a hurricane or something like that. They told us to get into this little boat and get to the island. They didn't call it a lifeboat, though. Something else."

"A tender?"

"Yeah, that's it."

"There was just one?"

"Uh-huh. So they had to make lots of trips to get us all on the island. Destiny and me was on the second trip. Eventually there was only one trip left. It was supposed to bring Mr. Smith and the captain and the crew people. We waited, but it never showed up. It musta gotten caught up in whatever horrible thing—" Suddenly she stopped. The look on her face was as if someone had slapped her. Hard.

"Maybelline, what is it? Is something wrong?"

"You know what? I *am* a stupid bitch. If you thought I was stupid, you was right."

"I don't," I told her.

"Well, you should. You know, even after all this, the rescue and being back in America and all, I only just now, just this very second, realized there *was* no horrible thing that happened like they said. It was all a trick."

Oh.

"Right? I mean, we couldn't see the ship from the beach we was on. It was behind this sticky-out part of the island. But we all thought that whatever big, horrible thing that was supposed to happen musta happened. We thought that big ship and the tender thing just got all swallowed up or something. We thought we was shipwrecked and no one would ever come looking for us. It was so weird, you know. Because we was all happy we was still alive, but we was scared, too. All we could do was figure out how to live on this island."

And suddenly, I too was struck dumb with a shocking thought.

Maybe that was the point.

Chapter Thirty-Four

"Was Peri with you through all of this?" I asked.

Maybelline pushed aside her glass of water and emptied the rest of the Pinot Grigio into her glass. It had to be warm by now, but she didn't seem to care. Destiny was nearly motionless, sitting on her hands, still looking at the blank screen where we'd just witnessed the unspeakable carnage that occurred on Skawa Island.

"Nah. We didn't really know her then. She was so young, maybe only twelve or thirteen?" She looked at Destiny for corroboration but quickly discarded the glance. She knew there'd be no help for her there. "And she was always hanging around with this other young kid, a boy. Never knew his name. And then after we got to the island, they was the first two to disappear. Actually, nows I think about it, they was gone long before the Indian guys started taking us."

"Algerian."

We both looked at Destiny. It was the first word she'd said in a while.

"What's that, girl?" Maybelline asked her friend.

"Someone said they were Algerian. Those men. Not Indian. Algerian."

"Okay," Maybelline huffed, a bit put out to be corrected on such a small point. "Algerian, then."

"I need you to go back," I said. "Take me through this one step at a time. We can go as slow as you need to. Start with when you first ended up on the island. You realized the last boat wasn't coming; what did you do then?"

"Well, like I says, we thought the whole world was probably destroyed and that we'd be stuck there forever. So we started to figure out how to live. You know, food, water, someplace to sleep, the kind of stuff like they do on that *Survivor* TV show. Except it seemed none of us was real good at it. Far as I could tell, all of us was city folk. A lot of us was used to living rough, but not on some deserted island in the middle of nowhere. But real quick it was obvious that the *Algerian* guys did not want to live with us. Before we knew it, they was gone."

"Gone where? Did they try to leave the island?"

"Dunno. I suppose at first they may have tried. But there was nowhere to go. Just a bunch of deep water out there. No, I think they just took off for another part of the island. The rest of us, we just stayed pretty close to where we landed."

"How many of you were left after the Algerians disappeared?"

"Dunno. Thirty, maybe forty. Too many really. We was having a real hard time finding enough food and water. There was some stuff brought over on the tender, but that got used up real quick. And no one was taking control. At least not in a good way. We was like a henhouse with no rooster. You know what I'm saying?"

I was quite certain people like my sister and ex-wife would not appreciate the simile, but I nodded my understanding. "What happened to Peri?"

"Like I says, she was hanging around with her little boyfriend, always sneaking off together into the woods. You can guess what they was doing. Then one day they just didn't come back. Before we knew it, days went by. We figured they died out there or got eaten by a tiger or something."

There were no tigers on Skawa Island, or any other predatory animals for that matter. But at that point in their experience and knowledge, I suppose anything would have seemed possible.

"So when did she come back? How did the three of you end up together?"

She made a whistling sound through her lips. "Ooh boy, a whole hell of a lot happened before we ever saw Peri Winkle again." What she said next came as a surprise. "It was probably a year or two before we saw her face. And let me tell you, was we ever glad. That little Peri? She saved our lives."

"Some of the men started calling it the wars," Maybelline continued with her tale of their early days on Skawa Island. "It started after we was there for about a year. We hadn't seen or heard from the Indian…or Algerians…whatever they was…in all that time. We thought they either got off the island somehow or just ended up dying.

"Our group was having a really hard time. We had water but hardly any food. There just wasn't enough stuff on the island or in the ocean for all of us to eat. And not enough of us who knew how to get it. Some of us got sick right away and died. When the wars started, there was maybe only twenty-five or thirty of us left."

Outside the windows of the suite atop the Royal York

Hotel, the bustling world of urban Toronto with its sky-scrapers filled with corporate headquarters and busy, important people buzzing about at hectic paces hadn't skipped a beat. Yet, that world, so close, seemed so remote, so foreign compared to what Maybelline Johnson, once known as Debbie Kilmer, was describing. I was far from unfamiliar with the stark and sometimes brutal contrasts that exist in the modern world, but never had I found myself anything but awed and saddened by them.

"What exactly do you mean by the wars?" I asked.

Once again, Destiny broke her silence with eerie words. "When they started to come for us."

Maybelline nodded. "At first, we didn't know it was them. We thought, kind of like what happened to Peri and the boy, that people just got stupid, wandered off, and either got lost or ended up dead in the jungle somehow."

"But that's not what was happening?"

I'd thought all their tears had been used up, but that was far from the case. Maybelline pressed down on the puffed, up area below her eyes in a failed attempt to stanch the flow. She reached out to Destiny, who pulled a hand from under her thigh, and they held onto each other like that for a moment, fingers intertwined and squeezing tight.

"It took us a while, you know," Maybelline said between harsh, moist intakes of breath, "before we knew what they was doing to us. What they was using us for. It started real slow. A few people would disappear and then nobody for sometimes months. But then some others would suddenly be gone. Always men. But then one of the women too. And then, well, you know."

She stopped there. Like a clock run out of ticking. I

gave her a minute, then urged her on. "I know this is difficult, Maybelline…."

"You saw it!" she screeched, using her free hand to point at the TV screen. "You saw what they was doing! Those men, those Algerians, they was starving too. But they had one thing going for them. There was more of them than us. So they started picking us off. Stealing us away from our camp and taking us to theirs. They was hungry. So they ate the men. They was men. So they raped the women."

Oh God.

Having been on the island and seen the clues, having watched the video, my brain had come to understand what had been happening on that godforsaken island. But to hear a first-person account, to hear the mental and emotional agony, was nearly overwhelming. The stronger camp, driven to the unthinkable by a killing hunger, utter desperation, and certain mental breakdown, treated the inhabitants of the weaker camp as livestock and sex slaves.

It was a while before any of us could continue. We had been talking so long that Alexandra texted to see if there was a problem. Theo was asking for his mother. But I couldn't end this here. I couldn't let the women go. Although it seemed we were on a treacherous, depraved, spiralling road straight to hell, I knew we hadn't gone quite far enough yet.

The sky was beginning to dim outside when I re-started the questioning. We'd moved to the sitting room, where the soft couches did little to comfort us.

"Was Peri the first? Instead of dying in the jungle with her boyfriend like you thought, were the two of them the first to be taken prisoner?" As I asked the question, I thought the possibility amazing if true. When I'd first set eyes on the women of Skawa Island, Peri was the one who appeared the healthiest and the least victimized by the ravages of the last decade.

Maybelline shook her head. "No. Neither of them was in the other camp." She shot Destiny a sad look. "And we wouldn't know about that, anyways. Destiny and me, we was almost the last ones left."

"How do you mean?"

"Long, long time passed. Probably a couple years or so in all. Eventually, all our men was gone. Taken. We knew our days was numbered, and there was nothing we could do about it. We couldn't protect ourselves. We could barely feed ourselves and keep clean. So when they finally came for us, we just went. We didn't try to fight or nothing. It was no use. I think—" She choked on the next words. "I think we kinda wished it would be over already. We just wanted to die."

I understood. The pure hell of living through years of watching every one of your companions be stolen away and never returned would break anyone's spirit.

I said, "To go through what you went through and still survive, it's an amazing feat. Maybelline, Destiny, you need to be very proud of yourselves. You are stronger than you think."

Maybelline tipped her head and quietly said, "Thank you." She took a short breath. Now she needed to get the story out, and I couldn't have stopped her if I tried. "The day they came for us…all our men were gone, Destiny and me was the only ones left. Only two of them came for us.

They knew we wouldn't give them a fight. They marched us to their camp. What we saw there was…." She stopped there and buried her hands in her face.

Destiny's hand moved to Maybelline's shuddering back. She rubbed it in slow-moving circles, a movement which, I guessed, had been repeated many times over their long, lonely years together.

"It's okay," I said. "I saw it. I saw the camp." Visions of the makeshift prison, the bones of the dead, the kettle polish in the cook pots, all of it flashed through my mind, and I willed the images to stop. "You don't have to tell me that part."

She looked up, eyes red, relieved. "What surprised me… surprised us…was that there was only four of them left. Four of these men. But they was still bigger than us. Stronger than us. We still couldn't understand a word they said. They seemed to have enough food to survive. So they just used us. You wanted to know where Theo came from? That's where."

My eyes met Destiny's, and I nodded my sympathy. She nodded back.

"That's when Peri came back," Maybelline continued.

"Came back? From where?"

"Can't say really. You'll have to ask her that. Alls we know is that she came back like some kind of superhero woman. She told us later she couldn't do anything sooner because she was just one scrawny woman against all those big men. But with only four left, and them using us like they was every day, she decided she had to try to take them on. She came in, real quiet-like, and killed them. One by bloody one. She didn't get us to help her or nothin'. When it was over, she just gathered us up and took us away. To her camp. The same place you found us. We never went back to that place. Never ever. We just wanted to forget it and live our lives.

"Nine months later, Theo was born. Thank goodness there was no problems with that. Peri looked after it. Younger than me and all, but she did it. She did it all. She saved our lives. We owe everything to that girl." She took a deep breath. "And then lots of years later, that boat shows up and wants to rescue us. That's it. That's what happened. That's your story."

Maybelline might have thought so, but I certainly didn't. For here was the crux of the matter. I repositioned myself so we were eye to eye. "And yet," I said slowly, "you didn't want to be rescued by the people on that boat."

Quick as a whip's lash, we were back to the old Maybelline, the one with the bad attitude and sour look on her face. "Yeah, so what?"

I moved even closer. "Why, Maybelline, did you ask for CDRA?"

Her answer was about to change everything.

Chapter Thirty-Five

The Canadian Disaster Recovery Agency is not—in theory—a clandestine organization. They do not operate undercover or in top secret. And still, the typical Canadian on the street is not familiar with the agency's mandate and would barely be aware of its existence. Not unlike a good insurance policy whose premiums slip out of your account each month almost without notice, it's only on the worst day of a person's life—when disaster hits close to home and they're in desperate need of assistance—that most people come to be aware of CDRA. The organization is a public service paid for in much the same way as any other government activity: by the people it serves to protect, via income tax. So having a prostitute from the streets of New Orleans be familiar with CDRA and request—no, demand—its services after being abandoned on a deserted island for ten years seemed...unlikely.

I knew what Maybelline was going to say before the words came out of her mouth. She wasn't the ringleader here. She was only the spokesperson for the women of Skawa Island, and reluctantly so.

It was Peri.

Peri had told Maybelline and Destiny to lie to us. Peri had come up with the story about them being the only survivors of an imagined shipwrecked yacht. They agreed because she'd been their saviour, the one who'd had the strength and tenacity and plain old pluck to keep them alive all these years. She was the one who hunted and fished and kept the fires burning. She was the one who not only helped Destiny give birth but also helped raise the boy when his own mother was too weak, too sickly, too…unwilling?...to do it herself.

Peri had come from out of nowhere. After being gone for years, she swooped in and killed their oppressors, the murderers, the cannibals, the rapists who'd imprisoned them. Then she took them under her wing and coaxed them to live—if not to flourish, then at least survive. By the time the Australian day trippers arrived, the other two women would have done anything for her. I didn't blame them.

But what they didn't know, couldn't know, didn't care to know probably, was that Peri had a secret. One that taught her the skills to do all she did. One that allowed her to know the name of the island they were on. One that informed her of why they were really stranded there. One that demanded their rescue come at the hands of CDRA and no one else.

Peri had an agenda.

I just had no idea what it could be.

Alexandra had knocked on Peri's hotel room door a couple of times over the hours while I was questioning Maybelline and Destiny. There was no answer. Alexandra's priority was to look after a five-year-old boy, and not wanting to leave him alone longer than a minute or two, she'd relented, thinking Peri was sleeping off her illness.

As a precaution, I'd instructed Alexandra to ask for two sets of keys for each room when they checked into the hotel and to keep one set for herself. Even as I opened her door, I knew I was too late. Peri had planned well. She'd even bothered to make it look as if someone was sleeping in the bed should anyone look in on her. But the misshapen lump I found under the bedcovers was nothing more than a collection of bath towels.

"Holy hell," Alexandra announced. "Where would she go?"

I was already busy searching the room, for one item in particular. Peri had been the only one to bring something with her when leaving the island. A briefcase she'd told us contained keepsakes. I was betting those "keepsakes" would go a long way to helping us understand what was going on here.

"Why would she run away from us?" Alexandra asked, half-confused, half-pissed off that the young woman had given her the slip. "She knows there's someone out there who wants her dead, so why risk it? Doesn't the stupid bitch know we're the best thing she's got going for her? Jeez! I could just wring her scrawny little neck!"

Alexandra didn't have the benefit of knowing everything I now did after my interview with Maybelline and Destiny. There was no time to fill her in. I needed to find Peri immediately. I had many more questions than my sister did.

Was the girl running away from whoever it was who wanted her dead?

Or was she just running away?

At the top of my list was a new question: Had Peri somehow been responsible for what happened on Skawa Island?

As I tipped over the last few cushions and searched drawers for the briefcase, I called Anatole.

"Yeah?"

"Anatole, do you still have access to the IIA computer?"

I heard something that sounded like it might be a snigger. "I doubt it. But let me check. Why?"

I ignored the question and waited for my answer.

"Nope. Shut out with a slam. Want me to try getting in...my way?"

"No time. I want you to email Peri's picture to Maryann Knoble. I'll call her and tell her to expect it and what to do with it. Do it now."

"Peri? Why?"

"Peri's gone. We need to find her. I can't explain it all right now, but I think she may have ties to CDRA, or a woman named Jacqueline Turner. It's our only lead right now. Send the picture."

"Wait! I think I know where she might have gone!"

"What? Where? What are you talking about?"

"I know I shouldn't have been wasting my time with it, but she asked me for a favour. She was all alone and out of touch with her family for so long. I didn't see the harm...."

"Anatole, I don't need to know the explanation right now. I need to know where she is. What do you know?"

He stuttered a bit, and I immediately felt bad for being harsh with him. His mother's glare icing up my skin didn't help much either.

"She knew I could do stuff on the Internet. She wanted my help in finding her family, her dad and her grandfather. I found the grandfather. He lives near Toronto. I bet that's where she went. To see him."

"I want you to text me the address and whatever else you think I need to know to get to her. I don't know how much of a head start she has on us, but she couldn't have gotten far. She doesn't know the city or have any money."

"Uhhhhhh, that's not exactly true."

This wasn't going to be good news.

"Where her grandpa lives is kinda hard to get to, and she can't drive. So I didn't really know how to get her there except with a cab. I gave her money."

"Text me the information now," I ordered through clenched teeth.

"Texting, boss!"

I heard the ding that told me I had a message. "Hold on." I checked the display.

Holy hell. The name of Peri's grandfather: Sergiusz Belar.

"Anatole!" I yelled into the phone. "Peri's father! What was his name?"

"I never found where—"

"What was his name?!"

Peri Winkle's real name was Amanda Knotts. She was thirteen when "Mr. Smith," convinced her to come with him. She was a homeless kid living on the streets in Vancouver. Sergiusz Belar was not Peri/Amanda's grandfather. He was just one of the two men whom she blamed for everything she and the other women went through on the island.

Anatole told me he'd set Peri up with money and directions for how to get to Aspen Downs, where Sergiusz Belar was living out the rest of his delusional days. My heart sank when I heard it was a ninety-minute drive away. I had no idea if Peri was five minutes ahead of me or five hours. If she got there first, I had no idea what her plans were. I had to assume the worst. My only choice was to involve local law enforcement.

I was too late.

By the time the cops arrived at the peaceful campus of the long-term care facility, Peri had already finagled her way into Belar's room. She'd posed as a long-lost granddaughter come to see her grandfather before he died. It would seem the high price tag paid by residents didn't come with stellar security measures. Then again, why would a place like Aspen Downs need to protect itself?

When the responding police officers burst into Belar's room, they found the man still fast asleep. Peri was sitting next to his bed, head in hands, weeping, quietly chanting: *I am strong. I am strong. I am a killer.*

They'd found a knife in her possession. But she couldn't go through with…well, whatever it was she'd thought she needed to do.

I arrived half an hour later. With the aid of a bellowing Maryann Knoble on the phone, the police agreed to allow me to take Peri into custody, and we headed back for Toronto. After all, I argued, she'd committed no crime other than impersonating a granddaughter. Not exactly accurate, but I left the officers with a suggestion to flip through the pages of Canada's criminal code and call me if they determined this was an indictable infraction they were interested in pursuing. I doubted we'd ever hear from them.

A starless night made for a road home that resembled a tunnel through a tar pit, the perfect sort of cocoon in which Peri felt comfortable telling her story.

Her voyage began much like Maybelline and Destiny's. She met "Mr. Smith." He gave her cash. He promised a great deal more in return for her involvement in some mysterious government experiment. To take part and get the big payout, she had to disappear from her life without causing suspicion. That was easy for Peri. From all she could tell, her parents hadn't tried very hard to look for her in the eighteen months since she first ran away. No reason to suspect they'd start now. There'd be no milk cartons emblazoned with her face to worry about.

When she first boarded the ship in Australia, she was scared. She knew no one. Most of the other people were older than she was, or men, or foreigners she couldn't understand. Some of the others were runaways too, some just plain old homeless people. A lot were prostitutes, male and female. Too late, she wished she'd taken the first five grand and run.

But then she met Darren. He was a few years older than she. He was cool and fun and made her laugh. Around him, she could be her usual confident, kick-ass self. Like her, he was a runaway. The man had found him in Toronto. Although Darren didn't say it in so many words, Peri was pretty sure he'd been selling himself just to stay alive. She got it. She didn't want to talk about it, but she got it.

Peri corroborated Maybelline's version of what happened next. Once they were stranded on the island, thinking the world was ending, Peri and Darren pursued a romantic relationship. This wasn't easy to do in an environment where the main focus was survival. What was easy was sneaking off for romantic interludes. No one really cared. No one was looking after them or out for them. If they weren't there at dinnertime, the most common sentiment probably wasn't worry or concern but selfish glee that there would be two fewer mouths to feed. This wasn't *Lost*.

Being young and adventurous as well as in the throes of puppy love, with each excursion, Peri and Darren ventured farther and farther away from the main camp. Part of them thought they might even solve the mystery of what happened to the dozens of Algerian men who'd simply disappeared. But it was something else that set their course on a tragic path.

Peri's eyes flickered opened.

Footsteps. Someone else was out there.

Careful not to move too fast or make a noise that might startle Darren, she nudged him with her shoulder. They were nestled together on the jungle floor, nearly asleep after a strenuous session of lovemaking. Darren moaned, a dreamy look on his face.

"Shhh," Peri warned. "Wake up."

"What is it?" he asked, suddenly alert, turning on his side to face her.

"Be quiet. I think I hear somebody."

She could tell he heard it too because his eyes suddenly grew wide and his arm fell across her in a protective gesture. The footfalls were growing louder, whoever it was coming closer.

Even though they were deep in the jungle and far from their own camp, they'd chosen a spot in a shaded gully encircled by bush, where only the most observant passerby might spot them.

Putting a finger to his mouth, then pulling away, Darren snaked his way up to the berm of the gully for a better vantage point. Peri was not far behind.

When they saw who it was, their mouths fell open in shock. Peri barely swallowed an exclamation. Darren silently mouthed the words: "Fuuuuuck me."

It was a ghost.

It was the man.

It was Mr. Smith.

But he'd gone down with the ship…hadn't he?

Tons of time had passed since they'd been stranded on the nameless island. In all that time, no one had reported seeing anyone other than the original group who'd come over on the tender. No captain. No crew. No Mr. Smith.

Yet there he was. Sneaking through the underbrush.

As soon as Darren felt Mr. Smith had moved far enough away that he dared speak, he had only two words: "Holy. Shit."

"Let's go." Peri pulled herself up to her knees, gathering clothing, bobbing her head this way and that to see if she could still catch sight of the disappearing man.

"Go? Where?"

"After him. Don't you want to know where he's going? What he's doing here? Where he's been all this time?"

Dumbfounded, Darren mumbled, "I guess."

As usual, his opinion wasn't particularly required to inform Peri's actions. The young girl was up, dressed, and after Mr. Smith in no time.

Having practice in being furtive, Peri and Darren easily followed the man, who seemed oblivious to their presence. Before long, he slowed his pace and eventually came to a stop in a nondescript section of the jungle Peri and Darren had passed often but had had no reason to investigate. Even if they had, it was doubtful they would have discovered the superbly camouflaged building. And then, just like a magician on stage, they watched in awe as Smith disappeared, leaving behind what seemed to be nothing but a thick draping of vines and leaves.

"Fuuuuck me."

"You can say that again," Peri readily agreed.

It wasn't until many days later, on their fourth visit back to the spot where they'd first witnessed Mr. Smith disappear, that Peri and Darren got lucky. A short while after settling into their by now familiar hidden roost several metres away from the concealed entrance, they watched as Smith left the cabin. They couldn't know how long he'd be gone, so they had to move swiftly. As soon as the man was out of sight, they stormed the wall of vines and located the unlocked door leading into the structure.

"What is this place?" Darren breathlessly wondered as he pushed it open.

"Let's look around," Peri suggested, pushing Darren inside, eager eyes already busy prowling the interior.

Darren looked doubtful. "Five minutes. Then we're out of here."

Vibrating with a mix of fear and excitement, hand in hand, the two began moving about the room. What they found was at first confusing to them. There was power here. Lights. Air conditioning. Food. Bottled water. How could this be?

But nothing was as shocking as what came next.

"He's got TV?" Peri exclaimed as she studied a wall of screens, each flashing different images. "We're starving out there and he's watching TV!"

"Wait, Peri. Look." Darren was staring at the screens, his face flickering dark and light with the reflection. "This isn't TV."

"What do you mean?"

"This isn't TV," he repeated, his voice darker and insistent. "This…this is real life. Our life!"

Peri studied the images more closely, questioning eyes moving slowly from one monitor to the next. Darren was right. These weren't TVs broadcasting a fictional show or news program. Hidden somewhere in the jungle were cameras, lots of cameras, transmitting their recordings back to this cabin.

"Oh my God, there's Twila…and the guy with the limp…and…oh my God, Darren, that's our camp! He's taping us! He's watching us!"

Their mouths fell open as they watched their fellow shipwreck survivors go about their usual daily routines: wandering, chatting, napping, digging for roots, searching for berries, going to the bathroom. Half of the screens were dedicated to their own camp.

"What the hell is going on?" Darren muttered, wanting to look away but unable to.

"Look!" Peri was pointing at one of the screens showing a location unfamiliar to them. "Those are some of the Algerian guys."

Darren studied the image of three men, talking, obviously entirely unaware they were being videotaped. "Yeah, you're right. Man, they look bad. They were skinny before, but look at those guys; they're like skeletons."

"Oh shit!" Peri cried out, stepping closer to one of the screens. "Darren, look at this one. I thought this guy was sleeping, but I think he's dead!"

Darren wrapped an arm around Peri and gently pulled her away from the bank of screens. "Come on. We don't need to look at this anymore. Let's just get out of here."

"Wait, wait," Peri resisted, pulling away. "We have to keep looking around, figure out what all this stuff is."

They saw computers and sophisticated recording, data storage, and communication devices but didn't know what they were. Surfaces were covered with reams of paper overflowing with data and complicated statistical analysis they'd never understand. They saw clothing and personal items that told them someone was living there. And then they saw Mr. Smith. Standing in the doorway, a disturbed look on his face and gun in his hand.

Chapter Thirty-Six

A single shot. That's all it took.

Darren collapsed, barely making a sound as he hit the floor.

He was dead.

It was over that fast.

Peri stared at her young lover, then up at the man who'd just murdered him, then back. The bullet had hit the dead centre of his forehead.

She was too shocked to react. She didn't cry. She didn't scream. She barely kept herself breathing.

Mr. Smith very slowly moved closer to the girl, eyeing her warily, judging whether or not he needed to fire a second time.

"Why?" was all she managed to utter.

"I can't tell you," he answered.

Peri stared at the man. He looked different from when he'd first come up to her that night on the street in east van. different from on the ship. His hair was a mess, and he looked as if he hadn't shaved in days. His fingernails were long, and his eyes looked bloodshot and bleary. There was something wrong with him. not drugs or alcohol. She knew what that looked like. This was something else.

"Why not?" she asked, instinctually knowing the longer she kept this guy talking the longer she stayed alive. The next moments would tell everything. life or death. one of them had ultimate control. The only thing Peri knew for sure was that the decision was going to be made very soon.

"I told you when i first met you. This is a top-secret government experiment."

"Still? I thought all of that was over when the ship sank—or whatever bad thing happened."

"No," he said with a grizzled grin. "That was part of it." He made an all-encompassing gesture. "This *is* the experiment."

She thought about that for a minute. "You mean you fooled us?"

"Nobody fooled anybody. i needed a year, you gave me a year. So did everyone else. Bought and paid for. What I do with you, what i do with that year, is up to me, up to the Canadian government."

"Canada is doing this?" incredulous.

"And me," he crowed. "Me and Canada."

Her eyes moved downward again to the dead body only inches away. Her throat tightened. She didn't know if she wanted to gag or howl in sorrow. Finally a tear. She saw it land on the floor and disappear. She looked up. "But why kill darren? He didn't do anything to you. or Canada."

Smith's eyes hardened. "What about 'top secret' don't you understand? This experiment doesn't work if the subjects know about it. You have to believe that you've been deserted on an island while the rest of the world has been destroyed. You have to learn to survive with nothing and no one to help you." He glanced at the TV monitors. "And frankly, everybody's doing a piss-poor job of it."

Peri held her tongue. She wanted to tell him how much easier it would be if they had power and frozen TV dinners in the fridge like he did. Instead, she stood her ground and glared at him. She would be the one in control, she decided.

She wanted to live.

"I can't go back," she said.

The man shook his head.

Pointedly, she looked at the gun. "You have to kill me too, I guess," she said. "Or…." She let it hang. Her only hope was if he filled in the blank with what he wanted. Whatever it was, she'd provide. Her life depended on it.

"Or what?" he asked.

I win. "Or I could stay here with you." She'd had little practice, but she'd heard how other girls, the prossies on the street, would change their voice whenever a possible John appeared. They made it higher, more girlie. She did it now. "I could take care of you. If you want." She hated how she sounded. She hated the words themselves. She hated this man. When she first set eyes on him all that time ago, she'd thought him handsome, in a devilish way. now he was just repugnant. Most of all, she hated how she was being forced to offer this pig what until now she'd only shared with the man lying dead next to her. now it would become nothing more than a bargaining chip. She also felt the sting of guilt. For the not very nice thoughts she'd had about the girls on the street who did what she was about to do. She'd been too stupid and naïve to understand that maybe they hadn't had a choice either.

As far as Peri was concerned, there were two facts of the matter. darren was dead. She would do whatever Smith wanted her to do to stay alive. Someday, this despicable man would pay for both.

In the weeks and months that followed, Peri saw herself as having become two things. First, a prisoner. Although the man shared his food and water as well as his bed with her, he never let her out of his sight. except for the rare occasions when he left the cabin. When he did, he used plastic zip ties to fasten her to the bed, where she stayed until he returned.

Second, she was a witness. never being allowed to be anywhere he wasn't, Peri saw everything Smith saw. As such, when he was monitoring the events playing out on the TV screens, so was she. She was witness to the goings-on at both camps, the one she used to belong to and the one where the Algerian men were living their lives. She was also witness to the devolving and disintegrating mental state of Mr. Smith as he lived this solitary (except for her) life and carried out his bizarre "experiment."

The worst came as the disgusting, unimaginable images passing before them forced him to admit that things were going horribly, irreversibly, devastatingly wrong. The "Algerian" camp was slowly but surely ravaging and decimating the "American" camp.

In the first months, realizing the island simply could not provide them with enough food to survive, the Algerians forced themselves to eat their own dead, and even then, only those who'd died of natural—in these circumstances—causes. But eventually, driven by indescribable hunger, the men returned to the other camp. For days, they watched their former shipmates, learning their routines and habits, gathering courage, fighting doubt. And when the time was right, they captured three men. no one in the American camp was aware that an annihilating war had just begun.

It was a desperate measure. They kept the men in a cage they'd fashioned from jungle wood and vines. Immediately, they killed one of the men and ate him. Their minds were repulsed, but their bellies were sated and cried out for more.

Weeks passed before they killed again and consumed the second man and eventually the third.

At first, the Algerians attempted to string out the abductions and killings and cannibalism as long as they possibly could. They weren't animals. They weren't crazed beasts. They were simply trying to survive. But hunger screams loud. The more they ate, the more they wanted. Capturing groups of two or three men soon became four or five. Instead of lasting a month or more, feedings would take place in half the time.

Peri could not watch it. on the first occasion, she pleaded with Smith to do something. She reasoned that if he was truly in control of this experiment, he could stop it. Smith would never hit her, but his rage at her insolence left mental bruises all the same.

Eventually, though, even Smith began to see the situation had grown unacceptable.

The final straw was broken when the Algerians took the first woman.

On one screen, Smith watched as four men took their turns forcing the already pitiable and frightfully thin woman to have sex with them. If Peri hadn't shielded her eyes, she'd have recognized her as Twila, the woman with the margarita who'd stopped to talk to her and darren on the day they abandoned the ship. on another screen, a group of men was preparing a meal by cutting the flesh from their latest victim.

Suddenly, Smith, crying out something indecipherable, jumped up from his chair, sending it crashing to the floor, and dashed out of the cabin into the jungle night.

It took Peri a minute to realize that for the first time she was alone and unshackled. She was free to run away, something she'd been good at ever since she was a child.

But instead of running away, without giving it a second thought, Peri ran with a better purpose. Without bothering to take anything with her, she too ran out the door, and followed Mr. Smith.

Smith rushed through the blackened jungle with reckless abandon. Unlike the first time she'd seen him sneaking about with practiced stealth, this time he ran without a care for the noise he created or if someone was behind him.

And there was.

For many minutes, the procession of two threaded its way through the humid wilderness, ignoring the nighttime sounds of animals and insects as they went about their own business, oblivious to the drama unfolding in their home.

They ran and ran and ran.

Sweat blurred Peri's vision, her breathing grew jagged, her legs ached from muscles rarely used.

Smith didn't stop until he was smack dab in the centre of the Algerian camp. Peri remained hidden behind a nearby clump of bush from where she could see and hear everything.

The unexpected arrival of the man they'd not seen since the ship had left them on this island caused a major and immediate uproar. Those who weren't sleeping began to yell for the others to waken.

Smith launched into his own tirade. He was imploring the Algerians to stop what they were doing. To use only what the island provided—as was intended—for sustenance. To immediately cease the killing and raping and cannibalism in the name of whatever god they worshipped or family member they loved.

In any other circumstance, it would have been a bravura performance, a stirring plea, but the men understood none of it. on the ship, the man had communicated with them through an interpreter, one of their own. But that man was long gone, one of the island's first victims.

When she thought about it later, Peri decided that the only reason the Algerian men did not immediately attack and kill and eat Smith (wouldn't that have been a lovely sight?) was because they recognized him, even in his current condition, which was only slightly less degraded and deranged than their own. They probably wondered if he was there to rescue them.

But soon that hope faded. The Algerians were becoming angry at the incessant yelling and senseless gesticulating of the crazy man. even Peri, a good distance from the action, could sense the turn. She bit her lip, knowing what was coming next. The Algerians would attack.

Smith sensed it too. His eyes took on a whole different gleam altogether. Instead of being enraged at what his "subjects" were doing, he became frightened for his life. The recklessness of what he'd done in the heat of the moment dawned on him like a stunning blow. He was going to die.

Smith ran.

Peri ran after him.

The Algerians took time to collect weapons and wake their remaining comrades, and then they too took to the dark forest.

At first, Peri was surprised by the route. Instead of rushing back to the safety of the cabin, Smith was heading in an entirely different direction. But then, it made sense. If he led the Algerians to the cabin, it would never be safe again. They would find a way in and do what they wanted with him. And her. no, Smith was trying to lead them away from his secret command post, hoping to lose them. only then would he return, his secret place intact.

Glad of the moments to rest while Smith unsuccessfully made his case to the cannibals, Peri was refreshed and easily able to keep up with Smith. Somewhere behind her she could hear the rustling sounds and pounding feet of several men who were in close pursuit. She needed to be especially careful. If—when—they caught up with Smith and killed him, she didn't want to be caught in the same net.

After several minutes, it was apparent to Peri, less so to the Algerians who were little by little falling behind, that Smith knew exactly where he was going. each step he took was assured, made with a confidence that told her the path he chose was one of his own design. Where was he going?

Without warning, Peri tripped over an exposed root and tumbled to the ground, costing her valuable seconds. Frantically pulling herself up and shaking the pain from where she'd struck her head, she chastised herself. Another misstep like that one would be her last. She'd lose Smith and be overtaken by the killing horde behind her.

She scanned the area. Instantly, she knew where Smith

was headed.

The water.

He was now many metres ahead of her, but by the light of a bright silver moon, she could easily see Smith flying across a field of sand. He was taking a big risk. The trees and branches and swinging vines of the jungle had slowed his progress but had also kept him hidden. He could cover more ground much faster on the beach, but now he was entirely visible. When the Algerians made it this far, which by the sounds coming up behind her Peri judged to be only a matter of seconds, they would know exactly where he was.

She had only a split second to decide. If she followed Smith, she too would be revealed and would become a secondary target for the pursuers. If she stayed put and hid, she'd lose him. There really was no good choice. Although she'd have preferred to kill him herself or watch the Algerians do it, her priority was the same as it was on the very first day she met Smith and made a deal with the devil: survival.

She hid. And waited. And watched.

He'd crossed the beach and reached the shoreline. She watched as Smith dived into a copse of reeds near the water's edge. At first, she thought he was using it as a hiding place. They'd find him for sure, she believed.

But then she saw his head bobbing up and down.

What the hell?

What she saw next almost made her cry out loud. Inside her head, she silently screamed, "Nooooooooooooooooo! Stooooooooooooop!"

Chapter Thirty-Seven

She should have known he'd have a way off the island. The Canadian government wouldn't send anyone to do an experiment like this without giving them some time off. It's not like *he* was the guinea pig, unwittingly forced to try to survive on this hellish island. There was probably another island nearby, a populated island, where he could replenish food and water supplies, have a bit of human contact. She could see now that the boat was located at the perfect spot, far enough away from both camps so the chance of anyone hearing the sound of his comings and goings was low.

Of course there'd be a way off.

If only she'd had the chance to find it herself.

As Peri crouched in her hiding spot, watching Smith's boat glide effortlessly into the safety of deep waters and the Algerians storm the beach like a battalion of warring skeletons, her mind rotted with bitterness and anger.

He was leaving her here to be eaten.

The Algerians rallied on the beach for quite a while, uselessly screaming after the departing vessel. Some of them even rushed after it, but were quickly overcome by the depth of the water. Peri waited. Finally, the men settled down. eventually, they began to disperse, leaving the beach for the long trek back to their camp. She used the time to debate her next move. When she was sure the Algerians were gone, she pulled herself out of her hiding spot and headed for home: the hidden cabin.

It was selfish, she knew. But she could find no good reason to go back to the American camp. She'd be a member of the losing side in a war that could not be won. To go back was to commit suicide. She would be taken by the remaining Algerians. They would first use her as a sex slave. Months of torture later, when they were done with her, they would kill her and then eat her. She'd seen it happen. over and over again.

She'd be safe in the cabin. There was no chance Smith would come back. It was one thing to watch nameless "test subjects" being tortured in the worst ways possible, and another to think it might actually happen to you. no, Smith, the coward, would not be returning. ever. The cabin, and everything in it, was now hers. The first thing she did on her return was clean the bedding. She wanted the smell of the man gone. Then she inventoried her supplies. She'd have to make them last as long as possible. But she knew that eventually she would have to learn how to hunt and fish and forage for herself. She knew nothing about such things. But she would learn.

The equipment was a problem. If she knew little about surviving in the wilderness, she knew even less about computers. Living on the streets was not conducive to being techsavvy. She didn't even know how to turn off the screens that even in Smith's absence continued their round-the-clock, unblinking reporting of the travesty transpiring at both camps.

At first, the relentless images came near to driving her mad. Then she decided it wasn't such a bad idea to know what was going on out there. She covered the screens with blankets and old shirts, but every so often she would watch. If things continued on the same course as they were now, some day the tide would turn. She would be the strong one, and the Algerians would be weak. It was a lesson she'd learned on the street. What goes around comes around. Maybe one day she would do to them what they'd done to the Americans.

The Americans.

Them.

With wry awareness, Peri realized she'd been gone so long she'd begun to feel it. Separate. Them versus me. She was no longer a part of the American group. It was wrong. They were her people. They needed her help.

But first, she had to learn how to help herself.

And so, little Peri Winkle went about her business of building a life inside the concealed cabin, hoping that one day she would be able to do something, something heroic, before it was too late and all the Americans were dead and gone.

For weeks, Peri taught herself to forage for roots and berries and other weird things to eat, careful never to stray too far from the cabin or for too long. She couldn't bring herself to be away long enough or far enough from her safe place to figure out how to fish. Instead, she ate bugs and slugs to fill up that achingly empty spot in her stomach that roared with demands for some kind of protein. only when she was desperate did she defrost or rehydrate one of the goodies Smith had stored in the cabin.

During the same time, Peri forced herself to spend at least a couple of hours each day experimenting with the equipment. She knew that something in this room had to have been used for communication with the outside world. If only she could reach someone, they could all be saved. But day after frustrating, mind-numbing day, she met with nothing but spirit-crushing failure. She wouldn't give up trying, but a little voice inside her head told her this would never work.

One thing she could do was read. And there was no shortage of material to consume in this cabin. She spent hours going over every single document, many of them far beyond her comprehension. Still, she made herself read each word and think about what it might mean. Just as with the computers, in this pursuit she repeatedly found herself wallowing in the shadowy depths of frustration, often to the point of tears. But every so often, she uncovered a piece of information she thought one day might be useful. This was how she learned the island's name. Skawa. She was glad to know it. If this was to be her home for the rest of her life, it needed a name.

She also found out the true identity of Mr. Smith. And that he'd been sent here by someone named Sergiusz Belar and an organization called the Canadian disaster Recovery Agency. There were printouts of emails between the two men. Most dated back to the days right after Peri and the others had been abandoned here. And then, suddenly, there were no more. Although it was sometimes difficult to follow the thread of their conversations, Peri could tell that Belar was in full support of the experiment. At first. Then something changed. The tone of their communications became terse. Then almost threatening. Then they stopped altogether. Search as she might, Peri could find no further communication between Belar and "Smith." All she knew was that they were responsible for everything that had happened and was continuing to happen on Skawa island. She had the proof, on paper, which she carefully stored in a leather briefcase that never left her sight.

First, one of the TV screens went blank. Then a second. Then more. Until she was down to only three. Two at the Algerian camp and one at the American camp.

She didn't need the American camp feed. The picture was always blank.

There was no one left.

The Algerians had taken everybody. Including all the women.

By her count, there were only four Algerian men left. They were keeping two women prisoner in the cage. luckily—sort of—for the women, these remaining men seemed to prefer using them for sex over food. With so few mouths to feed, they were able to subsist on what they could scrounge from the jungle. And one of the men returned regularly with fish he'd caught somewhere off-camera.

The idea developed slowly. But as it formed, Peri grew more and more committed to it.

Now was the time.

If she was smart about it, she could take the men out. It was a risk—four men against one little girl. But she had the benefit of having eaten more and lived in relative luxury.

She was certainly stronger than one man. But four? Yet, seeing the despair that oozed from the faces of the two remaining women, Peri knew she couldn't wait much longer. They certainly couldn't. She had to save them.

Other than the gun Smith must have taken with him, the cabin had no weapons, but she did have forks and dinner knives and other sharp and potentially dangerous objects. Armed with determination and a plot two days in the strategizing, Peri set in motion her rescue mission.

She began with the fisherman. As far as she could tell, he was the only one who regularly left the camp on his own. He'd be gone, without suspicion, for hours at a time. He was her first kill. She snuck up behind him as he searched a rotted stump for bait. With a swift swoop, she sliced open his neck with a deep cut. She was surprised at how utterly silent and untrumpeted the moment was. His death, although bloodier, reminded her of darren's. one minute he was alive and breathing, the next minute he was gone forever. Not even some sort of essence left behind.

Matching the furtiveness she'd seen from Smith, Peri snuck back to the Algerian camp. She posted herself in a spot where she could easily keep an eye on the firepit area. She waited until one of the men moved into the woods by himself. She knew what he was doing. As he defecated, she ended his life.

Now things would get serious fast. The fisherman wouldn't be missed for hours, but the man she had just killed would be.

It was now or never.

She chanted to herself: *I am strong. I am strong. I am a killer.*

Running into the camp, she made as much noise as her throat was capable of without exploding. It had been a very long time since she'd had the freedom to yell. It felt good. She felt blood coursing through her veins and lightning sparks ignite her skin.

"I am strong! I am strong!" she screamed.

The two remaining men were momentarily shocked into inactivity. They barely managed to stand up on thin, wobbly legs before Peri was upon them.

She thrust a knife into the first man.

In horror, she realized that not only was the cut nowhere near deep enough to kill the Algerian, she also couldn't seem to pull the blade out of him to try again.

Still, he was stunned and bleeding and confused. She pushed him hard, and he stumbled away just as the other man came at her from behind.

Peri swung around wildly, pulling a fork from her pocket and swinging it up into the man's groin.

She met her mark this time. The man shrieked with pain and tried to back away to deal with his injury. But Peri knew she couldn't allow it. She pulled another two dinner knives from the same pocket. Holding them up in front of herself so they were horizontal and pointing inward, about a metre apart, she rushed toward the man. He looked up in fear, and for a moment, Peri was taken aback. She cried out with sincere sorrow over what she was about to do. Had to do.

With every bit of strength in her shaking arms she rammed the knives against each other, like two racing cars crashing head on, the only thing in their way the man's head.

Leaving the knives in place as the man's eyes rolled up and he fell dead away, Peri swivelled about to ward off the sole remaining Algerian who'd likely recovered sufficiently to wage another attack.

But she was wrong.

He wasn't prepared to attack her.

He was on the ground. Cowering at the sight of her.

Retrieving the last piece of cutlery from her pocket, a steak knife, Peri approached the man. Standing above him, the first knife still protruding from his wasted, concave chest, moving up and down in rhythm with his staccato breath, she wavered.

The look on the man's face was a mask of mixed emotions, revealing to Peri everything he was feeling at that moment, the moment of his death. Fear. Guilt. Shame. Sorrow.

His lips began to move. Words she had no hope of ever understanding came burbling out between rasping gasps for air.

Was he begging for his life?

Was he begging for forgiveness for what he'd done?

Somewhere, deep in her young, inexperienced heart and mind, Peri knew she wasn't looking at an inherently evil man. He wasn't a devil. He wasn't even a killer. or a cannibal. He'd been forced into committing horrible deeds. More than likely, he'd have once considered himself incapable of all of them.

A noise, little more than a whimper.

It wasn't the man.

Peri's eyes followed the sound to the right.

The cage.

Behind the crude bars huddled two figures. They were barely recognizable as women, never mind as people she might have once seen on the ship or on the island before

Smith had captured her and darren. She would save them. Nothing would stop her. And when she did, she would take them to the new camp she'd built. not the cabin in the woods. That would remain her secret.

She sensed the motion rather than saw it.

Her attention swung back to the man.

Not unlike the trembling moment between life and death she'd faced so long ago when Smith had killed darren, the Algerian man was making his own bid for life, his dirty, trembling hands held out to her in supplication.

This was different. They couldn't both survive. It was her or him. He knew it. She did too. out here, in the wilderness, it was the natural order of things.

Peri buried the knife in the man's chest and whispered, "I am a killer."

Chapter Thirty-Eight

Canberra is known as the bush capital. To keep rival cities Sydney and Melbourne from duking it out like two bratty teenagers who both want to be captain of the team, the inland site was chosen in 1908 to be Australia's capital city. And like the district of Columbia in the U.S., Canberra was planned to be a city outside of any state. Its design was heavily influenced by the popular ideal of the time where all areas of a city should be balanced between residence, industry, and agriculture. especially agriculture. Which is why Canberra is nearly overrun by green space and bush. Which is what Addison Graham-Taylor was gazing at through the panoramic windows of his plush office when the call came in. Bush. Bush. Fucking bush. He hated it. The swank of Sydney or hipster vibe of Melbourne would have been more to his liking, but as a politician who played the power game, this is where he needed to be.

"I'm sorry, Mr. Graham-Taylor," the receptionist's voice drawled into his headset. "I know you didn't want to be disturbed, but the caller insists. It's Maryann Knoble, with the international intelligence Agency. She told me to tell you it's about the video."

Despite being in his mid-sixties, Graham-Taylor prided himself on looking decades younger. He maintained a strenuous physical fitness regime from which he rarely deviated, and regularly accepted "treatments" to combat aging. But with the sound of the unexpected words, he felt the skin at his neck begin to sag.

He accepted the call.

"Addison, it's Maryann," came the distinctive, decidedly masculine voice. one he hadn't heard in many years. They knew each other, of course. They'd attended the same conferences and meetings back in the days when he was an agent with CDRA and she was clawing her way up the ladder of IIA U.K.

In those days, when he was a much younger man, everyone knew Addison Graham-Taylor. He was famous in the world of intelligence organizations and aid agencies. It all began when he was working for USDRA. He'd been dispatched to the dense, nearly inaccessible rainforest near the Tumuk Humak Mountains of the Brazilian frontier. An American team of scientists had been waylaid there, believed overcome by an outbreak of an unidentified tropical disease. Graham-Taylor led the dangerous expedition team.

They found and safely extracted the Americans, including the daughter of a powerful U.S. congressman and a B-list TV actress. Graham-Taylor was lauded a hero, and his exploits were well publicized—and of course slightly exaggerated. A heavily fictionalized HBO movie based on the true events further propelled his fame and personal fortunes. But all too soon, his five minutes were up and he was forgotten.

"One moment, please," he said in a calm voice, putting the call on hold before she could say anything more. He punched in the number code that would disable the recording and tracking systems that automatically went live with any call that came into his office. He knew Knoble would already have done the same at her end.

He reconnected. "Maryann, what a pleasure to hear your voice. Are you here in Canberra?"

"Addison, I have neither the time, the skill, nor the patience for chit-chat and social niceties. And neither do you. Let's not beat around the bush. I know you sent the Skawa video. don't bother to ask how I know."

Of course, that was the primary question on the tip of his tongue, although he had a sinking feeling he knew the answer: Jacqueline Turner. They'd been lovers, although the "love" part had existed entirely on her side of the relationship. She was the one who'd first introduced him to Sergiusz Belar. An introduction which had led to the two men working together on Belar's top-secret project. Turner knew little about Skawa and even less about the role Graham-Taylor had played on the island. But she'd known enough. enough to have landed Knoble's suspicions directly on him.

Turner had contacted him immediately after Saint visited her in Tallinn. The foolish woman thought her loyalty to him might rekindle their relationship. He'd played along only because he needed her. She'd been the perfect lure in new orleans. once her usefulness expired, so had she, but obviously not soon enough. Had the bitch been playing him all along?

What could he say? He sat back in his chair and filled his eyes with more of that damned bush, and went with: "Well, then."

"What the hell were you up to on that goddamned island?" Maryann hissed.

"It wasn't just me, Maryann. I'm not the one who came up with it. You have your predecessor, Sergiusz Belar, to thank for that."

"A man with Alzheimer's," she pointed out with disdain. "That's who you're passing the buck to?"

"There was no Alzheimer's at the beginning," Graham-Taylor shot back. "It wasn't until the island was purchased and the experiment well underway that he first heard the news…that I knew about anyway. By then it was too late."

"Too late? Too late to stop women from being raped and men from eating one another?"

Graham-Taylor swallowed a sour bit of bile. "That happened much later. And of course that was never the intent. Never. It was a horrible, entirely unanticipated result of the experiment parameters."

"You keep talking about an experiment. What exactly was going on out there?"

"It was about Juliet. The aster—"

"Yes, yes, I know about Juliet. The asteroid that might have hit earth and never did."

"I don't appreciate your being so flip about the matter, Maryann. It's easy for you to play Monday morning quarterback, but at the time, Juliet was a very serious and credible threat to the American continent, to the world. Belar was a social scientist. His first and most abiding love was learning about people, why they did what they did, and, in this case, what they would do in circumstances they could never even begin to imagine."

"That's what Skawa was for? To carry out a social science experiment to see how people would react to world devastation?"

"Yes. He knew this was cutting-edge work. He knew there'd be dissenters and critics from every direction. So he wisely chose to pursue the experiment in hiding. exactly in the same way governments all over the world were hiding the existence of Juliet from their own people."

"What did he need you for?"

"Belar was a scientist. A thinker, not a doer. That's where I came in. I made everything possible for Belar," Graham-Taylor boasted. "The timing was perfect. I had access to—how shall I describe them?—suitable test subjects."

"Come again?"

"I was a DRA agent responding to a flood in Algeria. Over three hundred people were killed, mostly in the district of Bab el oued. Three and a half million people in the city, mostly the poorest of the poor. You offer them two hundred thousand dinar in exchange for a year of their lives, and they think they've gone to heaven."

"The women weren't Algerian."

"I recruited seventy-three participants from Algeria. Belar wanted more. Fortunately, the United States and Canada have a growing problem with homelessness. Shameful but, in this case, useful.

"Imagine, Maryann, if we'd been successful and Juliet hit. our findings would have become the model for how people would react, survive, and eventually thrive and re-populate the globe. We would have been heroes. Some of history's greatest scientists were derided in their time, but their work turned out to be—"

"Can it," Knoble barked. "You agreed to this because your star was on the decline. You left USDRA and joined

CDRA to see if you could make a big splash in a smaller pond. I know your story. You two idiots made a colossal mistake."

Graham-Taylor said nothing. Knoble needn't know it was he who insisted on continuing the experiment even after Juliet was determined to be non-threatening. Belar strongly disagreed. He'd implored him to call it off. But by then it was too late. He was atop a throne on Skawa island, his subjects in place. Graham-Taylor now knew he'd fallen into a delirium of sorts, drunk on playing God. And Belar had grown too ill, unable to exert enough influence to make him stop.

"Don't deny it," Knoble railed on. "I know Sergiusz Belar. If he'd been in his right mind, he'd never have allowed this to go so far. Face it, Addison, you're an accomplice to murder and crimes against humanity, with a mentally incompetent man as your partner."

For a moment, Graham-Taylor was struck dumb. no one talked to him that way. And if they did, they lived to regret it.

And she wasn't done yet.

"When everything fell apart, you ran off to Australia with your tail between your legs." She hesitated only long enough for a short pull of smoke from her cigar. "I have to give you credit. I looked you up. once again, you recreated yourself. This time as an entrepreneur. You built from scratch one of Australia's largest corporate and personal security firms, on the back of your artificially enhanced reputation as a disaster recovery agent."

"Nothing wrong with that," Graham-Taylor decreed, his voice low.

"Then you parlayed that success along with the political and star-fuck currency you saved up from your early days into a heavy-hitter career as chief whip."

"Yes. That's so."

"I'm not regurgitating all this for your listening pleasure, Addison. You can masturbate to your accomplishments on your own time," Knoble's sharp tongue continued to slash. "I only tell you this so you're aware that I know why you sent the video. I know what you're trying to protect. If your role on Skawa island ever got out, you'd be destroyed. not to mention wearing orange prison overalls for the rest of your days. do I make myself clear?"

A brief pause, then: "Crystal."

"So now we get to the good part. What the hell are we going to do about this?"

Graham-Taylor jumped at the offer to stem the barrage of threats and insults. "You have as much to lose as I do, Maryann."

"Do I? I don't think so." She puffed again on the Arturo Fuente opus X A. "But I will admit there are significant losses to be mitigated."

Graham-Taylor had had enough. His voice turned antagonistic. "Not to mention the hellfire I will bring down upon you if you ever dare pursue this."

Knoble chuckled. "Pursue this? Why would I ever pursue this? I just wanted you to be aware of my disdain for you and to know that I believe you to be an utterly detestable human being." Another puff. "That being said, I don't entirely disagree with your solution—bungled as it's been."

Once again, Graham-Taylor was stunned. This woman, this bulldog of IIA as she was known, truly was a piece of work. He disliked not knowing what someone might do next, but with Maryann Knoble, uncertainty was the only given.

After a moment of consideration, Graham-Taylor doled out careful words: "Our problem has expanded since I sent the video. It's no longer just the women of Skawa who need to be silenced."

"You're talking about Saint." Knoble already knew the problem he had in mind.

"And the woman he was with on the island."

"His sister."

"Yes."

"I assume your men came to Toronto after they missed Saint in new orleans?"

Graham-Taylor grunted. She knew about that too. "Yes. It was the only move until we caught his scent again."

Knoble's next words were spoken with cool precision. "Then let's make a deal. They've been separated, so we'll split the work. I'll take Saint and the one woman. Your men take the sister and the other two. I'll tell you where they are. We do it now."

With reluctant admiration for the bulldog of IIA, a smile any shark would be proud of formed on Graham-Taylor's lips.

Peri had fallen into a restless sleep. We were on a lonely bit of road. dark. Quiet. I was glad to have the time to consider everything she'd told me about her time on Skawa island.

Every so often, my eyes left the road and fell upon the delicate face of the young woman in the seat next to me. In the forgiving gentleness of diffused moonlight, I could

386 — Anthony Bidulka

see how she might have looked as a thirteen-year-old girl, getting on that ship, looking for adventure, finding first love, dreaming of a better life. Instead, she'd ended up in hell, surrounded by death and depravity.

But Peri Winkle, Amanda Knotts, whoever she ended up being, was a fighter. A survivor.

A killer.

With whatever time and influence I had left, I would fight for Peri. And destiny. And Maybelline. The women of Skawa island. And young Theo, who'd had the misfortune of growing up there.

Peri had been at war. In war, you kill people. That was what she had done on Skawa island. even her actions tonight, seeking out Sergiusz Belar, were part of the same battle. not only should her actions not be criminalized, I believed, but she and the others needed to be compensated for the wrongdoings of the Canadian government via the IIA. They would need help to get their lives back. or at least the best version of lives they'd be capable of after all they'd been through.

With good reason, Peri's sleep was fitful. She was twisting and turning in her seat, trying to find a comfortable position when the lights first appeared. It was as if someone had flipped a switch. Glaring white beacons up ahead on the road grew larger and brighter as we sped closer.

"What's that?" Peri croaked, peering out through the windshield, shielding her weary eyes with her right hand. "Is it an accident?"

Suddenly I knew.

My brain blared a warning: This was no accident.

Alexandra's eyes grew wide when the hotel suite door burst open with the speed and force of a tornado. She was behind the kitchen counter and only had a second to count four men before she dropped down out of the line of fire.

"Where are they?" the lead mercenary demanded to know as he inched into the room behind a powerful rifle.

Alexandra did what she thought best in the circumstance. If they were here to kill her, she really wanted these guys to know exactly what she thought of them.

"Fuck off and die, assholes!" she screamed.

Chapter Thirty-Nine

The man in the SWAT uniform who'd pulled Alexandra down behind the kitchen counter gave her a peculiar look as he radioed the order for his team of IIA agents to converge upon the room.

Alexandra heard a quick volley of harsh shouts followed by a single pop and the sound of a body slumping to the floor.

Someone was down. She hoped it was one of the bad guys.

The skirmish was short-lived. After more ominous commands from the IIA team leader who made it clear they were not afraid to put down every single one of Graham-Taylor's men, it was over. Alexandra kept on trying to jump up to see what was happening, but the freakishly strong bodyguard assigned to her continued to weigh her down. He kept her in a motionless state much longer than she felt was truly necessary.

When she was finally allowed to stand, there was nothing left to see. no mercenaries. no heavily armed IIA agents. not even any overturned furniture or crimson splatters of blood. This had been much less exciting than the daring escapade she'd been promised by Maryann Knoble's head guy, who'd impassively explained her role as bait. All she'd really had to do was look surprised when the assailants burst into the room. Frigging lame. little Miss Muffet could have pulled it off. At least she'd managed a few well-placed insults.

"Where are Adam and Peri?" she asked the bodyguard. "Are they back yet?"

"Agent Saint and Subject one were detained on the highway. To ensure they didn't inadvertently interrupt the operation."

Alexandra grinned. "So I was involved in the takedown of the bad guys and he wasn't? That's really gonna piss him off. Can I tell him?"

Until now, the face of the bodyguard appeared to have been permanently set at stern, but Alexandra detected the flicker of a smile.

"You'll have to discuss that with Maryann Knoble," he told her.

Alexandra scoffed and headed for the mini-bar. "No thanks. The less I have to do with that tank, the better. You want a drink?"

"If everything is all right, I'll be leaving now to rejoin my team."

Alexandra ignored the fact that the man was anxious to get on with his job. He probably hadn't enjoyed his babysitting assignment any more than she had. Too bad. "Where did you put Maybelline and destiny and Theo?"

"They've been moved to a secure IIA facility."

"Great. So I gotta entertain myself until Adam and Peri get back?"

"They've also been taken to the IIA facility, where Agent Saint will need to be debriefed."

As she poured a shot of vodka into a glass, she looked up at the agent, incredulous. "That's going to take all night!"

"I'm unaware of the exact time requirements," he reported.

She shrugged. "There's another vodka in the fridge if you're interested."

Another flicker. "Good night, ma'am."

Alexandra downed the drink. "Don't call me ma'am!" She yelled after his departing figure, which moved a little faster than was necessary.

Never before had Shekhar Kapur understood the American term "floating on air" when used in reference to a human being. Aside from being physically impossible, as a state of euphoria, which it seemed to imply, he could think of a great many alternatives that would describe the sensation more accurately.

But no more.

Now he knew. He felt it as he made his way home on foot from the corner where the city bus had just dropped him off. He'd just come from…time spent?…a date?…with Arla Tellebough. His head was so consumed by light, fluffy thoughts it was as if it was full of helium and might cause his feet to leave the ground.

Floating.

Including the initial short visit after her shift ended at the Yonge Street bar, Kapur had now been in the woman's company three times. each time, he left the situation feeling increasingly confused and increasingly joyful.

Was this love?

What should he do next?

Such things were not approached in the same way here as they were in india. Would she soon expect sexual intercourse? Was he willing to participate in such activity? These were serious questions for a serious man. only days ago he had suspected this woman of being nothing but an empty-headed, large-breasted, silly creature. And, in many ways, she was all those things. But she was also kind, sympathetic, gentle, thoughtful, and good-humoured. even more shocking, she seemed to enjoy spending time with him.

At first, their meetings were arranged under the guise of her telling him more about Adam Saint. She believed the CDRA agent was deceived into believing his life was about to end due to a fictitious tumour in his head. But in truth, after their first discussion, there was very little else to learn from her. She'd told him everything. He believed her. He'd pretty much proven the allegation to be true. At least to himself.

That first night, when the woman readily agreed to meet again, away from the unclean drinking establishment, the die was cast. Something had happened between them that could not be denied.

The timing, however, could not be worse. Shekhar Kapur had so many other things to worry about. Such as his belief that his superior, Maryann Knoble, and perhaps the entirety of IIA, had been complicit in the deception of Adam Saint. How his only attempt to speak with Agent Saint in person had been thwarted by Knoble, further fuelling his belief in her guilt.

But tonight, floating down the pathway to the house much too large for a single man—or even one with a family of six—his thoughts were elsewhere. on the long, dark hair of Arla Tellebough. How her eyes looked like little bowls of chocolate pudding. How she laughed at his awkward attempts at levity. How she laid a warm hand over his whenever he said something that touched her heart, something not difficult to do because her heart was so big.

As he inserted the key into the door lock, he wondered about bringing her back here. Certainly, sexual intercourse aside, showing her his home would be a sensible expectation on her behalf. That, he decided, would be a practical next step.

Stepping inside, he reached for a light switch. What the illumination revealed caused him to jump back and shout in alarm.

"No need to yelp," the cool voice suggested. "It's only me."

Regaining his composure as best he could, Kapur stepped forward and demanded to know: "What are you doing here, Maryann?"

"Lovely home you have here, Shekhar," Maryann Knoble declared from where she stood at the far end of the foyer.

"You have no right to be in my home without an invitation!" he snapped.

Knoble too stepped forward, intense pewter eyes menacingly magnified behind oversized spectacles. For a brief second, she assessed the man, the first time she'd seen him outside of a work environment, something she never sought to do with any of her colleagues or underlings. How ironic, she noted to herself, how this man with his undernourished frame appeared more terminally ill than Alzheimer's-ridden Serguisz Belar was, and Adam Saint was expected to be by those who knew of his diagnosis. "And you have no right to be in my computer system without *my* authorization. So I'd say we're even on that score, wouldn't you?"

Kapur was shocked. He didn't know what to say as a million thoughts ran through his mind. Could she possibly know he'd been digging into Adam Saint's records? What else? Was she following him too? Was she aware he'd found information at the office of deceased IIA physician Milo Yelchin that supported his belief that Saint was actually in good health? did she know about Arla? Was Arla in danger? At that last thought, an unflattering Hindi word escaped from beneath his breath.

Kapur would not be bullied. He marched across the empty space until he was directly in front of Knoble, his intensity and height, if not his bulk, an equal match for hers.

"I know what you've done!" he shot back. "I know what dirty game you've been playing with Adam Saint. I know he isn't dying."

"It's true," Knoble admitted.

Again, Kapur was surprised. He hadn't expected the bald honesty. "He must be told!"

"Of course," Knoble smoothly agreed.

Kapur stuttered. He'd expected a battle royale, not this quick, unruffled admission and agreement.

"Saint is no fool," Knoble said. "And i, even less of one. I know the sham can only go on for so long before he finds out the truth himself."

Bolstered, Kapur shouted, "He needs to be told now!

not later!"

Knoble moved closer. nose to nose. Kapur could feel her hot, tobacco-polluted breath on his cheek. "He will be told. By me. When I wish it."

"You are responsible," Kapur accused, holding his ground.

Knoble made a dismissive sound in the indian's face and brushed against him as she moved toward the door. "I don't know what you think you know, Kapur. But whatever it is, keep it to yourself." She turned the knob, opened the front door, and then turned to face her new head of CDRA. "I know how much you enjoy your work, Shekhar. I'd hate for that enjoyment to come to an end."

Kapur was shaken. no threat was as potent as one laced with ambiguity.

The woman stepped out of the house, tossing one last coldly cheerful message over her thick shoulder: "See you at the office, Shekhar."

The summery scent of freshly cut hay and late-blooming alfalfa hung in the warm evening air. With a few citronella tiki torches keeping mosquitos mostly at bay, we decided to eat outside at the old wooden picnic table. It was getting dark, but we'd agreed to wait until dad finished in the fields for the day before we sat down for dinner.

I'd picked up takeout from Tong's Wok on the way to the farm from the airport. Alexandra, who'd flown home about a week earlier, provided a case of cold beer from dirks. Anatole promised dessert. our hopes weren't high. A previous attempt at Jell-o had resulted in a gooey disaster.

Doris and Judy, the labradoodles, thrilled to have company and a break from the daytime heat, gambolled about.

Conversation during the first part of the meal consisted of little more than appreciative slurps and chewing noises, interspersed with dad's meagre reports on the crops, the horses, and the garden.

I loved it.

"I bet you're happy to have the house back to yourselves again," I said to dad and Anatole. "I hope having three young women and a kid around didn't upset too much of your routine."

"I suppose sometimes that's not a bad thing," dad murmured as he accepted a second beer from Alexandra.

Really? That didn't sound like my father. He was a man who preferred the invariable.

People change.

"Screw off, you fuckin' bloodsucker!" Alexandra groused at a persistent mosquito.

Some people.

"No swearing." My father's soft and oft-repeated reprimand.

Never mistaken for a big chatter, Anatole had been even quieter than usual since I'd arrived. I had at least expected a "hello" or a "pass the fried rice." Something was bugging him. So in the spirit of my newly developing interest in family and open communication, I went ahead and put my foot firmly in it. "Anatole, is something wrong?"

His shaggy head moved imperceptibly. I couldn't see his eyes, but they might have moved from where they'd been glued to his iPad to somewhere in my general direction.

396 — Anthony Bidulka

"No," he barely managed to get out.

"Anatole had a crush on Peri," Alexandra blithely stated.

"Awwww jeeeeeeez!" Anatole squawked. "That's not true!"

"Yup," she said, reaching into the cooler next to her high-heeled boot for another beer. "It is. A mother knows," she proclaimed reverently. "A mother sees things."

"You weren't even here most of the time Peri was!" he countered. As if that mattered.

Alexandra sucked in her cheeks. "Okay. Well, then, she might have said something to me when we were holed up in that hotel in Toronto."

Suddenly, we had my nephew's full attention. "What? Did she say something about me?"

I found myself both jealous of and regretful for the look that splayed itself so brazenly across his face. A face so young. So hopeful. So full of yearning. Blooming with insatiable adoration for another person. But I knew some small part of that youthful naïveté was about to be damaged.

"She said a lot," my sister said. "She couldn't stop talking about you and what a great guy you were."

I wondered if the feeling I was experiencing at that moment was my heart swelling a little, with pride for what my sister was doing for her son: lying.

Good God, she really was turning out to be a good mother.

"I got kinda tired of it after a while, actually," Alexandra said, pretending to be distracted by a scallop that was resisting capture by her chopsticks. "I finally stopped listening."

Anatole was rapt, taking in every word. He'd even

brushed aside his hair so as to have an unimpeded view of his mother's face and any telltale hints of information he might glean from it. "And what else?"

"Nothing, really. Just that she was sorry she didn't live closer to Saskatoon."

And there it was. A paper cut to the heart. Small. Seemingly insignificant as far as physical wounds go, yet with the potential to cause great pain.

"Where is she going to live?" Anatole asked, his voice high, looking to me for an answer.

"I don't know," I told him. "There are lots of things she and the other women have to figure out first. It's not easy being away from everything and everyone you know for so long. And they went through some pretty rough stuff on that island."

The chin dropped. eyes followed. "I guess."

We ate in silence for a bit.

"I'm sorry." From Anatole.

I looked up from my plate and found that my nephew was staring at me. "Why do you say that, Anatole? I don't know anything you should be sorry for."

"I screwed up."

"What are you talking about?" Alexandra asked.

"You trusted me to do all this cool stuff for you. But I believed it when she told me she wanted to find her family. I wanted to help her because…well, I did kind of like her, and I know I shouldn't have been wasting my time on it—"

"Anatole! Snap out of it," my sister crabbed. "What is this about? You didn't do anything wrong."

"I'm the one who told her about Serguisz Belar and where to find him. And I did it without telling you or Uncle

Adam. If it wasn't for me, what happened in Toronto wouldn't have."

I pushed my plate aside and leaned across the table, bringing me eye to eye with my nephew. "Anatole. You did nothing wrong. I was the one who screwed up. I gave you a lot of responsibility. I asked you to do a lot—"

Anatole threw up a hand, his long, narrow fingers twitching. "I know, I know, and I don't want you to stop. I don't want you to regret asking me to do stuff for you."

"I don't," I told him. "Not for a minute. That's my point. You are part of my team. I was the one who withheld information from you. I should have told you the whole story from the beginning. If I'd told you about Belar, you'd have known something was up when Peri said he was her grandfather. You would have told me about it then, right?"

"Yeah." The word pulled slowly from his mouth like uncooperative taffy. I could see my point had hit home.

"So you have nothing to apologize for. I do. And I'm sorry, Anatole. It won't happen again."

His lips did a thing that might have been a grin. "You've got a team?" he asked.

"I do."

"I'm on it?"

"Yup."

I heard my sister mutter under her breath. "Keeee-rist."

I could tell she was pleased though.

"Well, even so," Anatole said, "I have something that will make up for it."

"Oh?"

"I found Aunt Kate for you like you asked."

My heart did a little leap. I hadn't expected this. "Is she

okay?"

"I guess so…" he began.

If my heart had been leaping before—with relief ? hope? love?—his next words sent it hurtling off a cliff.

My eyes flew across the picnic table to my sister's. They burned with fear.

I should have known better.

Kate Spalding was no wounded bird. My ex-wife hadn't gone off somewhere to lick her wounds or cry rivers of tears to mourn her lost fiancé.

She'd gone off to declare war.

And now I knew.

If my tumour didn't kill me, Kate would.